More praise for
AMARI AND THE NIGHT BROTHERS

New York Times Bestseller • Indie Bestseller

Junior Library Guild Selection

Winner of the Barnes & Noble Book Children's
and YA Book Award

"In this thrilling debut, Alston thrusts his intrepid heroine into a
setting packed with magic, mythical creatures, and danger."
—*Publishers Weekly* (starred review)

"Fast-paced adventure and cutthroat pre-adolescent contempt
make for a delightfully challenging journey."
—ALA *Booklist* (starred review)

"An excellent middle grade fantasy."
—*School Library Journal* (starred review)

"Sharp, funny, and brightly imaginative."
—JESSICA TOWNSEND, *New York Times* bestselling author
of the Nevermoor series

"Gives an electrifying jolt to middle grade fantasy.
B. B. Alston's debut is a rousing success!"
—SOMAN CHAINANI,
bestselling author of the School for Good and Evil series

"I want to live in Amari's world and watch her save it (or have
her come here and save ours)!" —TUI SUTHERLAND,
bestselling author of the Wings of Fire series

"I loved every magical page." —J. C. CERVANTES,
New York Times bestselling author of *The Storm Runner*

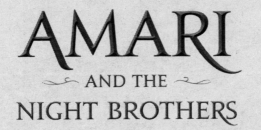

AMARI
AND THE
NIGHT BROTHERS

B. B. ALSTON

AMARI

~ AND THE ~

NIGHT BROTHERS

Illustrations by

GODWIN AKPAN

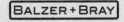

BALZER + BRAY

An Imprint of HarperCollinsPublishers

Balzer + Bray is an imprint of HarperCollins Publishers.

Amari and the Night Brothers
Copyright © 2021 by Brandon Alston

Names: Alston, B. B., author.

Title: Amari and the night brothers / B. B. Alston.

Description: First edition. | New York : Balzer + Bray, [2021] | Series: Supernatural
    investigations ; 1 | Audience: Ages 8–12. | Audience: Grades 4–6. | Summary:
    Twelve-year-old Amari, a poor Black girl from the projects, gets an invitation from
    her missing brother to join the Bureau of Supernatural Affairs and join in the fight
    against an evil magician.

Identifiers: LCCN 2020028609 | ISBN 978-0-06-297517-1 (paperback)

Subjects: CYAC: Supernatural—Fiction. | Magic—Fiction. | Missing persons—Fiction. |
    Brothers and sisters—Fiction. | African Americans—Fiction.

Classification: LCC PZ7.1.A4755 Am 2021 | DDC [Fic]—dc23

LC record available at https://lccn.loc.gov/2020028609

Typography by Carla Weise
21 22 23 24 25   PC/BRR   10 9 8 7 6 5 4 3 2 1
❖
First trade paperback edition, 2022

For my wife, Quinteria,
who always believed

1

I'M SITTING IN THE PRINCIPAL'S OFFICE. AGAIN. IN THE hallway, on the other side of the glass door, Principal Merritt is getting an earful from Emily Grant's mom. With all those wild hand gestures, you'd think I did a lot more than give her stuck-up Little Miss Princess daughter a tiny shove. Emily got up in my face, not the other way around. Wasn't my fault she lost her balance and fell on her butt in front of everybody.

Emily stands behind her mom, surrounded by her squad. They cover their mouths and whisper, eyeing me through the door like they can't wait to catch me alone. I lean back in my chair, out of view. *You've really done it this time, Amari.*

I glance up at the picture of the brown-skinned boy on the wall behind Principal Merritt's desk and frown. Quinton proudly holds up the trophy he won in the state math competition. You can't see, but me and Mama are just offstage, cheering him on.

There's not much to cheer about anymore.

The door swings open and Mrs. Grant stalks in, followed by Emily. Neither makes eye contact as they settle into the chairs farthest from me. Their dislike for me seems to fill up the whole office. I frown and cross my arms—the feeling is mutual.

Then comes Mama in her blue hospital scrubs—she got called away from work because of me again. I sit up in my chair to plead my case, but she shoots me a look that kills the words in my throat.

Principal Merritt takes his seat last, his weary eyes moving between us. "I know there's history between the two girls. But seeing as it's the last day of school—"

"I want that girl's scholarship revoked!" Mrs. Grant explodes. "I don't pay what I pay in tuition to have my daughter assaulted in the hallways!"

"Assaulted?" I start, but Mama raises a hand to cut me off.

"Amari knows better than to put her hands on other people," says Mama, "but this has been a long time coming. Those girls have harassed my daughter since she first set foot on this campus. The messages they left on her social media pages were so ugly we considered deleting her accounts."

"And we addressed that matter as soon as it was brought to our attention," says Principal Merritt. "All four girls received written warnings."

"How about the stuff they say to my face?" I lean forward in my chair, face burning. "They call me Charity Case and Free Lunch and remind me every chance they get that kids like me don't belong here."

"Because you don't!" says Emily.

"Quiet!" Mrs. Grant snaps. Emily rolls her eyes.

Mrs. Grant stands, turning her attention to Mama. "I'll have a talk with my daughter about her behavior, but your daughter got physical—I could press charges. Be thankful this is as far as I'm taking it."

Mama bristles but bites her tongue. I wonder if it's because Emily's mom is right about pressing charges. Practically the whole school saw.

"Up," says Mrs. Grant to her daughter, and they head for the door. Mrs. Grant stops short and looks back at us. "I expect to be notified the moment her scholarship is revoked. Or the Parents' Association will have a lot to say at the next meeting."

The door slams behind them.

I can barely sit still, I'm so mad. This is all so unfair. People like Emily and Mrs. Grant will never understand what it's like to not have money. They can do whatever they want with no consequences while the rest of us have to watch our every step.

"Are you really taking away Amari's scholarship?" Mama asks in a small voice.

Principal Merritt drops his eyes. "We have a zero-tolerance policy when it comes to physical altercations. School rules dictate she be expelled. Taking her scholarship is the smallest punishment I can offer."

"I see . . ." Mama sinks in her chair.

My anger melts into shame. Mama's already sad because of Quinton. I shouldn't be adding to her troubles just because I can't handle a few bullies.

"I know that it's been . . . difficult," says Principal Merritt to me, "since Quinton's disappearance. He was a great kid with a truly bright future. It doesn't take a rocket scientist to connect the dots between that incident and the start of your behavior problems, Amari. I can arrange for you to talk to a counselor, free of charge—"

"I don't *need* a counselor," I interrupt.

Principal Merritt frowns. "You should talk with someone about your anger."

"You want to know why I shoved Emily? It's because she thought it was funny to joke that my brother is dead. But he isn't. I don't care what anyone says. He's out there somewhere. And when I find him, I'll show you all!"

I'm shaking, tears streaming down my face. Principal Merritt doesn't say anything. Mama stands up slowly and pulls me into her arms. "Go to the car, Babygirl. I'll finish up here."

We ride home in silence. It's been almost six months since Quinton went missing, but it doesn't feel that long. Seems like just the other day he was calling Mama's phone to say he'd be home for Christmas. It was a big deal because Quinton was always gone once he got that fancy job after high school. The kind where you can't tell anybody what you do.

I used to swear up and down that Quinton was some super-secret spy like James Bond. But he would just give me this little smirk and say, "You're wrong, but you're not *totally* wrong." Whenever I tried to get more out of him he'd just laugh and promise to tell me when I got older.

See, Quinton is *smart* smart. He graduated valedictorian from Jefferson Academy and got full scholarship offers from two Ivy League schools. He turned them both down to work for whoever he was working for. When he went missing, I was sure his secret job had something to do with it. Or at least that somebody who worked with him might know what happened. But when we told the detectives about his job they looked at me and Mama like we were crazy.

They had the nerve to tell us that—as far as they could tell—Quinton was unemployed. That there were no tax records to indicate that he ever had a job of any kind. But that just didn't make sense—he'd never lie about something like that. When Mama told them he used to send money home to help out with bills, the detectives suggested that Quinton might be involved in something he didn't want us to know about. Something illegal. That's always what people think when you come from "the 'Wood," aka the Rosewood low-income housing projects.

The car rattles as we pass over the railroad tracks, letting me know we're in my neighborhood now. I'm not going to lie, it feels different coming back here after being on the other side of town. It's like the world is brighter around Jefferson Academy and all those big, colorful houses that surround it. Where I'm from feels gray in comparison. We pass liquor stores and pawnshops, and I see D-Boys leaning up against street signs, mean mugging like they own the whole world. Jayden, a boy I knew in elementary school, stands with a bunch of older boys, a big gold chain around his neck. He recognizes the car and shoots me a grin as we pass.

I try to smile back but I don't know if it's convincing. We haven't spoken since Quinton went missing. Not since he started hanging with the guys he promised my brother he'd stay away from.

Once we pull up in front of our apartment building, Mama buries her face in her hands and cries.

"Are . . . are you okay?" I ask.

"I feel like I'm failing you, Babygirl. I work twelve-hour shifts, five days a week. You should have somebody around who you can talk to."

"I'm fine. I know you only work so much because you have to."

Mama shakes her head. "I don't want you to have to struggle like I do. That scholarship to Jefferson Academy was your ticket to a good college—to a better life. Lord knows I can't afford to send you to a place like that on my own. I don't know what we're supposed to do now."

"I'm sorry, but I never fit in at that place." I cross my arms and turn to look out the window. Just because my brother made it look so easy doesn't mean I can too. "I'm not Quinton."

"I'm not asking you to be your brother," says Mama. "I'm just asking that you *try*. That school was an opportunity for you to see that there's a big, wide world outside this neighborhood. A chance to broaden your horizons." She sighs. "I know it's unfair, but the truth is that when you're a poor Black girl from the 'Wood, certain people are gonna already have it in their minds what type of person you are. You can't give them a reason to think they're right."

I don't respond. She acts like this isn't something she's already told me a million times.

"If you're not acting up in school," says Mama, "then you're sitting in front of that computer for hours. It's not healthy, Amari."

I mean, I know she's right. But it's hard to concentrate on schoolwork when you can hear other kids whispering about you. And posting photos of Quinton on as many websites as I can lets me feel like I'm helping with the search. I know it's a long shot, but it gives me hope.

Mama continues, "When you get inside, I want you to slide that laptop under my door and leave it there."

"But Mama."

She waves her hand. "I don't wanna hear it. Until you

decide to take your future more seriously, that computer stays with me. We'll talk more about this tomorrow. I've gotta get back to the hospital."

I slam the car door after I get out. And I don't look back once as I stomp toward our building. What am I supposed to do now?

Once I'm inside the apartment, I fall over onto the couch and bury my head in the pillows. This has been the *worst* day.

Finally, with a groan, I pull myself up to a sitting position and grab my old, beat-up laptop from my book bag. Quinton won it after placing second at some international science fair forever ago. He gave it to me after he won a better one the next year.

I'm not even surprised when the screen stays black after I open it up.

I open and close it a few times, but it still won't work. Since it's clearly in one of its moods, I set it down and head to the kitchen to get myself some food.

Except, even after I've calmed my grumbling belly, the laptop still won't turn on. I close my eyes and bring it up to my forehead. "Mama says I've got to give you up, and there's no telling when she'll give you back. *Please work*."

This time it powers right up. *Thank goodness*.

The free neighborhood Wi-Fi is super slow, but I'm still

able to copy and paste Quinton's missing persons poster onto a dozen websites.

Normally I'd check his email next (I figured out his password months ago—*Amari-Amazing*—my fake superhero name from way back), but my curiosity gets the best of me and I pull up Emily Grant's Instagram page to see if she posted anything about today. And what do I find? A photo of me on her profile with the caption:

Summer Break! And guess what?
We finally took out the trash at Jefferson. Expelled!

The post has a ton of comments from other students. I only read a few before I slam the laptop shut. Never wanted her here . . . I heard she used to steal from the lockers . . . All it took was her dumb brother to drop dead . . .

I didn't get expelled, and my brother isn't dead. Jaw clenched, I open my laptop again to write a reply to shut them all up. A notification appears at the top of the screen, and my whole body goes stiff. It's a new email for Quinton.

1 New Email: From Discreet Deliveries

Which may not sound like a lot, but Quinton never gets new emails. Ever. I've been checking since the day I figured out his password.

I open the email:

Package Delivered.

You shall receive a separate email once Amari Peters has signed, as requested.

Thanks for using Discreet Delivery service, where they get what's coming to them, whether they know it or not!

This email will self-destruct in 3 ... 2 ... 1 ...

The email vanishes.

I jump in surprise. Did that email really just . . .

And what am I supposed to sign?

A knock sounds at the front door. "Delivery!"

2

I SPRINT TO THE FRONT DOOR AND YANK IT OPEN.

A man in tattered clothes stands hunched over in the doorway. I lean over him to look down the sidewalk in both directions. Where's the delivery guy?

"Hello there," he says without looking up. "Might I trouble you for a moment?"

I instantly feel guilty for overlooking him. "I don't have any money. But there's a Hot Pocket in the freezer you can have. Mama hasn't gone shopping yet."

"That's very kind of you but I've actually just left a very fine restaurant."

"Oh," I say. "So you're *not* homeless?"

"Homeless? Heavens, no." The guy finally lifts his

head—he's older, with a neatly trimmed gray beard. The thing he's been hunched over is a computer tablet. "Why would you think that?"

My eyes drop to his patchy clothes. "Um, no reason."

The guy follows my eyes and his face goes bright red. "I'll have you know that this is the height of fashion in—oh, never mind. Might your name be Amari Peters?"

Whoa! I take a couple steps backward. "How do you know my name?"

"It's right here on the screen," he says, pointing to his tablet. "I'll just need you to sign for your delivery and I'll be on my way."

"You're . . . the delivery guy?" I say warily. "And you've got a package for me?"

"Yep." He flips the tablet around. "From a Q. Peters."

I gasp. "You're saying you've really brought me something from my brother?"

The guy nods. "I do if this Q. Peters fella is your brother. Says here he's sent exactly one 'Broaden Your Horizons' kit."

Broaden your horizons? Wasn't that what Mama was just talking about? "Is this some kind of joke?"

"I should think not." He frowns. "I only do deliveries part-time, but I take it seriously."

"Well, whatever you're supposed to be delivering, I'll take it." That's when I notice he's not carrying any envelopes or boxes. "Where is it?"

"Only after you sign, I'm afraid." The guy offers the

tablet and I grab it, messily signing the screen with the tip of my finger.

I look at him expectantly. "The package?"

The man taps the screen a couple more times. "Left it in Q. Peters's old bedroom closet."

I just stare. "You've been inside my apartment?"

"With Q. Peters's permission, of course." He clears his throat loudly. "Now then, I'm afraid I'll be needing your memory of this whole encounter. You see, we at Discreet Deliveries take pride in our customers' anonymity. Don't worry, you'll still get your package. At some point during the day you'll feel the sudden, unexplainable urge to clean out that closet, and there the package will be."

"You need my . . . what?" I take a nervous step back.

"Just the one memory." The guy pulls out what looks like a TV remote control. Then he squints down at the tablet again. "Oh. My mistake! Seems your name is on the Memory Intact List. Someone's off to the Bureau, I'll bet. Best thirty years of my life. Anyways, good afternoon!"

I blink and the man is gone. What in the world just happened?

And what's in my brother's closet?

Even after all this time, I half expect to hear Quinton yell at me for barging into his room without his permission. I step inside and glance around at the wrinkled rap posters hanging alongside his framed photographs of Stephen Hawking and Martin Luther King. His bed is messy, like always, and all his academic trophies and honor roll certificates fill up the back wall.

The investigators tore this place apart looking for clues about what might've happened to him, but me and Mama made sure to put everything back exactly like it was. I think we both secretly hoped we'd find something the police missed, something only family might recognize. But that just didn't happen. Neither one of us has been in here since. It hurts too much.

It's not until I get all the way inside that the memories hit me. All the times Quinton and I used to play in here. Or how sometimes he'd put on a playlist while we lay on the floor, joking and talking about how we were going to take over the world one day. How we were going to show our loser dad who ditched Mama that we're worth something. How we'd always have each other's backs, no matter what. Sure, Quinton might be ten years older than me, but we've always been tight.

Tick . . . tick . . . tick . . .

Okay, so . . . Quinton's room has never ticked before. Suddenly I've got goosebumps all over.

Maybe that weird delivery guy *was* telling the truth. The package is supposed to be in Quinton's closet. And sure enough, with each step closer to the closet, the sound gets louder. Did he send me a clock?

I bite my bottom lip and pull open the closet door. It's

empty except for a huge, ugly old chest that Quinton got from the thrift store when we were younger. While I was digging through the doll bin for a Black Barbie, he had his eyes on this raggedy chest with half the leather cover missing. Claimed he needed a place to hold all his master plans.

By the sound of it, whatever Quinton sent me is inside. Thankfully, he broke the lock years ago, so getting in is as easy as lifting the top. I dig through countless beat-up folders and old notebooks, searching for anything that might tick.

It's not till I get to the very bottom that I find a loudly ticking black briefcase, a white Post-it Note on top with Quinton's handwriting.

For Amari's Eyes Only

Quickly, I take the briefcase out of the chest and set it on the floor. What could be inside? Fidgeting with the locks doesn't get it open, so I try yanking it apart. No luck. That's when I notice another Post-it on the other side.

Will open at midnight, after the last day of school

I swallow, my heart booming. Quinton never said anything about having a briefcase for me. But that's his handwriting.

Maybe he wants to explain where he is and what happened. After six months of worrying like crazy . . . could this be how to find him?

I glance over at Quinton's alarm clock. 4:13 p.m. Midnight is nearly eight hours away. But what is it I'm waiting for?

11:58 p.m.

I'm in my room, sitting at the head of my bed with my knees pulled up to my chest. The briefcase sits at the foot of my bed, looking suspicious.

I check the hallway again. Mama's been home for a few hours, but no light shines under her door. She must be asleep. *Good*. Whatever's inside this briefcase, Quinton made it clear that only I'm supposed see it.

11:59 p.m.

I pace back and forth. Okay, I'm totally tripping, right? What do I honestly think is going to happen?

12:00 a.m.

CLICK! HISSSSSSSSSS . . .

I swear I jump a whole foot in the air. I creep over to my bed and take a seat. After a calming breath, I lift the top of the briefcase. Green-and-purple stripes stare back at me.

I reach inside, pull the smooth fabric from the briefcase and hold up what seems like a suit jacket to the light. It might be the ugliest thing I've ever seen. I reach inside and pull out the matching pants. I have no idea what's going on but I can't help a smile. This is definitely Quinton's corny sense of humor at work.

And there's more in the suitcase—an envelope and a pair of thick metallic shades. Attached to the shades is a chain of Post-it Notes.

#1 Please lie down before putting these on

#2 I'm serious about lying down first

#3 Pinkie swear-level serious!

Okay, okay, I get it! I bring the shades closer. Aside from being heavy, they seem pretty normal. Certainly not dangerous enough for three warnings. Are they supposed to make you dizzy or something? Well, if it's pinkie swear–serious then fine, I'll lie down.

I shove the briefcase to the edge of my bed and lay back before sliding the glasses onto my face. I'm not sure what the big deal—

"Amari?" comes a voice I'd recognize anywhere.

Quinton?!

3

I WHIP MY HEAD AROUND TO SEE MY BROTHER STANDING in the middle of my bedroom, a nervous grin on his face. I scramble off the bed so fast I trip over my own feet. Next thing I know, I'm across the room with my arms wrapped around his middle. I'm shaking as his arms hug me back.

"I missed you too." He laughs.

I relax my grip on him and he steps back, out of my arms. I don't think I've ever felt so happy in my whole life. My big brother is here. Like really here. "How? Where have you been? We've got to tell Mama!" I can't get the words out fast enough as I stare up at his very alive face, a big, goofy grin sitting below his wide eyes and uneven hairline.

"I'll explain everything. But for now, I just need you to trust me. Okay?"

Of course I trust him. But how did he just appear out of nowhere? "Um, okay."

"Follow me!" He turns and runs out of the room.

I give chase, skidding to a stop in front of Mama's darkened doorway. I have to tell her Quinton is back. She won't need to be sad anymore. We won't have to fight anymore either. Everything can go back to the way it was before.

"There's no time," Quinton calls from the living room. "We've got to hurry." He opens the front door and dashes out into the hallway.

I glance back at Mama's door as I sprint through the living room, wondering if Quinton's voice might have woken her. Her light doesn't click on.

But I can't let Quinton go now. I run after him and it's all I can do just to keep up. "Where are we going?"

"The roof," he calls back.

The roof? Quinton and I used to sneak up there all the time, even though Mama said it was too dangerous. Like we didn't have sense enough to stay away from the edge.

We run up a dozen flights of stairs until we reach the wide, empty roof. Only it isn't empty tonight.

"Is that . . . a boat?" I ask.

Quinton grins over his shoulder. "Sure is." The boat is the size of a school bus and looks like someone literally dropped a small log cabin on the back of it. Smoke wafts up from the cabin's stone chimney. Shiny gold railings surround the front half of the deck.

I can't help but laugh at how ridiculous this all is. *What is happening right now?* "How did it get here?"

"Gotta hurry!" Quinton disappears around the other side.

I follow, running my fingertips across the smooth hull of the ship. The wood is so glossy I can see my reflection in the moonlight.

Quinton waves me over. He tugs on a lever and a section of the ship falls open, becoming a short staircase. Quinton climbs in first, with me behind him. One long room runs the length of the boat. I'm able to make out two bunk beds and—swords?—before Quinton leads me up another staircase at the end of the ship.

We emerge on the deck, and Quinton brings me over to where two large wooden captain's wheels are mounted. The wheel in front of us turns left or right like every other ship. But the wheel to our right is angled so that it can only be pushed forward or backward from where we're standing.

I reach out and let my fingers graze the wheel, then jump as the ship jerks forward a few feet.

He just laughs. "You're going to want to get some altitude first." He nods to the second wheel.

I step back, shaking my head in disbelief. "When you say altitude, you don't mean . . ."

"Oh, I *do* mean." He smirks and takes hold of the second wheel, gently pulling it forward. My whole body goes stiff as the ship rises in the air. I throw both arms around the railing, holding on with everything I've got. My apartment building, and everything else in my neighborhood, gets smaller and smaller as we continue to rise. How is this happening?

My brother is having the time of his life laughing at me. "Relax, the ship has been triple-balanced. It's impossible to fall off."

"Quinton, we're *flying*! You're just going to act like this is normal?"

Again with the smirk. "Maybe it is."

Quinton grips the first wheel with both hands and the ship surges forward. Everything becomes a blur, the stars above stretching into glowing streaks. I can feel the wind on my face, but for as fast as we must be going, my legs really do feel steady—like I'm still on the ground.

He releases the wheel and the ship glides to a smooth stop in midair.

The smell of sea salt tickles my nose. There's water in every direction. "Is this the ocean?"

My brother nods. "Take a peek through that telescope next to the railing and look down. Tell me what you see."

Down? Who uses a telescope to look down?

Still, I step over and peer through. "All I see is ocean."

"Keep looking. It's a special telescope so it might take your eyes a few seconds to adjust."

I squint a little. Nothing . . . and then something. It appears only for a second before it's gone again—a streak of white, like lightning arcing across the ocean floor.

"What was that?" I ask.

"Keep looking. And this time, use the dial."

As I turn the dial, my view through the telescope magnifies. Now I can see that those streaks of light are actually glowing trains, racing across the ocean floor. "No way," I whisper.

I zoom out a bit to find more trains and I'm nearly blinded by all the light. That train is just one of what seems like thousands of them, zigzagging and swirling in every direction. For as far as I can see, the ocean lights up, like it's trying to outshine the starry night above. The whole world becomes a light show, just for me.

I turn to Quinton, tears in my eyes. "It's beautiful."

But the big smile Quinton's been wearing since he showed up in my bedroom begins to fade. "The International Railways of Atlantis. I only wish I could've shown you this in person."

"I don't understand," I say.

"I wanted you to know just how vast and how wondrous the world really is. Everything you've seen, from those trains to this ship, is real, Amari. They're out there anytime you want to see them. Everything . . . except me."

I shake my head. "But I'm looking right at you."

"You're looking through the shades. This is only an interactive recording. We call it a Wakeful Dream. I left instructions for its delivery in case something happened to me. And I guess it did. I took a dangerous job I love dearly, and I knew the risks. Still, I really wish I was there with you now."

The world around us begins to dim.

I rush over and throw my arms around him. "What happened to you?"

"I don't know," Quinton says softly. "But this dream was only supposed to be sent to you if the Bureau declared me missing . . . or dead."

"You're only missing." I shudder. "I can feel it."

Quinton squeezes me tighter. "Whatever happened to me, please don't let it discourage you from exploring this world to its fullest. Some of the things I've seen will take your breath away. I've left you a nomination with instructions on it."

"A nomination?" I ask. "For what?"

Everything goes black.

"Time's up, Chicken Little. I love you."

"I love you too," I whisper. "I'm going to find you. The *real* you. No matter what it takes."

4

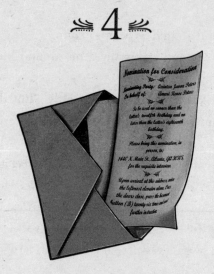

EARLY THE NEXT MORNING MAMA knocks on my bed-room door so that we can have breakfast together. Mother-daughter time or something.

I woke up wondering if that Wakeful Dream really happened, but once I took a look at what else was inside the briefcase I was convinced. . . . My brother made a dream for me, put it inside a pair of shades, and had it delivered to my apartment. What kind of place can do that?

I intend to find out.

"You all right, Babygirl?"

Mama's voice snaps me out of my daze. "Oh . . . um, yeah, I'm fine." I scoop up some cereal with my spoon.

Mama watches me from across our small dining room

table. I can tell she's worried about how I'm doing after what happened yesterday at school.

There's a huge part of me that wants to tell her about Quinton's Wakeful Dream. She deserves to know. But how do you explain being visited by your missing brother in a dream where you took a flying boat to go look at some underwater trains without sounding delusional?

And even if she did believe me (which I doubt), do I really want to risk getting her hopes up? She's only just gotten to where she isn't crying in her room every day.

So I keep quiet.

"What I did yesterday was for your own good." Mama sighs. "I miss him too. I really do. But right now, it's just you and me. It seems harsh, but it's my job to give you the best possible future. That can't happen if you keep your whole life on pause wishing for something that may never happen."

"I get it," I say quickly. Anything not to have that argument again.

"Then you'll also understand why you're grounded until I decide you aren't."

I nearly spit out my cereal. "Seriously?"

"You know better than to go around shoving people. Even *if* they deserve it." Mama stands up from the table and grabs her purse. "I've got to get to work a little early today. One of the girls has a sick baby at home. Don't let me find out you've been out that door. Understood?"

"Yes, ma'am."

The words stop Mama in her tracks, and she gives me a

good looking over. "Only time I'm ma'am instead of Mama is when you're up to something."

I put on my most innocent expression and shake my head.

"Well, before you get any ideas, I've got Mrs. Walters watching the place while I'm gone. And you know she don't have anything better to do than worry about what everybody else is doing."

"I understand," I say. Mama only said not to let her find out. She never actually said I couldn't go.

Back in my room, I spread out everything from the briefcase on my bed—the green-and-purple suit jacket and pants, two sheets of paper that were tucked inside the envelope, and the shades that triggered last night's Wakeful Dream. I try on the shades for like the tenth time this morning, but I still can't get them to work again.

I settle for reading over the paperwork from Quinton's envelope one more time. The first page reads:

(Mandatory: Staple atop all outgoing paperwork)
WARNING
WARNING
(in case you somehow missed the first one)
WARNING
(surely you get the idea by now)

The following information is classified, as it refers to a location that handles several million very well-kept secrets. As a result, reading this file without the proper permissions may result in any number of dire consequences that include but are not limited to:

Death by bottomless pit

Being locked inside a metal canister and shot into space

Being fed to a certain creature, in a certain underwater lair, that shall, for the purpose of keeping its existence a secret, remain nameless

I reread that first paragraph like three times. I mean, bottomless pits and secret underwater creatures?

Now then, should you happen across this paperwork by accident and wish to know how to avoid such consequences (and we'll know if you've peeked), you are to do the following:

Seal it up in an envelope, wrap that envelope in no fewer than three yellow blankets (preferably all the same shade), stuff it all in a box, tape that box shut, and mail it to the following address:

None of Your Business
Don't Ask Which St.
New York, NY 54321

Of course, if you have been deemed special, and thus do have the proper permissions, please feel free to move on to the next page.

—C. Kretts

Before last night, I would've laughed at that warning. But something tells me that whoever these people are that Quinton works for, they mean every word. Thankfully, Quinton made it pretty clear that this was meant for me. The second page confirms it.

<u>Nomination for Consideration</u>

Nominating Party: Quinton Javon Peters
On behalf of: Amari Renee Peters

≋ ≋

To be used no sooner than the latter's twelfth birthday and no later than the latter's eighteenth birthday.

≋ ≋

Please bring this nomination, in person, to: 1440 N. Main St., Atlanta, GA 30305, for the requisite interview.

Upon arrival at this address, enter the leftmost elevator alone. Once the doors close, press the basement button (B) twenty-six times and await further instruction.

Now it's just a matter of getting there. Unfortunately, that warning isn't the scariest part of what was inside the briefcase. One more Post-it is attached to the leg of the pant-suit:

WeaR this suit to the inteRview.

Clearly, Quinton has lost his mind. He wants me to go around *this* neighborhood in a green-and-purple suit? I won't make it out of the building before someone cracks a joke. And I can't afford to get into another fight. I sit down on the bed, biting my lip.

It all feels so unreal. This whole thing is crazy.

But what if it *is* real? What if this is my one chance to find out more about my brother? My one chance to bring him home.

Fine. I'll check it out. And I'll wear this hideous suit too.

I creep down the stairs of our building as if I'm hiding from the bad guy in a scary movie. The nomination is tucked inside my jacket pocket. Thankfully, the street is clear. Until a bunch of smaller kids rush out of the next building. They point and giggle, and I'm so distracted I forget to duck beneath Mrs. Walters's window. She looks right at me and gets to jotting in her little notebook. I'm *so* dead when Mama gets home from work.

Stupid ugly suit. I get to the bus stop in the worst mood and plop myself down on the bench. A peek at my phone tells me the bus should be here any minute. It can't come fast enough.

A clean, cherry-red Camaro screeches to a stop in front of me. The windows all roll down at once, and some boys around eighteen or nineteen poke their heads out.

One boy with long dreads grins at me. "Hey, lil mama, you lost or something? I think the circus left last week." The whole car bursts into laughter.

"Just leave me alone," I say, cheeks burning.

"Where the rest of the Skittles at?"

More laughter.

"Don't you have someplace else to be?" I growl.

That's when the back door on the other side of the Camaro opens. Jayden hops out and jogs around the car. "Y'all leave my little buddy alone."

The guys in the car make some more jokes about us being boyfriend and girlfriend before speeding off.

Jayden takes a seat next to me on the bench. He looks like he's grown another six inches since I last saw him up close like this. Still seems way too young for all that height.

His gold chain sparkles in the sunlight and those Jordans are brand-new. "Looking good, 'Mari. I'm feelin' the curly fro."

"Thanks," I say with a smile. "Feels like forever since anybody called me that."

He shrugs. "You don't hang with us anymore. Not since Quinton . . . you know."

"Yeah, I know." Truth is, even though we're in the same grade, I only know Jayden through the tutoring program at the rec center where Quinton used to volunteer. It's kind of embarrassing to admit, but all my old friends were kids my brother knew first.

Jayden laughs suddenly. "So I gotta ask. What's up with this suit? Is this how them rich folks dress?"

"Ha ha," I say. "No, this is for an interview. It's . . . well, it's hard to explain."

"Oh, so you trying to get a summer job or something?"

I nod. "Something like that."

Jayden's expression turns serious. He glances around before meeting my gaze again. "If you need some cash, I can loan you some." He reaches inside his pocket and pulls out a roll of twenty-dollar bills. "Pay you back for all the times you and your brother looked out for me."

Jayden doesn't look it now, but he's had it worse than a lot of kids living out here. Me and Quinton always had Mama to support us. I can remember going to visit Jayden and him not even knowing where his mom was that day. Or what he was going to eat that night. Me looking out for him was just me sharing whatever I had at the time. Sometimes it was just half my candy bar. He was always so grateful.

I search Jayden's eyes for a joke, but he seems totally serious. That is so much money. Enough that Mama wouldn't have to worry over bills for a good while. But there's no way I can take it. "I know whose money that is. Those boys are into some bad stuff. They're always getting arrested."

Jayden shoves the money back into his pocket. "Man, you don't know anything about them. At least they care what happens to me."

Quinton's old warning to me comes flashing through my head. *You're not going to change the world unless you hang with people who want to change the world too. Fast money and selling stuff that hurts other people ain't good. Be better than that.*

"My brother cares," I say. "And I know those boys don't give you all these nice things without wanting something in return. Tell me you didn't drop out of school to run with them."

"I do what I gotta do." Jayden frowns as he meets my eyes. "Getting good grades don't help me eat. And even if it did, there ain't nobody to help me study no more. Them people they got tutoring now don't understand. Always lookin' down on me, tellin' me what I should already know. Quinton wasn't like that. He could explain things in a way that made it all make sense."

Those words hit hard. It's a reminder that me and Mama aren't the only people who depended on Quinton.

That tutoring program is one more thing on a long list of stuff that's gotten worse since his disappearance.

I lean in closer to Jayden. "What if there's a way to get Quinton back here? Would you give the tutoring program another try?"

Jayden gives me a puzzled look. "You saying you know where he is?"

The bus turns the corner.

"Not exactly . . ." I say. "But I might've figured out a way to find him. Just promise me you won't do anything that could mess up your future. He'd be really disappointed."

I pause a second before getting on the bus, but Jayden doesn't give me an answer.

Once I've taken my seat, I meet his eyes again through the window.

Jayden shakes his head but gives me the biggest smile. "Okay, 'Mari," he mouths.

5

WHEN I GET OFF THE BUS, I'M SURPRISED TO FIND that 1440 North Main Street is a busy office building. It's a small skyscraper, all dark glass and metal. For a place guarding so many "well-kept secrets," I would've thought it'd be somewhere more . . . secret.

This place is packed even on a Saturday. I climb the stairs to the front entrance, doing my best to ignore all the eyes my suit attracts. And then nearly panic when I notice the security desk just inside the doors, but strangely the guard just smiles and waves me through, no questions asked. I spot the elevators at the back of the lobby and make my way through the crowd of adults. It's just my luck that I've come on the day of some business conference.

The instructions said I have to wait for the leftmost elevator to be empty. That's way easier said than done—it's the elevator that gets used the most. I get so tired of standing around waiting that I take a seat on a small bench. After around fifteen minutes, the traffic in the lobby begins to die down and I finally get my chance. But just when I think I'm home free, a frowning, bald guy slips into the elevator with me.

I reach out and hold the doors.

The man spins around to face me. "Stop that! I've got a meeting I'm already late for."

If I don't think of something quick, I'll never get where I'm going. "I've got a really bad cold." I throw in a sniffle and a couple fake coughs. "I don't want you to catch it."

The man scoots away from me, his frown deepening. "Yes, well, maybe I *can* wait on the next one." He dashes out the elevator so fast you'd think I had the plague.

Finally, I'm alone. The elevators doors shut. I take one more glance at the nomination form. Press the basement button twenty-six times.

On the last press, the lights dim and a red beam scans the elevator. "Nomination form detected," says a robotic voice. "Please proceed." A loud click sounds, and the back of the elevator opens up to a winding hallway with metal walls.

No way. How is *any* of this real?

I lean forward, hoping to get a peek at where this thing leads, but it twists out of sight. No turning back now, I guess.

Shaking off my nerves, I follow the hall to a small waiting room—six chairs with a magazine rack in the corner.

At the counter, a plump blonde lady smiles at me. "How can I help you?"

"My brother nominated me for . . ." What did he nominate me for, exactly?

"Of course," the lady says politely. "Unfortunately, our recruiter isn't in right now—"

A loud crash sounds from far off. "Ah," she says. "Seems he's just arrived. Use the door on the left and go on back. It's the last office on the right."

I do as she says and pop my head into the half-open doorway. Inside, a desk lays in pieces on the floor. Standing over the mess is a really strange-looking guy. He's taller than I am but just as skinny, with streaks of gray in his shaggy, brown hair. But it's not really *him* that's the problem. It's his clothes.

He's got on bright orange pants—traffic cone bright. His shirt is orange too. I've seen orange shirts before, but this guy's shirt has the nerve to be covered in orange and brown feathers.

"Come, come." The man waves me inside without looking up. "I'm just cleaning up a bit. I told the transporter to put me *at* my desk, not *in* my desk." He strokes his chin. "But then again, I was chewing a rather splendid steak sandwich when I gave the command."

I take one nervous step inside. Did he say transporter?

"My name is Amari—"

"And mine is Mr. Barnabus Ware, but full introductions won't be necessary, I'm afraid." He still hasn't looked up at me once. "This year's summer program has already begun. The kids'll already be assigned to rooms by now."

It's already begun? My heart sinks. "Does that mean I'm too late? I only just got my nomination."

"Rules are rules. Whoever nominated you should've filled out the proper waiver if your school year runs long. There's always next summer—" He finally looks up at me and his eyes go wide. "Many pardons, but if you don't mind me asking, is that suit a genuine Duboise?"

I glance down at the ugly green-and-purple stripes and shrug. "What's a Duboise?"

The man gasps. "Only the most brilliant clothing and accessories designer in the world!" He comes closer, stepping over the shattered pieces of his desk, then picks up the end of my right sleeve and rubs the fabric in his hand. "Very good. Yes. Very good, indeed. Would you mind removing the jacket? I'd *love* to try it on."

"Oh, um, sure." It's strange that anyone would be interested in this ugly thing except for maybe wanting to burn it and dance on the ashes. But then, this guy is comfortable wearing orange and brown feathers. I slide off the jacket and hand it to him.

He actually tries to put it on. He's almost a foot taller than I am! No way it'll fit.

But it does. Perfectly. My jaw drops. "How—?"

"Ah yes, it's certainly authentic. Never can tell with so

many knockoffs going around. But only genuine Duboises have the 'one size fits all' feature. Only way to be sure. The wife and I swear by them." Mr. Ware gestures toward his own outfit. "My ensemble is from the tropical collection, 'Essence of a Sandy Parrot.' Now, you might be wondering why it is I have on vacation attire. I'll explain. You see, we were on vacation, naturally, and having quite the time I should add, when I received an urgent message from my supervisor that a child had been added to the list and no one was in the office! You're supposed to be able to count on your coworkers to pick up the slack when you're on vacation—you'd expect that, wouldn't you?"

"I—I guess. Can we get back to how my jacket—"

Mr. Ware throws up his hands. "Exactly! It's a reasonable thing to expect! But not when Thesda Greengrass is your partner. Always going to pieces whenever one of her bloody cats gets taken away. Can't understand why her neighbors might object to a tiger in the neighborhood. No use, though, she'll have another by the end of the month. Can't *imagine* where she gets them—"

"MR. WARE!" I interrupt. My ears are ready to explode.
"Yes?"

"My jacket," I say. "How did it grow to fit you like that?"

"Why, a patented enchantment, of course. How else?"

"An enchantment?" I lift an eyebrow. "As in magic?"

"Yes." Mr. Ware crosses his arms. "If you don't mind me asking, how did you come by that suit, exactly?"

"It was in a briefcase," I say. "My brother left it for me."

"Ah," says Mr. Ware. "I understand now. I take it this brother of yours is the first in the family to go into this line of work?"

"Probably. But I don't really know what line of work this is."

He strokes his chin again. "Normally I'm not one to bend the rules, but how can I turn away a child with such splendid taste in clothing? However unintentional." He sighs. "Very well, have a seat."

I do what he says. It's pretty strange to be sitting across from someone over a pile of shattered desk pieces.

"It's *my* job," says Mr. Ware, "to offer *you* a spot in our rather unique summer camp. However, I can't tell you very much about said summer camp until I get an answer as to whether or not you'll take it. Think carefully. If you decide you're not interested, then our meeting will end right here, and you can go back to doing whatever it was you planned to do with your life. It's why we meet here in this office and not at the actual Bureau. But if you say yes, be warned that you *will* be obligated to attend this summer. Understand?"

I swallow and nod. "So the interview is just you asking if I'll take the spot?"

"Indeed it is," he says with a nod. "Would you rather it be more difficult? I can cook up some algebraic equations if you'd like."

I shake my head quickly.

Mr. Ware chuckles. "And your answer?"

As much as I want to say yes, I can't help thinking of Quinton right now. "My brother said what he was doing was dangerous. Is that true?"

At first, I think he won't answer. But eventually he says, "It very well can be."

I'm suddenly super nervous. Visions of disarming bombs and wrestling alligators sweep through my mind. "Is there anything else you can tell me?"

"I'm sorry, but I've said far too much already. I'm afraid I can offer nothing more until you've decided."

Even if it *is* dangerous, Quinton wanted me to experience all the things that he did. When has he ever wanted anything but the best for me? Just the memory of those glittering trains lighting up the ocean sends a rush of excitement through me I can't explain. And more than anything, this could be my only shot to find out what happened to him.

I meet Mr. Ware's stare and say, "I accept." And then hold my breath for whatever comes next.

6

One
Thousand
And
One
Careers

M R. WARE LEAPS OUT OF HIS CHAIR AND SHAKES MY
hand fiercely. "Congratulations! A fantastic decision. Always a pleasure to bring a fresh face into the Bureau
of Supernatural Affairs."

My hand is half numb by the time Mr. Ware releases it.
But I have a much bigger worry. "Bureau of Supernatural
Affairs?"

Mr. Ware grins. "Go to any corner of the world and you'll
find tales of beings and creatures that only seem possible in
our imaginations. What if I told you that living among us
are all the beings we've come to pass off as myth? Trolls and
sphinxes, mermaids and oddities you could see with your
own eyes and still not believe—these and countless more

dwell in our towns and walk our streets. One might be your neighbor or even your favorite teacher. And not only that, many supernaturals have vast cities of their own hidden just off the beaten path. The Bureau of Supernatural Affairs is the link between the known world and what is hidden. We are charged with keeping the secret."

I'm not totally sure I buy all that. An odd suit is one thing—hearing that creatures from books and movies might actually be real is something else. "Okay . . . so *if* that's true, don't people have the right to know if a werewolf is sitting next to them on the bus?"

"Thankfully, werewolves tend to be train people. But, yes, there is much in the supernatural world that is dangerous, and we do our very best to protect the innocent. As to your point about *why*, the supernatural world is kept secret for one very good reason. Peace of mind. People tend to fear what they don't understand. And fear can far too easily become hatred. Why, the Great Bug Conflict of '69 comes to mind. The Society of Sentient Insects had gone and invented 'people repellent' spray. You'd think a reasonable person would understand that turnabout is fair play, but you'd be surprised how quickly reason goes out the window when the bugs start spraying back. A particularly rough year for the Bureau, that one."

I cross my arms and lean back in my chair. "That's not in any history book I've ever read."

"We're very good at what we do." Mr. Ware smiles. "And we have been for a very long time."

I'll see for myself soon enough. Right now, there's something that interests me more than myths or magic. "My brother is missing. Is there anything you can tell me about him? His name is—"

My recruiter jabs a finger into each ear. "The Bureau is not always the safest place to work. It's likely that your brother worked in one of the more dangerous fields. I can't say I know of anyone that's died or gone missing. I very purposefully keep away from that sort of news. I'm the one who brings them in, you see. I'd take the news too hard."

"I understand." I remind myself there are probably lots more people I can ask about Quinton.

Mr. Ware reaches behind him and pulls a briefcase out of thin air. "An Invisi-Tote," he says with a wink. "Never leave home without it." Inside the briefcase is a stack of books. He tosses one onto my lap. I try to read the long title on the cover, but the words are some other language. French maybe? But then the letters flicker and fade, reappearing as *One Thousand and One Careers*.

Mr. Ware reaches over and starts flipping through the pages. "You'll train in the summers until you're eighteen, at which point you'll become a full adult member of the Bureau. So long as you pass the tryouts, you'll receive a scholarship to any school in the country, no matter how exclusive, and no matter the cost. If you wish, you can change your specialty at the start of next summer's session, but you'll have to go through the tryout process again to keep the scholarship." He finally settles on a page. "This is my job during nomination season. This publication lists every job classification the Bureau has to offer. What positions you are allowed to pursue depends on both your potential and your ability."

I nod and look down at the page he's selected.

DEPARTMENT OF SUPERNATURAL LICENSES AND RECORDS
Recruiter
Minimum badge allowed to perform this job:
    Wooden
Chief Responsibilities: Meets with nominated
    children to offer a spot in the summer
    training sessions in preparation for a career
    at the Bureau of Supernatural Affairs.

"What's it mean by 'minimum badge'?" I ask.

"That would be our next order of business—badge testing. Badges, you see, represent your current potential—intelligence, bravery, curiosity, all those kinds of things. If I had to guess, I'd say you're a cardboard badge. There's a chart on the very first page."

Cardboard? I frown and flip back to the opening page.

<u>Badges</u>
Gold
Silver

Bronze

Iron

Copper

Stone

Glass

Wood

Plastic

Cardboard

Aluminum Foil

Notebook Paper

My shoulders sag. Cardboard is all the way at the bottom, just above aluminum foil and notebook paper. Of course the Black girl from the projects would have an awful badge. Why would I think the supernatural world is any different from my own?

"I suppose you know how to use one of these?" Mr. Ware hands me a long, very thin plastic tube. "Works like a thermometer."

Except I notice there aren't any numbers. Welp, here goes nothing. . . . I blow off a piece of lint and stick the thing into my mouth. It's only under my tongue for a second before Mr. Ware asks for it back.

He holds it up for me to see. The red liquid rises all the way to the top, so fast it shatters in his hands. We lock eyes and he frowns. "*Interesting* . . ."

"Good interesting or bad?" I ask.

He doesn't answer. Instead, he pulls a small metal box with the words *Starter Kit* scribbled across the top from his Invisi-Tote and pushes it into my stomach. "Be at this address at six p.m. tomorrow."

"Tomorrow? But—"

He practically shoves me out of his office.

7

MAMA WORKS EVEN LONGER HOURS ON THE WEEKEND, so she won't be home until really late. That means I've got no choice but to call her at work about going to camp this summer. The phone call goes something like this:

Mama: What's happened? Are you hurt? Is everything okay?

Me: I'm fine, Mama—

Mama: Amari. Renee. Peters. You know not to call me at work unless it's an emergency.

Me: It kind of *is*, though. I have to be somewhere tomorrow and I need your permission.

Mama: You do remember that you're still *very* much grounded?

Me: I *know* but . . .

Mama: But what exactly?

Me: It's Quinton's old summer camp. He must've nominated me before everything happened.

Mama: (A long pause) Is that so. You got the number to the program?

Me: (Reads number listed in the "How to Deal with Non-Bureau Parents" pamphlet.)

Mama: I'll give them a call and let you know what I decide.

While I wait for Mama to call back, I go through the rest of the Starter Kit. Inside is my own personal copy of *One Thousand and One Careers, Protected Edition*. It's so protected that I can't even read it. All the pages are blank.

There's also a list of items I'll need to bring.

Items Needed

—Yourself, everything else will be provided

Last is a tiny vial of blue liquid. The attached tag reads:

TRUE SIGHT
BY VOILÀ PHARMACEUTICALS

One drop in each eye. Take immediately.

On the rare occasion that you find yourself

with X-ray vision, please consult a doctor.

It takes me a few tries but eventually I get the drops in my eyes. Nothing happens, though. Not even the X-ray vision. But I'm still so proud of myself I do a little dance in the mirror.

A knock sounds in the living room.

I dash to the front door, wondering if it's something to do with the Bureau of Supernatural Affairs. But one look through the peephole and I can see it's Mrs. Walters. Her permanent frown brings down my good mood even from outside. She's one of those people you can't ever imagine smiling. The type of person who looks annoyed even when they're on TV accepting a check for winning the lottery. I open the door and say in my most polite voice, "Hello, Mrs. Walters. How can I help you?"

"Don't you *Hello, Mrs. Walters* me! Your mama told me to keep an eye on you in case you tried to sneak out. And I caught you! Saw you at that bus stop, and I saw who you were talking to. Wait till your mama hears about . . ."

I'm right in the middle of coming up with a really sorry excuse when I blink, and Mrs. Walters's facial features begin to swell and shrink. And that's not even the biggest change. "Um, Mrs. Walters? How long has your face been green?"

Mrs. Walters stops midsentence, reaching up to touch the end of her suddenly long, pointed nose. Her beady eyes bulge in surprise. "You can see me? *Really* see me?"

I nod. "You look like the Wicked Witch of the West from that really old movie . . ."

Mrs. Walters shrieks and steps back away from my door. "That's what I get for buying that discount concealer!" She throws down some powder and disappears into a cloud of smoke.

No way. I step out into the hallway and wave my hand through the fading haze. Mrs. Walters is really gone. I guess Mr. Ware knew what he was talking about—there really are supernatural beings in the world. In my neighborhood!

Not that I didn't believe him—but seeing it is way different from just hearing about it. And I guess I know why those eye drops are called True Sight. I've seen Mrs. Walters a hundred times and never knew she was a witch.

What have I gotten myself into?

It's Sunday afternoon and Mama is late. When she finally called me back last night we agreed that she'd leave work today at 3:00 p.m. in order to make sure we had plenty of time to get across town.

Instead, it's after four when she comes stumbling through the front door with shopping bags in both hands. She drops the bags when she sees me and wraps me up in a great big hug. "This is so wonderful," she says. "Just what you need. When Quinton came back that first summer he was different. More mature."

"What's in the bags?" I ask.

"Oh, I just picked up a few things for you. I know they claim you don't need to bring anything but, trust me, you'll be glad. I grabbed you some new pajamas, all your hair products, ooh, those fuzzy socks you love . . ."

My ears automatically tune her out the moment I catch sight of the Best Buy bag. I scramble over and open it up, gasping once my eyes land on what's inside. The sleek wooden box contains the cell phone I've wanted practically my whole life. It's even the newest version.

"I thought we couldn't afford for me to get a new cell phone?" I ask. In fact, how can we afford *any* of this stuff?

Mama just smiles. "I won't have my daughter gone for most of the summer without a reliable way to keep in touch."

"But *Mama*," I say. She totally avoided my question.

She puts her hands on her hips. "Okay, I went to the payday loan place, but this won't be like last time."

I'm like a balloon with a brand-new hole, the way my excitement spills out of me. Last time Mama took out a loan, she had to use bill money to pay it back and we almost got kicked out of our apartment for missing rent.

"Don't look at me like that," Mama says, that familiar sadness creeping into her expression. "Just let me do something nice for you for once."

I don't have the heart to fight with her when she gets like this. So I just say "okay," and force a smile.

Mama smiles too and then adds, "I had a little bit stashed away in case of an emergency, and seeing as the program offers a scholarship, I won't have to put it toward your tuition next year."

"The scholarship isn't guaranteed," I say. "There's a chance I won't get it."

"You are my daughter and Quinton's baby sister. Ain't

a chance in the world they won't give you that scholarship."

I open my mouth to remind her I'm not nearly as good at everything as Quinton is, but I stop myself. That would only make her sad again.

"Remind me—what time did you need to be there?" she asks.

"Six," I say, glancing at the clock. It's 4:07 p.m. "How long is the drive?"

"Oh, we've got plenty of time," says Mama.

"Even with the big music festival going on downtown?"

"Is that tonight?" she asks. "I'm so sorry, I completely forgot. Traffic is going to be a nightmare." We exchange a panicked look and make a mad dash to get ready.

Mama swears she can get us to the address on time as long as she sticks to her side roads and backstreets. These aren't nearly as busy as the main roads but they are definitely way more . . . *interesting* than I remember.

First, Mama cuts off a man who waves a fist at us, except it's not a fist but a paw. And he isn't so much yelling at us as he is growling. My jaw drops and I turn to see what Mama makes of it, but she doesn't seem to notice. It has to be the eye drops, right?

It gets weirder. A man waiting at the next bus stop is literally on fire, but he doesn't seem bothered by it. Like, at all. He even lights a cigarette on his forehead. The lady that lets Mama turn in front of her? Snakes for hair. I try not to meet her eyes in case she decides it would be fun to turn me into stone, Medusa-style, but Mama just waves thanks and keeps on driving.

It isn't until we spend the longest red light ever next to a dark alley filled with glowing eyes that I decide maybe I'll just keep my own eyes inside the car from here on out.

I assumed supernaturals like Mrs. Walters were rare, but they're all over the place, hiding in plain sight. As it hits me where I'm going, I can't tell if I'm shaking with excitement or fear. Or maybe it's a little of both. I'm about to be part of their world. The supernatural world. Something I didn't even know existed two days ago.

I wish I could tell Mama about all of this. It doesn't feel right to keep secrets from her. Especially secrets that are this big. But something tells me she wouldn't be thrilled about her daughter going to the same secret agency that had something to do with her son going missing. Honestly, it makes me nervous too.

To keep myself from completely freaking out, I pull *One Thousand and One Careers* out of my bag. Only this time, thanks to those eye drops, every page is filled with words and pictures.

As I flip through it, Mama glances over and asks, "What's that?"

I panic and slam it shut.

"No need to be so dramatic," says Mama. "Is that your journal?"

Just that fast, I forgot that she isn't able to read it. Keeping all this a secret is going to be harder than I thought. "It's for camp this summer." Avoiding the question feels better than not being honest.

Mama just shrugs and focuses on changing lanes.

I open the book again and flip through until I reach a page that catches my eye. It's a full-page photo of a bulky, bearded guy in a cowboy hat, decked out in a dark gray suit. He's aiming a flaming ax toward the camera and his gray eyes are so intense it's like he's daring me to turn the page without reading first. So I read.

The caption says, "The closest thing to a superhero in the supernatural world. Join Agent Beauregarde Magnus at the Department of Supernatural Investigations and start your journey toward becoming a Special Agent today!"

On the opposite page is a job listing:

DEPARTMENT OF SUPERNATURAL INVESTIGATIONS
Junior Agent
Minimum badge allowed to perform this job:
   Bronze
Chief Responsibilities: To serve and protect
   both humans and non-humans alike against
   supernatural threats, foreign and domestic.
   Enforcement of the laws that govern
   supernatural entities living in the known
   world. Those who excel in this position may
   be promoted to Senior Agents, Surveillance
   Agents, Special Agents, and more.

Noteworthy Agents: Beowulf, Captain Ahab, Abraham Van Helsing, Captain Nemo, Dr. Jekyll/Mr. Hyde (part-time researcher/ part-time agent), Sherlock Holmes, Maria Van Helsing, and Quinton Peters

I can't believe it! Quinton's an agent. Just like this guy in the picture. Of all the crazy things I've learned, this might be the craziest. Agent Magnus looks like the person you'd call if a bear got loose at the zoo. Quinton is afraid of spiders. Even the tiny ones.

As the clock on the dashboard blinks to 5:26, a question pops into my head. "Mama, how much do you know about this summer camp?"

"It's a really fancy leadership camp," says Mama. "You guys take classes and go on trips to meet with CEOs and government leaders. Plus you'll get to mingle and make friends with other high achievers. These kinds of programs will really pay off later as an adult. When it comes down to getting those cushy jobs, it's not what you know but who you know."

So Mama thinks this is just a leadership camp. That must be what they told her when she called. And what Quinton used to tell her too.

"Just make me a promise, okay?" Mama continues. "Promise me you'll go to college. You won't follow Quinton into whatever he was doing."

"So you think this, um, program had something to do with Quinton going missing?"

"Of course not," says Mama, "or I wouldn't let you near it. I don't know what could've happened to your brother. I just want you to use this program to get into a good university somewhere and live a safe and happy life."

Safe and happy life. I can't help wondering if maybe deep down Mama does know that his job is the reason he's gone. "I promise," I say. I'm only entering this program to find out what happened to my brother. Once I do, I don't care if I ever see the supernatural world again.

Even with all Mama's shortcuts we don't turn onto the tree-lined entrance to the Vanderbilt Hotel until 6:02. I can't believe we're late.

The building looks so cool, like one of those famous cathedrals, topped with a beautiful golden dome. A large white guy in a gray suit is headed up the wide stairs at the front of the building. I recognize his cowboy hat.

"That's your escort," says Mama. "Catch him before it's too late!"

I push open the door and step outside. "Agent Magnus! I'm here!"

If Agent Magnus hears me, he doesn't stop or even turn around. I can't believe we've come all this way only to be too late.

"Hey! It's me. Quinton's little sister." I bounce back and forth, waving my hands over my head, praying that Agent Magnus will turn around.

At Quinton's name Agent Magnus pauses and turns to face me. He's twice as intimidating in real life. Those intense gray eyes size me up as he comes down to meet us.

Mama gets out of the car and thanks him. He says something that makes her laugh and then gives her hand a kiss. Mama blushes and giggles. Of course they know each other, Mama used to drop Quinton off here every summer.

"Babygirl?" says Mama. "Introduce yourself."

Now that he's right here in front of me, I can't find any of the confidence I had a minute ago. "Hello," I say, not able to meet Agent Magnus's eyes.

"You're late." His voice is deep, with a raspy southern twang. "Believe Mr. Ware said to be here at six."

"I know," I say. "There was traffic and—"

He puts up a hand to cut me off. "One thing you're gonna learn is we don't make excuses. If you were anybody else, you'd be headed back home. But you had one favor owed to you on account of being Quinton's little sister. That favor's used up now. Understand?"

I nod. "Yes, sir."

Agent Magnus turns his attention to Mama. "Always a pleasure, Renee. I'll make sure Amari is well looked after."

Mama smiles. "I know you will. You and Quinton were so close—I'm thankful you're taking the time to escort Amari on her first day."

"Great kid, Quinton." A flicker of emotion passes across Agent Magnus's face. "I'll send somebody down to collect Amari's things." His eyes find me again. "You ready?"

"I think so," I say.

Agent Magnus grins. "Oh, I doubt that very much."

THE INSIDE OF THE VANDERBILT HOTEL IS EASILY THE fanciest place I've ever been. The lobby is huge, probably bigger than most people's houses. The floor glistens like it's permanently wet and tall paintings hang on the walls.

The hotel guests all look like really important people—men and women lounge on plush chairs, sipping drinks brought to them by waiters in clean white uniforms as music from the string quartet set up in front of the large fountain fills the lobby. My stomach knots. And here I thought I didn't fit in at Jefferson Academy. This looks like the kind of place the royal family of another country might stay if they were visiting America.

I feel like a speck of dust on a beautiful painting.

"The Vanderbilt Hotel is one of many cover businesses the Bureau uses both to fund and conceal our organization. The building rests on a natural magic wellspring, which allows us an everlasting power source for much of what we do here. The hotel's a bit froufrou for my tastes, but they have a killer cigar selection."

I keep my head down as Agent Magnus leads me through the bright lobby to a small hallway marked *Authorized Personnel Only*. At the end of the hall is a big metal door with a keypad in the center. I try to see what code Agent Magnus types in, but his fingers move too fast. After a series of clicks, Agent Magnus twists the handle and pushes open the door to . . .

Another door. This one is even bigger, with a combination dial. Magnus turns it back and forth, like, ten times before the thing finally clicks and the door slides out of view. "Welcome to the Bureau of Supernatural Affairs."

An enormous hall greets us, and I gasp—it's filled with all kinds of strange sights. A flock of fairies twinkles past like floating Christmas lights, their laughter like tinkling bells. They all wave to me in unison. A bit dazed, I'm about to lift my hand to wave back when a loud shriek rings out. Witches zip by overhead on brooms, cackling madly and firing plumes of black smoke at one another. I look to Agent Magnus, wondering if maybe somebody should do something about the witch battle going on above, but he doesn't seem the least bit interested. *What in the world have I gotten myself into?*

"Follow me," says Agent Magnus, moving into the crowd.

I do, my head twisting in every direction trying to see everything at once. On my left, two hulking giants have a very polite discussion about the literary merits of Hemingway. It starts out polite anyway. Soon they're growling and stomping, and we make sure to give them plenty of space to avoid getting stepped on.

Just when I think this day can't get any weirder, I nearly bump into three dripping wet green . . . *somethings*, with a whole lot of eyes. They're flipping through "Places to See Away from the Sea" brochures.

It's not until we reach the clear elevators at the back that I realize I've been holding my breath this whole time. I wrap my arms around myself tight, my emotions all over the place. Is this real life?

"You all right, kid?" Magnus asks with a grin.

I nod stiffly and he laughs.

"We're all a bit shell-shocked in the beginning. Not to worry, you'll get used to it." Agent Magnus takes hold of my shoulder and gently turns me back around to face the lobby of supernaturals. "Now, one of the most important purposes of this here Bureau is to ensure that scenes like this one continue to exist. A safe place within human cities and towns for supernaturals to meet and gather and conduct business—no glamours or disguises necessary. Heck, they barely even have to behave within these walls."

I think about the supernaturals I saw on the ride here and how Mama couldn't see any of them. They all must've been wearing glamours and disguises.

He continues. "Supernaturals decided a long time ago that they'd be much safer hidden away from humans. And yet, outside of this place, the known world and the supernatural world are constantly slamming into contact in a thousand different ways every single day. So, for the privilege of remaining a part of their world, we here at the Bureau ensure these interactions occur in a way that keeps the supernatural world secret. Heck, we've got a whole department that does nothing but make up convincing stories to cover up some of the wacky things that happen."

Agent Magnus leads me to an open elevator and we step inside. Once the door closes, a warm female voice says, "Welcome to the Bureau, Special Agent Beauregard Magnus and Trainee Amari Peters. It's so good to see that you've trimmed that hideous beard, Agent Magnus. It was truly becoming an eyesore."

What the—? I glance around for the source of the voice. It seems like it's coming from all directions.

Magnus frowns. "Weren't you telling me how great it looked just the other day?"

"No," the voice answers. "If I remember correctly, my exact words were, 'you've certainly looked worse.' That hardly constitutes a compliment."

As Magnus chuckles, I have to ask. "Just to be clear . . .

you're having a conversation with the elevator?" I mean, sure, I talk to my laptop sometimes when it's not working, but it's never spoken back.

"That's right," Magnus says. "Amari, meet Lucy. She's the only elevator for me."

I raise an eyebrow and add talking elevators to my fast-growing list of things that are actually things. "Um, Lucy . . . are you supernatural?"

"Not in the slightest," she replies. "I'm what you'd call artificial intelligence. You'll find the Bureau operates on either advanced technology or magical objects. Whichever works best for the job."

"Cool," I say.

"Agent Magnus," asks Lucy, "I presume you're taking Trainee Peters to the youth dormitories?"

"That's right," he replies.

"Then down we go!" Lucy says.

We drop into the floor, descending through the clear tube. The elevator goes dark.

"Now approaching," says Lucy, "the Department of Supernatural Licenses and Records." A waiting room rises into view. Curious, I press my face into the glass to get a better look. Seated in the chair closest to the elevator is a cloud of smoke flipping through a newspaper. Next to it is a very bored-looking cyclops; it glances down at its ticket and rolls its large, bulging eye. An electronic sign at the center of the room flashes *Now Serving C26*, and behind it is a long counter with people stationed at little windows.

The elevator goes dark again.

"Now approaching the Department of Creature Control." Flashing red lights fill the elevator as another room comes into view. Something large and scaly is coiled a few feet from the elevator. People in plastic suits sprint back and forth with fire extinguishers. A wide, snake-like head emerges. The thing's cold yellow eyes find us in the elevator and it spits a whirling ball of fire in our direction.

With a shout, I jump to the back of the elevator just as flames reach it.

"No worries," says Lucy. "I'm fireproof. That's not the first Flame Serpent to get loose, I'm afraid."

Magnus laughs. "Kid, if you could've seen your face."

The elevator picks up speed.

"Now approaching the Department of Magical Science."

I only get a glimpse of the enormous room, but what I do see is amazing. Everyone floats, some upside down, like they're all in zero gravity or something.

"Show-offs," Magnus grumbles. "Tomorrow they'll all be invisible, just for the heck of it."

"Now approaching," Lucy says quickly, "the Department of Supernatural Investigations."

It goes by in a blur. Lucy keeps calling out names, but we're dropping so fast now that it becomes a garbled mess.

The elevator stops suddenly at a floor that looks like a

hotel hallway. Crimson doors are spaced out every few steps, matching the rug that runs down the center of the hardwood floor.

"We've arrived at the youth dormitories," says Lucy.

A tall, muscular woman in army fatigues steps into view. The doors open and she salutes Agent Magnus.

Agent Magnus returns the salute. "Got a late arrival, Bertha. See to it she gets a room and a good night's rest. Big day tomorrow."

Bertha nods stiffly. "I'll do my best to look after her while she's in my care."

"Kid," he says to me, "this is where you get off."

Quinton had a rule for whenever you find yourself in a new place: Fake it until you make it. That means doing your best to look confident even if you don't feel confident. I step off the elevator and give the lady a smile, even as my insides are doing flips. The lady returns a smile so forced it looks like she's in pain.

"Good luck," says Agent Magnus as the elevator doors close.

"Wait!" I shout. With everything there is to see in this place, I almost forgot about the reason I'm here. Agent Magnus holds open the elevator doors. "I want to ask you—"

"I know whatcha wanna ask me about," he interrupts. "Or rather, *who*. All information surrounding your brother's disappearance is classified. Nothing we're allowed to discuss with a trainee. It involves extremely dangerous matters you shouldn't concern yourself with."

"What do you mean?" I ask. "He's my brother."

"And he wouldn't want you in harm's way on his behalf. Focus on getting settled in."

His expression tells me he's not going to change his mind, so I set my face to show him I'm not budging either. If he won't tell me what I want to know, then I'll just have to find out on my own.

Agent Magnus frowns as the elevator whisks him away.

"Allow me to make one thing perfectly clear," says Bertha. Her forced smile is now a sneer. "I don't care who your brother is. I am your dorm leader and you will address me as ma'am and you will like it. Understand?"

I don't see that I have much of a choice. I nod.

Bertha continues her speech as she leads me through a maze of hallways. "It's bad enough I have to rearrange things because you've upped and decided to exist. I'll not tolerate any nonsense, do you hear me? Put one foot out of line and you'll find your stay here a short one. . . ."

The lady doesn't stop talking until we arrive at a door and she gives it a knock. No answer. She gives it another try, harder this time. Still no answer. Bertha takes both hands and beats on the door so hard it rattles on its hinges. Finally, the door opens. A lanky girl with light tan skin, curly black hair, and thick glasses leans into the doorway, yawning.

"Elsie Rodriguez, this is your new roommate," Bertha says.

The girl squints, her sleepy eyes going back and forth between me and Bertha. Then, like somebody flipped a switch, her eyes get big. "You're *you*! Come in, come in! Tell me all about you."

"An early start tomorrow means early bedtime tonight," Bertha cuts in. "There will be plenty of time for bonding tomorrow. Lights out!"

The door slams shut behind me. It's pitch-black in here.

"What's her problem—"

"Shh!" Elsie whispers.

I take Elsie's advice and keep quiet. After a few seconds I hear Bertha's loud shoes pound away. Once the footsteps fade completely, a small green flame pops to life, flooding the room with light. Elsie's face glows above a twisty little candle.

"She'll see the light under the door," I say.

Elsie shakes her head. "It's a sneakandle. Anyone more than three feet away can't tell it's lit. Invented it myself."

"That's pretty cool." I glance around the shimmering green room and notice two more beds. "Do we have any other roommates?"

Elsie's wide grin fades. "There were two other girls assigned to this room but they both requested transfers."

"You don't snore, do you?"

She lowers her eyes. "It's worse than that, actually."

"Okay," I say, a little off guard. "It can't be *that* bad."

She takes a slow, deep breath. "So . . . I'm kind of . . . a dragon."

"You're . . . a dragon." I repeat. I almost want to laugh but the look on Elsie's face tells me this is no joke. "You're serious?"

"Well, not a *dragon* dragon," she answers. "A were-dragon."

"Like a *were*wolf?" I ask. "Like, you can turn into a dragon?"

Elsie's shoulders slouch. "I was supposed to have my first shift years ago. But it just hasn't happened. And since I'm the last of my kind, there isn't anyone I can ask for help."

"Oh, then your parents are . . ."

"Both dead," Elsie finishes. "Weredragons were considered extinct like five hundred years ago. At least until my egg was found in a deep-sea shipwreck off the coast of Mexico. We can't hatch without sunlight. A dragon expert from the Department of Creature Control became my legal guardian and took me in." She sighs. "But once my twelfth birthday passed without a single shift, the Bureau declared me 'essentially human' and now I'm here."

"What's it like? Being the last of your kind?"

"Lonelier than you can imagine." She gestures to the two empty beds. "They told Bertha they didn't want to wake up one night to find a dragon snacking on their legs." She sighs. "Not an unreasonable request, all things considered."

"Well, I'm not afraid." I'm surprised by how much I mean those words. Maybe it's because I know how it feels to have people judge me before they even get to know me.

"Really?" she asks, beaming.

Nervously, I extend a hand. "Friends?"

She grabs hold and shakes it fiercely. "Absolutely!"

"Friends don't eat friends. Dragon or not."

Elsie gets a good laugh out of that. "Words to live by!"

It's then that I notice the wall above Elsie's bed. It's covered in pictures.

Elsie follows my eyes. "Ohmygosh, I am the biggest VanQuish fan on the planet. I've got all six of their action figures, even the super rare Junior Agent editions, a whole drawer full of T-shirts, a blanket, three coffee mugs, and like twenty posters."

"VanQuish?"

"Oh, that's right!" Elsie's eyes go wide. "You wouldn't have known anything about the supernatural world until your nomination. VanQuish is the nickname for the two most famous agents of the last fifty years—Maria Van Helsing and your brother, Quinton Peters. The *Van* is from Maria's last name and the *Qui* is from Quinton's first name—with a *sh* on the end. Get it? They 'vanquish' the bad guys? How cool is that?"

I double over laughing. There's just no way my dorky big brother is some celebrity. "Seriously?"

Elsie nods enthusiastically. "VanQuish singlehandedly defeated the last surviving Night Brother. It was the biggest arrest in centuries."

Before I can ask what a Night Brother is, Elsie holds up the sneakandle to show me her collection of magazine covers, centered around a small Mexican flag, stretching up to the ceiling. The magazines have names like *Elf Magazine* and *Harper's Bizarre* and *DeadBook: A Ghoulish Fashion Guide*. There's even a very sticky-looking *Slime Magazine* beside a *Supernatural Geographic*. Whatever the title, each cover shows a picture of the same pretty blonde girl next to my grinning big brother.

"Wow." There's a whole side to my brother that he kept hidden from me. I mean, while I was spending my summers doing cannonballs at the community rec center pool, Quinton was out saving the world.

"Can I ask you something?" I say.

"Sure," says Elsie.

"This might sound weird, but do you have any idea what happened to my brother? It's been six months since we've heard from him."

Elsie frowns. "No one knows. They vanished without a trace."

"Nobody went looking for them?"

"Sure," says Elsie. "Plenty of people did, from all over the supernatural world. The Bureau even set up a special hotline for tips. You wouldn't believe the kinds of rewards that were offered for information leading to their whereabouts."

"Did the Bureau find out *anything*?" I ask.

"If so, they didn't make it public. The last press report only said that VanQuish is considered missing in action and that all details surrounding the investigation are confidential."

My shoulders droop. I thought for sure that coming here would finally give me some real answers about Quinton, but it's just as big a mystery in the supernatural world as it is back home.

But I can't give up just yet. Not until I talk to everyone who knew him here. Somebody has to know something.

"Maybe some music will cheer you up." Elsie sets the sneakandle on the floor beside her bed and crawls underneath. She returns with a small black box covered in dials and buttons. Two long antennae rise out of the top.

"A radio?" I ask.

"Yep. Built it using spare parts."

I shake my head. "You're brilliant, you know."

My roommate grins. "Want to test it out?"

"Definitely."

Elsie sets it down on the floor and presses a few buttons. Suddenly a man's voice blares from the speakers: "HOT 159.7 FM. THE STATION THAT'S ALWAYS KEEPING YOU INFORMED ON THE LATEST NEWS FROM ALL CORNERS OF THE SUPERNATURAL WORLD—"

Elsie slams down on the large red button at the center of the radio, killing the sound. She blows out the sneakandle, and we both crawl into bed as fast as possible.

If Bertha is anywhere nearby, we're in trouble. I cringe at the idea of having to explain to Mama that I got kicked out an hour into being here. *Please don't let this cost me the chance to find Quinton.*

A few minutes pass but no one comes.

"That was close," says Elsie in the dark.

"Too close," I say.

"Want to try again?"

Now that my heart has stopped pounding, I have to admit—I *am* still curious. There's so much about this world that I don't know. "Only if you're *sure* you can get the volume right this time."

The sneakandle pops on again, and Elsie fidgets with the dials. The voice returns, quieter:

". . . Bureau has yet to release a statement regarding the string of incidents believed to involve monstrous human-animal hybrids occurring in both the United States and Europe over the past few months. These creatures, known for their extraordinary size, speed, and strength, as well as their disturbing ferocity, are perhaps the most devious product of magician-craft—a forced, unnatural fusion of man and beast. But with Raoul Moreau locked away in Blackstone Prison and his brother-in-arms, Count Vladimir, long deceased, the Supernatural World Congress has begun to express concerns that a new magician has surfaced—"

"A new magician?" says Elsie with a shiver. "That's a scary thought."

"Really? What's so scary about a magician?" I ask.

"Magicians in the supernatural world aren't like stage magicians in the known world," says Elsie. "They have *real* magic. Lots of it too—much more than the Supernatural World Congress allows humans to have. Remember what I said earlier about VanQuish being famous for capturing the last surviving Night Brother? Well, that's the same Moreau. The Night Brothers were two of the most powerful magicians there's ever been. They waged war on the entire supernatural world ages ago and almost won—"

"LIGHTS OUT MEANS GET TO SLEEP!"

Bertha's voice is like a crack of thunder outside our door and we scramble to put everything away and climb into bed.

But as soon as our dorm leader leaves again, Elsie says, "I can't wait to get my badge tomorrow. My overall potential rose really high on the Badge Tester, so I feel pretty good."

I think back on my own Badge Test and swallow. "What's it mean if the Badge Tester decided to self-destruct?"

In the dark, I hear Elsie gasp. "It means you've got so much potential the Badge Tester couldn't contain it all! Amari, I bet you're getting a moonstone badge tomorrow!"

"Moonstone? I didn't see that on the chart."

"They're extremely rare," she replies. "It means something about you is special—*legendary*. Quinton got one too."

Me, legendary? No way. What happens when they discover I'm not like Quinton at all?

"Hey, it's nothing to worry over," says Elsie. "You could be a hero, just like your brother."

I try to play it cool. "Who says I'm worried?"

"Um, I probably should've mentioned that I can see people's emotions, even in the dark. If you were a dragon, we could communicate telepathically, but with humans it's like an aura of different colors. And your yellow haze tells me you're plenty worried."

"Yeah, well, you should've been upfront about that too," I say angrily.

"You're right. I'm sorry." A moment passes and she adds,

"I really do think you could be a hero."

"I didn't come here to be a hero," I say, still annoyed. "I'm here to find out what happened to my brother."

My roommate doesn't say anything to that.

I know immediately I should apologize. That I'm too quick to get upset sometimes. Truth is, I *am* worried. Nobody would want me for a hero.

But she's already snoring.

Me, I don't sleep much at all.

9

An ear-shattering knock jolts my eyes open. Not that I'm fully asleep.

Elsie is still snoring, so I roll out of bed and drag myself to the door. As I turn the knob, another loud knock comes.

It's Bertha. "You're late!" she barks, pushing her way into the room. "Didn't you hear my knock an hour ago?"

"You didn't knock," I say, annoyed and still sleepy. "I would've heard it."

Bertha whirls around to face me. "You calling me a liar?"

I'm about to tell her just how much of a liar I think she is when Elsie grabs my shoulder.

"Must've overslept," Elsie says with a nervous laugh.

"You'd do well to follow your roommate's example and own up to your mistakes," says Bertha. "You two should've been in the underground auditorium five minutes ago. I suggest you change into your uniforms, make those beds, and hightail it down there." She turns and stomps out of the room.

"No way she knocked," I tell Elsie.

"I know she didn't, but we're just trainees. She's picking on us because she knows there's no one we can complain to yet. Just wait until we've been accepted into a department. Things will be different, promise."

Inside the small closet behind the two empty beds hangs two pairs of black pants, two neatly pressed white blouses, and polished black shoes. Elsie and I get dressed, brush our teeth, and make our beds in two minutes flat.

We race up the hall to find the elevator.

While we wait for one, I decide now is a good time to make things right. She's the first friend I've made in forever. I can't mess this up. "Hey—"

"No worries," she interrupts. "You're forgiven."

"But how did you know what I was going to say?"

"Your aura is white," Elsie explains. "Apologetic."

I can't help a smile. "That's pretty useful."

Elsie grins. "Has its moments."

Finally, an elevator slides into view, and we take it all the way down to what looks like a well-lit cave. Various tunnels with neon signs at their entrances veer off in different directions. One sign says, *International Railways Station—Bureau of Supernatural Affairs this way.* Another says *Department of Hidden Places this way, or is it?* A lady comes running out of the largest tunnel. Her name tag says *Secretary to the Chief.*

"Where on earth have you two been? The ceremony's about to begin!" She throws an arm around each of us and runs us back the way she came. We follow the winding passage until we walk through a golden door set into the tunnel wall. A long, narrow hallway ends in another set of gold doors. As we approach, the hum of a crowd begins to echo off the walls, raising hairs on the back of my neck. How many people are here?

We pass through this set of doors onto the floor level of an enormous auditorium. I was expecting something close to the fancy Jefferson Academy auditorium, but this place is more suited for a professional basketball team. Above us, on the ceiling of this great big cavern, are thousands and thousands of blue-green shimmers that I recognize instantly from my fifth-grade world geography class. They're the same glowworms found in the Waitomo Glowworm Caves in New Zealand. *Wow.* I never thought I'd see them in person—it's way cooler than Mrs. Varner's dusty film projector.

I don't realize I'm standing in a total daze until the secretary gives me a tug to keep moving.

The auditorium is dimly lit, with most of the lighting focused on the stage, where a stout white lady stands behind a wide glass podium. At the back of the stage, a massive screen displays her round face and neatly trimmed brown hair. My eyes pop at the sight of the fish gills on her neck.

Seated in the rows and rows of seats below her are kids of all colors, all around my age, and all wearing the same uniform.

A camera flash blinds me. A swarm of faces—some encased in glass tanks, some covered in fur, some with *way* too many fangs—quickly surround the three of us, hurling questions at me from every direction.

"Amari! Rumor has it someone's getting a moonstone badge today. Is it you?"

"Miss Peters! Will you follow in your brother's footsteps and become an agent?"

"If you join the Department of Supernatural Investigations, will you take up the search for VanQuish?"

I freeze up, stuck between wanting everyone to know I'm here to find my brother and hating being the center of attention. I just stand there, my eyes darting between them, until thankfully the secretary shoos them away. As she rushes me and Elsie down the aisle toward the stage, a full commotion breaks out in the seats. Kids stand to get a better look at us. Face burning, I pretend not to notice.

The secretary seats us in empty chairs at the very end of the first row, next to a tall, blond-haired boy whose posture is so perfect he might as well be a statue. The creases in his uniform look sharp enough to injure somebody. He cuts a glance at me, and then whispers something to the girl beside him. She snickers.

I sink in my seat a little. What is it about me that turns people off so much?

The secretary lady gives a thumbs-up to the stage.

The woman with the gills nods and steps to the podium. "Let's get started. My name is Elizabeth Crowe and I'm Chief Director here at the Bureau of Supernatural Affairs. I'd like to personally welcome you all. There's not a cooler summer camp in the whole world."

The auditorium applauds, and Chief Crowe continues. "The ceremony these young cadets are about to undertake is of the utmost importance. Each will be assigned a badge based on what we believe to be their current overall potential. But that's only half the reason for this occasion. The first law established by the very first Supernatural World Congress states that in order for one to be allowed entry into the supernatural world, one must *be* supernatural. For this reason, we will make each of you so. . . ."

I sit up in my chair. They're going to make us supernatural? How? I glance down the row at the other kids but no one else seems surprised by this.

"All of you possess a unique talent that we will enhance into a supernatural ability through an ancient gem gifted to us by the famed elf Merlin. For instance, if you are someone who is constantly being told how good a listener you are, once you've touched the Crystal Ball, you might find yourself capable of hearing through walls. Some of you will have a pretty good idea which of your talents will be enhanced; a great many more of you are in for a surprise. However, no matter the nature of your supernatural ability, rest assured there *is* a place for you somewhere within the Bureau."

So we get a supernatural ability based on our talents. But I don't have any special talents I can think of. At least nothing that could be turned into something cool like listening through walls.

"Allow me to say just one more thing to those of you receiving lesser badges today," Chief Crowe continues. "While it's true that badges are important in identifying those children we feel will be extraordinary additions to our ranks, don't allow your initial badge to define your career with the Bureau. Hard work can improve your badge over time. My position as Chief Director is a testament to that. I was only awarded a wooden badge when I first arrived at the Bureau." She taps on the shiny gold badge pinned to her jacket. "But now you can all see it's quite golden. So strive for excellence. Now, without further ado, let us proceed to the badge presentations and talent enhancements."

Please let Elsie be wrong about me getting that moonstone badge. The idea of having a badge higher than the Chief Director's makes me queasy.

While we all clap—me a lot less enthusiastically than the other kids in my row—Chief Crowe pushes her podium to the edge of the stage. From the other side, three men in dark suits push a hulking metal contraption front and center. Attached to the front is a Crystal Ball that stands around five feet tall.

The ceremony begins with the notebook paper badges. A short brunette girl named Aspen Matthews is the first to be called onstage to shake hands with the Chief Director, who hands her a smooth wooden box containing her badge. Then it's over to the machine to place her hand on the Crystal Ball, which glows faintly white at her touch. The giant screen blinks and then shows:

Talent Enhanced to Supernatural Ability:
Orderliness to Freakish Organization Skills

I turn to Elsie. "Freakish organization skills?"

"I know someone with that ability. If she was carrying a huge stack of papers and tripped, they'd all land exactly like she had them before." Elsie grimaces. "She'll probably end up in the Department of Supernatural Licenses and Records filing papers."

The crowd claps and Aspen is led offstage.

"Why would *anyone* want to be in a boring department like that?" I ask.

"Well, some people do prefer easier, less dangerous departments," says Elsie. "But usually it's one of two reasons. Either it's all you qualify for, or you make it to age eighteen without passing any tryouts and the Bureau just sends you wherever they need people. Noncompetitive departments like Supernatural Licenses and Records don't even have a tryout."

My name still hasn't been called by the time all of the plastic badges have been handed out. Uneasy, I glance over and catch statue boy watching me from the corner of his eye. He quickly looks away and then back to me. He says, "I wasn't staring."

"Didn't say you were."

"Oh . . . well, good then." He turns his attention back to the stage.

What's his problem?

Even with my growing knot of dread, things start to get more exciting by the time the bronze badges finally roll around. Not only does the Crystal Ball glow brighter when touched, but rarer abilities start popping up. A grinning kid named Billy Pogo's knack for being in the right place, at the right time, becomes Unnatural Luck. While he's onstage he gets a phone call stating he'll be inheriting his great-aunt's golden fleece collection.

Jonathan Zhang's talent is Hiding, and once it's enhanced, he happily demonstrates by turning his body into clear glass. He announces to everyone he's aiming for the Department of Spies and Secrets. Elsie elbows me and says, "Betcha he doesn't know that he'll have to get his memory erased every time he leaves the department." A dreamy-eyed girl named Julia Farsight's supernatural ability makes her a medium, a result she seems more than surprised to receive. Elsie bursts out laughing when I ask if it's better than being a small. I don't realize my mistake until Elsie says that she'll probably choose the Department of the Dead.

Elsie is one of only thirteen kids to receive a silver badge—meaning I've either got a gold badge or the scary moonstone badge.

Chief Crowe puts her arm around Elsie onstage and speaks briefly about the diversity benefits of having members who aren't fully human—she herself is half Atlantian. Elsie doesn't get a huge reaction from the crowd, so I make sure to stand up and holler, "Go, Elsie!" Statue boy frowns as I sit back down. Not that I care.

Badge in hand, Elsie moves nervously toward the Crystal Ball. She places her free hand against the crystal. It glows bright white, shimmering like a giant one-hundred-watt bulb.

Talent Enhanced to Supernatural Ability:
Inventiveness to Mastermind Inventor

Elsie beams. Her talent doesn't surprise me one bit. But then, having created that sneakandle and her own radio from spare parts, I'd have thought she was a mastermind inventor already. It's no wonder the Bureau has such amazing technology. They turn smart people into geniuses.

I try again to think of something I'm really good at. Falling asleep on the sofa after school? I doubt the Bureau would have much use for that.

As Elsie returns to her seat, Chief Crowe steps back to her podium. "Only once every few years do we get the honor of presenting an elite badge, and yet this year we shall present three. Dylan and Lara Van Helsing. Please come up and accept your gold badges."

Van Helsing? Why does that name sound so familiar? Then it hits me—my brother's partner! I nudge Elsie. "Are those two related to Maria Van Helsing?"

She nods. "Maria is the Van Helsing twins' older sister.

Their mom and dad are here too. The Van Helsings are one of the most important families in the supernatural world."

Is that why statue boy was staring? My whole body goes stiff as another realization comes. If they've got gold badges, that moonstone badge really does belong to me. So much for blending in.

Lara and Dylan both smile and wave toward the flashing cameras as they make their way to the stage—it's easy to see they're used to this kind of attention. Loud applause and cheers ring out in the auditorium. Lara's polite grin bursts into a big, toothy smile as she jogs up the few steps to the stage where Chief Crowe swallows her in a big hug. Dylan does a better job controlling his emotions and gives the chief a firm handshake. The whole auditorium hears the chief tell them how proud she is. All three pose for a few more pictures and then both Van Helsings are handed their badges. Dylan moves to the Crystal Ball first.

His cool smile is gone. In fact, he looks scared to death.

Guess I'm not the only one questioning what kind of supernatural ability they'll have. I lean forward in my chair, curious.

Dylan shakes out his hands and touches the Crystal Ball with just the tips of his fingers. The instant he does, blinding light pours out of the Crystal Ball, so bright I have to cover my eyes. Finally, his results show onscreen.

Talent Enhanced to Supernatural Ability:
Marksmanship to Physics-Defying Aim

Dylan looks as happy as I've ever seen anyone in my entire life. When his sister steps to the Crystal Ball, her talent starts off as Fitness and becomes Superhuman Athleticism. Lara decides to test out her supernatural ability, doing a long run of impossible jumps and flips across the stage. It looks like the special effects from a superhero movie. The crowd goes nuts. After a few bows Lara practically skips off the stage, her smirking brother right behind her.

The lights dim further as Chief Crowe returns to the podium. "And now for a very special presentation. The reason, I expect, that we have so many additional spectators this year. Amari Peters, please accompany me onstage."

Every eye in the auditorium watches me. Cameras flash like crazy. I'm not used to being the center of attention. Not for something good anyway. The walk to the stage seems endless.

My hands shake as I climb the stairs. My flushed face takes up the giant screen once I step onstage.

Chief Crowe smiles warmly and puts her arm around my shoulder. "It's very rare indeed that a moonstone badge is awarded. Rarer still to have two in the same family. There have only been thirteen in the whole history of the Bureau, and Amari here makes the second Peters to receive the honor."

The chief reaches into her suit jacket and pulls out a tiny wooden case. "I present to you the fourteenth moonstone ever awarded." She tilts it open and I peek inside. The round badge looks a lot like a medal without the ribbon. It's the size of my palm and twinkles in its case like a tiny star.

It's the most beautiful, most wonderful thing I've ever owned. It's also the badge my perfect brother received, and all those accomplished Bureau members before him. I don't deserve it.

Still, I take the case and everyone claps. Even with my doubts, I smile at the attention. It doesn't feel real—like it's happening to someone else. I spot Elsie bouncing in her seat in the front row. Then I spot the twins, both sitting stiffly, arms crossed.

Jealous much?

Now it's my turn to touch the Crystal Ball. I step past Chief Crowe and frown. I'm suddenly nervous at the prospect of revealing something about myself in front of all these people. What if my supernatural ability turns out to be something disappointing like superhuman knitting? I *was* really good at it when I was little. The truth is, I don't even know myself well enough to guess what it might choose.

But everyone's waiting.

Reluctantly, I place my hand on the Crystal Ball. . . .

And nothing happens. Not even the faintest glimmer of light. There's a collective gasp from the crowd. Cameras begin to flash again. I look to Chief Crowe, but she seems as confused as I am.

And then something does happen. A plume of black smoke appears, swirling and filling the ball completely. A crack reaches across the surface.

I yank my hand away. Take a few steps backward. So does Chief Crowe.

The screen flickers behind us.

Talent Enhanced to Supernatural Ability:
Dormant Magic to Active Magician (Illegal)

The auditorium erupts.

⪻ 10 ⪼

CONFIDENTIAL
MEETING
IN
PROGRESS

I SIT IN A COLD ROOM AT THE END OF A LONG, WOODEN table. After I was rushed offstage by Chief Crowe, she instructed two ladies in gray suits to bring me to a door marked *Conference Room*.

What happened back there? How could my talent be magic? I couldn't even pull off the simplest stuff in the "Magic Tricks for Beginners" playset I got for Christmas that one time.

I didn't even know that real magic existed until just recently.

I cover my face with my hands. If having magic makes me a magician and magicians are the enemies of the supernatural world like Elsie suggested . . . then what's going to happen to me now?

Raised voices and hurried steps echo in the hallway. Heart pounding, I sit up straighter in my chair. The door to the conference room swings open and half a dozen adults rush in.

I only recognize Chief Crowe, who dashes over and grabs me by both shoulders. "Are you all right, sweetheart?"

I nod. "What happened back there?"

"That's what we're trying to determine," says Chief Crowe. "But to do so, we'll need to conduct a very important test. Do we have your permission?"

I swallow and nod again. From the worried looks on everyone's faces, it's probably the only answer they'd accept.

Chief Crowe backs away. "Dr. Khan, if you wouldn't mind."

"Certainly," replies a jittery South Asian man in a long white lab coat. He steps forward to place a square piece of metal on the floor in front of my chair. The little screen near the top makes it look like a scale. Why would they need to check my weight?

"Remove your shoes and socks, please. You'll need to stand on it with your bare feet for the Magic-Meter to work properly."

Magic-Meter? Maybe there really was a glitch with the Crystal Ball, and this will prove that whatever happened back there was a mistake. It had to be.

The grown-ups all stare expectantly, especially a tall, stern-faced white guy who keeps pacing back and forth near the door. I pull off my shoes and socks and get to my feet. Then I take a slow, deep breath and step onto the Magic-Meter.

Numbers rise and fall on the little screen, until finally it settles on 97 percent. A second later it creeps up to 98 percent, then 99 percent, and finally 100 percent.

Dr. Khan gasps. "Every drop of this girl's blood is magical."

The adults rush to huddle near the door.

Dr. Khan just stares at me, eyes wide. So I ask, "What does that mean?"

"It means you're perhaps the most magical being that's ever existed." Dr. Khan lowers his eyes and frowns. "It also means your very existence is a crime."

A crime? But I haven't done anything. "The Bureau uses magical objects, don't they? So magic can't be all that bad."

"The Bureau isn't against objects being too magical," Dr. Khan replies. "It's against *people* being too magical. There's a big difference, I'm afraid."

Chief Crowe is back in front of me. "Amari, we're going to ask you some questions. It's important that you be completely honest with us, understand?"

But I've got my own questions. "How did I get magic?"

"It was my hope that *you* might tell *us*," says the stern-faced man. He crosses his arms, turning up his nose like he can't stand the sight of me. His golden name tag reads: *Director Van Helsing, Department of Supernatural Investigations*. He must be Maria's and the Van Helsing twins' dad.

My heart thumps faster.

"I don't know," I say. "I touched the Crystal Ball like everyone else—"

Director Van Helsing bangs his fist on the table so hard it makes everyone in the room jump. "The fourth law created by the first Supernatural World Congress states quite clearly that humans may receive magic from only one source—the Crystal Ball. A single 10 percent dose that gives us our supernatural abilities. Yet you have come to the Bureau with an overabundance of magic from an unknown source. Where did you get it?"

"I don't know," I say. "It's got to be a mistake."

"Tell the truth!" he says.

"I am!" I shout back, trembling.

Director Van Helsing won't let up. "You expect us to believe that you possess the highest magicality we've ever tested *by mere chance*?"

"No . . . I mean yes . . . I mean . . ." I'm shaking so much I don't even know what I'm saying.

"And I suppose we're also to believe it's a coincidence," Director Van Helsing continues, "that you showed up here at the same time hybrids are terrorizing our outposts around the country. It is common knowledge that only magicians can create hybrids. Tell me, girl, are these attacks your doing?"

"I don't know anything about that." I shrink back in my chair. "I swear—"

"Then perhaps," Director Van Helsing interrupts, "you

could simply tell us which other magician is responsible?"

The door swings open again and Agent Magnus steps through. "I'm here to speak on the kid's behalf." A tall lady with fiery red hair in a long ponytail hovers in the doorway behind him.

Director Van Helsing frowns. "This is a director-level meeting."

Magnus rolls his eyes. "Like I care a lick about that!"

"For the last time, you are not above the rules, Agent Magnus!" He looks to the chief, but she just waves him off.

"This is no time for you to quarrel," snaps Chief Crowe. "Let Magnus in. He was close to the girl's brother and might know something that could shed some light on how on earth Quinton's little sister is—of all the things in the world—a magician." She nods to the lady in the doorway. "Agent Fiona, I think we'd all feel a lot better if you could put that ability of yours to use and reveal the girl's intentions."

The red-haired lady nods and steps forward. She may not be a director like the other adults, but they all move aside for her. "No need to be frightened, lass," she says softly. "If you'll allow it, I'm going to check out your intentions for being here. You'll feel yourself go still for a bit but that's the worst of it."

"If you've truly got nothing to hide," says Director Van Helsing, crossing his arms, "then you'll have no objections to our proving it."

Again, I don't have much of a choice. If I refuse, then

they'll just assume the worst. I meet Agent Fiona's eyes. "Okay."

The room goes quiet as Agent Fiona puts herself right in front of me. Her fierce blue eyes widen and my whole body goes stiff. I try to look away, but my neck refuses to turn. My eyes are stuck on hers—I can't even close them. I'm totally helpless. I fight down my fear as best I can.

It's not until she finally blinks that I can move again. She cracks a smile. "Her intentions might as well be in big neon letters across her forehead they're so easy to read. She's an honest little thing. On the surface, the lass means to bolt for the door if she's not treated fairly in this meeting. Second, and most importantly, she's come to the Bureau to discover what happened to her brother and bring him home if she can. There's nothing dangerous in her intentions as far as I can tell."

I blink in surprise as the adults in the room exchange glances. Did that lady just read my mind?

"Normally I'd put complete faith in your ability, Fiona," says Director Van Helsing, "but magicians are known for their deception."

"It's true!" I say. "I just want to find Quinton."

"Do you imagine there's something you could be doing better?" Director Van Helsing scoffs. "My best agents were on that search—Magnus led the investigation himself."

Agent Magnus looks at me with sad eyes. "With the investigation being classified, the most I can say is we're currently out of leads."

Chief Crowe's tense expression relaxes a little. "We're all sorry about Quinton, and I'm quite relieved to hear that Amari means us no harm. I've got the utmost faith in Agent Fiona's ability. But there's still the troubling matter of *how* the girl became a magician. It's been more than two centuries since the last rogue magician emerged, and he quite famously blew himself up."

"Does the how even matter?" drones a pale, thin man. His name tag reads *Director Kript, Department of the Dead*. "The Bureau has had one policy for dealing with magicians for over seven centuries. Lock them up and throw away the key."

A few of the other directors nod in agreement. A serious lady in thick black glasses even suggests I be taken to her lab and studied. *Director Fokus, Department of Magical Science* is sewn onto her lab coat.

"Over my dead body!" Magnus replies. *And mine too*, I think. The red-haired lady moves to Magnus's side, leveling a withering stare at the directors who want me locked up. She and Magnus must be partners.

"*Please*, everyone just calm down," says Chief Crowe. "What we need right now is a thoughtful discussion about how best to proceed."

"Can I start by acknowledgin' that the kid's supernatural ability didn't pop up as evilness or spite," says Magnus. "So let's stop treatin' her like she did somethin' wrong."

"And yet we've all heard the terrible stories, haven't we?" says Director Cobblepot of the Department of Supernatural

Licenses and Records. "There's no such thing as a good magician. Let's not forget how close we came to canceling the training sessions this summer on account of those hybrid attacks."

More shouting follows. Chief Crowe closes her eyes and shakes her head.

Someone clears their throat loudly, quieting the room. "If I might have a word on the matter," says a gentlemanly voice.

I look around to see who's talking but no one's lips are moving. That's when Director Kript opens his suit jacket and places the head of an elderly brown man with a gray handlebar mustache gently onto the table. It takes my brain a few seconds to catch up to what my eyes are seeing, and when it does I jump in my seat.

"Where's the rest of you?" The words come out before I can stop myself.

But the man isn't offended. "Back in my office taking a most restful nap. What began as flexibility became detachability once I touched the Crystal Ball those many years ago." He winks at me. "Now then, as Director of the Unexplained, I believe the great many unanswerable questions surrounding young Amari here mean that she falls squarely under my jurisdiction."

I glance over at Magnus. He doesn't seem to like my being considered "unexplained" any more than I do.

"And what would *you* have us do?" asks Chief Crowe.

"When faced with a mystery, one must first determine

if said mystery presents a danger. We've established that the girl means us no immediate harm. The next step, then, is not to project our own prejudices onto the mystery, but rather to allow the mystery to reveal itself to us in its own time. Which is to say that I believe we should allow the girl to stay, if she wants to. She'd be monitored, of course, but discreetly. Also, it may be prudent to explain to her exactly why being a magician has caused such a commotion."

All eyes turn to me.

"That really would be helpful," I say.

"Allow me," says Chief Crowe. "In ancient times, long before the Bureau existed, there wasn't the separation between the known world and the supernatural world that exists now. Humans lived right alongside supernaturals and those supernaturals performed magic right out in the open. The thing was, with all the free-flowing magic that existed in the world, humanity had none of it. Not a single drop. Until the Night Brothers—Sergei Vladimir and Raoul Moreau.

"No one knows how the two of them obtained magic, just that they weren't satisfied with the 35 percent magicality of a common elf or even the 50 percent magicality of a woodland hag. They gave themselves more power than any single being has a right to possess. It's said that they could perform seemingly impossible feats. We know for a fact that they conquered old age and death, with a spell called Vampir, which requires consuming the blood of innocents. . . ."

I shudder. *Vampires?*

Chief Crowe pauses, visibly upset, so Agent Fiona picks up where she left off. "Ye can imagine that supernatural folk didn't take too kindly to humans terrorizing the land and upsetting the peace. And humans and supernaturals banded together to bring down the Night Brothers. But they were no match for the magicians. It seemed hopeless, that the Night Brothers would take control of the whole bloody world—"

"Until *my* ancestor," Director Van Helsing cuts in, "Abraham Van Helsing drove a stake through Vladimir's heart—a blow that sent Moreau into hiding and scattered their forces. On the strength of my ancestor's courage, certain humans were privileged to remain in contact with the supernatural world and enforce laws meant to keep its existence secret. These trusted men and women became the Bureau of Supernatural Affairs.

"For the nearly seven hundred years that the Bureau has existed, Moreau has continued to create new magician apprentices—until he was finally captured by my daughter and your brother. These newer magicians have been the cause of great tragedies and terrible disasters these many years. Humanity was never meant for such power. It corrupts the soul."

"That's quite enough," grumbles Magnus. "Leave your beliefs out of it."

I sit very still, trying to wrap my head around everything they've said. "You're saying the magic I have is bad?"

"At best we're saying we don't know," says the talking

head. "The amount of magic we receive from the Crystal Ball is but a fraction of what even the weakest magician possesses. At such high concentrations, we simply don't know what effects the magic, now that it's active, may have on you."

"I don't feel any different," I say.

"It does raise an interesting question. How can we be sure her talent was even enhanced?" asks Agent Fiona. "The ball didn't glow."

"In fact, it very nearly shattered," says Director Kript. "Let's not pretend that means nothing. Can you imagine how difficult it's going to be to explain to Merlin how we let a trainee destroy a priceless artifact of unending power?"

"No explanation will be necessary," says Director Fokus. "I rushed over right after with a couple of my best researchers to have a look at the damage . . . and there just wasn't any. The ball was in pristine condition, its magic functioning normally."

"What happened then?" asks Chief Crowe.

"In my professional opinion, the incident with the Crystal Ball revealed just what kind of magician Amari is." Director Fokus swallows. "She's an illusionist. If she possesses any other kind of magic in addition to this, such as what's necessary to create hybrids, it remains to be seen."

The directors look at one another with nervous glances. Even Magnus looks concerned.

So what happened onstage with the Crystal Ball was just an illusion? I'm not sure what to think about that.

"I just wish we had more information." Chief Crowe frowns. "If Horus were here he could peek into the girl's history, maybe discover how the magic was passed to her." She turns to Director Van Helsing. "I trust he's still away on sabbatical in the Wandering Isles?"

"Afraid so," says Director Van Helsing. "The isles were last seen just off the coast of Africa, but that was days ago. They could be anywhere in the world by now."

"Can we summon one of his underlings from the Department of Good Fortunes and Bad Omens to give us some advice on the matter?" asks Director Fokus.

The chief shakes her head. "I'd rather have Horus himself on something this important."

"Is this *really* a risk we're willing to take?" asks Director Van Helsing, throwing up his arms. "That she might not be so bad because her brother is a hero? Is it not the height of recklessness to allow a magician to roam freely inside the Bureau while there are still so many unanswered questions?"

"And just what do you suggest?" growls Magnus. "Lock her up for something she can't help? Fiona's already proven the girl isn't up to anything nefarious."

"Or perhaps she's been prepped to fool Fiona's supernatural ability," answers Director Van Helsing. "At the very least, we ought to erase the girl's memories of the supernatural world, erase her memories of being a magician, and then send her home to be carefully watched. She'd go back to being just an ordinary girl and no danger to the Bureau or the supernatural world."

"No!" I say, jumping to my feet. "You can't erase my memories. If you do, I'll never be able to find my brother. Let me stay. I'll prove that I'm just like any other trainee. *Please.*"

Director Van Helsing starts to say something more, but Chief Crowe asks for quiet. We all watch her pace back and forth a few times. Finally, she comes to a stop right next to me. "I can see benefits to both requests. But let's not forget it was Quinton himself who nominated her. There is not a person in this room who would question his judgment were he standing here. And so we shall give you the benefit of the doubt, Miss Peters. But understand that you'll be on the shortest possible leash. I won't compromise the safety of the Bureau, understand?"

A wave of relief and then nervousness rushes through me. "I understand."

"Good," she replies. "Prove that we're right to trust you. Prove you belong here."

11

AFTER THE MEETING, AGENT MAGNUS ESCORTS ME TO an elevator named Whispers, which surprisingly shouts out the name of every floor we pass. It's lucky for my ears that the Special Events floor is only a few stops up. As I follow Agent Magnus off the elevator, a voice comes over the intercom:

"This is your Chief Director speaking. With regard to this morning's unfortunate event, we are still working out the particulars of what exactly occurred and why. Rest assured that once we have this information we will be forthcoming with an explanation. In the meantime, Trainee Amari Peters is to be treated no differently from any other trainee. That is all."

"They were the ones who wanted to treat you differently in the first place," Agent Magnus grumbles. "Bunch of superstitious clucks. They'd jump off the roof if someone told 'em the building was unlucky."

"Thanks for having my back," I say.

"Don't sweat it, kid." Agent Magnus strokes his beard. "No way was I gonna let 'em throw you in jail or send you to some lab to be studied. But I ain't gonna lie, I'd rather the chief sent you home. I don't say it to be mean. I just want you to be perfectly clear on what you're signing up for here. Your brother's arrest of Moreau is still fresh in everyone's minds. And Moreau's awful deeds are well documented—as are the past seven hundred years of magician crimes in our world. People are going to form opinions and say nasty things about you based on nothing more than what you are. You sure you're prepared for that?"

I smile a little. Am I prepared for that? It's kind of like how being a Black kid from the projects makes Mr. Jenson feel the need to watch me extra close every time I come in his store. Or how surprised my scholarship interviewers were that I could speak *so* well. People assume stuff about you based on things you can't change about yourself. So I just do my best to prove them wrong, to be the person they're not expecting. Amari Peters, changing minds one person at a time.

"I'm prepared," I say. "I've been practicing my whole life."

Agent Magnus gives me a small nod and pats me on the back.

Unlike most of the other floors, the Special Events floor doesn't have a lobby. It's just a wide hallway that bends out of sight. I follow Agent Magnus down the hall past doors labeled *Ballroom*, *Meeting Room*, and *Formal Dining Room*. Finally, we reach one marked *Grand Theater*, where a young guy in a gray suit rushes over to tell Agent Magnus, "It's almost our turn."

"I'm right behind you," Magnus replies. Then he turns to me. "The presentations have already started, so go on in and take a seat at the back."

As much as I appreciate Agent Magnus's help, I realize I need to make something clear. "For as long as I get to stay, I'm going to be searching for my brother. Whether you help me or not."

Agent Magnus frowns. "Quinton would much rather you stay safe. This is dangerous stuff."

"I don't care how dangerous it is," I say. "I care about Quinton."

"And he cares about you. Heck, you're all he used to talk about. Amari this, and Amari that. So before you do something dumb, I'd ask you to consider how Quinton's gonna feel if he manages to get himself found only to discover something terrible has happened to his little sister because she went looking for him. He'd be devastated."

I don't know what to say to that. Agent Magnus knows he dropped a truth bomb right smack on my forehead. He's already started down the hallway.

Shoulders slumped, I step into a massive, darkened

theater with endless rows of seats curving around a wide stage. I'm thankful that whatever this is has already started. Everyone's attention is on the stage instead of me. I'm even more thankful to find Elsie waving me over to a seat she's saved for me in the last row.

"Your aura's yellow again," says Elsie. "What happened back there?"

I shrug.

She lowers her voice. "People are saying . . . Are you really a magician?"

"I think so," I say. "An illusionist."

Elsie thinks on this for a few seconds. "Well, if anybody gives you mean looks you let me know and I'll . . ."

"*Not* breathe fire on them?" I smile.

"Hey!" she says, giving me a playful punch. "I'm working on shifting, just you wait."

"Thanks for not freaking out," I say.

"Well, if you can handle rooming with a girl who could turn into a dragon at any time, then I can handle being friends with a baby magician. I'm really glad they're letting you continue on."

"Me too," I say, and then point toward the stage. "So what's this all about?"

Elsie hands me her copy of *One Thousand and One Careers* and says, "It's basically a presentation from each department explaining what they do and why we should choose them."

I flip through the pages. "What have I missed so far?"

"Not a whole lot," says Elsie. "Somebody from the

Department of Supernatural Licenses and Records nearly put us all to sleep with a demonstration of orderly filing techniques. And just now, Director Rub-Ish from the Department of Half Truths and Full Cover-Ups invited a few kids onstage and had them pick out their favorite historical event so she could explain what *really* happened. Did you know that World War One started because a few tiny alien ships accidentally crash-landed into Archduke Franz Ferdinand and his wife? Everyone thought it was an assassination. The aliens visit three times a year to apologize for the mix-up."

The departmental presentations are amazing. A man from the Department of Hidden Places steps out of a top hat, where he claims an entire city is kept. A woman from the Department of Dreams and Nightmares puts the entire front row of the theater to sleep with a snap of her fingers, and then convinces them that they're all being chased by a giant, evil teddy bear named Bubbles, Destroyer of Worlds. Two grumpy old men from the Department of the Unexplained tell us absolutely nothing at all about what they do, on principle. A girl from the Department of Supernatural Health has us clap along as she sings a man out of a coma.

I'm about to ask if Elsie has any idea how long that poor guy has been in a coma when shouts ring out from above us. Every head in the theater turns upward to find men and women in gray suits running across the walls. They leap into the air, doing flips and twirls overhead.

Wow! A couple of them swing whips of fire while others

twirl staffs of glittering light. Finally, each one stops to toss a plate in every direction. Out of nowhere Agent Fiona appears, standing upside down on the ceiling, and draws a bow and arrow. She fires a single arrow that explodes into a flash of lightning that branches out to destroy every plate. Eventually, they all land onstage, bowing to thunderous applause from the trainees.

I'm clapping, too, my heart pounding with excitement. That was *amazing*.

That's when Agent Magnus walks onstage to join them, frowning harder with every step. "I'm guessin' you all know an agent when you see one. And I'm guessin' a great many of you are thinking of trying out, am I right? Well, what they don't tell you is that there ain't a more dangerous job in the whole Bureau. Agents get hurt. Good agents too. In nasty, gruesome ways. I know I'm wasting my breath. You'll all be after the glory and excitement that comes with wearing this gray suit. You all want to be real-life superheroes, am I right? Well, just don't say you weren't warned."

Then he turns and stomps off the stage.

The demonstrations continue for hours but I'm barely paying attention. I'm thinking about trying out for Junior Agent. And not just because of how cool the Supernatural Investigations presentation was. Everything about Quinton is there—it's where he works, where the people who know him work, and even where the people who are searching for him will be.

But Agent Magnus's warning felt especially meant for

me—a reminder of what he just told me about putting myself in unnecessary danger.

Once the demonstrations are finally over, the lights come up and cards are passed around the theater. On them, you're supposed to write down your top five choices. I watch Elsie scribble Department of Magical Science as her top choice and then quickly fill in the other four slots.

I stare down at my own card and scribble Junior Agent in big letters.

I scratch it out just as fast.

"I think you'd make a great agent," says Elsie. "You're a Peters, you've practically got hero in your genes."

Her eyes are so full of belief that it almost convinces me. I shake my head. "I don't feel like a hero. Maybe Agent Magnus is right—Quinton would want me to be safe. And besides, my supernatural ability is illegal. They probably wouldn't even let me in."

"Do you want in?" Elsie asks.

I nod.

"Good, because if the situation were reversed, I don't think there's anything anyone could say to Quinton to convince him not to look for you."

She's got a point—if my stubborn, hard-headed brother decided he was going to look for me, no one would be able to stop him.

Elsie smiles. "Now go on and get yourself into Supernatural Investigations so we can start our *own* investigation."

Did she say *we*? "You mean you'll help me find out what happened to Quinton?"

Elsie nods. "I'll do whatever I can. Promise."

Just having one person with me is a huge weight off my shoulders. I instantly feel ten times lighter.

Grinning, I jot down Department of Supernatural Investigations. I'm still beaming when I hand it to the guy collecting them at the back of the theater.

He takes a quick peek at my card and nearly drops the entire stack in surprise.

Not only did I pick Supernatural Investigations as my top choice, I left the other four slots empty.

12

AFTER THE DEPARTMENTAL PRESENTATIONS, WE'RE GIVEN the rest of the afternoon off to get ready for the Welcome Social at 6:30. It's a chance for all the incoming trainees to get to know one another. Except while most of the other kids crowd the hallways joking and laughing and comparing outfits, Elsie and I lock the door to our room and begin our investigation into the disappearance of VanQuish.

"First, we need to come up with an actual plan and then make sure we follow it," says Elsie. "The best way to do that is to put it into writing." She uses her sleeve to wipe some equations from her whiteboard before she lays it down on the floor between our beds. "So what's been your plan so far?"

I bite down on my lip. "I don't really have a *plan* plan."

Elsie shoots me a look. "You were just going to make it up as you go along?"

My cheeks flush. "It does sound pretty dumb when you say it like that."

My roommate just shakes her head. "You can't investigate anything without a plan." She pulls the top off her marker and writes . . .

Step One
Come up with a plan.

"Did you really even have to write that?" I ask.

"Yes. Now let's think."

We're both quiet for a bit before I say, "I guess what I've been doing so far is just trying to get some answers about the Bureau's investigation. But all Agent Magnus will tell me is that it's classified. It's like the only word he knows."

Elsie nods and writes out:

Step Two
Find out what the Bureau already knows about Van-Quish's disappearance.

And that's when I realize I actually did have a plan. I slide off my bed onto the floor beside Elsie and pick up one of her spare markers.

I write:

Step Three
Use what we find out to launch our own investigation.

My roommate grins. "This is a good start."

"Too bad we're going to be stuck on Step Two forever.

It's not like they'll suddenly decide to make the VanQuish files *un*classified just for us."

"You're probably right," says Elsie. "But we don't need the files. We just need to find someone who knows something and might be willing to talk."

I think back on all the people I've met at the Bureau so far. Then it hits me. Elsie looks up at the same time as I do and we both say, "The Van Helsing twins!" Their dad is the Director of Supernatural Investigations, they're bound to have heard something about the search.

"Hope you feel like dancing," says Elsie, "'cause they'll definitely be at the social tonight."

When 6:30 comes, Elsie's all dressed and ready to go. She put on one of the dresses that made their way into our closet after the departmental presentations. Her dress is so cool—it looks like she's wrapped herself in sparkling blue ocean. Waves seem to ripple across the fabric, and a school of bright orange fish zips around her waist. The water looks so real I think my hand might get wet if I touch it.

Somehow, our closet seems to magically contain whatever outfit we need. I wish it would magic up some comfy pajamas, because that's how little I feel like going to a Welcome Social.

"You're still not dressed?" Elsie makes an exasperated face.

"There's got to be an easier way," I say. "Can't we just surprise one of them in the hallway or something?"

"The Van Helsing twins stay with their parents in the director apartments," says Elsie. "The only time they come down here is to visit one of their friends. It could take weeks to run into them by chance. We don't have that kind of time."

"Fine," I groan.

Elsie skips over to the closet. "Hmm, there's a white dress in here from Madame Duboise that would be *a-maz-ing* on you." She holds it up and it looks like it's made of actual clouds.

"Ugh. Like I need any more attention. It'll be bad enough just showing up as the magician who received a moonstone badge this morning."

"You're looking at this the wrong way," says Elsie. "Lara and her friends love anything that gets them more attention. Being the magician girl with a moonstone badge is the reason they'll want to hang out with you." She holds up the cloud dress again. "You're kind of a big deal. Might as well look the part."

Fifteen minutes later, the two of us take an opera-singing elevator named Luciano back to the Special Events floor. Music booms behind the golden ballroom doors. Two ladies in butler uniforms push them open for us.

I stop cold. When they said this year's theme is Winter Wonderland, they really meant it. It's snowing inside the huge ballroom. Snow-covered fir trees grow straight up out of the floor and huge ice sculptures of dancing penguins and laughing polar bears fill up the spaces between the candlelit tables. Kids dance in midair, squealing and laughing as they're carried back and forth by swirling gusts of wind.

I start to feel that same bubbly excitement I got the first time I saw those underwater trains with Quinton. This is incredible.

Elsie's freckled face beams as she takes my hand. "Ready?"

"As ready as I'm going to be."

As we make our way through the tables, I do my best to ignore all the stunned faces that turn my way. It's hard though. It feels like the whole room is staring. This is just what I was afraid of—having the same "outsider" spotlight shining down over me as I had back at Jefferson Academy. I honestly feel like I could throw up.

"There's Lara," says Elsie, nodding toward a tall girl in a dress that sparkles like diamonds moving through the crowd of kids near the snack table. "Let's go talk to her while she's alone."

I fight down my nerves and try to focus on why I'm here—to get answers. After a deep breath I say, "Let's do it."

"Be confident," Elsie says.

"Right," I say. "Confident."

"And whatever she says about me, just ignore it. We can't blow this chance."

Before I can ask what she means, Elsie reaches Lara and gives her a polite tap on the shoulder.

When Lara spins around, it's like she's posing for a photo or something. That girl is crazy pretty. Like, never-used-a-filter-in-her-life pretty.

Lara frowns and rolls her eyes when she realizes it's Elsie. "What do *you* want? Please tell me you aren't here to beg me to be friends again."

If Elsie's feelings are hurt, she doesn't show it. "I just thought you'd like to meet *the* Amari Peters."

Lara finds me over Elsie's shoulder and her whole face lights up. She brushes past Elsie like she's not even there. Next thing I know, Lara is throwing an arm around my shoulder and snapping a quick selfie.

"I'm Lara Van Helsing," she says confidently. "You may not know this, but your brother and my sister were partners."

All I can think to say is, "They're famous." So dumb.

"The *most* famous." Lara grins. "You have to come sit at our table," she says, leaning in close. "My friends are dying to meet you."

"Actually, I was kind of hoping to talk to you about VanQuish—"

"Just come and say hello," Lara interrupts. "It'll take two seconds. Then we can talk all about my sister and your brother. Deal?"

Lara looks at me like telling her no would break her heart. I glance around but Elsie is nowhere to be found.

"Don't worry about Elsie. We used to be besties, like, *forever* ago. But that was before she went and got boring. I mean c'mon, a weredragon who can't even shift. . . . Anyway, you coming?"

Who does this girl think she is? I'm just about to tell her about herself but remember Elsie's warning just in time. She knew Lara might badmouth her and told me to ignore it. So, hard as it is, I force a smile and say, "Maybe just a quick hello."

Lara squeals and takes my hand, then leads me to the other side of the ballroom where a few tables have been pushed together. The kids there all look bored silly. Lara clears her throat loudly. "Meet my new friend, Amari Peters."

That gets their attention. They all turn to look at me.

Feeling myself flush, I give a little wave. One of the boys stands up and says, "You can have my seat."

That's when Dylan Van Helsing catches my eye. He's seated on the other side of the table, arms crossed. Just like his sister, he's cute enough that he looks like he flies out to international modeling gigs after the last school bell rings. He mouths, "Don't."

But before I can react, Lara practically shoves me down into the seat. Dylan sighs and shakes his head.

"They're really letting you stay on after cracking the Crystal Ball?" asks a girl in a gown that looks like a starry night sky. "I'm Kirsten Kurst, by the way."

My heart sinks down into my belly. "I didn't actually

crack it," I say, quickly. "It was an illusion." I shrug. "An accident."

The others all look at one another with wide eyes.

"And they *know* you're a magician?" asks a boy in a shiny, metallic gold suit. "I heard all the worst magicians were illusionists."

I nod. "They're um . . . giving me a chance to prove myself."

A boy in a sky-blue suit holds up his phone. "Geez, her touching the crystal is trending at number one! Can you believe that?"

"I am?" I say. "On YouTube?"

"Not the *inter*net," says Kirsten. "The *other*net. It's the protected part of the internet we use in the supernatural world."

"Oh," I say.

"Well, it really was a killer entrance," he replies. "No way it'll ever be topped."

I crack a nervous smile. Lara is awful, but maybe her friends aren't? Maybe they understand? "I wish it had been a boring entrance. I'd even take a different badge if I could."

No one at the table returns my smile, and I wonder if I've said the wrong thing. I glance over at Dylan again, but he won't meet my eyes.

"Amari, settle an argument for us," says another boy. "One last vacation before you die: London or Rome?"

"I've never been to either," I say.

He looks shocked. "Oh, I bet your people are yacht people, right? Saint Tropez?"

I sit staring at the table in front of me. These kids really do live in a totally different world. Yachts and trips to fancy places. What do I know about that?

"My family isn't rich," I say. "It's just me and my mom. She's a nursing assistant at a hospital."

"A nursing . . . assistant?" asks Brian Li, who I remember touching the Crystal Ball right before Elsie. "Aren't nurses already assistants?"

Laughter. My fists clench beneath the table. It feels like I'm drowning.

"But if your family is broke," asks the boy in the gold suit, "then how did you and Quinton get in?"

"Didn't you know?" answers Lara, who's finally made her way around the table to take a seat next to her brother. "Quinton wasn't a legacy kid; he was merit."

The whole table goes quiet. They all stare at me like I've got two heads or something.

"What does *merit* mean?" I ask.

Kirsten leans in. "It means your brother got in for doing something noteworthy, like saving a family from a burning building or acing one of the national exams. Most kids at the Bureau get in because they have a family member who nominated them. Many of us can trace back our family history in the Bureau for hundreds of years."

"The Van Helsings founded the Bureau," Lara adds matter-of-factly.

"Merits are basically what the Bureau does to fill any leftover seats once the legacy nominations have all been sent out," says Kirsten.

"Well," says Lara, "I don't mind as long as they know their place."

"What's that supposed to mean?" I ask.

"It means they shouldn't set their sights too high," says Kirsten. "They should just take an unimportant specialty and be grateful."

Lara rolls her eyes. "But you know they won't. They'll all try out for Junior Agent anyway."

"So what if Quinton was merit?" I say. "My brother was one of the best agents there's ever been."

"Even a broken clock is right twice a day." Lara cocks her head to one side. "My father tells us about it every year. Merit kids who go out for fancy specialties only to fail the tryout and get sent home without a scholarship. And let's be real, they're the ones who really need the scholarships."

"You can only try your best," I say. "Why shouldn't they choose something that really interests them?"

"Did you read that off a poster?" Lara covers her mouth dramatically. "Wait, don't tell me you signed up for Junior Agent? I mean, *technically* you're a legacy kid, but barely."

"What if I did?"

Lara huffs and I see it—that same I'm-better-than-you attitude flashes in her eyes that I used to see in Emily Grant's. "*Please*. Do you really think lightning is going to strike twice? I mean one ghetto kid stumbling into fame is rare enough, don't you think?" She leans closer, lowering her voice so that she's practically growling at me. "Face it, fancy badge or not, you don't even have a supernatural ability. Not a real one."

Snickers ring out around the table.

"I do," I say.

"Then show us," says Lara.

I just sit there as the others try to hold in their laughter. Lara pokes out her bottom lip mockingly. "How tragic."

I stand up from the table quickly, knocking my chair over. "Leave me alone!" I'm shaking.

"Or what? You and your disgusting magician friends will sic your nasty hybrids on me? You shouldn't even be here!"

I don't only hear Lara's voice. I hear Emily Grant and her stuck-up friends too. Anger surges through me. And then, suddenly, a swirling blaze of fire erupts on the table between me and Lara. My breath hitches, and the kids fall over one another as they scramble to get away.

"Disgusting magician!" Lara glares at me over the blaze.

That's when I feel two hands steer me away from the table. "Hey!" I say in protest, but it's just Elsie. She's a lot stronger than she looks. I glance over my shoulder to see my fire fade away without a single burn mark anywhere. Thank goodness. Elsie doesn't let me go until we're back on the other side of the ballroom.

"Your aura was burning red," she says. "Figured I'd get you out of there before you did something you'd regret." She sets a plate in front of me. "Eat."

"Maybe I don't—" The aroma of the pepperoni pizza hits me and I don't even remember what I was saying. I start in immediately on a thick, cheesy slice.

I'm halfway through it when Elsie says, "I'm guessing things didn't go well, huh?"

I groan. "I don't think Lara ever wanted to talk about Quinton and Maria. She just wanted to get me in front of her stupid friends to make fun of me."

Elsie winces. "Sounds like Lara. I thought with how much she looked up to Maria, she might want to help us." She shakes her head. "She wasn't always like that. When we were younger, back before she cared about being a 'Van Helsing,' she used to be really nice."

"Well, that Lara is long gone."

Elsie nods.

Once I've finished my plate, I pull out my new cell phone and set it in front of Elsie. "Can you show me how to access the othernet? I want to be able to check social media."

"Do you really think that's a good idea?" asks Elsie. "The supernatural world isn't much nicer than the known world."

"I know," I say. "I just want to show everyone the real me. Can you do it for me?"

"Okay, but you've got to promise me something in return."

"Deal," I say.

Elsie not only downloads the app that lets me access

the othernet, she even creates a profile for me on Eurg-phmthilthmsphlthm, the leading social media site in the supernatural world.

"How do you even pronounce that?" I ask.

"You don't," she replies. "Humans don't have enough tongues."

"Oh, okay then."

Elsie's request is that I go with her to the aerial dance floor. She swears it'll lift my spirits. And even though I don't ask, she can't wait to tell me how it works. "It's basically a mini-tornado, but it's controlled so it isn't dangerous." Even down here on the ground I can feel the wind on my face. Kids whip around in fast circles high into the air and back down again.

"Okay, the next time a spot opens up we're jumping in," says Elsie.

I'm a little nervous, but with the way this whole day has gone, I just want to do something fun. And Elsie is so excited it's hard for me not to feel it too. She nods along to the music and next thing I know, so do I.

Elsie and I are next in line. "Ready?" she asks.

A hand lands on my shoulder. I turn to discover it's Dylan Van Helsing. I shrug it off, instantly annoyed. "Can't you guys take a hint?"

He raises both hands in surrender. "Not me. My father wants to talk with you."

"What does your dad want?" I ask Dylan as I follow him across the ballroom. Lara could've run off to tell her dad about my fire illusion. What if he thinks I'm out of control? The chief made it clear that I'm on a short leash.

Dylan shrugs. "No clue."

My heart is beating so fast. But not so fast that I don't realize I've got another chance at a Van Helsing twin. "Well, can you at least tell me if you know anything about what happened to my brother . . . and your sister?"

"My dad said that he'd let us know as soon as they learned something," he grumbles. "That was six months ago."

I shake my head. Another dead end.

Dylan stops to look at me. "But . . . I've done my own snooping around and managed to find out a few things on my own."

"Tell me."

He gives me a questioning look. "Why should I?"

"Because it's not just your sister that's missing. It's my brother too. You should understand how I feel. *Please*." I only hope he isn't as awful as his sister.

Dylan frowns. For a moment it seems like he won't answer, but then he says, "*Fine*. But over there." He points to an empty section of the ballroom.

Once we're there, he says, "The Bureau knows who took Quinton and Maria. They have for months now."

"Really? Who was it?"

Dylan drops his voice even lower. "It was one of Moreau's people. A couple months after VanQuish went missing, a letter arrived at the Bureau offering a trade. It said that if the Bureau refused, then no one would be safe. It was signed, *Moreau's loyal apprentice*."

My breath catches. "Does that mean Quinton and Maria are alive? That they're okay?"

"I hope so," says Dylan.

If the letter was from Moreau's apprentice, then maybe Quinton and Maria were taken so they could be traded for Moreau's freedom. "What did the Bureau do about the letter?"

"Doesn't seem like they did anything," Dylan says angrily. "And there have been hybrid attacks ever since."

Hybrids? My brain tries to process what I just heard. The magician who's been attacking the Bureau is the same person who took my brother.

I can't believe Director Van Helsing accused me of being that magician. Did he really think I'd kidnap my own brother? "Wait, so the Bureau just ignored the letter?"

"As far as I can tell." He looks me right in the eyes. "But don't tell anyone what I just said if you know what's good for you. It's supposed to be top secret. Classified."

I nod. "I won't say a thing."

Dylan nods and says, "C'mon. My dad is over with the other chaperones."

"Hey, wait a sec. So, um, Elsie and I are doing our own

investigating too. Maybe we could all work together?"

He shrugs. "Maybe." Then he turns and heads over toward his dad.

Maybe? I think, following.

Director Van Helsing breaks off from a group of adults once we get close.

"I saw you two head off by yourselves," he says. "What was that about?"

"Sorry," says Dylan with a smirk. "I was just telling Amari that she should leave the investigating to those with actual experience."

I glare at him. Why put me on blast like that? Especially in front of his dad?

Director Van Helsing narrows his eyes. "I see."

"Did you need anything else?" Dylan asks.

"No, that's all, son," says Director Van Helsing.

Dylan walks off and suddenly it's just me and Director Van Helsing. I just know I'm in trouble. I can't even meet his eyes.

Director Van Helsing pulls out my card. "You've only written Junior Agent here."

"That's . . . um, that's what I want to do," I say, trying to sound confident.

He sighs. "You want to follow in your brother's foot-steps. That's understandable—"

"That's not the reason," I interrupt. "I want to find out what happened to my brother. Everything there is to know about Quinton is in the Department of Supernatural Investigations. And the only way I can be there is to become a Junior Agent."

Even though he's trying to look calm, I can tell he's annoyed. "*Whatever* the reason, you are clearly underestimating just how difficult it is to earn a position as Junior Agent. It's not only the most competitive specialty here, but you'll be competing with students from longstanding legacy families who have known about the supernatural world their whole lives. Children with the means to visit the places you'll only have read about. Private tutors and the like. You're at a tremendous disadvantage."

"Maybe my chances aren't great," I say. "But Quinton had the same disadvantage and he was able to make Junior Agent."

"Your brother's supernatural ability was quite literally Super-Genius Aptitude—we could show him nearly anything once and he'd learn it, just like that. He's the exception, not the rule, Amari."

I feel my shoulders droop. "But it's still my choice, right?"

"Well, of course. I just want you to be realistic. It may not be fair, but our job is to choose the trainees who will make the best agents."

"My badge shows I've got as much potential as anyone," I say.

Van Helsing blows out a long breath. "Understand that you don't get to come back next summer and try again like the other children. You are a magician, a criminal, and should you fail to prove you belong here, the chief will have no choice but to implement my suggestion to take your memories and send you home to be monitored. Trainees have until the first tryout to transfer into a different specialty. After that you're on your own. There's never been a moonstone badge recipient who failed a tryout. But then, perhaps your being a magician is the only thing special about you."

He turns to leave but stops himself. "And if I hear about you using another spell in this building, *especially* in my daughter's direction, you're gone, understand? Consider yourself extremely lucky that a witness vouched for you. Goodnight, Miss Peters."

The director stomps off. I could cry I feel so discouraged.

My phone buzzes. It says I've got a new message on my profile, but last I looked it was still set to private. So how could anyone find me? Curious, I click on the flashing icon.

New Message from magiciangirl18:
Keep your head up, Amari Peters. You aren't alone.

THE NEXT MORNING ELSIE AND I JOIN A BUNCH OF trainees at the youth dormitory elevators. We found our uniforms—a gray suit for me and a white lab coat for Elsie—waiting for us in our closet. I nearly panicked when I saw my moonstone badge sparkling on the front. How did it even get out of its case? Doesn't matter. No way am I walking around with a shimmering "Look at Me" badge attached to my jacket. I took it off and reattached it under my lapel to keep it hidden.

All around us kids talk excitedly. Once again, I'm thankful for the distraction because no one pays much attention to me and Elsie whispering near the back of the crowd. After last night, we've still got a lot to talk about.

"I think Dylan was telling the truth about the letter," says Elsie. "He's been honest for as long as I've known him. I'll bet whoever took VanQuish tried to trade them for Moreau."

"But that would mean the Bureau ignored a chance to get my brother back."

Elsie frowns. "They'd have to. Otherwise, every bad guy in the supernatural world would start kidnapping agents to make outrageous demands."

I hate that Elsie is making so much sense. Because it doesn't make me feel any better at all.

"What are you going to do about magiciangirl18?" Elsie continues.

A jolt of unease zips through me again. How did magiciangirl18 even know I'd made a profile? "I already told you, I'm not doing anything about it."

"But what if she's the same magician the Bureau is looking for?" Elsie's face goes red. "What if *she's* Moreau's apprentice?"

"Why would that magician want to be nice to *me*?" I ask. "I'll bet it's actually somebody pretending to be a magician just to mess with me." Like when Emily Grant and her friends sent me friend requests out of nowhere just so they could post mean things on my page. "Besides, Director Van Helsing already thinks I'm a criminal. That message is the excuse he needs to kick me out."

We find a spot on a packed elevator next to a large group of boys in scuba gear. Clearly they're headed to the Department of Undersea Relations.

Two girls in safari gear squeeze on last. Their name-tags say they're trying out for the Department of Creature Control. "You don't think they'll make us walk through the Woodland Predators section, do you?" one of them asks. "Maybe," says the other. "When my uncle was twelve he went totally bald after getting too close to an African lighting bird nest during his tour."

My stomach is doing flips thinking about what my own first day will be like. Supernatural Investigations is the most dangerous, most competitive specialty there is.

"I'm pretty sure the first day is just a tour," says Elsie, giving me a soft nudge with her elbow. "Nothing to be worried about."

"Thanks," I say, remembering that she can see just how worried I really am. I don't think I'll ever totally get used to Elsie knowing exactly how I'm feeling. But right now I need a little reassurance. Director Van Helsing's words keep replaying in my head. Surely you can't fail a tour, can you?

I shake out my nerves. I've got to focus on why I'm here. I need to find out if Dylan was telling the truth about the stuff he told me last night. Elsie might believe him, but the way he turned on me in front of his dad makes me worried he might've just been messing with me.

I'll just have to find out for myself. Which means the plan stays the same for Elsie and me—find out as much as we can.

And this tour is the perfect time to learn my way around Quinton's department—like where Quinton and Maria's office is located and where all the files are kept.

As for how we'll get into those places? We'll figure that out later.

By the time the elevator arrives at the Department of Supernatural Investigations, it's half full. Around thirty kids in light gray suits all stand shoulder to shoulder.

Seeing the lobby for the first time feels like I've somehow stepped into one of those old black-and-white movies. The floors are covered with black-and-white tiles. The walls are glistening white, and two black pillars surround a white statue of Abraham Van Helsing driving a stake into Vladimir, one of the Night Brothers.

"Good luck," Elsie says as the elevator doors slide open. She gives me two big thumbs-up.

"Thanks," I say, stepping off. "You too." If I wasn't nervous before, I definitely feel it now. I gulp as the elevator lifts Elsie away. *You're on your own now, Amari.*

"It's not too late to turn back," sings a voice I recognize. Lara Van Helsing smirks at me from beside her brother at the far end of the line. Nearly all the kids from her table at the social are here too.

"See that statue?" Lara adds. "That's how the Bureau feels about magicians." She and her friends laugh. Only Dylan keeps a straight face.

I ignore them and find a spot at the opposite end of the line. The lobby stays pretty quiet except for the whispers coming from the twins' little group. Everybody else looks just as nervous as I feel.

After a few minutes, there's a loud click and a section of the back wall slides away. Agent Fiona steps into the doorway. "The Red Lady," someone murmurs. It's easy to see how she got the nickname. Unlike yesterday, her blazing red hair is flowing and wild, falling down over her shoulders like it might bite anyone who comes too close with a comb. Those piercing blue eyes dart around the room like they're watching everything at once.

"So none of ye are any good at heeding warnings?" asks Agent Fiona.

No one dares to answer.

"Well, don't go losing your nerve now," she says pacing back and forth in front of us. "If ye can't find your voice in front of me, what chance do ye have against a forest of tree zombies closing in for a bite? Or a score of stone-skinned gargoyles circling above ye with ill intentions?"

"I'm sure you'll see to it we're ready for whatever comes our way," says Lara Van Helsing, stepping forward from the line. "And I, for one, am ready for the challenge."

Ugh. Lara is so full of herself.

Agent Fiona stalks over, stopping directly in front of her. She towers over Lara, sizing the girl up. "You've got the look of a lass who's hunting glory, little Van Helsing. And trust me, there's a good bit of glory to be found as an agent. But there's no surer way to fail at this than to go seeking it out. You'd do well to remember that. Ye all would."

I'm enjoying the embarrassed look on Lara's face when those blue eyes find me. My heart skips a beat.

"Peters," Agent Fiona calls out. "Step forward."

And here I was hoping to stay invisible today. But I do as I'm told.

The way I feel as Agent Fiona approaches me is how gazelles must feel when a lion shows up. She puts her face really close to mine, staring into my eyes. It's completely different from how she looked at me yesterday and it's all I can do just to stand my ground. *Did I do something to make her mad?*

"I suppose ye think you're special with your fancy badge. Better than the rest of us?"

I shake my head. "No, I—"

"No?" says Agent Fiona. "Then can ye tell me what on earth made ye put down Junior Agent when ye ain't got a supernatural ability to speak of?"

"I *do* have a supernatural ability," I say. "It's just . . . illegal."

"Same difference in the end," says Agent Fiona. "When a werewolf's got ye by the throat, ye can be sure he won't be giving ye the courtesy of a time-out to let ye work out if it's okay to use your illusions or not. So, tell me, why are ye here?"

Agent Fiona read my intentions yesterday, so there's no point in lying. "T-to f-find my brother." I hate how shaky my voice sounds.

"So ye don't want to be an agent to help others—only yourself. That right?"

"I . . ."

"And if I said you're wasting your time? That in all my years of training agents I've never seen a worse prospect?"

A few kids snicker at that. Out of the corner of my eye, I see Lara clap a hand over her mouth to keep from laughing out loud. Agent Fiona might as well have punched me right in the gut. It's the same as always, somebody looks at me and thinks that I'm not good enough. I drop my head.

"Nothing to say, lass?"

Maybe I'm not Quinton, but I bet I could be a decent agent if I decided to be. I'm tired of being underestimated. "You're wrong about me," I squeak out.

"What's that?" she says.

"I said you're wrong about me. I *can* be an agent."

"So ye mean to prove me wrong, then?"

"I *will* prove you wrong."

"That so? Well it ain't just *me* doubtin' ye." Agent Fiona points to the row of kids behind me. "They doubt ye too. Same goes for all the higher-ups who were *so* eager to tell me to turn ye away. What have ye got to say to that?"

"I don't care. I *will* be an agent."

The Red Lady's expression softens so that she looks more like the woman who fought for me yesterday. She lowers her voice so that only I can hear her. "Keep that wildfire burnin' inside ye, lass. And let all of their doubts become kerosene. Because ye know what I see when a lass is maligned for something she can't help and yet she still shows up anyway?"

I shake my head.

"Courage," says Agent Fiona. "And that's what separates the wannabes from the agents in the end. Quinton didn't nominate ye 'cause he needed a rescuer, he nominated ye because he believed ye can thrive here. Only you've gotta believe it before anybody else will." She leans back and unclips my moonstone badge from beneath my lapel to place it back in its original spot. "Now, back in line with ye."

I glance at the other trainees as I step backward. A couple look back at me with hesitant smiles, but most everyone else looks wary or even mad. It doesn't matter. Agent Fiona is right about one thing—I can be brave. I have to be.

Agent Fiona cracks a wicked smile and opens her arms wide. "Welcome to Junior Agent tryouts. Of all the trainees who wrote down Junior Agent on their cards, the thirty-two of ye are considered the cream of the crop. Those fancy badges ye carry signify you've got plenty of potential, but you've already come as far as those'll take ye. For the privilege of wearing this suit you'll have to prove your worth in the tryouts. Now then, the name's Senior Agent Melanie Fiona and, as ye may have gathered, I'm the one in charge of training and tryouts. There'll be three tryouts in all, designed to evaluate whether or not you're cut out for this. Simple enough. Any questions?"

"Can you really tell a person's intentions just by looking at them?" asks a red-faced boy with a gulp.

"Aye . . . Billy Pogo," answers the Red Lady, reading his name tag. "It's my supernatural ability. And plenty useful when it comes to interrogating baddies." Her eyes flash. "Right now it's telling me ye can't wait to get this tour over with so ye can get back to that slice of sweet potato pie ye got stashed back in your room."

"You're amazing," says Billy, wide-eyed.

Agent Fiona gives him a wink. "Don't I know it."

"Could you give us a clue about what these tryouts are?" This is from Dylan Van Helsing.

"Not a chance!" The Red Lady laughs. "Ye should know better than most that these things are very well-kept secrets. And even if I did tell ye, who's to say I won't change me mind later?"

"Is there anything you *can* tell us?" I ask nervously.

"Three things," Agent Fiona replies. "For starters, while it's true we'll be training ye before and between the tryouts, your ability to pass won't just be a matter of how well ye learn. You'll need to have the right stuff already inside ye— the kinds of traits ye can't teach.

"Second," she continues, "the last tryout is called the finale. It's a culmination of all the training you've received. Comes in three parts. An exam on supernatural facts. A display of technique while dueling with Sky Sprints and Stun Sticks, and finally a demonstration of your supernatural ability. Don't expect ye to be masters, but you'll need to have gained some level of control over what ye can do. Peters, we're still debating what you'll do if ye make it that far."

"And the third thing?" blurts a very anxious-looking girl.

"Aye," answers Agent Fiona with a smirk. "First tryout comes this Friday. Meaning it'll be a short summer for a lot of ye."

The announcement sends the lobby into a commotion. Friday is less than a week away.

"I know there were eight spots last year," says Dylan Van Helsing. "How many spots are available this time?" The lobby quiets, waiting for an answer.

Agent Fiona frowns. "We had a few older agents who were set to retire but decided to putter on for another year. Means we can only offer four spots this summer."

If there was a commotion before, this sends the group into an all-out panic. I feel it too. Am I really capable of beating out twenty-eight other kids?

Agent Fiona raises her hands and the lobby goes silent. "Quit your whining and carrying on. Ye all knew this was the most competitive specialty." She grabs a short stack of paper from behind the Van Helsing statue. "Now then, let's get these schedules handed out."

I'm the first to get one, so I take a quick look.

JUNIOR AGENT TRAINEE
SUMMER CAMP SCHEDULE
Week 1
   –Supernatural Investigations Tour

   –Supernatural Knowledge Exam

   –Intro to Sky Sprints

   –Supernatural Immersion

FIRST TRYOUT—Thirty-two trainees drop to sixteen!

• • •

Weeks 2 & 3

–Sky Sprints-Wallrunning & Aerial Maneuvers

–Supernatural Immersion

–Intro to Stun Sticks

–Supernatural Knowledge (Self-Study)

SECOND TRYOUT—Sixteen trainees drop to eight!

• • •

Week 4

-???

FINALE—Eight trainees drop to four Junior Agents!

• • •

Weeks 5–8
JUNIOR AGENT TRAINING BEGINS

If I manage to get through the first tryout, I'll have two weeks to find out what happened to Quinton before I've got to prove myself again. But is that really enough time? It'll have to be.

"Now that you've had a moment to review your schedules," Agent Fiona calls out to the whole lobby, "let's get ye all separated into tour groups. When I call your name, come and stand beside me. Peters, ye stay put."

It's just my luck that I get picked for the first tour group along with Dylan Van Helsing. Why does he even need a tour? He must've seen this place hundreds of times growing up.

Agent Fiona addresses my eight-person group. "You're encouraged to ask questions while we tour the department, but more than anything you'll need to keep out of the way. A lot of important business is being conducted that can't be disturbed. Ready? Then follow me."

When Agent Fiona punches a code for the door, it hits me that I'm about to walk the same halls, see the same sights, that Quinton did. The thought puts a warm feeling in my chest, but it also makes me miss him terribly.

The door slides open and Agent Fiona leads us into a wide hallway. It's a fast-moving river of gray suits, SWAT team gear, and fatigues going in both directions across a black-and-white tiled floor. "This is the main hall," calls Agent Fiona over the noise. "Leads from one end of the department to the other, making a giant U. Every area in the department can be reached from this hallway. If ye ever lose your way, simply seek out this hall to right yourself."

We start up the left side of the U, keeping close to the wall to stay out of everyone's way. I stare up at the various wanted posters and Agent of the Month plaques. Agent Fiona brings our group to a quick stop when agents come bustling through a doorway struggling to control a ten-foot tall furry creature in ripped blue jeans and a green Save the Trees T-shirt. It's not making things easy at all for the agents, squirming and kicking its feet wildly as it howls, "I'm innocent. I swear! It was a Sasquatch, not me!"

Agent Fiona shakes her red tangles. "Again, Bigfoot? What've ye gone and done this time?"

The agents wrestle Bigfoot through another door on the opposite side of the hall. Agent Fiona tells us to stay put and follows them inside. Half a minute later she sticks her head back through the door and waves for us to follow.

"Line up just there and keep quiet," says Agent Fiona once we've all crowded into the small room. Bigfoot is nowhere to be found. "I've asked to take over so I can give ye a glimpse at what we do here."

A few minutes later, an angry little bearded man in a green suit is brought in. He looks like the grumpy uncle of the guy on the Lucky Charms box.

"Is that a real leprechaun?" I blurt out. I've really got to stop doing that.

The little man turns around. "Well, I ain't a bloody fake, that's for sure!"

Agent Fiona shoots me a look.

"Sorry," I mouth.

Dylan Van Helsing chuckles beside me. "I asked the same question the first time I saw one. That leprechaun still sends me hate mail."

I laugh but then quickly turn away from him. Maybe that's rude, but I won't forget what he said to me in front of his dad.

"Don't be like that," says Dylan. "Who do you think vouched for you with my father? I told him how Lara and her dumb friends were teasing you."

Dylan is the witness Director Van Helsing was talking about? He's the reason I wasn't punished for my fire illusion?

I turn back to face him. "This isn't a joke to me, okay? You can't be mean to me one second and then nice the next. I don't know if I can trust you. Or anything you told me."

Dylan goes quiet and I turn back to Agent Fiona.

"In a moment I'm gonna show ye five faces," she says to the leprechaun. "Point out the one who took your pot of gold."

He nods. "Gotcha."

Agent Fiona gives the far wall a knock and it shifts into clear glass, revealing a strange group of people. Things? Creatures?

First is an actual bear. Beside it is what looks like a man in a cheap Chewbacca costume. Next to him is Bigfoot from the hallway. Then another bigfoot, only its fur is gray, and it's dressed in a fancy red suit and sipping a cup of tea. At the end of the row is a person-sized ant in a trench coat.

An actual *ant* that's taller than I am.

How did I never have any idea that all of these things exist?

"That's him!" shouts the leprechaun. "Right there in the T-shirt and jeans!"

Agent Fiona gives the transparent wall three knocks and Bigfoot is led away grumbling. The other bigfoot, the gray one wearing the suit, just rolls his eyes and adjusts his monocle.

Agent Fiona is about to tell us something when the gray bigfoot steps into the room.

"Melanie, *darling*," he exclaims. "When they told me it

was you out here I simply had to come say hello."

"Sorry to keep draggin' ye down here every time your cousin gets out of line," says Agent Fiona. "I know it's a hassle."

"Nonsense," says the gray bigfoot with a wave of his hand. "Gives me a chance to try to talk some sense into him. Crime doesn't pay and all that. Falls on deaf ears but, as they say, you can never give up on family—" He gasps as his eyes land on me. "As I live and breathe. Is that *the* Amari Peters?"

I wince as Agent Fiona says, "That's her, all right."

The gray bigfoot sweeps into an elaborate bow. "Allow me to introduce myself. I am Sir Francis Sasquatch III of the Yellowstone National Park Sasquatches. Formally knighted in *both* Faerie Courts. An absolute pleasure to meet you. Sweetheart, you're all *anyone's* talking about."

"Really?" I say.

"A magician at the Bureau? The gossip practically spills itself!"

What kind of gossip, I wonder.

"Well, I simply must be going, but if you're ever in the market for a good cave hideout with reliable escape routes, or maybe even a nice underground lair off the beaten path, I'm the woodland real estate agent to the stars, honey. Think of me when you're done playing at this Junior Agent business and looking to start your criminal empire in style. Good or evil, when it comes to clients I don't pick sides. Here's my card. Toodles."

I take his notebook-sized business card and frown. A hideout? An underground lair? Is that what people think of me? That I'm destined to be the supernatural world's next supervillain?

Agent Fiona leads us back into the main hallway. We follow it past the Briefing Auditorium to the tall wooden door protecting the Great Vault that Agent Fiona says is impenetrable. We end up at an area that's glassed off, with people passing in and out of glass doors. "This is the Operations Bay," says Agent Fiona. "The central hub where the Director and Assistant Director oversee the missions carried out by our agents around the globe. We have outposts on every continent."

"Even Antarctica?" I ask.

"*Especially* Antarctica," answers Agent Fiona. "One of the seven great beasts, the abominable snowman, has been hibernating there for nearly three centuries, and sedatives must be given on a monthly basis to ensure he continues his slumber. He ain't called abominable for nothin'. Tell ye what, I'll give ye all a hint. Know your great beasts by heart. It's a question that gets asked every year in the finale."

Most of our group presses their faces against the glass to gaze into the huge space full of men and women sitting at long tables topped with computers. Massive screens cover the other three walls, making the Operations Bay look like a NASA control room. One screen has the words *Helmet Cam* written at the top and shows agents in gray suits raiding a haunted house. Zombies pour out of doorways and the agents keep slicing them to dust with burning swords. Another screen shows a smirking elderly man in a dusty rocking chair. This one is labeled *Moreau Interrogation*. That must be Moreau, the magician.

Like me.

"Is that really *him*?" Billy asks with a shudder. "Is it really Moreau?"

"It's gotta be!" says Brian Li. "Who else is that creepy?"

"I just hope wherever he is," comes another voice, "it's far away from here."

"Far?" says Dylan. "Heck, he's right here in this building."

Nearly the whole group gasps.

Agent Fiona puts both hands on her hips and presses her lips tight. "That's not for ye to go around repeating."

Dylan nudges me with his elbow and says, "Well, maybe if the Bureau were better at catching his apprentices, my sister wouldn't still be missing."

I watch for Agent Fiona's reaction.

She sets her jaw. "One more word from ye, little Van Helsing, and I'll throw ye right outta these tryouts. I don't care who your father is. Understood?"

Dylan folds his arms but stays silent.

Agent Fiona might be upset, but she didn't deny Dylan's claim. Maybe he was telling the truth about the Bureau knowing who took my brother—Moreau's apprentice.

Which means this is my chance to get some answers. But I can't let her know what Dylan told me. That stuff is supposed to be classified. So I clear my throat and say, "Has Moreau said anything at all about Quinton and Maria's disappearance?"

Agent Fiona sighs and shakes her head. "These talks

are nothin' more than a formality. We question him once a week and he refuses to answer a single question—says the Bureau is the enemy of all magicians."

No wonder he won't answer their questions. They've been sending agents to interrogate him—but *agents* are the reason he's locked away. An idea pops into my head. There might be an upside to my being a magician.

"Could I talk to him?" I ask. The rest of my tour group gawks at me but I focus on Agent Fiona. "Maybe he'd be willing since I'm also a magician?" If the whole supernatural world thinks I'm destined to be a villain anyway, maybe Moreau will too, and say something that could help us find Quinton and Maria.

Agent Fiona raises an eyebrow. "Not a chance, Peters. You're on shaky ground as it is. There's no way the higher-ups are gonna risk ye being corrupted by the single most dangerous being on the planet."

"Who says I'd be—"

I stop short as the hallway darkens and red lights begin to flash above us. What's going on? A siren blares, making me jump.

"Agent Fiona!" shouts a Junior Agent running up the hall.

"Tristan," says Agent Fiona. "What's happened?"

"There's been an attack on one of our outposts," he replies. "Thirty hybrids have overrun the place."

"*Thirty?*" Agent Fiona's face blanches. "How's that possible?"

He shrugs. "The Director wants all Senior and Special Agents to report to the Operations Bay immediately."

The rest of the tour is canceled. Instead, we're taken into a large computer room. But my mind is still back at that red alert.

If the Bureau refuses the trade, no one is safe. That's what the letter said, according to Dylan. The way Agent Fiona fussed at him, he had to be telling the truth. Just who is this apprentice that has my brother and Maria? And what's going to happen if we don't find them soon?

An agent sits at a desk at the front of the room, speaking in the most boring monotone I've ever heard. "I'm sure the red alert you all experienced must have been very disconcerting. Rest assured that we've got the very best people looking into it. Rather than have you kids idle, we've moved up tomorrow's Supernatural Knowledge examination to today. Do remember this is merely a diagnostic, meaning no studying was required. It will merely serve to inform us where you currently stand."

As much as I try to tell myself this exam doesn't count, I get more discouraged with each question. How am I supposed to know which two great beasts reside in the Atlantic Ocean? Or how old Merlin is? Or even what date the Bureau of Supernatural Affairs was founded?

Not to mention I keep getting distracted by the fact that Moreau is literally in the same place as I am. There's got to be a way for me to find out what he knows.

When the exam is over, we're called into the office at the back of the classroom to meet with the instructor. Lara is first up and returns a few minutes later red-faced. "A measly eighty-three," she tells Dylan. "I told that ridiculous tutor we were focusing on the wrong things. When I see Daddy, I'm demanding a new one."

If not even Lara could ace this test, I'm not looking forward to my own score. Unfortunately, I'm called in next.

"Take a seat, dear."

I do. As the instructor taps away at her computer, I brace myself for the worst. "I know I probably didn't do all that well . . ."

The instructor nods. "You'd be correct. You scored a four out of one hundred. And that's probably due to a few good guesses, am I right?"

I nod. *A four?!*

The instructor keeps typing away, not a trace of sympathy in her voice. "Just means you'll need to devote a good bit of your time to studying in order to perform well during the exam section of the finale. I won't sugarcoat it, dear, you've got quite the uphill battle ahead. Especially given your supernatural ability situation. I'll write you up a list of books to check out at the library. I suggest you begin your studies as soon as possible."

The list she gives me is the length of my arm. I'm supposed to read all of these? When will I have time to search for Quinton?

I leave the office in a daze.

My phone buzzes inside my pocket. It's another message from the mystery girl.

> **New Message from magiciangirl18:**
> **Bummer on failing the test. Wouldn't you rather be learning the truth about magicians?**
> **About Moreau?**

I spin around, searching the classroom. I look to Lara, then Dylan, then their circle of friends. Not a single person is on their phone right now. I type up a quick response.

> **From: Amari_Peters**
> **How do you know that? Are you here too?**
> **And what do you know about Moreau?**

The response is nearly instant as I scan the other trainees to see if anyone picks up their phone. No one does. I glance down at the message.

> **New Message from magiciangirl18:**
> **First, you have to prove you can keep a secret.**
> **Don't tell anyone about my offer and I'll contact you when the time is right.**

≫ 14 ≪

CONFIDENTIAL
MEETING
IN
PROGRESS

Y THE TIME LUNCH COMES AROUND, I'M ALREADY STRESSED
out about my chances of making Junior Agent. Maybe
Director Van Helsing was right. Maybe I am in over my head.

Feeling like I need to be doing *something*, I skip the first
few minutes of lunch and head to the Files and Evidence
Room in the Department of Supernatural Investigations.
Maybe if I can get permission to look at some of the files
on my brother, it'll help me understand what the Bureau
knows and what they're doing to find him.

Unfortunately, the lady at the front desk makes it clear
that trainees don't have access to classified files under any
circumstance. What's worse, Junior Agents don't either—
only the adults.

And if that's not frustrating enough, magiciangirl18 is spying on me somehow? I was so sure it was one of the other Junior Agent trainees trolling me, but none of them were on their phones when those messages came through. I made sure of it.

Now I can't help but wonder if Elsie was right and magiciangirl18 really is the magician who took my brother and Maria. But what should I do about it? If I accuse her and I'm wrong, there's no telling how she'll take it. I certainly don't appreciate being called a criminal just because I'm a magician. A false accusation—especially against someone trying to help—could mean blowing the best chance I have to learn anything at all about Moreau and being a magician.

I can't risk it.

"Ooh!" says Elsie when she sits down to lunch with me in the food court. "Tell me what you think about this—lip gloss that shoots knockout gas. The antidote would be in the lip gloss itself, so once you put some on, you'd be immune!"

She's been like this ever since she got her Mastermind Inventor ability from the Crystal Ball. Out of nowhere she'll get this intense look and then just start coming up with all sorts of ideas for cool new inventions. Yesterday she got an idea for a microphone that turns your voice into that really high pitch that only dogs can hear. As long as the person you're talking to has an earpiece that picks up the sound, you could have totally private conversations in a crowded room—assuming there aren't any werewolves around.

It feels weird not to tell Elsie about the new messages. But magiciangirl18 was pretty clear.

"You might as well tell me," Elsie says.

I blink and find my roommate staring right at me.

Elsie leans closer. "Your aura just went gray. What's wrong?"

"I . . . well, there's a . . ." I totally chicken out. "Um, just worried about my test score."

Elsie doesn't look convinced. "Are you sure that's all?"

Chief Crowe's voice booms over the intercom before I can answer. "Trainee Amari Peters is requested in the office of the Chief Director immediately. Her private elevator will be waiting for you in the food court lobby."

The food court goes completely silent and nearly everyone turns to look in my direction.

"Nobody gets to use that elevator," says Elsie, eyes wide. "Must be something really important."

Why would the chief need to talk to me?

I mean, unless I'm in trouble again. I swallow. Maybe they know about magiciangirl18 after all.

The chief's elevator is the last one on the row and is twice as big as the others. Normally there's an *Off-Limits* sign on its front, but today the doors are wide open. The floor is plush carpet and the walls are all tinted mirrors so those inside can see out but nobody can look in. A pair of slippers sit near the entrance.

"Are these slippers for me?" I ask, leaning inside. Man, this thing is fancy.

"Of course they are," says the elevator in a snooty voice. "This carpet is made of fine hand-woven unicorn hair—*shed* not shaven—and it will not be blemished by the likes of you!"

I can't roll my eyes hard enough. "Nice to meet you too," I mutter.

"What was that?"

"Nothing," I say quickly. "Wait, aren't you supposed to introduce yourself?"

The elevator groans. "I suppose I am. How I go from transporting His Royal Deviousness, the Goblin King himself, to some *trainee* is beyond me . . ." The elevator clears its throat. "The name is Lord Archibald Reginald Kensington, reluctantly at your service."

"Lord . . . of the elevators?" I ask. "Is that really a thing?"

"Of course it's a thing! Now get on!"

"Okay, okay. Sorry I asked." I step out of my shoes and into the slippers. I turn around as the doors shut and then immediately open up again.

"We've arrived at the Office of the Chief Director," says Lord Kensington in a bored voice.

Whoa! "That was fast!"

"As I am Lord of these elevator shafts, that should really be expected, shouldn't it?" replies Lord Kensington with a harrumph. "Now be gone with you. And don't you dare take my slippers."

I step out of the elevator and glance around the small lobby. There's only a fancy glass desk with a big *Office of the Chief Director* plaque across the front. The same secretary who escorted Elsie and me to our seats on Welcome Day is seated behind it. A giant picture of Chief Crowe in a business suit fills the back wall.

My smile fades at the secretary's serious expression. She points to a door marked *Conference Room* and says, "This way, please. They're waiting for you."

They? My mind flashes back to the last time I was in a conference room—when everyone had just learned that I was a magician. A few of the directors wanted me locked away. What if this time they mean to go through with it? *Please, oh please, don't let me be in trouble.* If they really do know about magiciangirl18, I'm toast.

This time the conference room is a lot emptier. Agent Magnus is seated at one side of a long table, his big arms folded across his chest. Agent Fiona and Chief Crowe both sit on the opposite side. Agent Fiona shoots an annoyed look at Magnus as the secretary leads me into the conference room.

"Amari!" says Chief Crowe with a wide smile. "I do hope your afternoon is going well. Please take a seat."

It can't be that bad if she's smiling, right? I glance over at Agent Fiona, and she gives me an encouraging nod.

I start to relax a little until Magnus pats the chair next to him.

"Don't you go getting comfortable. Wait till they tell you

about the reckless idea that's brought you here," he says to me. He shakes his head. "In all my years . . ."

Agent Fiona chucks a pencil past his head.

Reckless idea? I take a seat beside Magnus, my eyes going back and forth from adult to adult. "What's going on?"

"Well, Amari . . ." Chief Crowe gets to her feet and puts her hands behind her back. The gills on her neck flap open and shut as she clears her throat. "You're no doubt aware of this morning's attack on one of our outposts?"

"It happened right in the middle of our tour," I say. "There were flashing lights and everything."

Chief Crowe sighs and begins to pace. "It was an especially violent attack that resulted in terrible injuries to a number of our members. These weren't agents, mind you, rather very specialized researchers studying wild magical flurries. The new batch of hybrids appears to be especially bloodthirsty creatures. These hybrids exhibit superhuman speed and strength far beyond the ones of the past." She shakes her head. "It's quite unlike anything we've seen before."

"Truly," says Agent Fiona. "The entire research team had to be flown to the nearest supernatural health center."

"That's awful," I say.

"The long and short of it is that we've become quite desperate," says Chief Crowe. "As far as we know, Moreau is the only magician with enough magic to create hybrids. A spell that can warp nature so perversely is typically far beyond his apprentices. Until you showed up here, we had no idea a single person could even be so magical."

That must be why they were so quick to accuse me. I swallow. "It wasn't me. Everything I've done with magic has been a complete accident. I wouldn't even know how to use a spell."

"No one in *this* room is accusing ye," says Agent Fiona. "Why, you'd have had to be in two places at once to order the attack on that outpost."

"What we are saying is that someone we believe to be connected to Moreau *is* creating these hybrids. And we don't know the first thing about this new magician. So when Agent Fiona came to me with what I'll admit is a rather outlandish proposal, I found myself forced to consider it," says Chief Crowe.

That's when I realize why I'm here and why Agent Magnus is so upset. I lean forward in my seat. "You're going to let me to talk to Moreau."

Agent Fiona and Chief Crowe both nod.

Agent Magnus gets to his feet, knocking over his chair. "Amari won't have any part in it."

Agent Fiona reddens. "It's not your decision is it, ye great big oaf!" Her blue eyes come back to me. "We wouldn't ask ye if it wasn't important. Innocents are getting hurt."

"Oh, do sit down, Magnus," snaps Chief Crowe.

Magnus picks up his fallen chair and drops into it dramatically. That guy can sure throw a tantrum.

"Now, Amari," Chief Crowe continues, "I know you were quite eager before but I'd like to be sure you've properly thought this through. We would be placing you near the most terrible villain in the history of our world. Desperate or not, it's not a decision I'd have you take lightly."

"This kinda thing ain't her job yet," grumbles Agent Magnus. "She's just a kid, for crying out loud."

"And it's still *her* decision," says Agent Fiona.

I lean back in my chair and pretend to think it over. I get that Agent Magnus feels like it's his job to keep me safe, and maybe that's what Quinton would've wanted. But this is the opportunity I've been waiting for. "I'm doing it."

Agent Magnus throws up his hands.

Agent Fiona blows out a heavy sigh of relief. "Ye have our thanks, Peters."

"Indeed you do," says Chief Crowe.

"But I have a condition too," I continue. "I want to know why you refused the trade to get my brother back. And whatever else you know about my brother's disappearance."

Agent Fiona and Chief Crowe both exchange a startled look. Chief Crowe asks, "How on earth do you know about that?"

"It's classified." Agent Magnus crosses his arms.

"If she already knows about the letter," says Agent Fiona, "then it's only fair we fill her in on the details. It's nothing she couldn't learn from Moreau himself."

After what feels like forever, Chief Crowe gives a stiff nod. "We'll tell her everything we can within reason."

Agent Fiona and Chief Crowe huddle for a moment,

speaking in low voices. While they talk I sneak a peek over at Agent Magnus. He's seriously unhappy. Well, too bad. I'm about to complete step two of me and Elsie's plan. I'm about to discover what the Bureau knows about my brother's disappearance.

Chief Crowe and Agent Fiona return to the table. The chief speaks first. "The letter we received came from one of Moreau's apprentices. And it made not just one, but two impossible demands, one for each member of VanQuish."

Two demands?

Chief Crowe continues, "The first was releasing Moreau from prison."

"Ye weren't here when Moreau was free," Agent Fiona cuts in. "Horrible things would randomly happen without any rhyme or reason. The worst part is we'd all know it was Moreau who did it but there was nothing we could do. The fact your brother and Maria were able to track him down is nothing short of a miracle."

Elsie and I figured Moreau's apprentice would want him free. "What else did the letter ask for?"

"That, I'm afraid, really *is* classified," says Chief Crowe. "Just know that it concerns an item of immense destructive power. An item that would put many, many innocent lives at risk were it placed in the wrong hands."

It takes a few seconds for the words to sink in. When they do, I try to blink back my tears. "Whoever has my brother must be a horrible person to want something like that. If we can't give them what they want, what's to stop them from hurting Quinton and Maria? How are we supposed to get them back?"

"By catching whoever has them," says Agent Fiona, coming around the table to crouch in front of my chair. "And our best hope right now is getting something out of Moreau that will help us do just that. *Ye* are our best hope, Amari."

"I'm in," I say. "I'll do whatever it takes."

15

I T'S ALMOST TIME.

I'm sitting in the lobby of Chief Crowe's office, watching a whole bunch of adults rush in and out of conference rooms in preparation for my meeting with Moreau. When I agreed to it, I didn't think they meant right away. But, as Agent Fiona explained, the Bureau has no clue when the next attack might come. The quicker they find Moreau's apprentice, the safer we'll all be.

Agent Magnus and Agent Fiona gave me a list of questions that Director Van Helsing typed up himself, and I prepped with them all afternoon. "Moreau is wicked smart," said Agent Fiona. "He'll try and mess with your head if ye let him."

"He'll also try to distract you with his illusions," said Agent Magnus. "Remember, no matter what he claims, you're completely safe. His magic can't penetrate the enchanted glass that holds him."

"It's important to show confidence," said Agent Fiona. "He'll be able to sense if you're scared. Ye won't be alone down there—we'll be keeping an eye on the whole thing through the security cameras."

"That being said," added Agent Magnus, "if at any point you *do* get scared and feel like you need to leave, you are free to do so, understand?"

"I do," I said. "I won't let you down."

I put on the slippers and step into Lord Kensington alone, trying not to let my nerves show as the elevator doors shut and the adults wish me luck.

"Apologies for my earlier behavior," says Lord Kensington. "Trainee or not, what you're doing is very brave."

"Thanks," I say. "But I don't feel very brave." My knees feel wobbly just standing here.

Lord Kensington zips me down to a floor I've never seen before. It's not even really a floor, just a solid wall of black metal.

"Could you tell me more about where I'm going?" I'm realizing I didn't ask Magnus or Fiona nearly enough questions.

"There are a number of walled-off floors in the Bureau—typically quite dangerous or very secret places.

Blackstone Prison is both. To earn a place there you must be found guilty of truly vile acts. All visitors must be approved by the Chief Director herself. Thus, I am the only way for you to enter. Are you ready?"

I try to stand a little taller. "Ready."

"Now entering Blackstone Prison," says Lord Kensington. "I'm afraid there's a speed limit while traveling through here."

As the elevator lurches forward, a gap in the metal wall slides open. Everything goes dark as we pass through the thick wall; the shimmer of my moonstone badge is the only light. My heartbeat booms in my ears.

And then we're inside. Curious, I press my face against the glass.

Turns out, Blackstone Prison is just one long hallway with giant glass walls on both sides. The floor and ceiling are so black I'd think we were floating if I couldn't see the metal rails that guide Lord Kensington through the center of the space.

The prison is like those indoor exhibits at the zoo, with long walls of glass cages, only a thousand times scarier. Scary creatures slither and skulk about; some scream constantly, while others have laughs so cold I can feel it in my bones. A pack of drooling beasts claws at the glass. Some things are so awful they're kept in complete darkness. But their fiery eyes follow me down the hallway.

"There's no harm in covering your eyes," says Lord Kensington.

"Good idea," I squeak out.

It feels like a whole hour passes before Lord Kensington finally says, "We're here."

Trembling, I open just one eye and glance around before opening the other. We're in a different section of the prison now. There is only one glass cage here, and inside it is a gray-haired man in a rocking chair facing away from me.

"Find your courage," says Lord Kensington. "You can do this."

I take a slow deep breath. *I can do this.*

The doors open and it's deathly quiet—the kind of quiet where you can hear yourself breathing. I take a shaky step onto the glossy black floor of the prison. It's pitch-black everywhere, like Moreau's cage is floating in an ocean of shadow. My eyes dart to Moreau in his chair, expecting him to turn around to face me at any moment. Only he doesn't.

Not even when I come right up to the glass.

"Moreau?" I say in a small voice, wishing I sounded braver.

Suddenly Moreau and the chair vanish and a different scene emerges inside the cage—a fancy living room with plush chairs and a large fireplace.

I blink, and Moreau is face-to-face with me, so close that he could reach out and grab me if not for the glass.

I yelp and stumble backward.

A wide smile reaches across Moreau's face, and he watches me for a moment before placing his palms against the glass.

"No need to be frightened. Hardly any of my power reaches beyond this cursed fishbowl. Besides, why would I harm someone I've looked forward to meeting so very much?"

"Why do you care about meeting me?" I ask.

Moreau doesn't answer. Instead, he closes his eyes and drums out a beat on the glass using the tips of his fingers. "Do you hear that? It's your song, child. The magic in your blood, it sings such a strong melody. Can you hear my magic as well?"

I shake my head.

"You don't possess any blood magic then." Moreau frowns and steps away from me. "A pity. There are blood spells that allow one to live forever."

I remember what Chief Crowe said about the Vampir spell and how the Night Brothers used it to conquer death. "I don't want to live forever if it means I have to hurt people. It's wrong."

"Right and wrong are relative, my dear. For instance, is it right to keep another human being trapped in a cage? Of course not. And yet I doubt you'd agree with me that I should be set free. Remember this—there is only weakness and strength. The strong have imposed their will on the weak since the beginning of time. 'Tis the way of the world. Because your Bureau was stronger on the day they raided my island, I now find myself here."

"I have questions," I say. Let's get this over with.

"As do I." Moreau turns and begins to pace beside the glass wall. "But we mustn't forget our manners. I am Raoul

Moreau." He dips into an elaborate bow. "And you are?"

"Um, Amari . . ." I lift my chin. "Amari Peters."

He flinches at my last name, then laughs. "How very . . . unbelievably . . . ironic. It all becomes clear now. *Yes*. How could the Bureau ever justify locking up the sister of the famous Quinton Peters?"

I swallow and ask, "Do you know where he is?"

He smirks, his voice mocking. "Of course not. How could I lay hands on your brother from inside this cell?"

Agent Magnus and Agent Fiona warned me that would be his answer. I take another look at the paper in my hands. "I'm supposed to ask you some questions."

"And I have questions for you too," he replies. "Whatever will we do about this little conundrum?"

I think for a moment. "You and your apprentice like to make trades, right?" I ask bitterly. "Well, let's trade questions. We'll take turns."

Moreau strokes his chin. "Very well. But you must promise to be truthful in your answers. There shall only be one lie between us, and I've already told it. Agreed?"

He's already lied to me? "Does that mean you really do know where my brother is?"

Moreau frowns. "It *means* what it means."

I set my jaw. "That's not fair!"

Moreau snarls, and the cage becomes a tempest of swirling black clouds. "I am not some inconsequential lackey the Bureau can bully for information. You can either accept or you can leave empty-handed whilst utter chaos is wreaked upon your precious Bureau." And then the man smiles, the scene returns to a cozy living room, and he's pleasant again. "Now then, shall we begin?"

I shudder and close my eyes. *Be confident.* "Fine."

"First question." Moreau turns to pace a few steps before meeting my eyes again. "When the day comes that you have to choose a side—and that day will come—will you join your fellow magicians or would you side with this Bureau that hates everything we are?"

Fellow magicians? The question catches me off guard. "How many other magicians are there?"

"Hundreds, I'd wager."

Hundreds? Are there really that many?

Moreau laughs at my surprise. "Come now, you didn't think yourself so special as that, did you? Though I'll admit you *are* unusually strong. And so very young. Now then, for my second question—"

"Wait, it's my turn."

"No, you asked me about the current number of magicians and I answered to the best of my knowledge. That was our agreement."

I kick the glass in annoyance. I've wasted an entire question.

"Quite the temper." Moreau smiles darkly. "Don't be angry, child. Be *better.*"

I ball my fists at my side. "Ask your next question."

Moreau narrows his eyes at me. "Has anyone claimed you?"

"What do you—" I catch myself and start again. "I don't know what you mean by that."

"In the world of magicians, there are masters and there are apprentices. One to offer the power, the other to receive it. One to possess the wisdom, the other to need it. Whoever gave you such powerful magic should have claimed you by now. Unless . . ."

"Unless what?" I ask. "No! Don't answer that. That isn't my question."

Moreau lets out a low snicker. "*That* I shall answer for free. Only a very powerful magician could bestow the kind of magic you possess, the likes of which no longer exist aside from myself. It is far more likely that you were born a magician. And if that's true, then you are quite special indeed."

As much as I want to know what being special is supposed to mean, I've got to remember why I'm here. I look down at my list of questions and decide to ask one of my own. Before he can trick me again. I meet Moreau's amused stare. "You said you don't know where Quinton is. So tell me what you *do* know about my brother's disappearance . . . please?"

"Clever girl. If only your brother had been smarter in his choices. You might think his being taken was a simple matter of revenge, but I can assure you that we have far more substantial schemes at play. What I can tell you is that Quinton was looking into things he shouldn't—things your precious Bureau would frown upon. I suppose he found something we wanted."

"Like what?" I ask desperately.

"I've answered your question. You now know far more than you did when you came down here." Another dark grin. "Earlier, you asked me a question. . . . You wished to know why I wanted to meet. Care to offer a guess?"

My mind is still spinning. "I don't know."

"Then by all means," he says. "Allow me to explain. There is a plan being carried out that is many years in the making. A plan so perfect that not even my capture has prevented it from coming to pass. When the dust settles, this wretched Bureau will be destroyed and magicians shall take their rightful place in the world. I had been content to wait out the destruction here in my cell. But then I felt your magic awaken, like a clap of thunder that vibrated my very bones."

Moreau waves his hands and the scene inside the cage changes again. I see myself covered in expensive jewels, a shimmering moonstone crown atop my head. "*You* could be great, my dear. Truly special. With the proper guidance, you could have anything your heart desires. Anyone who has ever wronged you would bow and scrape at your feet. You need only join us, Amari Peters. Join your fellow magicians."

I just stare, unable to find my words. "I . . ."

He bares his lengthening canines in a grin. With a twirl of his fingers a hulking beast suddenly fills the space, ten-feet tall and as wide as a truck, with the growling head of a tiger and the muscular fur-covered body of a man. It stalks right up to the glass and lowers its snarling jaws to flash razor-sharp teeth. A low growl rattles the glass cage.

Is that what hybrids look like? I'm backing away before I

even realize it. I've never seen anything scarier in my whole life.

"This is what your Bureau is up against, child. Do you imagine that anything could stand against an army of these deadly creatures? But what if *you* didn't have to? What if creatures such as these were yours to command? What would you do with such power? What *could* you do?"

His voice drops to a whisper. "With magic as strong as yours, I could teach you to create your own."

For a moment, I imagine myself back at Jefferson Academy surrounded by Emily Grant and her friends. Then I imagine those taunting smiles fading away as a pack of scowling hybrids show up to help me. I'll bet they'd wet their pants at the sight. As much as I hate to admit it, a part of me likes that idea.

I shake those thoughts out of my head. What am I thinking? I turn to run back to Lord Kensington before Moreau can mess with my head anymore.

Still, I stop short of the elevator and make myself stand my ground, even though I feel like I could throw up. "I'm on the Bureau's side—on my brother's side. Always."

Moreau sighs heavily and the illusions fade away until only he and his rocking chair remain. "The Bureau has long believed themselves beyond our reach. That arrogance will be their downfall. The hour draws near when we shall regain what was taken from us." His voice hardens into a snarl. "Remember that I gave you a chance, little magician. In the end, we are all bound by our choices."

16

ONCE WE LEAVE BLACKSTONE PRISON, LORD KENSING-ton brings me to the Department of Supernatural Investigations to be debriefed, same as the adult agents whenever they get back from an important mission.

I can't get there fast enough. I walk so quickly that I almost run over Director Van Helsing. He isn't amused.

The debriefing room is the size of a closet. Inside, Agent Magnus and Agent Fiona sit at a square metal table. As soon as I'm through the door, I blurt out, "What was Quinton working on? And what did Moreau mean when he said he was looking into something he shouldn't? What did my brother find that got him kidnapped?"

"VanQuish worked directly under me," says Agent

Magnus. "If he or Maria were looking into anything out of the ordinary, I'd have known about it."

"Then why would Moreau say that?" I ask.

"We believe Moreau was merely mocking us," says Agent Fiona. "Or, at most, it was an attempt to turn you against the Bureau and recruit you to his way of thinking. I had worried as much might be true, but we've had so little success until now that I thought it worth the risk."

"I would never help him," I say. "Not for anything."

"We know you wouldn't," says Magnus. "Just don't go taking anything that man said as fact."

"Well, how about what he said about regaining what was taken?" I ask. "Is that the item of immense destructive power that you won't tell me about—that's supposed to be classified? Moreau seemed pretty sure he could get it even without trading VanQuish."

Agent Fiona winces.

Agent Magnus looks smug. "This was *your* brilliant idea, Fiona."

Agent Fiona lowers her voice to a whisper. "That item is none of your concern, Peters. Just know that we have taken every possible precaution to keep it safe."

So not everything was a lie. But couldn't that also mean none of it was a lie? Moreau made such a big deal out of telling each other the truth. "He said they would destroy this place. Aren't you worried?"

"Buncha mumbo jumbo," says Agent Magnus. "This

place is a fortress. Nothing in the known or supernatural world could harm it."

I lean forward. They didn't see his face like I did. "But he seemed so sure . . ."

Agent Fiona answers. "And ye can be sure that we've taken every precaution to be certain the Bureau remains safe. Trust us, Amari."

I wasn't supposed to tell anybody what happened with Moreau today, but as soon as Elsie gets back from Junior Researcher training everything spills out of my mouth.

"What are you thinking?" she asks.

"I don't know," I say, pacing the floor between our beds. "I just keep wondering, what if Moreau was telling the truth? What if he's so sure about his stupid plan that he doesn't care who knows?"

"You think he just wanted to rub it in?"

"I think he knew the Bureau wouldn't take his threats seriously because he's locked away," I say. "But maybe you and I should." I glance at the Elsie's whiteboard. "We know what the Bureau knows about VanQuish's disappearance. So let's move on to step three."

Elsie goes over to grab the whiteboard. "Launch our own investigation. But where do we start?"

I think for a moment. "I'll try and figure out what Quinton might've found that got him taken. Maybe it'll help us track down Moreau's apprentice."

"That's a good idea," says Elsie. "I'll try to research what this item of immense destructive power might be. I just wish we had more to go on besides that it was taken from Moreau." She sighs. "Well, even if there's nothing in the main library, there are a few other places I can try."

"Good," I say. "The more we know the better. I like our plan."

Elsie starts to smile but it fades. "Be careful, okay? Now we're the ones looking into stuff we aren't supposed to. If we get caught . . ."

"We won't," I say. "We can't."

The next morning, I do my best to not think about my trip to Blackstone Prison. It isn't easy. Even now, standing in one of the training gyms, when I'm supposed to be listening to Agent Magnus give us our first lesson on Sky Sprints, my thoughts keep going back to yesterday.

The size of that hybrid—are they really that scary or was Moreau exaggerating with his illusion? And what about Moreau's perfect plan to take down the Bureau? Or the fact that he wants me on his side—the side of the magicians.

Concentrate, Amari. If you fail the tryouts it won't matter what Moreau said.

I force myself to pay attention to Agent Magnus's lecture.

"These boots give the wearer the ability to walk

horizontally across open air, run up walls, even hang upside down from the ceiling. When used correctly, they'll give you an advantage over a great many ground-based nasties. And if you encounter a nasty that can fly, well, you'd better be right strong in your technique because these here Sky Sprints will be your only chance. Everybody got that?"

We all nod.

I can't help but stare at the Sky Sprints worn by the other trainees. Unlike me, they brought their own boots from home, and they all look so cool—and crazy expensive. The Van Helsings each have shiny chrome boots with *Duboise* written in cursive along the sides. Others wear LaBoom brand Sky Sprints made of polished wood. Only three of us have to go into the equipment room to pick out a pair of standard issue Sky Sprints. Mine look like worn-out sneakers and smell like feet.

Still, I'm pretty surprised at how easily moving in the Sky Sprints comes for me. After about an hour, I'm keeping pace with the legacy kids as we race along the walls and take turns avoiding the obstacles Magnus puts in our path. After three hours I'm able to walk across open air without losing my balance.

At noon Magnus allows us to take a shot at a practice course the agents use to keep their skills sharp. "We call it the Invisible Bridge," he says. He plops down behind a control panel, presses a few buttons, and poof! Two diving boards rise to face each other from opposite sides of the room. A few seconds later, a dozen gigantic punching bags descend from the ceiling. With the push of another button the bags begin to swing back and forth at different speeds.

The goal is pretty clear. We've got to run across open air from one diving board to the other without getting knocked down by the punching bags. It sounds a lot easier than it looks.

Magnus grins. "Who wants to give it a shot?"

Not many hands go up. Even the legacy kids look wary. It's easy to see why. Your reflexes have to be lightning fast in order to stop and start fast enough to avoid the bags. The scariest part, though, is definitely getting by the final bag. It swings so fast it's pretty much a blur.

Of course both the Van Helsings raise their hands. They've probably got a course just like this in their mansion back home. I lift my hand too. As bad as my test score was, this might be my first chance to shine as a trainee. Or fall flat on my face—a really long fall.

"You sure you're up to this, kid?" Magnus asks.

"Not really," I say.

He chuckles. "Gonna try anyway?"

"Yep."

"Good." He raises his voice. "A round of applause for our five brave volunteers." He leads the applause. "Tell you what, let's have you five line up out in the hall. Ain't exactly fair to the first volunteer to let the others watch."

I head into the hallway with the others. The Van Helsings move to the back of the line, so I've got no choice but to take the spot behind them.

For a second, I think maybe Lara will be so focused on completing the obstacle course that she might leave me alone, but then she turns to face me with that little grin of hers. "Nice Sky Sprints. Those might be the first pair ever made."

With so much on my mind already, I'm really not in the mood. My words just come pouring out. "What's your problem with me? I get that you don't like magicians. Guess what? No one does. But you're the only person who's made it their life's mission to annoy me."

My outburst catches her off guard, but not for long. She crosses her arms. "Like you don't know."

"Know what?" I ask. "I barely know anything about the supernatural world." My test score yesterday is proof of that. "Is it all the attention I'm getting? Because my life would be a lot less complicated if nobody knew my name."

Lara goes red. "You think this is about attention? You really are as dumb as you look. I've got over two million followers on Eurg. I've got all the attention I need."

"Then why?" I ask desperately. "My brother and your sister were partners. Shouldn't we try to be friends?"

"*Your* brother is the reason *my* sister wasn't there to watch me get my badge. The reason she's never come back—" Emotion cuts her words short.

I stand there, stunned. "What are you saying?"

"If Quinton hadn't convinced Maria to help him on some secret case, she'd still be here. She never even liked being a

Special Agent. She wanted to be a trainer, like Agent Fiona, but your brother would always convince her to come back. And when she finally ignored him and put in her transfer papers, he guilted her into helping one last time. No one's seen them since."

Secret case? Is that what Moreau meant when he said my brother was looking into something he shouldn't? But Agent Magnus said that he'd know if VanQuish was working on anything out of the ordinary. Unless, maybe they kept it a secret from him too. "I . . . didn't know," I say.

A loud *oooh* comes from inside the training gym. The others crowd the doorway and Lara lets Dylan pull her over too. Still in a daze, I get to the doorway last, just in time to see Brian Li lying on the floor rubbing his shoulder.

"Bobbed when you should've weaved," says Magnus, tossing him an icepack. He looks over at the rest of us in the doorway. "Who's next?"

Billy Pogo heads inside and me and Lara don't speak again. She keeps to one side of her brother and I stand on the other. The worst part is that I could imagine Quinton doing what Lara said if he felt like it was the right thing. He was always so good with words. How many times had he convinced me to do something I didn't want to do?

Cheers ring out and we all rush back to the doorway.

Agent Magnus is shaking Billy Pogo's hand. "Never seen anyone trip and stumble their way past every bag. Kid, that Unnatural Luck ability of yours is really somethin'!"

Now it's Lara's turn. Once she's gone, it finally feels like I can breathe a little.

"She's really not as bad as she seems," says Dylan. He tries to smile. "Well, she is, but she isn't usually *this* bad."

"Is it true?" I ask. "What she said about Quinton and Maria splitting up?"

Dylan leans his head back against the wall and nods. "But Maria and Quinton were partners for years before she decided to try something new. It only makes sense that Maria would still have Quinton's back if he needed her. Partnership is a sacred bond for agents—there's even a ceremony where you take an oath."

"You don't blame him, then?" I ask.

He shakes his head. "My sister is smart and brave and wouldn't have let anybody make her do something she didn't want to do." Then he adds, "I miss her."

"I miss Quinton too," I say. "Everything would be different if he were here. I wouldn't feel so . . ." I stop myself from saying too much.

"Alone?" Dylan says with a sad smile. "I know the feeling. Lara and I are twins, so everybody assumes we're super close. But we're nothing alike. Never have been. Lara likes to be the star of the show, but I'm more like Maria, happy to stay in the background."

He laughs at my raised eyebrows. "I know she was famous, but you don't catch the most dangerous magician of all time and not get famous. Maria was cool with giving Quinton the spotlight, though, letting him do all the interviews." He shrugs. "It's just who she was."

Cheers go up in the training gym. Lara must have made it too. Dylan starts for the door but stops short. "You're a natural in Sprints. Just take your time. The last bag moves so fast that you can't stop to think, though. You've just gotta take a leap of faith. Do that and you've got a chance—but hesitate, and you're going to get clobbered."

Dylan goes through the door, leaving me alone with a million thoughts swimming through my head. No surprise, he makes it through the obstacle course too. Now, it's my turn.

I can feel everyone watching me as I make my way across the training gym. When Magnus gives the signal, I start up the ladder to the first diving board. Except my hands are so sweaty from nerves I nearly fall. Snickers ring out.

When I finally do get to the top, I make the mistake of looking down. The diving board is even higher than it seems from the floor. I swallow.

You can do this, I tell myself. I squeeze my toes together to activate the hover feature and race toward the diving board on the opposite side of the room.

Getting by the super slow bags is easy. The next few are a little faster, and I have to slow down a couple times to avoid them. I pass bag five, then bag six. So far so good.

My arm is clipped by bag nine and it nearly knocks me off balance, but I'm just barely able to catch myself. I sprint past bag ten and stumble past bag eleven by accident. I come to a stop in front of bag twelve. Even up close this thing moves so fast I can barely keep track of it.

Dylan said to make a leap of faith. That means I just have to believe I'll make it, right?

But what if I don't? What if I'm not cut out for this?

I tense up at the thought but then force myself to stagger forward . . .

I don't even see the bag coming. I just feel a sudden impact and I'm falling. At some point my shoes light up and the hover feature activates, so that I'm hanging upside down in midair. My eyes are level with Magnus.

"Gave it a good shot," says Magnus. "Almost got there on your first day."

Too bad it wasn't good enough.

To say that I'm grumpy after sucking at the Invisible Bridge would be an understatement. Am I even good enough to pass Friday's tryout? The reality that I could fail and be sent home sends a shiver down my back. Director Van Helsing made it clear I won't get another chance. And what's worse, they'll take my memories too.

These might be my final days in the supernatural world. I could be running out of time to get any of the answers I came here for. But I know of at least one answer I can get right now. I pull out my phone and message magiciangirl18.

From: Amari_Peters
How do I know YOU aren't Moreau's apprentice???

The moment I hit send, I regret it. Accusing someone of being evil isn't how you treat someone who wants to help. If she gets upset and never messages me again, could I really blame her?

So far, no response. Usually she answers right away. That worries me so much I slide my phone in my pocket and try to think about something else.

Fifteen minutes later, my phones finally buzzes as I'm sitting down for lunch in the food court. I'm so anxious that I fumble and drop the thing.

It's not a new message. Instead, it's an Eurg notification suggesting I send a friend request to Lara Van Helsing. Like she needs any more friends. I glance over at her joking with a group of Junior Agent trainees on the other side of the food court and then click on her page.

Scrolling through her pictures only worsens my mood. She really does have 2 million followers—2.3 million to be exact. I see her hugging her father in front of Van Helsing Manor—the place looks like the outside of a mall. In another photo she's on a street made of gold, blowing a kiss to the camera. The best photo is one where she's staring out the window of an underwater train at a city that glows. The caption reads, *Headed to Atlantis with Mom for a weekend of shopping!* Our lives really couldn't be any more different. In every way.

Dylan must've been telling the truth about him and Lara not being close because I don't see him in any of her photos. He doesn't even have an Eurgphmthilthmsphlthm page.

My phone buzzes in my hand.

New Message from magiciangirl18:

I'm not, I promise!

Tell you what, since you've proven you can keep my secret, why don't we meet face-to-face?

I read the message twice. She wants us to meet up? In person?

"Your aura is extremely purple," says Elsie as she plops down at my table. She sets a copy of *Physics in Magic: The Often Lack Thereof* on the table in front of her.

I frown and shove my phone back into my pocket. "What's that mean?"

"Purple can be tricky, but it usually means somebody's feeling overwhelmed. Still thinking about Moreau? Or is it the plan—your part does seem a lot harder than mine."

I hate that I still can't be honest with her about magiciangirl18's messages. At least not yet. I'm not exactly thrilled about the idea of meeting up with a stranger, especially after Moreau, but if this girl really is willing to help me, then I also don't want to do anything to mess it up.

"It's this tryout," I tell Elsie. "You know how bad I flunked the first test. They said you really can't prepare for the first Junior Agent tryout, but I'm sure you have to know *something* about the supernatural world."

Elsie shrugs. "Maybe you don't."

"Maybe . . ." I say, unconvinced. "Do you know what your first tryout will be?"

Elsie frowns. "A test—but Junior Researcher and Junior Agent are very different."

I think back to how confidently she wrote down Junior Researcher at the departmental presentations. "Do you like it? Junior Researcher training, I mean?"

Her whole face brightens, and she goes on this long rant about all the amazing things she's learned and seen and done. Because of all the great ideas she's constantly coming up with, she's even been asked to sit in on some brainstorming sessions with the adult researchers at the Department of Magical Science. Just seeing her excitement lifts my own spirits.

After ten minutes of catching up, a few researcher trainees stop by our table.

"Hey, Els," says a smiling Korean girl in a lab coat.

Elsie explains that this is her Junior Researcher trainee lab partner, Gemma, and I instantly feel jealous. It hasn't even been a full day of training and she's already given Elsie a nickname. *I* haven't even given Elsie a nickname.

Gemma gives me a little wave. "The Junior Researchers have a table near the taco stand and they're inviting the trainees to come watch them demonstrate all seven kinds of explosions. The magical ones are supposed to be really cool."

Elsie's eyes flash with excitement, but she tries to hide it. "No, thanks. I'm just going to hang with my roomie today."

"No," I say. "You should go. We can hang out later." I glance toward the Van Helsing table. "I should probably try to get to know the Junior Agent trainees."

"If you're sure . . ." Elsie eyes me like she's waiting for me to change my mind. I wonder what my aura looks like right now.

Once Elsie is gone, I reread magiciangirl18's message. Do I really want to meet this girl? What if she's not even who she says she is? There might be some kind of creature out there that eats magicians for dinner and lures them to its den through social media. Okay, that sounds dumb, but still, it's so obvious to me that meeting up is a bad idea.

But then, the same could be true for my next move.

I pick up my tray and start toward the Junior Agent trainee table. My heart thumps in my chest. This might be worse than when I had to go onstage and accept my moonstone badge. *This will be fine.* Some of those kids cheered for me earlier.

I can't go the whole summer without making more friends. And Elsie shouldn't have to blow off her new Junior Researcher trainee friends just to keep me from sitting alone.

I can do this. Lara may hate me but Dylan seems okay when he wants to be. I manage to get most of the way there before Brian Li notices me and gives Lara a nudge.

Lara groans. "You can't be serious."

"Um, I thought I'd sit with you guys today." I put on my best smile.

"Sorry," says Lara. "Only people with legal abilities are allowed. Besides, we wouldn't want to catch whatever it was you gave the Crystal Ball."

A few of the others laugh. Some even throw their feet atop the empty chairs at the table to keep me from sitting. I look around for someone to have my back but even the kids who cheered me on in the training gym won't meet my eyes now.

Finally, I look to Dylan, hoping to find some hint of the boy who talked to me when we were alone in the hallway. But he just pushes his food around his plate. Guess I'm only worth being nice to when he doesn't have family around.

It's Jefferson Academy all over again.

I turn and walk straight out of the food court. No way I'm gonna let them see me cry.

New Message from magiciangirl18:
They're never going to accept you. But I will if you give me a chance.

How does she know already? You know what—I don't even care. I type up a quick reply.

From: Amari_Peters
When and where?

New Message from magiciangirl18:
Tomorrow. I'll message you in the morning with a time and place.

17

WHEN I WAKE THE NEXT MORNING, THE FIRST THING
I do is check my phone to see if magiciangirl18 has
messaged about meeting up. If she really has info about
Moreau, even just about being a magician, this could be
major.

Unfortunately, when I click on the Eurg icon, I get this
message:

Error! Please update Othernet App

And because I have the worst luck ever, Elsie's bed
is empty. She's not even in the food court for breakfast.
Apparently the Junior Researcher trainees all have to attend

a presentation from some really old, really famous magical scientist who's visiting from the Bureau's London outpost. Which means I have to skip breakfast and go to the lobby of the Department of Magical Science to wait for her.

Whispers the elevator shouts, "NOW ARRIVING AT THE DEPARTMENT OF MAGICAL SCIENCE," as its doors open to a wall of purplish-blue flames. At first, I figure he must have the floors mixed up. Then I remember the lobby of the Department of Magical Science is constantly changing to reflect current breakthroughs in the field.

"Whispers?" I ask. "Is it safe to walk through that?"

"YES!" Whispers shouts.

"Okay," I say, covering my ears. I stretch one foot out through the burning wall. Thankfully I don't turn into Amari-flavored BBQ, so I hop the rest of me through the fire. Once I'm safely on the other side, a tiny metal drone floats over to where I'm standing.

"You just stepped through a wall of Nightfyre. What you may not know is that Nightfyre isn't actually a true fire at all, but rather a convergence of naturally occurring free magick and ultraviolet light energy that combusts harmlessly!"

"That's great," I say, not caring at all.

"Would you like to hear more about the scientist who discovered Nightfyre?" asks the drone. "He's visiting today."

"No, thanks," I say. The drone sighs and floats away. The rest of the lobby is covered in giant screens showing different experiments taking place at Bureau facilities around the world. Each screen has a couple drones hovering nearby to answer any questions passersby might have.

I find a bench beneath a live feed of Brazilian researchers studying the growth rates of various grasses. It's right next to a darkened screen flashing the words *Outpost Under Repair Due to Recent Attack*. It's not hard to guess why no one else has chosen to sit here.

Elsie finally comes out, surrounded by a huge group of Junior Researcher trainees. They smile and laugh as they talk, and she looks so happy—it's the complete opposite of how I feel whenever I'm with the other Junior Agent trainees.

I wave her over.

"What's wrong?" she asks, looking concerned.

"I don't know how to update the othernet app." Realizing how ridiculous that sounds, I add, "I'm waiting for an important message on Eurg."

Elsie raises an eyebrow. "Really? From who?"

I probably said too much. "Uh . . . no one you know."

"Okay . . ." says Elsie. "Well, it's my mistake. I could've sworn I set the app to auto-update. It can be a pain to do manually."

She taps away on the screen for a couple minutes.

"Got it," she says. "And don't worry about your missed messages. They should all come . . ." Elsie frowns. "Who are you supposed to be meeting?"

I snatch the phone and have a look for myself.

New Message from magiciangirl18:
6:00 p.m. Room 307 in the Vanderbilt Hotel.

It's really happening then. My stomach does a flip. As exciting as this is, I'm also terrified.

Elsie crosses her arms. "You can't really be thinking of meeting this girl."

I should make up a story, I know I should. But nothing I say will erase what she just saw. I'm caught. And besides, if I'm really going to go through with this meeting, somebody should know where I am. Just in case something bad happens.

"She claims she can tell me more about Moreau and about being a magician." I've been so focused on finding my brother that I haven't even given much thought to my magic and how it works. "Promise you won't tell anyone."

"I don't know," she says. "There's probably a reason this magiciangirl18 is hiding from the Bureau. What if she's Moreau's apprentice? What if this is how they get to you? You could be walking into a trap."

"She told me she wasn't. And I'm not going to assume the worst just because she's a magician—I'm one too and I'm not bad."

"I guess not," says Elsie. "But then, we're assuming she even *is* a magician. There are probably a lot of bad guys who wouldn't mind using you for revenge since they can't get their hands on your brother."

I didn't even think about that. There's no way for me to know if these messages are really from another magician. This mystery person could be lying about everything.

"I have to try. She can't be that bad if she wants to meet so close to the Bureau, right?"

"Maybe I should come too. Just in case."

"You're the only person who knows about this," I say. "If you're right and I don't come back, then someone has to let people know where I went."

Elsie frowns. "I guess that does make sense. But be careful, okay? I mean it. Your brother had a lot of enemies."

I blow out a huge sigh of relief. "I'll be as careful as I can."

With the first tryout tomorrow, the only thing scheduled for Junior Agent trainees today is something called Supernatural Immersion. Elsie described it as a supernatural entity show-and-tell. Whatever that means.

I'm one of the first to get to the classroom so I take a seat near the front. As the other trainees come in, they do everything in their power not to sit next to me. Even when the seats get full, kids decide they'd rather take up spots on the floor. I just sit there in a full classroom with a circle of empty desks around me like I've got some terrible disease no one wants to catch. I don't get it.

Dylan and his sister are the last to come in. At the sight of me sitting alone, Lara shoots me a little smirk. They're both about to take up a spot on the floor next to some other legacy kids when Dylan stops, turns around, and comes to sit next to me.

He gives me a small smile and I honestly feel like I could burst into tears, it's so nice. Lara looks ready to explode.

A chubby white guy in a gray suit comes in a few minutes after the class is supposed to have started. "Name's Senior Agent Kozy," he says. "Before we get started, I have a message to pass on from Agent Fiona." He clears his throat. "There will be a sleep-in taking place in the training rooms tonight with the goal of fostering camaraderie in the midst of competition. Further details to be provided. Now that that's out of the way, who knows what today's class is about?"

Dylan answers. "The purpose of Supernatural Immersion is to get us used to being around supernatural entities."

"Very good." Agent Kozy claps. "Our first guest got spooked and canceled on us after this most recent attack on the Bureau. But not to worry, I called in a favor, and do I ever have a treat for you." He dims the lights. Shouts and shrieks go up as a pitch-black puddle slinks across the floor to the center of the room. I jump in my seat as it passes in front of my desk.

Billy Pogo goes red and points a shaking finger. "I know what that is! It's a boogeyman! Had one under my bed for years!"

A boogeyman? I lean in closer as the shadowy shape of a woman emerges from the puddle, her glowing white eyes searching the room.

"Boogey*person*," says the shadow-lady. "It's the twenty-first century, for heaven's sake."

Agent Kozy hoots in delight. "Isn't she grand? Well,

class, this is your chance. Immerse yourself in this experience. Have a listen to her story."

The boogeyperson tells us that her kind resides in the deep, dark shadows of sketchy places. She explains that certain creatures are allowed to scare and harass unsuspecting people if they wander someplace generally acknowledged to be spooky—like graveyards, old abandoned mansions, dark caves, and under beds. As long as the area has a current Permission to Terrorize zoning permit from the Department of Supernatural Licenses and Records.

Makes me wonder if that's why Quinton always warned me about taking a shortcut through the creepy junkyard down the street from our apartment. There's no sign out front and I've never ever seen anybody go in or out of there.

Once the boogeyperson is done telling us about a few of her favorite frights, Agent Kozy lets us ask questions.

I want to know more about that Permission to Terrorize stuff, but Billy Pogo gets his question out first. "Are you related to the boogey, um, person who haunted the upstairs bedroom at 231 Knacker Boulevard in Charlotte, North Carolina?"

The boogeyperson strokes her chin. "I do have a second cousin I simply adore in Charlotte. Can you describe him?"

"Well, he's sort of shadowy and terrifying and he made these creepy noises . . ."

"We're *all* shadowy and terrifying, love. And creepy noises are in the job description. You'll need to be more specific."

"Sometimes he'd make this 'Booga Booga' sound out of nowhere, right when I was drifting off to sleep."

"Oh, that *was* Clarence! Firm believer in the 'Booga Boogas,' he is. Myself, I'm more of a 'spooky whispers in the middle of the night' gal."

"Why do you scare people?" asks Brian Li. I wouldn't mind hearing the answer to that myself.

"Everyone's got to eat," she shrugs. "Boogeypeople eat fear."

"What does fear taste like?" asks Dylan.

"I have it on good authority that it tastes like chicken, but as I've never had chicken before, I can't really say how true that is."

"Fair enough, but why children?" asks a girl.

"Because nowadays adults just don't fear us like they used to. They hear something under the bed and they're grabbing the flashlight to have a look. Children are far more likely to let their imaginations run wild. And that makes for some tasty fear, let me tell you."

"I have a question . . ." says Lara Van Helsing. "Well, really more of a statement."

I roll my eyes. Of course she does. Anything to get everyone's attention back on her.

"Says here," Lara continues, squinting at her phone, "that boogeypeople date back seven hundred years to the war with the Night Brothers."

Looking uncomfortable, the boogeyperson glances at

Agent Kozy. "We don't really like to talk about those days. Dark times and such."

Lara keeps reading. "It's believed that boogeypeople were created by the Night Brothers and sent into the camps of enemy armies to terrify them in the night. The result being that armies would arrive on the battlefield drowsy and sluggish." Lara looks at the boogeywoman. "Such a scandalous beginning for your kind."

Agent Kozy steps forward. "That's quite enough, young lady. This boogeyperson is our guest. I don't see how any of that is relevant."

"But there's a magician right here in this room," Lara says. "Don't you recognize one of your masters?"

The boogeyperson sniffs the air a few times and then looks to me. She drops to her knees. "Apologies, my lady. I didn't recognize you."

"Oh no, you don't have to bow." I hate that she sounds so afraid all of a sudden. "Please stand up."

The boogeyperson scrambles to her feet and looks up at me with frightened eyes. "Us boogeyfolk know what you magicians are planning, and we don't want any part in it. Please don't force us, I'm begging you."

"I'm not—do you mean Moreau?"

"*Please*, just leave us be!" The lights flicker and the boogeyperson fades into the shadows.

Her fear of me makes me sick to my stomach. Is this what it means to be a magician?

The rest of the trainees just stare in stunned silence.

I swear I could melt right into this chair.

Even though we agreed she wouldn't come, after hearing about my Supernatural Immersion class, Elsie begged me to at least let her take the elevator ride with me up to the third floor of the Vanderbilt Hotel. I told her no, for her own good—but let me tell you, no one's overpowering a were-dragon if she wants to go somewhere.

On the bright side, without her help I never would've known about Mischief, a part-time service elevator known for pranking kids with out-of-order signs and self-destruct countdowns, and for a willingness to assist in any type of general rule-breaking. As Elsie and I are lifted up through the Bureau, Mischief has been giggling nonstop in the background saying, "I'm helping a real-life magician escape! It's my crowning achievement!"

I'm so nervous I'm bouncing from foot to foot. "If I don't come back, you have my permission to add my moonstone badge to your VanQuish collection. Think about the bragging rights you'll have at the next convention."

"You can make all the jokes you want," says Elsie. "You're forgetting again that I can *see* how worried you are."

Mischief says, "Now entering the Vanderbilt Hotel." About ten seconds later the elevator stops and the doors open up inside the closet of an empty hotel room. I'm confused for a second but then I realize it makes sense to have a secret entrance like this. Our elevators aren't exactly open to the public.

"Be careful," says Elsie.

"I will," I say. "Thanks for coming with me."

The second I step off, Mischief squeals, "Magician on the loose!"

Elsie quickly mashes the button to shut the doors and they both drop down out of sight. I take a deep breath and dash out into the hallway before I lose my nerve.

When I reach room 307 I spend forever standing in front of the door trying to gather up the courage to knock. Also, how are you supposed to greet a fellow magician? Is there a secret handshake or something?

I knock. I'm so nervous I can't stand still.

But nothing happens—until I hear the door behind me click open.

I spin around to find a tall, pink-haired girl leaning into the hallway. Tattoos cover her arms.

"Hurry," she says. "Before anyone sees."

"Are you—"

"Yes!" she says. "Now come inside."

I follow the girl into room 308. She waits by the door a few seconds, peeking into the hallway. "You came alone, right?"

"I did," I say.

"And nobody followed you?"

"I . . . I don't think so."

"Good." The pink-haired girl nods, drops the fancy

wooden *Do Not Disturb* sign onto the doorknob, then shuts the door. She takes a few steps backward, away from me. "I'm going to show you something, but you have to promise not to freak out. Okay?"

"Um . . . or maybe you could just tell me what you're about to do?"

"It's better if I just show you." Slowly, the girl raises her right hand. As it passes in front of her face she whispers something that sounds like "Misspell." Suddenly her face begins to blur as though somebody went at it with a giant eraser. I jump back.

The blurry-faced girl tilts her head and lets out the creepiest laugh—it sounds like multiple people are laughing at once.

I turn and dash for the door.

"Wait!"

I know that voice.

I turn and feel my jaw drop open.

DYLAN VAN HELSING SMILES AND WITH A WAVE OF HIS hand all traces of the girl are gone. "Okay, maybe I should've warned you."

"No way . . ."

"Yes way." He chuckles. "Surprised?"

"But . . . I don't get . . . I mean . . . how?"

"How do you think?" Dylan grins like it should be obvious.

"You're a magician?!"

Dylan blows into his hand and three fiery butterflies burst into life. They fly smoky circles around my head and then fizzle out.

A million different questions pop into my mind. They

must all come out at once because he says, "Whoa, one at a time!"

My face flushes. "Sorry. Why in the world did you call yourself magician*girl*?"

He flushes. "It was part of my cover. I wasn't sure if I could trust you. The Bureau doesn't know about me yet and I want to keep it that way. I didn't know if you'd report me or not."

"Okay . . . but why didn't your magic show up on the Crystal Ball like mine did?"

"Because I crafted an illusion," he says with a smile. "Made it look like I was just another trainee. Took me months to get it just right."

I think back to how relieved he looked when he came back to his seat. I thought he was just nervous about his supernatural ability. He was relieved that he'd pulled off his illusion. "Well, what about the boogeyperson? Why couldn't she smell you?"

"Illusions can fool any of the senses, not just sight," says Dylan, grinning. "I wrapped myself in an illusion that can only be smelled instead of seen. You never know what supernaturals you'll run into at the Bureau, so I make sure to always hide my magician's scent."

"That's incredible," I say.

"Not as incredible as your illusion," says Dylan. "You made it seem like the Crystal Ball filled with smoke and cracked."

"But that was just an accident," I say.

"Exactly!" says Dylan. "Only an extremely powerful magician could've pulled off an illusion of that size without realizing it."

I'm not sure how to feel. That Magic-Meter, Moreau, and now Dylan have all told me how powerful I am. But that's not how I feel at all.

"Compared to you, I'm a pretty average illusionist," adds Dylan, "but I'm a really strong technologist."

"What's a technologist?"

Dylan smiles and my phone buzzes. "Answer it."

I pull my phone out of my pocket and take a look. I gasp.

New Message from Dylan
Pretty cool, huh?

"No way!" I can't help a smile. "That's *so* cool."

"Isn't it?" says Dylan. "Magic isn't the curse my dad and everybody else at the Bureau make it out to be. I'll bet they gave you that whole speech about how too much magic turns you evil, blah blah blah. Am I right?"

I just nod.

"Well, nobody gave the Night Brothers their magic. They were born magicians."

"Moreau said I'm probably a born magician too," I say. The idea that I've always had magic seems so impossible.

"So it's true, then? I overheard my dad talking to the chief about you going to Blackstone to meet with Moreau."

"Yeah," I say. "He claims there's some big plan to destroy the Bureau. Kind of like what that boogeyperson was saying. Remember what you said about Moreau's apprentice wanting to make a trade for VanQuish? Well, it wasn't just to free Moreau, it was to obtain some kind of destructive power too. Something Moreau says was taken from him."

Dylan starts to say something but then stops himself.

"What?" I say. "Do you know what it is?"

"I . . . might," he says. "Some magicians believe that the Night Brothers created their own spell book—something called the Black Book. Supposedly the most powerful spells a magician can wield. Vladimir was probably the strongest weaver the world's ever seen."

"Weaver?" I ask.

"It's a kind of magician, like an illusionist or a technologist. They weave together new spells. It's why the Night Brothers were so powerful. They were a perfect team—Vladimir created the spells and Moreau carried them out. After Vladimir's defeat, the Black Book was supposedly locked away in the Great Vault in the Department of Supernatural Investigations. If it's even real."

From the way Chief Crowe and Agent Fiona acted, it sounds like it could definitely be real. "Do you think it might contain spells that could destroy the Bureau?"

Dylan shrugs. "But I can tell you one thing. They'd be far beyond the abilities of an ordinary magician. You'd need to be incredibly magical to even use them. Like, born magician magical. Like Moreau himself or . . ."

I look up to meet his eyes. "Or like me."

He nods.

I shiver. "What makes a born magician so special?"

Dylan leans back in his chair. "Born magicians are really rare. The Night Brothers are the only ones I've ever read about. It's like nature itself chose you to be a magician. The rest of us inherit our magic from another magician."

"But how can we be sure I'm a born magician? Couldn't someone have given me their magic without me knowing?"

"Not exactly," he replies. "The Apprenticeship spell isn't the kind of thing you'd forget. It's pretty intense, and it binds you to that magician forever. You two basically share the same magic."

"Who gave you yours?"

Dylan sighs and runs his fingers through his hair. "I'm going to trust you with another really big secret, okay? I'm only telling you this to prove that being a magician doesn't automatically make you a bad person."

"I won't tell anyone. Pinkie promise."

After Dylan and I lock pinkies, he says, "You know the story of how my ancestor Abraham Van Helsing drove a stake into Vladimir's heart, right? Well, there's a reason Vladimir trusted him so much. Abraham Van Helsing was one of Vladimir's magician apprentices."

"Are you serious?" I ask, leaning forward in my chair.

"Totally serious. Van Helsing magicians have passed that magic down through our family for generations, keeping it secret from the rest of the family. The magic was passed to my uncle, who passed it to Maria before he died. And once she made Special Agent she passed it to me—"

"Wait!" I interrupt. "You're saying Maria is a magician too?"

"There's a reason I knew how to beat the Crystal Ball," says Dylan. "Members of my family have been doing it for nearly seven hundred years."

It takes me a few seconds for that to sink in. "So we aren't the first magicians to join the Bureau . . ."

"Not even close! And not one of the magicians in my family went on any terrible crime sprees. They were as normal as anyone else. If anything, they used their magic to make themselves better at their jobs. It sucks that people hate magicians so much that they had to take their secret to the grave, though."

"Did Quinton know about Maria being a magician?"

"I don't think so," says Dylan. "We *really* aren't supposed tell anyone."

That's an awfully big secret to keep. It means a lot that Dylan told me. I *so* want to believe him when he says that I don't have to be the awful thing people say I am. But magicians are known for their crimes. And Moreau . . . "Then why do the bad magicians go bad?"

"Beats me," Dylan replies. "Maybe they get tired of being automatically hated because of the Night Brothers and they just snap. Doesn't it make you angry how Lara and the other Junior Agent trainees treat you? It's one of the reasons I took a risk and messaged you. I couldn't stand the thought of you believing the hateful stuff the supernatural world wants you to believe. We're different from every other person in the Bureau—but that just makes us special."

I smile. "Where did you learn all this?"

"You probably know from my sister that my family has money. Rather than spend it on dumb shopping trips, I buy up whatever I can find about magicians. My parents think I'm going through a phase. Or at least that's what they're hoping. My dad is so paranoid about it he forbade me from talking to you. It's why I haven't exactly been the most outgoing person whenever my sister is around. She'd rat me out in a heartbeat." He pulls a small book out of his jacket. "Bought this book of spells at a collector's auction last year. It once belonged to Madame Violet, one of the most famous illusionists who's ever lived."

Dylan hands the book to me. It looks like one of those fancy leather diaries. It even has a little golden key attached by a string of black velvet.

I feel nervous just holding the thing.

Dylan's expression turns serious. "This secret is a really big deal to me and all the magician Van Helsings that came before me. We aren't even allowed to tell the non-magician members of our family what we are. And believe me, my mom and dad would freak if they knew the truth about me and Maria. I guess I'm asking if you're somebody I can trust."

I lower my eyes and think. Not until right now do I realize just how much I've needed a magician friend. Someone who understands what it's like. I smile. "You can definitely trust me."

Dinnertime is almost over by the time I get back to my room. Elsie is probably still in the food court. If Mama were here, she'd tell me to get my butt down there and put something in my belly, especially since the first tryout is tomorrow. But there's no way I can pass up a chance to see what this spell book has to offer. For as much trouble as it's caused me, I'm so curious to know what kinds of things I can do with my magic. I practically sprinted the whole way here.

I plop down onto my bed and pop the key into the tiny lock on book's gold clasp.

But the key doesn't work.

I try again and again but the thing just won't open. Did Dylan trick me?

There I go not trusting him again. He took a big chance telling me his secret; there has to be a way to get this thing open.

After a few more tries, I'm about ready to throw the dumb thing across the room, when my finger grazes the slightest little bump on the spine of the book.

Bringing the book closer to the light, I spot a tiny, golden button. I give it a press and the clasp unfastens. Then, on its own, the book opens to the very first page:

WELL DONE!

The first lesson in the training of an illusionist is this: Never trust. Take absolutely nothing at face value. In viewing anything, assume its appearance is false until proven otherwise. To this end, the very first spell the novice illusionist must learn is the extremely simple spell that casts aside illusions set forth by others.

DISPEL

Once you've read this entire page, shut this book. Then, with only your pointer and middle fingers extended, wave your hand in front of it and speak the word *Dispel.*

This must be what Dylan used to get rid of his tattoo girl illusion. I close the book and extend my two fingers. Slowly, I move my hand over the book and say, "Dispel."

A warm sensation fills my chest, like when you drink hot chocolate on a cold day. Instantly, the book begins to tremble on my bed, and bright red spots peek through the black leather cover. As it continues to shake, the edges of the book expand to twice its original size, and it gets thicker too. When it finally stops moving, I'm left with a large red leather book with a new lock and clasp and shiny gold lettering across the cover:

SO YOU WANT TO BE AN ILLUSIONIST?
THE SPELLS AND MUSINGS OF MADAME VIOLET,
FOREMOST ILLUSIONIST OF HER ERA

"I *knew* you were up to something!" comes Lara's voice from behind me.

I nearly fall off the bed before turning to find my door barely open and Lara eyeing me through the crack. Except that's not all—she's recording me with her phone too. She must've seen me rushing down the hallway and followed me.

I swallow. "How much did you see?"

Lara steps into my room and kicks the door shut behind her. She lunges for the book but I clutch it to my chest. I make a run for the door.

She easily beats me there.

With a smirk, Lara yanks the book out of my arms like it's nothing. Her Superhuman Athleticism ability must make her super strong too.

Lara holds the book up to her face and shakes her head. "You are in so much trouble. They're going to kick you out for this. I hope you know that. They might even arrest you."

"Please," I beg. "Don't tell." How could I be so dumb as to let Lara catch me? If I get kicked out, they'll take my memories and there goes any chance of finding my brother.

Lara grins. "On one condition."

My heart sinks. "What condition?"

"I want you to quit Junior Agent training."

"But I can't quit!" I say, shaking my head. How am I going to search for Quinton if I can't even get into the Department of Supernatural Investigations? How am I supposed to join the Bureau's official search if I can't become a Junior Agent?

Lara shrugs and leans back against my door. "There are only four spots and I won't risk you stealing one because everyone loves your stupid brother so much. It's either quit or get kicked out of the Bureau. Your decision."

It's not much of a choice at all.

19

WITH THE FIRST TRYOUT TOMORROW, LARA INSISTED I quit right away.

For as much as I dreaded possibly failing the tryout, it would've been nice to at least get the chance to see what I could do. Maybe I only saw Supernatural Investigations as a way to learn about what happened to Quinton at first, but I've done so much in just a few days. Elsie and I launched our own investigation, I got to question Moreau and used what I learned to get Dylan to tell me about the Black Book. I think I actually started to see myself as a real Agent.

It would've been so great to prove Director Van Helsing and all the others rooting against me wrong. The worst part is that people like Elsie and Agent Fiona were rooting *for* me. It would've been nice to not feel like such a disappointment for once.

I take Lucy up to the Department of Supernatural Investigations. It's late, but the halls are just as busy as they were during our tour the other day. Makes sense, I guess. Protecting the innocent is a twenty-four-hour job.

Like it or not, I screwed up big-time. All Lara has to do is message that video of me to her dad and I'm toast.

I'm pretty sure I remember where the offices are, so I head to the right side of the main hall and enter another hallway. The first door I come to has a plaque that reads *Strategy Room*. I peek through the crack in the door to find men and women in army fatigues arguing as they huddle over a Battleship board game. Whatever they're talking about, it sounds serious. The next door has no plaque but shouting comes from inside. Nosy as ever, I stop to listen. "You tell the Governor that if he didn't want his house pushed into the lake, then he shouldn't have cleared that forest. Seems to me the yetis were only returning the favor."

I find Agent Magnus's door locked. Just my luck. But then I hear his gravelly laugh from somewhere behind me, so I follow the sound until I reach Agent Fiona's office. Well, that's just great. I've got to quit in front of both of them.

I give the door a knock.

Magnus appears in the doorway. "Kinda in the middle of something, kid. What do you want?"

When I practiced on the way here, I imagined myself meeting his eyes and confidently saying, "I'm looking to do something different. I'm over the whole Junior Agent thing. Just need you to fill out the paperwork."

But now that Agent Magnus is front of me, the words are a lot tougher to get out. "Okay so . . . the thing is . . ."

"Spit it out."

Deep breath. "I need to switch to another department."

The door swings open fully. "Don't tell me you've given up before you've tested yourself even once." Agent Fiona stares down at me with those scary blue eyes. Except she's not nearly as frightening with her hair all done up in pretty curls. She's wearing an emerald gown that looks amazing on her.

Confused, I peek into the room to see that there is a candlelit dinner for two on top of Agent Fiona's desk. "Are you guys on a date? Like a *date* date?"

Agent Magnus stands up a little straighter. "What's it to you if we are?"

"Oh nothing," I say. "Just, good job, I guess. Agent Fiona is *way* out of your league."

Agent Fiona smothers a laugh as Agent Magnus goes red.

"I like to think I make up for the rather significant, err . . . beauty gap in other ways. Devilish charm and impeccable character, for instance."

Agent Fiona eyes me. "I've got half a mind to take a look at your intentions, see what's really behind this sudden change of heart, Peters."

If she does that, then she'll know about me using a spell inside the Bureau. That would be a disaster. I've got to think of something, fast.

"But I won't . . ." Agent Fiona adds. "Instead, I want ye to take the rest of the evening and think this through, ye hear? This is a big decision and it shouldn't be made without at least a wee bit of reflection. If ye come back in the morning and still feel the same, then I'll gladly sign the paperwork meself."

"But I *am* sure," I say.

"Do it as a favor to me," says Magnus. "Don't forget you owe me one for speaking up for you a few days back."

I sigh in defeat. "Fine."

The sleep-ins are being held in two of the training rooms. One for the girls and one for the boys. We're supposed to use the locker rooms inside to change into our pajamas. The whole purpose is to relax and build friendships with other trainees before the stress of tomorrow's tryouts.

As soon as I step into the training room, Lara hops off her bed and comes right up to me. "Well?" she says, hands on her hips.

I can't even meet her eyes. "They said I have to wait until morning. They want me to be sure."

Lara huffs. "You'd better be sure." Then she turns and stomps back to her bed.

I pick the bed the farthest away from everyone else. I'm

not in the mood for Lara tonight, and all the other girls have chosen beds that surround hers. She's like the sun and they're a bunch of little planets. They all talk excitedly about what tomorrow's tryout might be. Lara assures everyone that she's seen the rules on her father's desk and that it's basically a massive obstacle course with little stations where we have to answer supernatural trivia questions.

Hearing that makes me feel a little bit better. I'll get to save myself the embarrassment of being the only moonstone badge recipient to fail a tryout and be sent home. For all the reading I've been doing, it feels like I haven't even made a dent in my supernatural booklist. While the other girls press Lara for more clues, I lie back on my pillow, pull out my cell phone, and plug in my earbuds. I close my eyes and before I know it, I'm drifting off to sleep.

What feels like just minutes later, my eyes jump back open. Dylan crouches over me, flicking my cheek with his hand. I sit up and freeze. *What's going on?* I'm not in the training room anymore. I'm on the floor of a small library. A dusty desk sits to my left and there are battered bookcases all around me.

"Good," says Dylan, standing up. "You're finally asleep."

"You mean awake?" I say groggily.

"No, I mean asleep. We're sharing a Wakeful Dream. I think this is the first tryout."

For real? I think back to Agent Fiona and Agent Magnus wanting me to wait and make my decision in the morning. They didn't want me to quit before the first tryout.

I groan. I'm not a fan of being tricked.

But I'm also wondering if maybe it means they think I actually have a chance of passing.

Ugh. But I can't pass. Not with Lara holding that video over my head.

"Are we partners?" I ask him.

Before Dylan can answer, a ball of red flame bursts into existence between us. It grows, burning white-hot before it explodes into a fiery message. Dylan circles around to read it with me.

WELCOME TO THE FIRST JUNIOR AGENT TRYOUT.

GET TO THE BASEMENT DOWNSTAIRS AND RETRIEVE WHAT WAS STOLEN.

HINT: IT'S THE MOST VALUABLE THING YOU'LL FIND.

BE PREPARED TO EXPLAIN YOUR CHOICE.

AND REMEMBER,

YOUR EVERY DECISION WILL BE JUDGED.

GOOD LUCK!

The words disappear into a cloud of smoke.

"Be prepared to explain your choice," Dylan repeats.

"Maybe there's more than one object to choose from?" I say.

Dylan laughs. "Well, it wouldn't be much of a challenge if there wasn't. I think we need to figure out the answer to your first question—are we supposed to work together or is this a me versus you competition?"

They can't expect us to work together. "It has to be a competition," I say. "If they eliminate the loser of each pairing, then that leaves the sixteen trainees that move on to the next tryout."

"True, but don't forget that real agents always work in pairs."

I bite my lip. He makes a good point.

"Hmm," says Dylan. "Maybe we should agree to work together until something tells us we can't."

"Okay." Hopefully that comes sooner rather than later so I can just get this over with and let him win.

"We should start by observing our surroundings," Dylan says, looking around. "There's probably a reason we're in this room."

"All I see is a lot of books."

"Look for details," Dylan says. He points to the corner of the ceiling. "How about those cobwebs?" He sniffs. "And there's dust everywhere. Maybe we're in an abandoned house."

I point to a pot full of pretty white and violet flowers. "Someone has to be watering those."

"Good find. Let's keep that in mind while we head to the basement. Uh, okay if I lead?"

"Sure," I say. "You've got more experience in the supernatural world."

Dylan pulls open the squeaky door and pokes his head

out. "We're at the end of a hallway. It seems empty."

"Seems?" I say, but he's already stepped into the darkness.

Here goes nothing. I follow Dylan into the hall. It's dark as far as I can see, the only light coming from two open doorways on the right side of the hall. Unless one of those rooms leads down to the basement, I don't know where else the entrance might be.

We tiptoe through the darkness, the floorboards creaking loudly beneath our feet. Twice, we hear what sounds like voices up ahead and Dylan has us stop and wait. Both times it just gets quiet again and we continue down the hall.

It seems like forever before we reach the first doorway. Dylan stops us short of the entrance. "We should check out both rooms. We don't want any surprises."

"Good idea."

Dylan leans into the open doorway and whispers, "A weapons room."

We both slip inside and close the door behind us. The sunlight and warm air coming through the large, busted-out window make the room feel like an oven. Outside a wide desert stretches into the horizon. A cactus that's been chopped down is all there is to see.

"Maybe we should choose something," Dylan says, picking up a dagger from the weapons rack. Axes, maces, a javelin, and a couple swords hang from metal hooks. There's even a crossbow.

I grab a really cool-looking ax—which is surprisingly

light—and give it a couple swings. Then I get a scary thought. "Does this mean we'll have to fight something?"

"No clue. I'm as much in the dark about this as you are."

That might be true, but the way he twirls the dagger between his fingers like a pro makes it clear he at least knows how to fight. "We should get going," he says.

I nod and follow him out the door.

The hallway feels even darker than last time. Probably because the weapons room was so bright. Dylan moves quicker this time, ignoring the loud floorboards. Having that dagger must be a confidence boost. Or maybe he's as ready to get out of this spooky place as I am.

Dylan's breath catches, and he stops suddenly. I don't have to ask why. Gleaming red eyes appear in the dark. A hulking frame in tattered clothing steps into the light of the second doorway, its head hanging unnaturally to one side. It's missing an arm and one of its legs is turned the wrong way.

It moves toward us with jerky steps. A growl fills the hallway.

Dylan lifts his dagger. That's when I see it.

"No!" I shout, and grab his arm.

"What are you doing?" says Dylan.

The creature stumbles right past us.

"Look," I say. Lit by the sunlight pouring out from the weapons room doorway, I'm able to point out the bouquet of flowers in the creature's hand.

"Just because we're afraid, doesn't give us the right to

attack," I say. "Where I'm from that happens a lot—you get labeled as bad or scary just by how you look or what neighborhood you're in. Remember that flowerpot in the library? I'll bet whatever that was is just going to put some flowers in it."

"Thanks," Dylan says in the darkness. "That was a good call."

I smile. "Maybe I should lead."

He laughs. "Good idea."

I move to the front and into the next doorway. Another room with a view of the desert landscape. "It's empty."

Dylan joins me in the doorway. "Are you sure?"

Before I can answer, something whimpers. Looking harder, I'm able to make out a girl tucked into the shadows directly beneath the window.

"Help," the girl says. "Please."

Wait, she's a Junior Agent trainee like we are. Stephanie something. A sword lies at her side.

"I don't wanna be a Junior Agent anymore," Stephanie says. "Did you see that thing in the hall? Can I come with you guys?"

"No," Dylan says firmly.

"Seriously?" I ask. "Can't you see she's scared?"

"Where's your partner?" Dylan asks.

"When I told him I wanted to quit, he left me here," answers Stephanie. "Said he wouldn't let me ruin his try-out."

"So you haven't left this room?" Dylan asks.

Stephanie shakes her head. "I never should've picked this stupid career. I don't know what I was thinking."

Enough of Dylan's questions. I'm going to help her.

I make it all of two steps before Dylan shouts my name. He adds, "Don't go any closer."

"I'm helping her," I say.

"Ask her where she got the sword," says Dylan.

I stop cold. She would've had to go to the weapons room to get that sword. But she just told us she hasn't left this room.

A wicked grin spreads across Stephanie's face, revealing fangs. The sight makes Moreau's fangs flash in my head and I totally freeze up. She lunges for me, but Dylan shoves her back just in time. The girl stumbles into the sunlight, where she dissolves into a cloud of ashes.

"Thanks." I close my eyes and shake out my nerves. "How did you know?"

"Since the first test was about something scary being harmless, it only makes sense that this test would be the opposite."

Why didn't I think of that? Having a partner is working out pretty well so far. Which is probably the point—we're supposed to work together. My heart sinks. Dylan trusts me. Am I really going to let him fail because of me?

For so long I've wished for real friends—for someone to have my back. Is this the kind of friend I want to be?

No. I've got to at least try my best. I can always quit after this tryout.

Near the end of the hallway, Dylan and I find a staircase hidden away in the darkness. We both ease down the steps as quietly as possible.

A dark stone room waits at the bottom of the stairs. A row of pedestals runs down the middle, leading to a tall red door in the middle of the back wall.

Dylan raises his dagger, his eyes darting around the room. I grip the handle of my ax and move to his side. As we near the pedestals, I keep waiting for something to jump out. For some alarm or booby trap to go off.

Nothing happens.

Dylan presses his lips tight. "This feels . . ."

"Too easy?" I finish.

"Way too easy," Dylan agrees. "Unless this test is just deciding which of these treasures is the most valuable."

I take a look at the pedestals. There are four in all, each a little taller than the one before it. The first pedestal holds a painting of a giant sea dragon crushing a large wooden ship. Electricity sparks across the beast's massive body.

"The leviathan," says Dylan, coming up beside me. "One of the seven great beasts."

Dylan continues to the second pedestal where a bowl of clay sits. It's covered in primitive markings.

"I bet that's beyond ancient," I say.

Dylan's eyes go back and forth between the two pedestals. "Does that make it more or less valuable than the painting?"

"Good question."

Dylan shakes his head in frustration. "This is impossible."

On the third pedestal is a glittering diamond bracelet. The fourth holds a golden crown covered in jewels. I stare at the last pedestal. The diamond might make me rich, but a crown would make me queen. But it can't be that simple, can it?

I want a closer look. But the moment I step beyond the diamond bracelet, a loud boom echoes through the room as something crashes into the other side of the big red door.

I turn to find Dylan staring wide-eyed.

"Take another step," says Dylan.

I move closer to the crown.

Boom! Another bone-rattling crash. Every step I take toward the crown causes something to slam into the door.

"Grab the crown!" Dylan shouts.

I sprint the rest of the way and snatch the crown from the pedestal. The red door bursts open, sending a wave of water through the room. It knocks me off my feet and carries me back to the third pedestal.

I whip my head around looking for Dylan and find him sliding, waving his arms for something to hold on to. He slams hard into the back wall and vanishes.

He must've woken up.

Meaning I'm on my own now. I dropped my ax when that wave hit me, but at least I managed to hold on to the crown. Seeing as how the dream hasn't ended yet, it's pretty clear that just having it isn't enough. I need to get back up the stairs.

The room beyond the door is full of water, but it isn't pouring out. It's like the water has been magicked to stay inside. A huge, dark shadow appears. I swallow and grip the crown more tightly. What could that be?

Shimmering gray scales emerge from the watery room. I recognize them from one of Quinton's old nature magazines. A water python. Actually, the *king* of water pythons—that thing's head is the size of a car.

The giant snake hisses and bares it fangs, its beady yellow eyes glaring.

Can't give up. I need to think of a plan. But what? Maybe if I can get to my ax I can fight it off?

I crawl through a foot of water back to the last pedestal, putting it between the snake and me. I glance around for my ax. *Yeah, because it'll do a lot of good against that thing. Dumb plan, Amari.*

I'll have to make a run for it.

Another menacing hiss fills the room.

I sprint for the stairs, but the giant snake doesn't give chase. A realization strikes me like lightning—the crown isn't what we came for. I stop just short of the stairwell and drop it.

The instant my foot touches the first stair the world around me vanishes. I wake up in my bed, a pair of Wakeful Dream shades over my eyes.

An agent lifts the shades from my face. When I sit up, I'm surrounded by the other girl trainees.

"How do you feel?" asks the agent. Her name tag says *Special Agent Meredith Walters*.

"Sleepy," I say. "Did I pass?"

"You made it the longest," she replies, "and that's usually a very good sign."

"And Dylan, he's all right?" I ask.

Agent Walters nods and stands. "Now that everyone is awake, please go to the locker rooms and get changed into your trainee uniforms. Once everyone is dressed, we'll head to the briefing auditorium to meet with Agent Fiona and Agent Magnus for the results. I must stress that the tryout hasn't concluded, so no talking among yourselves."

"It seems the girls have arrived," says Agent Magnus from up onstage. "Please come up and stand next to your partner."

I see Dylan near the end of the stage and take the spot next to him. His eyes ask me how it went but I can only give him a small shrug. I've either got this thing all figured out, or I screwed it up big-time.

Agent Fiona clears her throat and steps to the center of the stage. "Now that everyone's here, allow me to start by saying that no matter how ye did during your tryout, ye should be proud of yourselves. This tryout is designed to trick ye, to test your instincts and your ability to work as a team. Instincts and teamwork are the foundation of what makes a great agent."

She continues. "Every single action was judged, but there were three automatic disqualifiers. The first test was simple: Did ye leave the library together? There were quite a few close calls but ultimately only two pairs failed that task. When I read your names, please exit the stage and meet with Agent Walters at the entrance for further instruction."

Once those trainees are gone, Agent Fiona shoots the rest of us a sneaky smile. "Next, we offered ye the chance to get yourselves a weapon. And then we gave ye a chance to use it. Depending on the combined level of familiarity with the supernatural world, there were more or less clues that Mr. Zombie was absolutely not a threat. For instance, a pair with no familiarity had Mr. Zombie appear in pink polka dot pajamas humming happy birthday whilst carrying a bouquet of flowers."

Chuckles erupt in the theater.

"Still, this one tripped up a few of ye," says Agent Fiona. She reads off some names and more trainees leave the stage.

Agent Fiona crosses her arms. "Seems the most effective of the disqualifiers was the stranded trainee room. A dirty trick, to be sure, but also a way to take measure of your instincts and how well you analyze a situation. There was no range of difficulty for this test—it was the same for all of ye."

This time eight trainees hear their names called.

"Good news, all," says Agent Fiona. "Since we're already at the sixteen trainees we expected to keep, it means everyone left onstage has passed the first tryout . . ."

I blow out a huge sigh of relief. *Thank goodness.*

"But dontcha go gettin' comfortable, because the second tryout will be a doozy! Lucky for two of ye, the pair that scored the highest in this tryout gets a head start at the next one. Now then, the objective was to retrieve what was stolen, and we gave ye a hint that it was the most valuable thing you'd find. Curiously, every pair but one left with the crown in hand. Would ye believe the odd pair is none other than Dylan Van Helsing and his partner, Amari Peters? I wonder, does that make ye more or less confident in your choice?"

Dylan spins around to face me, eyes wide. I open my mouth to defend myself, but remember we aren't allowed to speak yet. Was I really the only one to leave the crown behind?

"I'm going down the row," says Agent Fiona. "And I want each of you to tell me why ye made the decision ye did."

All the others have similar answers.

"Crowns are priceless."

"Crowns give you power."

"Crowns represent a whole nation of people."

Finally, Agent Fiona stops in front of me and Dylan. "I'd ask ye about the decision, little Van Helsing, but ye didn't make it to the end, did ye?"

Dylan goes red.

Agent Fiona steps in front of me. "Tell me, was it a bit of genius or a severe case of overthinking that led ye to drop the crown before retreating up the staircase?"

I clear my throat. "I'll say . . . genius?"

Agent Fiona begins to circle both me and Dylan. "Go on, then. I'd love to hear the reasonin'."

"Well," I say. "I didn't actually know until I tried to escape with the crown. The water python didn't chase me and I wondered why. Then I realized it was because the snake wasn't guarding the crown. It was guarding the water."

"Hmm," says Agent Fiona. "Interestin' theory. But why would the water be so valuable?"

"Because the dream took place in a desert," I reply. "I noticed it when we were in the weapons room. The land was so barren, the only thing alive was a cactus. And even that had been chopped down for the water already. Put a king in that desert and he'd gladly trade his crown for a drink of water."

"Shots fired!" Agent Fiona laughs. "Okay, Miss Smarty-Pants. Why then would the water python attack when ye grabbed the crown?"

I grin, feeling more confident. "The crown was on the last pedestal," I say. "Every step closer to the crown was also a step closer to the water room the snake was guarding. Behind that door, the python only knew that I was getting closer. It couldn't have known if I was going for the crown or the water room."

"Still," Agent Fiona says, coming to a stop in front of me. She eyes me closely. "Ye were asked to *retrieve* what was most important."

"I did," I say. "I was dripping wet when I got to the last stair."

"You're absolutely correct. Congratulations! A perfect score. First time since your brother did it. Ye and Dylan will both receive a thirty-second head start at the next tryout. Should ye decide to split up and choose new partners, then it'll apply to both your new teams."

Agent Fiona winks and adds in a lower voice, "Trust you'll be sticking around then, Peters?"

Dylan picks me up and spins me around the stage. My arms are flailing and I'm grinning and laughing so hard my stomach aches.

"That was so epic!" he says, finally putting me down. "We really did it!"

I nod, my face flushing. "We really did."

Lara steps between us. "Give me one reason why I shouldn't send that video to my father right now."

"What video?" says Dylan.

"I recorded your *partner* using a spell book inside the Bureau," says Lara. "Caught her red-handed."

"Prove it," says Dylan.

Lara pulls out her phone and starts tapping away at the screen. Her face falls. "It's gone! I don't get it. It was right here!"

"There you go making stuff up again, sis." Dylan shakes his head. "Oh, and the book is mine, by the way. Amari's just borrowing it. You tell Dad I brought it here, and I'll tell Mom who *really* maxed out her Duboise Cosmetics credit card."

Lara just stands there, stunned. Then she huffs and stomps away from us.

"Make sure you put my book back where you found it," Dylan calls.

If Lara was shocked, it's nothing to how I feel. "You erased the video with magic?" I ask.

"Tech-magic has its benefits."

"Thank you so much," I say. "If I'd thought of that earlier, I could've saved myself a whole lot of worrying."

Dylan just shrugs. "Partners have each other's backs, right?"

Definitely.

"CONGRATULATIONS TO OUR TOP SIXTEEN TRAINEES!" says Director Van Helsing, raising a glass of strawberry punch. "And a special congratulations to my son, Dylan, who finished at the top of the rankings. I want all of you to eat, drink, and be merry before our first weekend break. You've earned it. On Monday, return to us focused, refreshed, and ready to get back to work! Cheers to you all!"

The trainees gathered in the large conference room let out a cheer. The conference table is completely covered in desserts—tall frosted cakes, huge plates of cookies, steaming pies. Kids gather around, munching and laughing. They're gathered around Dylan, too, giving him high fives and pats on the back. Even the Junior Agents who put this whole thing together for us tell him good job. Lara makes sure to stand right next to him, soaking in the attention as though she was his partner and not me.

I'm left standing alone by the door, arms crossed, staring down at my feet. None of those same kids come over to congratulate to me. But then I guess Dylan wasn't the one who showed them up in front of Agent Fiona. Even though that's not what I was trying to do at all.

It bothers me a little that Dylan is hogging the praise. Because if they knew the truth, that he's a magician like me, things would be totally different. I almost want to blurt it out to everyone, but I know it's just me feeling jealous. Plus, I'm so grateful that he bailed me out of the situation with Lara. And that he's trying to help me with being a magician.

Still, I wish that I could pretend to be something I'm not too. Things would be so much better if nobody knew I was a magician.

Who am I kidding? It's not like people like me anyway. The Bureau isn't any different from Jefferson Academy. I'm the outcast here too.

"Is there some terrible threat we don't know about?" Agent Fiona's voice comes out of nowhere.

I lift my head to find the Red Lady in front of me. "Huh?"

She smiles. "You've been guarding the door all afternoon. Thought maybe ye know something the rest of us don't."

"Oh," I say, feeling embarrassed. "I'm just waiting for

this to be over so I can go back to my room."

Agent Fiona glances over at Dylan, who's posing for a picture with a pretty Junior Agent girl. "There's not a name more famous in the supernatural world than Van Helsing." She sighs. "Ye get used to them getting all the credit. Especially in this department. But dontcha go worrying yourself, those of us who count know who was this morning's star."

I give a little smile, and Agent Fiona rubs my shoulder.

"Uh, Amari?" Dylan has come over. He looks awfully fidgety.

"I'll leave ye two to celebrate," says Agent Fiona, moving back toward the party. "But Peters, do make sure *he* remembers who got you two that first place."

I nod and then frown as I give Dylan my attention. "What do you want?"

He startles at my tone. "Can we maybe talk in the hallway?"

"Why?" I ask. "You don't want your fancy friends to see you talking to me?"

"Huh? No—" He pauses to let two Junior Agents through the doorway, and then drops his voice to a whisper. "You said you wanted to start investigating together, right?" He flashes me something shiny up his sleeve. "This is the key to the VanQuish office in the Hall of Special Agents."

Did he really just say he has a key to my brother's office?

"C'mon," he adds, waving me into the hallway.

We start toward the main U-shaped hall.

Dylan walks and talks. "I told everybody I was taking you to meet my mom. She's a Crisis Manager in the Department of Half Truths and Full Cover-Ups. She comes up with the cover stories whenever there's a major secrecy breach. Remember that really bad hurricane we got last year? That was actually all-out war between the merpeople and the ocean nymphs." A grin lights up his face. "My mom really does want to meet you, by the way. Big fan of Quinton. It just won't be today."

I make sure to keep my voice low when I ask, "How are we supposed to get into the VanQuish office without anybody seeing us?"

"All the Special Agents on duty today were at the party. I counted." He laughs. "I've had Maria's spare key for months. This is the first chance I've had to use it."

We step into the main hallway. "Just play it cool and nobody will even notice us."

He's right. None of the adults seem to care at all where two trainees are headed. We move a little farther up the right side of the U, toward the Great Vault, but take a turn through a skinny doorway we skipped on our tour.

The walls in this hallway are lined with gold trimming. Fancy.

"The Hall of Special Agents," says Dylan. "There are only ever thirty agents per outpost. They take on only the most dangerous missions."

I glance around the hall until I see a smooth wooden door with a fancy cursive *V* etched onto it.

Dylan leads me over to it. "The department left their office intact out of respect."

I trace the *V* with my finger. I never would've been able to get into Quinton's office on my own. It feels like I'm so bad at this investigating stuff sometimes. Like I'm letting my brother down. "They've already looked in here for clues?"

"It's the first place they checked," says Dylan.

"Let's go inside before anyone sees us."

Dylan nods and slips the key into the door. I get goosebumps as he pushes it open.

"You first," he says.

I take a couple deep breaths to calm my nerves. Once I step inside, the lights flicker on by themselves. Only . . .

It's more like a trophy room than an office. The walls are lined with shelves of photos, awards, medals, and other things. Elsie would love to see this. It's a VanQuish fan's dream.

In the center of everything, there's a really big photo with Quinton and Maria crouching down beside a short elf with a head full of dark leaves and skin like mottled tree bark. "That's Merlin himself," says Dylan, trailing me. "He almost never lets anyone take his picture."

I follow the shelves around and let my fingers graze a big golden Medal of Honor. Beside it sit two Agent of the Year certificates in shiny silver frames. Farther down the shelf are a pair of shiny purple Sky Sprints in a glass case. The same fancy *V* is written across the side. There's a little sign beneath that reads:

DUBOISE AIR VANQUISH:
Limited Edition

"They had their own Sky Sprints?" I ask.

Dylan grins. "I'd have gotten a pair myself but the lines were crazy."

I laugh.

I step past a few more magazine covers with headlines like "Supernatural Citizens of the Year" and "Ten Most Influential Members of the Supernatural World."

"They're a really big deal," I say.

"They really are," says Dylan.

"I can't believe Maria would want to give this up."

He shrugs. "Being a Special Agent is hard. It has to be a lot of pressure having to protect the whole world. Especially when you get crazy famous and the older agents start to resent you for being promoted to Special Agent ahead of them. I know my sister had a hard time with it."

"Is that why she wanted to be a trainer?"

"I think she and Quinton were starting to get into arguments."

I stop and look at Dylan. "They didn't get along?"

"Something must've happened," says Dylan, shaking his head. "Because one day it was just different between them. It was really weird."

"No idea why?" I ask.

Dylan shrugs.

That *is* weird. I look at a giant video game poster of

VanQuish and ask, "Didn't you say this was an office?"

"Say 'up,'" says Dylan.

"Up?" Lights flicker on above us and my feet lift off the ground, like there's some invisible elevator carrying me upward. I tilt my head back to find office furniture floating above me. My body doesn't stop rising until I'm standing right in front of Quinton's floating desk.

"Whoa," I say, testing my balance. "A floating office?"

Dylan beams, floating up to my side. "Quinton loved working in a cluttered office. But my sister is the cleanest person you'll ever meet. She threatened to start chucking stuff into the hallway if he didn't agree to get the office enchanted for more space."

"That sounds like Quinton. He's still got a perfect attendance certificate from the third grade on his bedroom wall."

I take a look at my brother's desk. It's covered by a large stack of folders marked *Classified* and a sleek silver laptop. The stack is so tall it nearly hides the two picture frames behind it. One is Mama's high school yearbook photo from *forever* ago that she gets all embarrassed about when anyone sees it. Me and Quinton would always joke that she looked pretty dope for a cavewoman.

The other photograph is me sitting on a bright red bicycle, with a big ole snaggle-toothed grin. Just seeing it makes me close my eyes and cover my face with my hands. Next thing I know, I'm ugly crying. Like full on bawling. Dylan wraps a shaky arm around my shoulder. I try my hardest to get it together, to stop crying like such a baby in front of him, but I just end up crying harder.

Once I'm finally done, he says, "That picture must mean a lot to you, huh?"

I nod. "It was the first time I realized that Quinton always had my back, no matter what." Mama and Daddy had just separated, and Daddy had promised me for months that he was going to get me this bright red bike we'd seen in Walmart for my birthday. Mama warned me not to get my hopes up, but I didn't listen. I knew my daddy would get it for me because he said he would. And daddies didn't lie to their little girls.

Well, Daddy didn't even show up for my birthday. When Mama called to ask where he was, they got in this big argument on the phone. At some point Mama must've hit the speakerphone by accident because all of a sudden I heard my daddy's drunken voice say, "She probably ain't even mine. Tell whoever her real daddy is to get her the stupid bike."

Mama hung up on him and looked right at me. She started to say, "He didn't mean it . . ." but I wasn't hearing it. I ran straight to my room and cried like I'd never cried before. Quinton brought me into his room that night after Mama fell asleep, and we had the first of our thousands of talks lying in the middle of his bedroom floor. He told me he would always have my back. When Christmas came around, my brother didn't get one present.

But I had a brand-new red bike.

"We're going to find them, okay?" says Dylan. "We just have to keep believing."

I nod and try to smile. "I do believe that."

Dylan takes a seat at Quinton's computer and mashes the power button. I crouch next to him. "Cross your fingers."

I do, but all that appears onscreen is:

Please Enter Password

The words keep flashing.

"Could you use your tech magic?" I ask.

"On a computer this advanced?" He shakes his head. "It would take me at least an hour. We don't have that much time."

I bite my lip. What are the odds Quinton uses his email password for more than just his email? "Scoot over. I want to try something."

Dylan slides over to give me some space, but he stops me before I can type anything. "Just so you know, these computers are highly classified. If you put in the wrong password even once, it'll alert security. So . . . no pressure."

I swallow. "Sure, no pressure."

"Just be sure this is your best guess," he says. "You got this."

It's my only guess. I type out *Amari-Amazing,* one nervous keypress at a time. All that's left is to hit Enter.

My finger hovers above the key.

Dylan leans over and presses it for me.

I shut my eyes and hold my breath, preparing for the worst.

"We're in!" says Dylan. "You did it."

Relief washes over me. Quinton's schedule appears on the screen. He must've left it open all this time.

> **Schedule:** Quinton Peters
> November 18
> **12 p.m.:** Contact KH
> **11 p.m.:** Meeting with Horus

Dylan gasps. "That's the day Maria and Quinton went missing."

I pace fast circles around the elevator on the ride down to the youth dormitories. Dylan wanted me to come back to the victory party with him but I have to let Elsie know what we found. Maybe she'll know what KH means. Could it be someone's initials, maybe? If so, maybe they'll have an idea about where my brother is. Or at least what he was working on.

The second entry was a lot easier to figure out. Horus has to be Director Horus from the Department of Good Fortunes and Bad Omens. Unfortunately, he's not due back from the Wandering Isles until Monday. It feels like a lifetime from now.

I want to know what his meeting with Quinton was about. He might've been the last person to see my brother before he disappeared.

I'm still pacing when the elevator opens up to the youth dormitories. The sight of so many kids packed into the hallway raises my eyebrows.

Bertha's nowhere to be found either. It's not until I start to make my way through the crowd that I realize that all eyes are on me, staring. A few kids nudge one another, whispering.

I'm used to getting weird looks, but this is on another level. What's going on?

The farther down the hall I get, the more it happens. People start to step aside, making a path for me to my room.

"Do you think she's seen it?" a girl whispers.

When I finally turn the last corner to my room, Lara and a few of her friends are huddled next to a couple adult agents. The girl looks scared.

I get there at the same time Bertha steps out of my room. Agent Magnus is right behind her and he looks furious. Bertha keeps shaking her head.

"What's going on?" I ask.

They turn to look at me. Bertha winces.

Magnus points over my shoulder. "Turn around and go back to the elevators. You don't need to see this."

"See what?" I step forward.

Bertha tries to shut the door, but she isn't fast enough. Painted over my bed is a Black girl with two X's for eyes and a stake in her heart. *NO MAGICIANS ALLOWED* is written just below it.

My stomach turns. I ball my fists and storm over to Lara. "You did this?"

"It wasn't me," she says quickly.

"Liar!" I scream.

I go to shove her, but Lara twists and pushes me down instead. My back hits the floor so hard it knocks the air out of my chest and I start coughing.

Lara glares down at me. "If I had done that, you can be sure I would claim it. Face it, nobody wants you here. It was bound to happen sooner or later."

Someone shouts, "No magicians allowed!" Then a few more join in. Soon the hall echoes with the chant. Everywhere I look, kids shout at me. Does it even matter who put that message on my wall if they all agree with it?

I've never felt so small.

Magnus stretches out his arms, his hands transforming into solid metal. With one booming clap, the hall falls quiet. "Next person who says a word gets a one-way ticket outta the Bureau and ya ain't comin' back. Think I can't do it? Try me and find out!"

No one says a word.

"Amari!" Elsie appears out of the crowd and takes my hand. "Come on. We're leaving."

I can't get out of there fast enough.

≫ 21 ≪

"YOU CAN DROP ME OFF AT MY APARTMENT," I TELL
Maxwell, the driver of the town car Elsie's guardian
sent for her. He was supposed to take her straight home but
she told him to just ride around for a bit while I cooled off.
He was even nice enough to go and get my things from the
dorm room.

I decide not to text Mama that I'll be coming home.
She'll just have a million questions and wonder if I'm all
right.

Thing is, I'm not all right. That ugly painting above my
bed was just so cruel. Those *X*'s over the eyes and the stake
in the heart. . . . I feel like I could throw up. Do they hate
magicians enough to really want to hurt me?

I lay my head against the car window. Is there *anywhere* that I belong?

Moreau's voice echoes in my head. *Join us, Amari. Join your fellow magicians.*

"I know you're sad right now," says Elsie, "but not everyone is against you. I'm not."

I don't answer. I keep staring out the backseat window. It's started to rain.

Realizing I'm being rude, that she's not who I'm mad at, I open my mouth to apologize but Elsie cuts me off.

"I know," she says. "You don't have to say it."

I nod and close my eyes. I can still hear that chant in my ears. Still see those faces looking at me with hate just because I'm different. For being something I didn't even choose to be. "I don't know if I can go back."

"But . . . your brother," says Elsie, scooting closer to me on the back seat. "You can't let them make you give up. They *want* you feeling ashamed of what you are. They want you so scared you'll quit."

"I don't care," I say. "I'll just have to find another way."

"You can't quit and keep your memories. You'd go back to being the person you were before you knew about the supernatural world."

I think about the clues Dylan and I found on Quinton's computer. I'd lose them if my memories were taken. But then, I'd also lose the memory of people hating me.

"You're being a coward," says Elsie.

I whirl to face her and she flinches.

But then she lifts her chin. "Quinton would fight for you if the situation was reversed. You know he would."

"Quinton was my brother, not yours," I snap. "You don't know anything."

"I may not know him like you do," she says. "But I know I'm right."

I don't have a comeback for that. Because deep down I do know she's right.

"This is my neighborhood," I say as we pull up to a red light. Elsie presses her face up to the window and I wonder what she's thinking. Outside, Mr. Jenson is fussing at a group of boys hanging outside his shop. They're all wearing black bandannas. They just laugh at the old man. As soon as we stop, though, all eyes turn to us.

"Don't stare." I pull Elsie away from the window.

"Do you know those kids?" asks Elsie.

"Nah," I say. "They're just being nosy 'cause we're in a nice car. Probably wondering what it's doing out here."

I glance over Elsie's shoulder to be sure and realize I'm wrong. "Actually, I do know one of them. See that tall, skinny boy off to the side? His name is Jayden. He used to come to Quinton's tutoring program. Now he's running the streets with the Wood Boyz."

"Wood Boyz?"

"It's a gang. If Quinton were around, he'd be so

disappointed. He really cares about Jayden." I think about our talk at the bus stop. I hope he doesn't get himself in trouble fooling around with those guys.

"Sounds like you care too," Elsie says.

"I guess I just know how easy it is to fall into that life when you're struggling. A lot of them really have it rough, you know?" Everyone wants to feel like they belong somewhere.

"Maybe you could do something," says Elsie.

"I'm not Quinton. He just had a way with people." I shake my head. "The best thing I can do is get my brother back here. He'd know what to do."

It's not much longer before we get to my apartment. As we pull into the parking lot, I start to feel nervous about Elsie seeing where I live. If Elsie's guardian is rich enough to send a driver, then I'm sure her life outside the Bureau is a lot closer to Lara's than my own. What if she thinks less of me for not having all the things she does?

"It's this building," I tell Maxwell, Elsie's driver. He pulls the car into a spot right in front of my apartment and I reach for the door handle.

"Can I come inside?" asks Elsie.

My stomach does a flip. "Um, I guess."

Elsie grins all the way to my front door.

I push it open and step inside. It's so clean. I guess with me gone and Mama always at work, there's no one around to make any messes. Elsie comes in behind me.

"I know it's not much, but it's home," I say with a shrug.

Elsie looks around wide-eyed, a weird little smile on her face. She stops to check out the photos of me and Quinton that Mama has all over the front room. I look a hot mess in a few of them.

I'm so nervous I can't stand it anymore. "What are you thinking?"

Elsie just looks at me. "It's just . . . well, this is where my hero grew up. And where my best friend grew up too. I don't know, it just feels really special being here."

"Best friend?" I ask, my face flushing.

Elsie goes red. "Oh, I mean . . . I'm sorry, I shouldn't have just assumed—"

"No," I say quickly. "We can be best friends. It's just that I've never had a girl best friend before. Or any best friend besides my brother, I guess."

Elsie picks up a picture of me and Quinton splashing around at the rec center pool. "What's it like having Quinton Peters for a brother?"

"Normal?" But then, after I think for a bit, I say, "To me, he was just regular old Quinton. But he was always looking out for me. I couldn't imagine having anyone better."

"I wish I had a brother or sister," says Elsie. "I mean, my adopted parents are really nice, and I owe them so much, but they're also really busy. It would've been nice to have someone to talk to or play with. I think it's why I'm always in my head so much. Kind of sad, huh?"

"Not at all," I say. "Being in your head so much is

probably why you're the smartest person I know. And besides, now you've got a best friend. And that's almost as good."

There's a noise at the front door. If it's Mama, she's going to flip about me having somebody over without her permission. Not to mention the fact that I never even told her I was coming home this weekend.

But it's only Maxwell. He's such a big, muscular guy he could probably serve as Elsie's bodyguard too. "I'm sorry, Miss Rodriguez, but your mother requested I bring you home immediately. She asked me where you were, and when I told her she got very upset." Maxwell looks to me and then drops his eyes. "She doesn't think it's safe for you to be in this part of town. She threatened to fire me for even bringing you here."

Elsie sighs. "And she'll do it too, just to prove a point. I'm sorry, Amari, but I have to go."

"I get it. It's cool." I do my best to hide how much Maxwell's words sting.

"Are you sure you're okay?" Elsie asks.

"Mm-hmm. I'll be fine."

Elsie comes over and gives me a hug. "I put my number in your phone. Call me, okay?"

I stand at the window and watch as Maxwell opens the car door for her. And then they're gone.

To keep from thinking about what happened back at the Bureau, I dig around in my bag for the spell book.

I place it on the table and stare at it for a while. I know I'm safe at home and that Mama is at work, but it still feels like having this book is wrong.

But maybe Dylan is right. Maybe it's okay to explore what I am. Even after everything, I'm curious to know more about being a magician.

I flip open the book to a random spot. On one page is a really cool picture of the sun. The other page has a spell.

SOLIS

Create the outward illusion of blinding sunlight from within yourself. Cross your arms at your chest and throw them open while exclaiming *Solis!*

That's it? Seems simple enough. I get to my feet and step back from the table. I throw out my arms and say, "Solis."

A bright flash makes me jump, but it disappears as quickly as it came.

"Did it work?" asks a voice I recognize.

"Dylan?" I whip my head back and forth. "Where are you?"

"I'm kind of inside your TV at the moment," he says. "I tried sending you messages on Eurg, then I tried calling your cell phone but it kept going straight to voicemail. So I thought I'd try a more creative approach. If you press the power button we can see each other."

I grab my remote and turn it on. Sure enough, Dylan's face appears on the screen. "How in the world are you inside my TV?"

"Tech magic," he says with a grin. "Mind if I come over?"

"When? Like now?"

"Yep," he replies.

"Um, okay, just let me—"

Dylan appears right in front of me and I fall onto my couch in surprise. He points to the metallic band around his forearm. "Borrowed my dad's transporter. He has so many he won't even notice."

Mr. Ware used a transporter to get to my interview, I remember. Once I'm over my surprise, I slouch down into the cushions. "Are you sure your parents won't get mad at you for being in this neighborhood?"

"Maybe," says Dylan. "But I don't usually make a habit of telling them where I'm going."

"Must be nice. My mom might work all the time but she's got the neighbors trained to keep an eye on me. Whenever I sneak out I know she'll hear about it."

He plops down on the couch next to me and looks around. I cringe when his eyes find my baby pictures. For some reason him seeing those pictures feels way more embarrassing than Elsie seeing them.

"Um . . . so I guess you heard what somebody did to my room."

Dylan turns to face me, his expression serious. "You can't let ignorant people get you down, Amari. I mean it."

"Easy for you to say." I roll my eyes and fold my arms. "Nobody even *knows* you're a magician. Everyone wants to be friends with you."

"I might smile and play along, but I know they'd treat

me the same as you if they learned the truth. Maybe worse because of who my family is. Trust me, I know who my real friends are." He sighs and crosses his arms too. "I wish Maria were here, I'd ask her how she dealt with having to lie about being a magician literally all the time."

It never dawned on me that it might be just as hard to keep being a magician a secret. At least with me, everything is out in the open. Maybe I'll never be popular but I know the few people who do like me, like the *real* me. Even the magician part.

"I wish there was some way we could just magic Van-Quish home," I say.

"If only." Dylan cracks a small smile. "But, hey, we're becoming Junior Agents, right? We can find them ourselves."

My shoulders droop and a nasty chill spills down my back. "That drawing . . . They *hate* me, Dylan."

"So you're really just giving up? When you could be the one to find them?"

"Can we just not talk about it? Please?" I want to tell him that I'm scared to death of going back. But I can't get the words out.

Dylan looks so disappointed that I can't even meet his eyes. Finally, he says, "Well, all right then, let's see that spell you were trying."

My cheeks flush, remembering how easy Dylan said illusions are supposed to be for me. "I don't know if I did it right."

"Try again. I'll help you."

"Really?"

"Really," he says. "I know you're not a quitter. So let's see that spell."

I wish I was that sure. Still, I pull myself off the couch. After a deep breath, I throw open my arms and say, "Solis."

This time the tips of my fingers begin to shimmer but that's about it.

Dylan tips over, laughing.

"It's not funny!" I say. But even I'm fighting back a giggle.

Dylan finally calms for long enough to say, "It's just that you could try to be a little enthusiastic when you perform the spell. You sound like the last thing you want is for it to work. Remember, your magic is alive. It can sense your doubt."

"Fine," I say. I repeat the move, only this time I nearly shout, "Solis!"

My whole body suddenly feels warm and tingly.

Dylan's eyes go wide. "It's working! Look at your hands."

I bring my hands in front of my face, and sure enough, they're glowing. A few seconds later my whole body burns bright.

"Dispel!" says Dylan, holding up a hand to shield his eyes. "You almost got too bright there for a second."

"That was *so* cool!"

"You think that was cool?" asks Dylan. "Check this out."

He waves over the spell book and opens it to the last

page. The only thing written on there is *The End* with a picture of a black leather book beneath the words. It's the old cover, before I used Dispel to turn the book red. Dylan extends two fingers and waves them over the page. "Dispel."

The book begins to shake and suddenly this isn't the last page anymore, it's closer to the middle. And more words appear under *The End* so that the page now says:

The End

of

Fair Magick

and the beginning

of

Magick Most Foul

Dylan turns the page.

That you have found these pages speaks to a willingness to wield more than what fair magick can provide. However, this pursuit comes with a dire warning. The foul magick contained on the following pages is not for the faint of heart. As I learned in their creation, uttering these spells will cost you. For once innocence is lost, it cannot be regained.

MAGNA FOBIA

Allows an illusionist the ability to pull the very darkest fears from your opponent's mind to craft an illusion around them that they shall believe is real. As its name suggests, this spell can inflict great mental harm. Do not use it lightly.

Stare into your opponent's eyes—

I slam the book shut. "Why would you show me that?"

Dylan blinks, his face flushing. "I know these spells sound awful. But we need to be able to protect ourselves. You saw how far people are willing to go because they don't like us. I just don't want anything to happen to you is all. Self-defense only."

"I don't care," I say. "I don't want to learn anything like that." I didn't realize my magic could be that dark. Is it any wonder people fear magicians?

"You might not have a choice, Amari. If you were ever to be challenged by another magician, you could have your magic stolen. Magicians don't survive that."

"I said no," I say firmly. I get that he's only trying to protect me. And maybe I'm being dumb, but the thought of having that kind of power over people scares me a lot more than another magician does. "I don't want to learn magic to hurt people. I won't be like Moreau and those other bad magicians. And you shouldn't use that stuff either."

Dylan raises his palms in surrender. "Sorry. You're probably right. I guess I just thought—well, let me make it up to you. There's something else I've wanted to show you. But it'll mean using my dad's transporter."

"I don't know." Fair or not, I'd be lying if I said I don't look at Dylan a little differently now.

"It's about teaching you to use your illusions," says Dylan. "Something that's not in your spell book."

"Fair magick, right?" I ask, remembering what the book called it. "Not foul magick."

"Totally fair magick," Dylan says. "I promise."

Maybe I am being a little harsh. He's only ever tried to help me. "Okay, then."

"Grab hold of my arm," says Dylan. "It's going to feel a little weird the first time you transport."

I nod and wrap my arm around Dylan's. It can't be that bad, can it? He reaches over and presses a button on his metal armband. Suddenly I get the strange sensation that I'm falling, my living room blurring around me. A moment later, there's something solid beneath my feet, and a cool breeze whips across my face. It takes me a few blinks to shake my dizziness, but once it's gone I stare out at a large lake that sparkles in the moonlight.

"Where are we?" I ask, my knees still a little wobbly from being transported.

Dylan turns to look over his shoulder where a huge house sits between the trees. "The old Van Helsing lake house. It's been in the family for ages, but I'm the only one who comes here anymore."

"Follow me!" He dashes toward the house.

I follow, excited to see what he has to show me.

We head through the front door and into a big, empty living room. Dylan leads me to a doorway near the back. "I may not be as strong an illusionist as you are, but it's still my favorite kind of magic. Painting illusions is sort of my hobby."

"Is that what you wanted to show me?" I ask. "One of your illusions?"

Dylan nods and pushes open the door, revealing a staircase leading down to another door. "I've been working on this one for a couple months now. I thought maybe you could add to it if you wanted."

"I don't know if I'm good enough . . ."

"Don't worry," says Dylan. "I'll show you how."

He opens the second door and I gasp. Dylan's illusion is a whole forest of twinkling neon lights. Trees and bushes with shimmering leaves of blue and pink and purple. "I've got almost the whole basement covered. C'mon, I'll lead you through."

I follow Dylan down a little winding path, my eyes darting back and forth trying to see everything at once. A butterfly with red-and-gold wings flutters by my face, and squirrels with glittery silver fur race up trees when we get too close. It all feels so real that it takes a second to realize that I can actually hear the sounds of animals. I didn't know illusions could do so much.

"You made all this?" I ask.

Dylan looks back over his shoulder and smiles. "Pretty cool, huh?"

"Really cool," I say.

We continue until we reach the point where the forest ends and the stone basement begins. "This is as far as I've gotten. I thought this would be a great spot to put something of yours."

"Of mine? Is there a spell for forest-making or something?"

Dylan laughs and shakes his head. "The spell book shows you how to create automatic illusions, but you can also paint them manually too." He reaches out with his pointer finger and draws a glowing white bird onto my shoulder. It hops to life with a few chirps and then flutters off into the forest.

"It even sounds like a real bird."

"Once you practice enough, there'll be no sense you can't fool. Your illusions can make sounds, have bad smells, or even feel real to the touch. I've never actually tried to taste one, but it seems like it would work."

"Can you show me how?" I ask.

Dylan says the secret to making an illusion is to focus on an image in your head and imagine it pouring out of your fingers. He says to start off with something small and not alive, so we begin with making an extra button on his shirt. It takes me like thirty minutes, but finally a button appears just like I imagined it in my head. Painting manual illusions is a lot harder than the automatic illusions.

"Awesome!" says Dylan. "Let's do one together." He leads me over to the path and paints a tiny green sprout that grows through a crack in the concrete. "This reminds me of you."

"How come?" I ask.

"Because you haven't let where you come from or what you are make you give up. At least, not yet. You just keep fighting through it."

I feel my cheeks flush and we're both quiet for a while. Suddenly my hand reaches out on its own and with a twirl of my fingers, Dylan's sprout grows and blooms with petals of sparkling clear glass. It twinkles like a rainbow in the neon lights of Dylan's forest.

"That's beautiful," says Dylan.

"I don't know how I just did that," I say, staring at my hand.

"Sometimes your magic will take over for you if you let it," says Dylan. "Hmm, how about we call it an Amari Blossom?"

I smile. "I think I like that."

22

THE LAST THING I EXPECT TO HEAR WHEN DYLAN transports me back to my apartment is voices in the living room. A tall white guy sits in one of our kitchen chairs facing away from me—*DETECTIVE* written in big yellow letters across the back of his dark blue jacket. Mama sits on the opposite side of the room with her head down.

I push Dylan into the hallway before Mama can look up. "You have to go."

"I will," he says softly. "But am I going to have a partner on Monday?"

"I . . . I don't know," I say. "But you *really* have to go, okay?"

"I'm going. But I hope you do come back." Dylan taps his armband and vanishes.

I close my eyes and lean my head against the wall. That was so close.

What in the world is Mama even doing home this early? Did the police call her? Could they have found something?

With so many questions bouncing around my head, I decide to slide to the end of the hallway and have a listen.

"I know it's not what you wanted to hear," says the detective. "But please don't think we're giving up on Quinton. We're simply out of leads at this point. Our detectives have to move on to new cases. But rest assured that if anything new comes in, we'll be right back on your son's case."

Mama nods. "I understand." She looks so small, bunched up on the couch like that. So defeated. I hate it.

The detective leans back now. "You know, I've worked this neighborhood for twenty years, both as a beat cop and a detective. Seen the same pattern again and again. A son gets tired of seeing his mother struggle and decides to do something about it. Starts to participate in activities that ain't exactly on the up-and-up. He don't want his mom to be disappointed in him so he keeps it under wraps. Claims he got a job. You see where I'm going with this?"

"I do," says Mama. "But I told you. Quinton was *working*."

"Working, you say?" asks the detective. "Ever been to this job? Seen a paycheck or even a check stub?"

Mama drops her eyes and frowns.

I've heard enough. I stomp into the living room. "Leave her alone!"

Both the detective and Mama jump in surprise.

"Amari?" says Mama. "What are you doing here?"

I'm so focused on the detective I barely even hear her. "She's already answered your questions, so just go."

"I know this ain't easy," says the detective, "especially coming from somebody like me. But—"

"I don't care, okay? You can't just come in here and say stuff like that when you don't know. You can't assume what my brother is like just because of where we're from. Quinton is a good person. The best person. And I'm not going to let you just say whatever you want about him."

"Amari!" says Mama.

"All right," says the detective, getting to his feet. He ignores me and speaks directly to Mama. "Wasn't my intention to start any trouble."

Mama takes a shaky breath. "Thank you, detective."

I slam the door shut behind him.

Mama covers her face, crying. I go over and take a seat beside her and say, "I meant what I said. You should hear the kinds of things they say about Quinton."

But Mama just shakes her head. "What Quinton did in that leadership camp doesn't matter, Babygirl."

What can I say to make her understand the truth? I could try to come up with a way to explain the Bureau to her, but how can I do that without sounding like I'm making it up? I could show her a spell but then she'd freak. And there's no telling how the Bureau would react if they found out. Would I get in trouble? Would we both get in trouble?

But watching her cry like this is too hard. I have to do something.

"You shouldn't have blown up at that detective like that," says Mama. "He's just trying to help."

I can't believe what I'm hearing. "But he was wrong about Quinton. You know that."

"I *don't* know that," says Mama, her voice harsh. "I have no idea what Quinton was doing. For all we know he got caught up in the same mess as so many of the young men from around here."

"*Mama.*" I'm too stunned to say anything else.

She gets up and trudges into the hallway. I hear her bedroom door close.

And that's when I realize I'm crying too. But not because I'm sad.

I'm *mad*. Mad at whoever's keeping Quinton away from us. And mad at myself for ever becoming so scared that I'd consider giving up on my brother. I've got to be stronger than I've been. No matter how bad those other kids make me feel, nothing's worse than seeing Mama hurt like this.

I've got to bring Quinton home, if only to prove to Mama that her son is everything she's always thought him to be. And more.

After munching on a Hot Pocket, I go ahead and iron Mama's work uniform and hang it up on her doorknob. The light in her room is out so hopefully she was able to fall asleep. Even though it's been a couple hours since that detective left, I'm still so frustrated that there's no way I'll be falling asleep anytime soon. So I grab my cell phone, plug in my earbuds, and head upstairs to the roof.

The night sky is still cloudy so it's even darker than usual. Cautiously, I take a seat right at the edge of the roof and let my feet dangle over the side. I can hear both Quinton's and Mama's voices in my head telling me to come back to where it's safer. But honestly it feels good not to listen for once. To be scared of something and do it anyway. If I'm going back to the Bureau, this is good practice.

"Amari?"

I whip around to see Jayden coming up behind me. "What are you doing up here this late?"

He just smiles and plops down beside me. "Ma's new boyfriend don't like having me around so I come up here till they fall asleep. How about you? Thought you were out doing fancy kid stuff."

I laugh at that. "Trust me, there's nothing fancy about Amari Peters." The kids at the Bureau make sure I know it too.

"Yeah, right," he says. "You're practically a legend in the 'Wood."

I raise an eyebrow and he laughs.

"I'm serious," he adds. "People in the neighborhood love

them some Peters. And not just your brother either—you too. We all think you're gonna be president or something."

"No, they talk about me *because* of my brother, there's a big difference. I'm not good at everything like he is."

Jayden looks at me like he has no clue what I'm talking about. "So you didn't get *all* the school awards back in elementary school? And I guess they just give anybody a scholarship to those rich kid schools, huh?"

"Oh, be quiet," I say, blushing a little.

"I get it, though," he says. "Can't be easy having Quinton Peters as your brother. It's like being the second-best basketball player in the whole world but your brother is the best—you'd grow up losing all the time and thinking you suck. But everybody else, the people watching, we see you pulling off moves we only wish we could. We able to see how great you are."

I open my mouth, but don't know what to say.

Jayden's phone rings and his whole expression sours. He sighs as he gets to his feet.

"Jayden . . ." I say.

"I'm trying to get myself out of the Wood Boyz, I really am," he says. "You and Quinton will still help me when I do, right?"

I nod. "Definitely."

He grins and nods too, then disappears down the stairwell.

Jayden's words stay on the roof with me. I *have* always compared myself to Quinton and never felt like I measured up. My brother is good at everything without even trying . . . because that's his supernatural ability, I realize! Quinton has super-genius aptitude—Director Van Helsing said it gives him the ability to learn anything with ease.

Why haven't I ever realized this before now? My whole life I've been comparing my best efforts to my brother's *supernatural* efforts. Of course I'd fall short.

My phone rings. I take a look at the screen, thinking it has to be Elsie. But the phone number is blocked out, and the caller ID just says "Surprise."

Huh? Maybe Dylan, then. That tech magic of his. I tap to answer and say, "Hello?"

At first there's nothing, then a robotic voice comes on the line. "ENEMIES OF MAGICIANKIND, YOU WERE WARNED WHAT WOULD HAPPEN IF OUR DEMANDS WEREN'T MET. NOW SUFFER THE CONSEQUENCES."

The call ends. Consequences?

A message pops up on my screen. It's a video, shot from overhead. I squint down at my phone at footage of massive creatures sprinting across someone's front lawn. They look like those hulking creatures Moreau showed me back in Blackstone Prison. Hybrids.

Once they reach a mansion, the monsters don't even break stride, bursting through the front doors and shattering the wall of windows.

No! I recognize that house. I saw it on Lara's Eurg page. That's Van Helsing Manor. The scene changes to another mansion, then another, all overrun by hybrids. When it finally ends, I get to my feet and open up my own Eurg page.

Hands shaking, I contact Dylan the only way I know how.

From: Amari_Peters
I just got a weird video showing your house being attacked. Are you OK?

I pace back and forth across the roof waiting for a reply from magiciangirl18, aka my partner. Instead I get a call from Elsie.

"Ohmygosh, do you know if the Van Helsings are okay?" she asks.

"I don't know—wait, you got that video too?"

"Yeah," she says. "So did my mom and her coworkers at the Department of Creature Control. I think it went out to the entire Bureau."

~ 23 ~

I DON'T HEAR FROM DYLAN UNTIL THE NEXT DAY. He video calls me from inside the Department of Supernatural Health sporting an ugly bruise on his forehead. I must make a face because he says, "You should've seen me before the Healers."

"But you're all right?" I ask. "Is your family okay?"

"Well, Mom and Lara were touring this year's Heartland Crop Circle Art Festival, so it was just me and Dad there when the hybrids stormed in. I tried to fight them off as I ran to find him, but one of them clawed me pretty good. We barely made it out of there."

"Thank goodness," I say. "I wasn't sure what to think when I got that strange phone call and video."

Dylan's expression turns serious. "I just keep thinking what if everyone was home for the weekend like usual. Would we all have made it out? Lara's room is on that side of the house. Moreau's people went after my family, Amari. Again."

"I know," I say. "It's awful." Lara and I might not get along, but I'd never wish for her to get hurt.

"Dad says the attacks were against old legacy families. Our house wasn't even the worst hit," he says. "A lot of people got hurt. Some didn't make it. Billy Pogo's unnatural luck saved him, but he lost both his parents. He's not coming back to the Bureau this summer."

I shudder at the realization of what he's saying. I couldn't imagine losing Mama.

"I want to be the one to stop them," Dylan says solemnly. "Promise you'll help me make Junior Agent. You know we make a great team."

"I've already decided to go back," I say. "Because *I* plan to be the one to bring Quinton and Maria home."

"Are we going to be VanQuish 2.0?" he asks with a small smile. "We made a pretty good team the other day."

I nod. "From now on we share whatever we find."

"Deal."

Mama's doing a lot better by the time Sunday comes around.

Neither of us brings up the other night. We mainly

just talk about how well I'm doing at "leadership camp." It seems to lift her spirits some.

As we turn onto the tree-lined drive of the Vanderbilt Hotel I tell her how I'm ranked first in my group. I leave out the part about me feeling like an outsider, just like I did back at Jefferson Academy. That would only make Mama worry, and she already looks exhausted from the extra shifts she's been working. She even worked a half shift this morning.

"I'm so proud of you, Babygirl. Doing well here can open so many doors for you."

"I know, Mama." I meant to give a more cheerful answer, but the sight of the hotel sends a shiver through me. As much as I've tried to prepare myself, the thought of facing the other kids is still pretty scary. Especially after the latest hybrid attack. If the other kids weren't fond of having a magician in the Bureau before, I can only guess what they'll be thinking now.

Mama looks at me for a second. "You'd tell me if anything was wrong, wouldn't you?"

"I'm fine," I say. "Just feeling a little sleepy." I even throw in a fake yawn.

I'm not sure if a well-rested Mama would buy my excuse, but since she's as tired as I'm pretending to be, she just nods. "Okay, well make sure you get some rest once you get to your room. Mama loves you."

"I love you too," I say.

I glance up at the hotel as we come to a stop in the drop-off area. Welp, here goes.

I keep my head down as I move through the lobby and into the elevator. I stand all the way in the back, behind a couple of mummies headed for the Department of the Dead. Once they've shuffled off into the gloom of the department's lobby, I ask the elevator to give me a few minutes to think.

The second tryout is the Friday after next, meaning I've got about eleven days to learn as much as I can about Quinton and Maria's disappearance before I have to prove myself again. It's not a lot of time.

My usual doubts creep in but then so do Jayden's words. I've been comparing myself to Quinton for too long. I passed the first tryout well enough, so why can't I pass the second?

And maybe I'm capable of finding VanQuish too. It's time I start believing in myself.

I think back on what I've learned so far: Moreau's apprentice tried to trade Quinton and Maria for Moreau's release and possibly the Black Book. But the Bureau refused, and Moreau's apprentice started attacking the Bureau with hybrids, including that awful attack the other night.

Moreau said the reason my brother was kidnapped was that he found something Moreau's apprentice wanted—something Quinton shouldn't have been looking for. And Lara said Maria was helping him, even though they weren't partners anymore. But what did they find?

Our only clue? A calendar entry on Quinton's computer from the night they went missing. Something about contacting KH and a meeting with Director Horus. Thankfully, the Director is supposed to return from the Wandering Isles soon.

Seeing as I've got no clue what KH stands for, there's really only one thing to do. "Take me to the Department of Good Fortunes and Bad Omens," I tell Lucy.

"That department can only be visited by appointment," she replies. "Would you like to schedule one?"

"I guess. When's the soonest I can speak to Director Horus?"

"That would be the middle of next week," says Lucy. "People tend to book up spots for readings in uncertain times such as these."

"That long?"

"Afraid so."

"Fine. Just tell him it's really urgent."

I take a second to shake out my nerves once the elevator arrives at the dormitories. The kids in the hallway just stare. I keep my eyes focused straight ahead until I get to my door.

But the second my hand hits the knob I hear, "Why are you here?"

I look up to find Lara and Kirsten coming up the hall.

"Same reason you are," I say. "I'm going to be a Junior Agent, and I'm going to find my brother. And hopefully your sister too."

"My sister doesn't need any help from a Peters, got that?" Lara jabs a finger in my direction. "You just focus on your own dumb brother."

I just shake my head and turn back to my door.

"Guess you thought those hybrid attacks were fair payback for that picture *somebody* left on your wall," says

Kirsten, crossing her arms.

I whirl back to face them. "Are you serious? I had nothing to do with that."

"So you say," says Lara.

"You're being dumb," I say.

Kirsten steps closer. "Watch your back, *freak*."

I take a step back. "What's that supposed to mean?"

"Exactly what it sounds like," answers Lara.

"You three! Break it up!" calls Bertha from down the hall.

But I can't let that be the end of it. I won't let anyone intimidate me anymore. I look them both square in the eyes and say, "I'm not scared of you."

"You should be," spits Lara.

For as brave as I'm trying to be, the words still give me chills.

Elsie arrives at the dorm just before lights out only half awake. She texted me earlier to say she and her guardian were up all night volunteering to help those who were hurt in last night's hybrid attacks. My best friend smiles, gives me a quick hug, and then falls over onto her bed fast asleep.

I had hoped to update her on what Dylan and I found on my brother's computer, since I haven't gotten the chance yet, but it's clear she needs the rest.

Lights out comes and goes and I sit cross-legged on my bed with *Noteworthy Agents: Heroics, Scandals & Everything in Between.* I borrow Elsie's sneakandle and put it right up against the wall, so its light won't reach her. After reading VanQuish's loooong entry near the end, I flip back a few pages and skim through Agent Magnus's paragraph to find that his talent for being tough-skinned got enhanced to steel-skinned after touching the Crystal Ball. And Agent Fiona nearly caused an international incident when, as a Junior Agent, she greatly offended the Origami Hive Mind by insisting that scissors beats paper in a game of rock, paper, scissors.

The lightest knock—really more of a tap—sounds on my door. I slide out of bed, tiptoe across the room, and just barely crack open the door to have a look.

A pretty girl in a white flower tiara peeks through the sliver of doorway. "Hello, Amari. I'm here to escort you to the Department of Good Fortunes"—she grins wide—"and Bad Omens." Her face falls.

"Really? I thought my appointment wasn't until next week."

"You've been granted a special 'top priority' appointment by the chief herself. Something about ensuring that your being here won't bring doom and despair to the Bureau. . . . The usual. No biggie."

"Oh, um, okay." It sounds like a pretty big deal. "If I wanted to ask Director Horus something important, could I?"

"Of course," she replies. "But maybe wait till the end so you don't interrupt the show. Now get dressed. Oh, and bring your raincoat."

"Why do I need a raincoat?"

"For the rain, silly!"

I close the door, a little dazed by the sudden turn my night has taken. In the closet, my favorite pair of jeans and the jet-black *I Heart Books* T-shirt Quinton got me last year are waiting for me. Matching black sneakers sit just below them. This must be what I'm meant to wear because there's even a bright yellow raincoat with my moonstone badge attached to the front.

I dress quickly and turn off the sneakandle. In the hallway I get my first good look at my Junior Fortune-Teller escort. She's wearing a fancy white dress that glows in various places.

"Cool dress," I say.

"Isn't it? I made it myself," the girl replies. "The secret is to weave Christmas lights into the fabric." She twirls and then curtsies. "The name is January. Very pleased to make your acquaintance."

I try to return the curtsy, but it ends up being an awkward bow. January doesn't seem to mind.

"Shall we?" she says.

As we move through the halls of the youth dormitories, more kids slip out of their rooms. One girl emerges with a purple velvet cape and crown. A boy skips into the hallway in a thick fur coat, a large pair of antlers perched atop his head.

"Are all of you from the Department of Good Fortunes and Bad Omens?"

January nods. "Our dress code is to wear whatever

makes us happiest. We're a free-spirited bunch."

"Do you all make your own clothes?"

"A lot of us do. But honestly, if you go to the Duboise clothing website on the othernet you can almost always find exactly what your mind has dreamed up."

That's when I realize I've never seen anyone dressed like this during the day. "Do you guys only work at night?"

"We do, but it's not that unusual. There are quite a few departments with nighttime business hours—the Department of Dreams and Nightmares, the Department of the Dead, and I believe the Department of the Unexplained as well. Oh, and the Department of Supernatural Health is always open twenty-four hours a day."

A girl dressed like Santa Claus rushes over to January and clutches both her hands. "Let me guess. . . . Strawberries?"

January giggles. "You're always getting your Futures and Histories mixed up. Strawberries Jubilee was my name yesterday. Tonight I'm January Winterfrost."

The other girl nods her approval and then runs off to catch up with a group up ahead. One of them is wearing a fully inflated blue balloon.

The others have already stopped an elevator for us. I scan their faces for any sign of magician-hate, but they appear much more interested in each other's costumes. January gives them her thanks as the elevator doors shut. I instantly recognize the elevator as Lucy.

"Not used to seeing you out and about this late at night," says Lucy.

"She's to meet with the Starlight Shaman himself," says January.

Lucy coos. "That Director Horus sure has a dreamy voice."

January blushes and they both laugh.

It surprises me when Lucy announces we've entered the Vanderbilt Hotel.

"Are we going outside?" I ask, thinking about the raincoat in my arms.

"Yes and no," says January.

Finally, Lucy says, "Now approaching the Department of Good Fortunes and Bad Omens."

The doors open to a huge circular room that I realize must be the inside of the large golden dome atop the hotel. The dome is split into halves—the walls on the right side show cute furry animals in green meadows filled with flowers of every color. Happy cherubs take aim at grinning couples, and children laugh and dance.

The left side of the dome is totally different. Ugly monsters twist themselves around dark spaces filled with angry green eyes. Some bare sharp fangs, others have sneaky grins. All the people on this side look sad, terrified, or furious.

I guess one side represents good fortunes while the other side represents bad omens. I just hope my visit falls on the good fortunes side of things.

There's a big white pillar in the middle of the room. A black staircase wraps around it, leading up to the viewing end of a telescope that stretches up to the ceiling.

Most of the room is filled with curved tables arranged in concentric circles around the pillar. It reminds me of the solar system. If the pillar is the sun, then these tables are like the orbits the planets take, making bigger and bigger circles the farther you get away. The only difference is there's a walkway that leads straight from the elevator to the pillar.

As January leads me to the pillar, I glance at the little stations spread out along the tables. Some have crystal balls that cloud up as we pass. A few have stacks of tarot cards, and others have bowls with small bones inside. On the bad omens side, I see a book titled *Cursed or Blessed with Bad Luck? A Subtle but Important Difference*. Further ahead a blazing fire burns with little pillows spread out around it.

January follows my gaze. "That's for pyromancy. If you really concentrate and stare into the fire for long enough, you'll start to see glimpses of the future amidst the flames. We're trained in twelve different methods of fortune-telling."

Once we go around the pillar, I spot a doorway with a plaque that reads *Office of the Director*.

We pause in the doorway. It's pretty empty for an office. No desk or chairs or anything on the walls. There's only a big, dark-skinned guy in deep blue robes and a matching blue African kufi hat embroidered with silvery stars. He sits with his back to us on a wide blue carpet with silver trim.

"Hello there," he says in a deep, rumbling voice. The sound makes me smile—it's like far-off thunder. "Welcome to the Department of Good Fortunes and Bad Omens."

"Thanks," I say. "Um, glad to be here?"

Director Horus stands and turns with a swish of his robes. Golden eyes gleam above his neatly trimmed goatee. "January, thank you for escorting Amari. Do me a favor and check the conditions."

"Will do," says January. Before leaving, she glances to me and says, "He *always* guesses my name right."

Those golden eyes look to me now and Horus waves me inside. "Please remove your shoes and have a sit on my carpet."

I do what he says, and we both sit cross-legged across from one another. If I wasn't nervous about this meeting before, I certainly am now. "If you decide my being here is a bad omen, does that mean I'll be kicked out of the Bureau?"

"Don't worry yourself," says Director Horus. "Tonight's reading is merely a precaution. Atlantians like Chief Crowe see every oddity as an omen for calamity. So when a magician shows up at the Bureau around the same time it's being attacked, it's only natural that the chief would want answers."

"Then you don't think me being here is a bad omen?" I ask.

"I have learned to wait for what will be revealed to be revealed," says Director Horus.

That isn't exactly the "no" I hoped for. But then, it isn't a "yes" either.

"It's pouring outside," says January from behind me.

Director Horus grins. "Perfect." He stands and stretches. "Are you ready for a ride?"

I stand up too. "Um . . . sure."

"Stand next to me on the center of the carpet," says Director Horus.

January pulls open a hidden drawer in the wall, then reaches inside and takes out a long silver staff. She tosses it over and Director Horus catches it in one hand. January closes the drawer and then presses herself tightly against the wall. Almost as if she's trying to keep out of the way.

Pieces begin to click into place in my mind. "Wait . . ." I say looking down at the fancy blue carpet beneath our feet. "This isn't a flying—"

"Go!" shouts Director Horus.

The carpet comes to life beneath our feet. It bucks and wriggles and then jumps forward, bending at the edges to fit through the open doorway. We fly in fast circles around the top of the dome, while a crowd of upturned faces cheers us on. A panel slides away and Director Horus spins his staff until it becomes an umbrella that he opens with a flick of his wrist.

We dash out into blinding rain. I can sort of make out the lit-up windows from tall buildings. Enough to figure out that we're rising higher and higher.

I grab hold of Director Horus's arm. The rain comes at us sideways. I try to get a look to see how he's handling all this rain, but I can only just make out the golden glint of his eyes. We continue like this, soaring through the storm until suddenly the rain stops.

Next thing I know we're above the clouds, a starry night

sky all around us. My teeth chatter as I pull my jacket on tighter. It's cold up here.

Director Horus closes the umbrella and sets it down next to his bare feet. That's when I remember my own wet feet.

"A beautiful night," he says, staring up at the sky.

"I'm soaked and freezing," is all I can manage at the moment.

Director Horus grins. "As am I. But what we're here to do won't take very long, I promise."

How can he be so calm when I'm halfway to becoming an Amari popsicle? "What *are* we here to do?"

"We're here to cast constellations." He points to the stars above. "These constellations have been set for tens of thousands of years. They describe the history of our planet itself, moving ever so slowly with the passage of time."

"What do they say?"

"I have no idea." Director Horus laughs. "They're written in language long forgotten. But as you are very young, your constellation should be easy enough to figure out."

"My constellation?"

Director Horus nods. "Hold out your hand."

I do. And then I watch as Director Horus reaches up to pluck a star right out of the sky. He drops the speck of twinkling light into my palm. Then another . . . and another. He continues until my hand is covered in a pile of warm, shimmering flecks.

Finally, he says, "That should be plenty." And with one

broad swipe of his staff he knocks loose the remaining stars from the sky. My eyes widen as they drop down around us like glowing dust. An inky dark sky now stretches out above us.

"Am I really holding whole stars in my hand?" I ask.

"Not the stars themselves, but their spirits. Every natural thing exists in two places, both here and there. If we are physically here, then we are spiritually there. Likewise, if the stars are physically out there, then it only makes sense for them to be spiritually here. Do you understand?"

"Not really," I say.

Director Horus lets out a low chuckle. "Well, if you wish to learn more about these things, you are more than welcome to come try out for my department next summer. It's been many a century since a moonstone badge has graced our doors."

"That moonstone badge is only because I'm a magician, I think."

"Don't sell yourself short. From what I've heard, you've done quite well so far."

I smile at that.

"We'll begin with a look at your history," Horus says next. "To understand where you're going, we must first understand where your blood has been. Separate the stardust into two even piles on the carpet."

I do as he says, carefully molding the mounds of light.

"Gather up the first pile of stardust and toss it as high as you can. Jump if it helps."

I scoop up a pile, cupping it with both hands. Then

I bend my knees and leap into the air, tossing the glowing sprinkles as far above me as I'm able. The glowing pile soars, exploding against the sky like fireworks and then re-forming into a woman with an elaborate headdress. It shifts into a crouching man with a spear lifted over his head. It changes again to a boy on the edge of a cliff, his gaze on the horizon.

I try to be patient as the images continue to shift above me, but my curiosity gets the best of me. "What do these images mean?"

"These are your ancestors. You are descended from great African tribal queens, from fierce warriors who protected the innocent, from renowned travelers who sought the thrill of adventure. Greatness, like all other traits, can be passed down in the blood, from parent to child."

The image continues to shift, this time into a young girl on her knees before a man with a whip. It changes again to show men and women marching, even against the blast of a fire hose. "There is resilience in your blood too. The willpower to endure seemingly insurmountable obstacles. Though your ancestors were once slaves, their descendants fought for equal rights."

At the sight, I hold my chin high.

Then I see Mama's face in the starlight, smiling as she holds a baby in her arms. I hold my breath at the sight of Quinton's proud face as he loads the briefcase that started all this.

"These are the people who know you best," says Director Horus. "You've been greatly loved."

My chin quivers. "I love them too."

Director Horus spins his staff until the whole sky is filled with the faces of my ancestors all at once. "Not a single magician in your family history." He spins the staff over his head and the stars wink out. "This is the history of your magic, Amari. Completely blank. As if the magic truly began with you. Fascinating."

"It's true then? I was born a magician?"

"Apparently so," says Director Horus. "Though I've no idea what that will mean for you. So let's move on to the present and future. Cast the second pile of stardust."

I repeat the same motion as before, tossing the stardust high above my head. There's another explosion of white light and a twinkling bird takes form.

"That bird represents you as you are right this moment. Notice it hasn't yet taken flight, its wings are outstretched, its head turned upward. The pose suggests that you are capable of becoming truly special, reaching great heights—"

Director Horus goes quiet and steps forward. The bird isn't the only thing being shown. The head of a snake emerges, and the creature winds itself through the legs of the bird, coiling up around it. The director stares intently, and I watch him, anxious to learn what this might mean.

A much larger two-headed snake appears. I jump when both its heads bare their fangs. Instead of backing down, the smaller snake shows its fangs too.

"This isn't good," says Director Horus. "I've seen that two-headed snake before. During my own castings while I was away in the Wandering Isles. It's why I cut my trip short and announced my return."

"What's it mean?" I ask.

Director Horus lifts his staff to the sky and waves it in wide circles. The stars swirl above us until the image of a mighty elephant appears. "This represents the entire Bureau of Supernatural Affairs." Seconds later the two-headed snake emerges, coiling itself around the elephant's leg. It waits there for a moment before climbing up to the elephant's neck where it strikes, bringing the animal to its knees.

This time when I shiver, it isn't from the cold.

Director Horus narrows his eyes and strokes his chin. "Snakes have typically represented magicians in these constellations, chiefly for their potential to do great harm to the caster. You do not appear as a snake, likely because it is your casting. I must admit, however, I don't know what a two-headed snake might represent. It's puzzling. Whatever the case, it would seem you and the Bureau share a common enemy. And that concerns me."

"Do you think the two-headed snake could be Moreau and his apprentice?" I ask. "That's who's planning to destroy the Bureau."

"That would be the most logical guess," he replies. "There is much in your constellation that isn't clear. The snake that sought to protect you, for instance. I don't suppose you have any idea who that magician might be?"

Dylan. It has to be. But I can't give away his secret. "I don't know."

Director Horus frowns. "I'll need to inform the chief about what we've witnessed tonight."

"Do I get to stay?" I ask.

"Absolutely. I saw nothing to indicate that you are a bad omen for the Bureau. If anything, this constellation re-inforces the need for protective measures to be put in place to ensure your safety. I don't advise you going home for any-more weekend breaks."

"But what if I fail a tryout?" I ask.

"We'll cross that bridge when we get to it. But drastic measures would need to be taken. Whatever this two-headed snake represents, it has taken an interest in you, Amari. And that appears to be a very dangerous position to occupy."

While I think on those words, Director Horus twirls his staff and the stars scatter, returning the night sky to normal.

"Before we go back," I say, "could I ask you something? About my brother?"

Director Horus nods thoughtfully. "You want to know why Quinton came to see me on the night VanQuish went missing."

"Yes," I say. "Was it about his future?"

"He came to see me about reading the future, but not his own." Director Horus sighs. "It's why I had to refuse. Unless it is an emergency, I can never reveal the future of one per-son to another. Such things are as private as thoughts."

"Was he asking about my future then?" I ask.

"Not yours," he replies. "Maria's. Your brother wanted to know if she would ever betray the Bureau."

I WAKE UP EARLY THE NEXT MORNING AND WAIT FOR
Dylan near the elevators in the lobby of the director
apartments. Since I've got no clue where the Van Helsings'
apartment is located, I figure it's the best place to wait for
him. A group of Junior Record Keepers awaiting Director Cobblepot shoot me nasty looks and mutter something
about "unfair badges" and "stupid magicians," but I ignore
them.

Dylan and I promised to share whatever we learned, so
that's what I'm doing. But I've been dreading it all night.
Maria, a traitor? When I finally spot him, I run over.

His eyes go wide. "Amari? What's up?"

"Can't talk here," I say. "Come with me to the library."

"Okay . . ." he says. "Should I be worried?"

"Just come on. It's important."

We take an elevator down to the library and dash into a study room.

"What's going on?" he asks.

"I was casting constellations with Director Horus last night and I asked him about that meeting we found on Quinton's computer."

He leans closer. "And what did he say?"

I tell him.

Dylan looks stunned. "But why . . ."

"You said it yourself—they weren't getting along anymore. They were splitting up! What if Quinton realized she was keeping secrets from him?" I meet Dylan's eyes. "Maria is a magician. What if she accepted Moreau's offer to join them?"

Dylan looks so hurt by this accusation that I can't help wondering if I made a mistake telling him. "You think my sister is a traitor?"

"I don't know," I say. "But there had to be a reason for my brother to go behind her back like that."

Dylan pushes himself to his feet. "I'm outta here."

"Wait," I say. "That's not all. Director Horus knows about you being a magician."

Dylan goes stiff. "He does? How?"

"I shouldn't have said it like that," I say, shaking my head. This whole thing has me flustered. "I just meant that he knows there's a magician who wants to protect me. The constellation showed a two-headed snake baring its fangs at me. But there was another snake by my side. He said that snakes are supposed to represent magicians."

Dylan thinks for a moment. "Of course I'd have your back. That's what partners do. That's why it doesn't make sense for Quinton to think my sister would ever . . . Let me prove it, okay? You keep looking into what Quinton was up to, and I'll show you my sister isn't a traitor."

"Okay." I don't know what else to say.

Dylan turns to leave but stops short. "Did Director Horus get suspicious about there being another magician on your side?"

"Well," I say, "he asked me about it, but I just told him I didn't know."

Some of his anger fades. "You kept my secret?"

"You should tell people when you're ready." It's a choice I wish somebody had given me.

Surprise shows on Dylan's face and he flushes. "Thanks."

Now that training has restarted, it's time to learn Stun Sticks. Agent Magnus paces in front of us, holding up a metal rod. It almost looks like a really fancy pen. "First thing to know about a Stun Stick is that it's for self-defense purposes only. Once you make Junior Agent in a few weeks, you and your partner will be assigned to a Senior or Special Agent. Wherever that agent goes, you go. Needless to say, things can get a little hairy when you're out fighting crime.

These Stun Sticks have the power to down an eight-foot yeti mid-pounce. Which one of you brave souls wants to volunteer to demonstrate it?"

"I think Amari wants to volunteer!" shouts Kirsten.

I turn to glare at her but Agent Magnus steps in front of me.

"That so?" he asks.

Which is worse? Getting zapped by a Stun Stick blast or chickening out in front of everybody? I swallow. "Sure, I'll volunteer."

I step up in front the group and Agent Magnus offers me the Stun Stick.

"Wait, you want *me* to zap *you*?" I ask.

"That's right."

A slow grin spreads over my face. Now we're talking. This might be worth it for how much he teased us about our sloppy Sky-Sprints technique last week.

"Now you'll want to hold it out in front of you and press—" I press the button and Magnus goes stiff as a board, his thick arms clapping against his sides. He bursts into loud guffawing laughter.

Huh? I touch the Stun Stick to my own arm and tap the button. Instantly, both my arms snap to my sides. It's a lot like one of those bear hugs I used to get from my great-aunt at Thanksgiving. A few seconds later I get the sensation of being tickled on the bottoms of both my feet.

We pass the Stun Stick around the room and let each

trainee experience what it feels like. "The Stun Stick works in two ways," says Magnus. "First, it immobilizes your opponent, preventing them from attacking. Second, it can lessen whatever ill will your opponent bears you with laughter. At the finale, you will duel against one another in pairs using Sky Sprints and Stun Sticks. So go ahead and get your Sky Sprints on."

I turn to head to the equipment room to get a pair of standard-issue Sky Sprints.

"Amari," calls Dylan, waving me over. It takes me by surprise. The two of us haven't talked much since the whole "Maria might be a traitor" thing. He keeps glancing down at his gym bag.

"Yeah?" I say.

"I, uh, picked up something during weekend break." Dylan reaches inside and pulls out a black box with Duboise written in silver across the top. "Didn't have a chance to give it to you before so . . ."

I'm so stunned, it takes a second for my brain to catch up. "These are for me?"

Dylan lifts off the top. A pair of really cool Sky Sprints sit inside a velvety box. The white boots have a ghostly shimmer. The tag reads *Dead but Dazzling Collection*.

All I can do is shake my head in disbelief. "Thank you."

Dylan's whole face reddens. "I mean, uh, you won't get far in those dusty old Sky Sprints you were using before. And if you fail, so do I."

"Right," I say. "That makes sense."

I wish things with me and Dylan could go back to normal. Please don't let Maria really be a traitor . . .

Over the next week there's a new report about some outpost or legacy family's home getting overrun by hybrids practically every other day. Elsie said the only reason they haven't canceled the summer training sessions is because Bureau headquarters is probably the safest place for us to be.

My days are pretty busy just trying to keep up. Every day I wake up and take classes, study for the finale in the afternoon, and hang out with Elsie at night, which usually means the two of us in a study room not coming up with much about Moreau, KH, or the Black Book.

Elsie has been doing her part. She borrowed nearly every book on magical objects from the library and even brought a few from Director Fokus's personal collection, but hardly any of them mention the Black Book. And if they do, it's info we already know.

On the days I miss Quinton the most, Elsie and I spend the last few minutes before curfew looking at old magazines about VanQuish. It helps me feel closer to him. On better days, either I'm Elsie's guinea pig for whatever wild invention she's working on or she's barricading the door and helping me practice my magic.

I'm getting better and better at painting illusions by hand. One time I even changed the color of Elsie's frizzy brown hair to bright pink. She nearly freaked when I pretended that I couldn't remember how to change it back. I can even paint moving illusions now, which are tricky because you have to concentrate so hard to make the movements look natural.

The only downside is that in order to keep Dylan's secret, I can't tell Elsie how I got the spell book or how I learned to paint illusions in the first place. I wonder if my aura shows how much I hate hiding things from her. If it does, Elsie never says anything.

It's the week of the second tryout and I'm trudging to the food court when Gemma, Elsie's lab partner, hands me a note to meet her in the library instead.

When I get there, she rushes me into a study room.

"Did you find something?" I ask.

Elsie sighs dramatically. "This is the last book I have access to. It's taken so much sucking up to Director Fokus to get her to lend me *Rasputin's Directory of Dangerous Doodads and Doohickeys.* It's the magician's handwritten notes. If there's not anything new about the Black Book in here then I don't know where else to look."

I bite down on my lip and take the seat next to her. "Let's see then."

Elsie carefully flips through the pages until she finds an entry for the Black Book. Her eyes scan it top to bottom before her face falls. "Nothing new."

As bad as I feel, Elsie looks even more upset. I know she's been working crazy hard to find something that would help, so I pull out my own spell book to cheer her up.

Elsie looks over as I slip the key into the lock and she sits up. "Of course! I'm such an idiot. All this time . . ."

She reopens the book, flipping past the Black Book entry until she lands on a new page:

THE BLACK KEY

If only a spare few know about the Black Book, even fewer are aware of the key necessary to open it. After Vladimir's death, the Bureau of Supernatural Affairs was tasked with protecting the Black Book from Moreau and those magician apprentices who avoided capture. Not trusting humanity to possess both the Black Book and the Black Key, the inaugural Supernatural World Congress bestowed the Black Key upon an anonymous Key Holder whose duty it was to hide and protect it. This duty is to be passed down through generations, with each new Key Holder honor bound to never reveal themselves.

The Black Book and the Black Key are never to be brought together under any circumstances. Therefore the Supernatural World Congress forbids the Bureau from ever seeking out the key. For if it does, then it has broken its foremost oath and shall be forever dismantled, its members immediately banished from the supernatural world.

"KH means Key Holder," says Elsie, eyes wide, pointing to the page. "That's what, or I guess *who*, VanQuish found."

I bite my lip and nod. "No wonder Moreau's apprentice went after my brother. If there really is some master plan to take back the Black Book, then they'll need the Black Key to open it."

"This is bad," says Elsie, dropping her voice to a whisper. "If anyone finds out about this, the entire Bureau would be shut down for breaking its oath."

"Then for now we don't say anything to anyone," I say.

"What about Dylan?" asks Elsie.

"I . . . don't know yet." Because Maria Van Helsing might be Moreau's apprentice.

Now that Elsie and I are out of clues, and the second try-out is only a couple days away, we decide to shift all our focus into not failing. It would be different if *we* knew who the Key Holder was, then we could at least send a warning somehow. If it's not already too late.

Hopefully Quinton hasn't told Moreau's apprentice anything. But I don't like to think about the ways a magician might go about making someone talk . . .

A couple times I've wanted to tell Dylan about what we found, but it seems like he's avoiding me. He's even been pairing up with Lara instead of me in Sky Sprint training. I almost wish I'd never said anything about Maria.

All the trainees from every department have been

studying and practicing like crazy. Hardly anyone shows up for lunch anymore. If not for Elsie, I'd be right there with them. My roommate doesn't believe in missing meals, and apparently that rule goes for me too. Last time I told her I planned to skip lunch to finish *Uniforms of the Bureau of Supernatural Affairs: A Guide*, she picked me up and carried me here.

As I finish off a taco, Elsie goes on and on about some new flea grenade that the Agent Support Division of the Department of Magical Science is working on. That's where she wants to end up when she makes Junior Researcher. They come up with all the cool gadgets that agents use to fight crime.

"A flea grenade isn't as mean as it sounds," says Elsie. "My fleas tickle the yetis into submission. It's actually a lot like how a Stun Stick works now that I think about it." I just smile at Elsie. If I thought I was doing well by ranking first in the previous tryout, that's nothing compared to how much the researchers love Elsie. She's the only trainee to be invited to Director Fokus's Movie Night for the Intellectually Inclined. Apparently, they just sit around watching really boring documentaries that only geniuses would find entertaining. Whatever the second tryout for researcher trainees is, it'll be no sweat for that girl.

"Are the yetis really as bad as everyone makes them seem?" I ask.

Elsie nods. "The *worst*. They think they own the whole forest! They throw the most ridiculous tantrums. Some sports team just *mentioned* one of their forests as a possible spot to build a stadium, and the yetis proceeded to buy the team and trade away all the good players."

"They're that rich?"

"Yep," she answers. "They own a really popular ice cooler company."

"Hey, Amari, you got a sec?"

Elsie and I both look up to find Dylan standing over us. "Um, sure," I say.

I follow Dylan to an empty table.

"So . . . I have a friend, who heard it from another friend, whose brother is a Junior Agent, who walked in on Agent Fiona telling my dad about the second tryout being a treasure hunt—*inside* the Bureau. He said Agent Fiona made it clear that the only way to pass is to have a really good understanding of the Bureau."

"Are you sure it was real?" I ask. "Because Lara seemed pretty certain she knew what the first tryout would be too."

"That was just my sister wanting to be the center of attention. This is legit."

I chew on my lip. "How many people know about this?"

"All the agent trainees. But you weren't there so I came to find you."

He's being nice about it, but I know what he really means. The magician wasn't invited to the secret meeting.

"Thanks for telling me," I say. "But I bet all the copies of *Ins and Outs and In-Betweens of the Bureau* are checked out by now."

"No worries," he says. "I have my own. We can study together."

"Oh," I say, surprised. "That would be cool."

He goes a little red. "I've been thinking and . . . I know you only said what you said about Maria because that's where the investigation led you. If the situation were reversed, I'd have done the same. Just please keep an open mind, okay? Let's treat my sister like she's innocent until we know for sure."

"I can do that," I say.

A smile spreads across his face and he holds out his fist. "VanQuish 2.0?"

I smile and bump his fist. "VanQuish 2.0."

≈ 25 ≈

AGENT FIONA THROWS HER ARMS OPEN AND SHOUTS, "Welcome to the second tryout! By the end of the day, we'll be sayin' goodbye to half the remaining trainees, bringing our numbers down from sixteen to eight. But if ye do pass this tryout, then all you'll need to worry about is the finale next week. No more surprises. I'm sure the lot of ye could do with a bit more certainty in your lives."

The sixteen of us sit in the briefing auditorium of the Department of Supernatural Investigations. Agent Fiona and Agent Magnus stand onstage next to a large basket of eggs. You know you've been here for a while when weird stuff like that doesn't even faze you. I've been looking around for Dylan since I got here, but there's no sign of him or his sister.

"In a moment, we're gonna ask that ye partner up and send one representative from each pairing up to the stage to collect your first clue—"

Magnus leans over and says something in Agent Fiona's ear. "My apologies! I haven't even said what you're getting a clue for, have I? This tryout is a treasure hunt, seeking to test your ability to puzzle out clues in high-pressure situations. An agent has gotta be quick on their feet to determine the next move. To that end, we'll be sending each pair on a unique path through the Bureau. In each location you'll receive a new clue that leads to the next department. The first four pairs to finish the treasure hunt will receive an invite to the finale. Go on and pair up."

Kids jostle to get a seat next to their partners. I look for Dylan but he's nowhere to be found. If he waits much longer I might have to go it alone. With everything that's riding on this tryout, just the thought makes me nervous.

Dylan and Lara finally walk in together. From the way they glare at each other, I can tell they've probably been arguing. Lara turns her back on him as he's talking and goes to partner up with Kirsten. Dylan just rolls his eyes and glances around the auditorium. I wave a hand.

He comes over and takes the seat next to me.

"You and Lara not getting along?" I ask.

Dylan sighs and shakes his head. "I might've promised her that we'd be partners once we were able to choose. But that was before the summer. Things change, you know? I bet she's going to rush off and whine to Dad if she doesn't do well in this tryout."

I can't believe Dylan is willing to anger his dad and Lara just to be my partner. "Well, um, thanks for not bailing on me."

He shrugs. "Partners, remember?"

Agent Fiona calls out, "Our first-place team decided to remain partners it seems. Both of ye come on down and collect the first clue. You'll get a thirty-second head start on the rest of the trainees. Doesn't sound like a lot, but you'll get the benefit of not havin' to share an elevator."

I let Dylan reach into the basket to select our clue. It comes in an egg that looks so real I'm half expecting to find a yolk inside. Once every team has one, Agent Fiona says, "And dontcha give us a hard time about our clues either. We aren't poets, after all. Dylan and Amari, go on and start us off!"

Dylan crushes the egg in his palm and unfolds the paper inside. I read as fast as I can.

That thing in the shed, was it even real?
The girl on the phone says, "It's no big deal."
He can't believe it. "It tried to eat me!"
The girl on the phone disagrees completely.
"I'm a surgeon, I'll fetch my laser!"
"Please calm down. Help's on the way, sir."
A bit more fussing, then, "Finally, they're here."
And with the press of a button she erases his fear.

"Has to be the Department of Half Truths and Full Cover-Ups," says Dylan. "They're responsible for any accidental contact between humans and the supernatural world."

"Right," I say. "All 9-1-1 calls that deal with the supernatural get forwarded to the Call Center."

Dylan and I race out of the auditorium and down the main hall of the Department of Supernatural Investigations to the elevators. I glance over my shoulder as Luciano the elevator opens up in front of us. As our doors close, the rest of the trainees come storming out of the auditorium. The treasure hunt is officially on.

I'm actually glad that we got Luciano. He may not move as fast as Lucy, but he sings us a soft ballad that calms my nerves. Dylan can't keep still, he's so worked up. He keeps bouncing back and forth from foot to foot.

"Now approaching the Department of Half Truths and Full Cover-Ups," croons Luciano.

The doors open up to what I think is the coolest lobby in the whole Bureau. It's pretty much the wall over Elsie's bed on steroids. Every inch is lined with covers from famous magazines from the known world, like *Time* and *National Geographic*, only they've changed the pictures to show what really happened. I've only seen the lobby a few times, when somebody else would get off on this floor, but I've got a favorite cover that I look for every time. Instead of that famous *Life* magazine cover showing an astronaut on the moon, it says "Apollo 11 Gets Tow from Friendly Alien Cruiser after Running Out of Fuel." The image of Neil Armstrong reaching out into space to give a hitchhiker's thumb cracks me up every time. The invasion of mutant concrete-eating termites that brought the Berlin Wall down is definitely second place. The giant termites are all wearing *Mutants for World Peace* T-shirts.

Me and Dylan rush through the lobby and into the main hall. It's like ten times as busy as the Department of Supernatural Investigations. Who are all these people? It's a good thing we learned these floors by heart or I'd have no idea where to go next.

We keep close to the wall and move around the right side of the U till we get to the Call Center. The place is enormous. Rows and rows and rows of people sit in little cubicles in front of bright red telephones. The place seems to go on forever.

"What now?" I ask.

Dylan shrugs.

So we wander the aisles, listening to Double-Talkers and Junior Double-Talkers at work.

"You say your mother-in-law is haunting you? Assuming what you're saying is true . . . might you deserve it?"

"Try two plus two. . . . The calculator said it equals five? Oh, this is serious. The math gods are clearly upset with you. You'll be wanting to make an in-person apology. You can make an appointment at the nearest tax office."

One Junior Double-Talker puts his caller on hold to ask the girl in the cubicle next to him, "Jenny, any chance you brought a spare hypnosis radio?"

Jenny rolls her eyes. "Yes, but this is the last time I'm letting you borrow it. You don't have to replace *everyone's* memories, you know." She reaches into her bag and hands the boy something that looks like a TV remote. I recognize it from the delivery guy who dropped off Quinton's briefcase.

"You're a lifesaver." The boy mashes a few buttons and soft music starts playing. He places his caller on speakerphone. "Are you listening . . . ? Yes, that is some smooth jazz, isn't it? Now then, repeat after me. 'That wasn't a mummy I saw in the woods, but rather an unfortunate fellow who survived a plane crash and needed a full body cast. . . .' Yes, I daresay the bloke might be a bit put off by you running away in terror and all. . . . No, definitely don't go back and apologize . . ."

Dylan and I walk the entire first two aisles before we spot an empty cubicle with a little sign that says *Reserved for Junior Agent Trainees* attached to the phone. I plop down in the chair and Dylan drops to a knee beside me. It starts ringing.

"I bet we're supposed to answer it," says Dylan.

"But . . . oh, okay." I pick up the phone. "Hello?"

"I've got a bit of an issue," the voice responds.

"Okay. Maybe I can help?" I ask. "What's wrong?"

"Well, I seem to have a clue and no one to tell it to," says the voice.

My eyes go wide and I turn to meet Dylan's curious gaze. "It's the next clue." I put the caller on speakerphone. "You can tell it to us."

The voice clears his throat. "Finding this clue was easy

enough. But don't you get cocky, 'cause now it gets tough. Head to a room of dangerous things—fangs and claws and barbs that sting. Locate the beast that's not like the rest, with a heavenly name created in jest."

I swallow. "The only department that keeps beasts is the Department of Creature Control. Fangs and claws? It must be the predators section, right?"

"No way they'd really let us get eaten." Dylan lets out a nervous laugh. "At least I don't think they'd let us get eaten . . ."

We get Lucy this time, and she zips us up to the Department of Creature Control.

I know from cramming *Ins and Outs* that the Department of Creature Control is the largest floor in the entire Bureau. It's as big as all the other departments combined. Aside from the lobby, it's all wilderness. Well, an indoor wilderness.

"I'm the Senior Wilderness Ranger assigned to you guys today," says a lady in safari gear. "Name's Becca Alford." She gives each of us a gloved handshake. "So . . . where to?"

"The predators section," says Dylan.

The lady smiles. "Scary place for newcomers. You sure?"

"*Pretty* sure," I say.

Ranger Alford gives us a thumbs-up. "Follow me outside. I've already got the jeep running."

We step out of the lobby onto a grassy hilltop, and my jaw drops. You'd never know we were still indoors. The massive hologram on the ceiling looks just like a cloudless blue sky. I can even feel the warmth of the sun on my face. Real wind whips around us—it even smells like the outdoors.

And this view! A wide forest stretches below us, and beyond that is a lush green jungle. To our right, way in the distance, is a snowy valley. It's the exact opposite of the sandy desert far off to our left.

I reach down and pluck a blade of grass. "No way. This is real!"

Ranger Alford laughs. "Sure is. The only thing that's fake out here is the sky. We've done everything in our power to give these critters as authentic a habitat as we can while they're here."

"Cool," I say.

We hop in the jeep and Ranger Alford drives us down a winding dirt trail. As the woods thicken into jungle, we pass all kinds of wildlife—everything from a silvery white unicorn to a pack of flying pigs, and even a kaleidoscopic serpent that leaves a shimmering rainbow trail in the sky.

We slow to a stop in front of a sign that says *Jungle Habitat*.

Ranger Alford turns to face us in the back seat. "The jungle predators are all kept in this first section. Remember, the things we're about to see in here are called predators for a reason. Don't leave the jeep unless I say it's safe. You two are allowed to ask me as many questions as you'd like but if I have to step in to save either of you, you'll both automatically fail the tryout. Got it?"

"Got it," we both answer.

We continue down the dirt trail, but a lot slower. Ranger Alford's expression is serious now, and she's constantly watching the trees.

I jump in my seat when, out of nowhere, a streak of gold flashes across the trail in front of us. It disappears into the bushes. A deafening roar rattles the jeep doors. Dylan and I both lean into one another and duck our heads, just in case whatever that was tries to take a swipe at us. As the trail curves we catch sight of a gigantic lion made of pure gold atop a small hill.

"That's a Nemean lion," whispers Ranger Alford. "The true kings of the jungle. At least when there aren't any dragons around."

And that's not even the scariest thing we encounter. A swamp beast covered in horns peers up at us through the murky water. Dylan points out a griffin that swoops down in the distance and emerges with some poor creature in its beak.

"Stop!" Dylan shouts. He points to a large flowery bush in a small clearing. "There, that's it! It has to be."

"We're here for a flower bush?" I ask, unimpressed.

"That's no flower bush," he says. "That's a Mars mantrap. Think about it. 'Locate the beast that's not like the rest.' All the other predators are animals; this is the only plant. And the second part, the 'heavenly name created in jest'? Well, the planet Mars is in space, making it a heavenly body. And it's called a Mars mantrap as a joke comparing it to the Venus flytraps of the known world."

Ranger Alford grins at us in the rearview mirror. "Shucks, you nailed it." She steers the jeep into the clearing.

"Good job," I say, a little stunned. "I'd never have figured that one out."

"My tutor would be proud," Dylan says with a laugh.

We jump out of the truck. Becca and Dylan are quick to squeeze their noses shut. But why—

The sweetest scent hits my nose and I suddenly get lightheaded. Not that I care. I just want to go over and smell those beautiful flowers up close. I take a few steps and then feel myself get yanked back. Somebody has the nerve to throw an arm around me and put their hand over my nose. "Let me go! I want one of those flowers . . ."

I blink a couple times as my head clears.

"The scent lures you in close so it can eat you," says Dylan.

"Be *careful*," Ranger Alford warns. "If it looks like one of you two are in real danger, I won't hesitate to step in."

That was a close one. I reach up to hold my own nose. "Thanks. I'm good now."

Dylan points to a small white rectangle just in front of the flower bush. "I'll bet that's the next clue."

"But how do we get to it without becoming that thing's dinner?"

"Good question," he replies.

Good question. I remember what Ranger Alford said earlier. "You said we could ask questions, right?"

"That's right," she replies.

"How does it know when you're close to it?"

"Some of those blossoms are actually eyes," she answers. "It's watching us right now."

Well, that's creepy. But it also gives me an idea. "Hey, follow me."

I lead Dylan and Ranger Alford out of the clearing. We all crouch behind the Jeep. "Okay, don't freak out, but I want to show you something."

They look at me, confused.

"You want to show us something now?" asks Dylan.

"Just watch." I make a fist and cover it with my other hand. "Duplicarta."

A second me pops into existence. Dylan holds in a laugh, but Ranger Alford swallows, then asks, "Is that magic?"

I nod. "But I think I can use it to help us, if you'll give me permission." I just have to hope our chaperone is open-minded enough to give me a chance.

"Well . . ." Ranger Alford looks uncomfortable. "Spells aren't really allowed inside the Bureau." She shakes her head slowly. "But it doesn't sit right with me for all the others to be allowed to use their abilities and you not. And I suppose no one *said* it was against the rules of the tryout."

A few minutes later we're all in position. Me underneath the jeep with a view of the clearing. Dylan and Ranger Alford wait in the brush at the edge of the clearing. Dylan gives me a thumbs-up. This had better work, because if it doesn't, Ranger Alford made it clear she'll disqualify us.

"Duplicarta," I whisper. An illusion of me appears in the clearing. I try to give Illusion Amari a dazed look as she stumbles toward the flowers. From here, I see the bush shiver as she gets closer. Just a few more steps . . .

A great big mouth emerges from the bushes, chomping at the air where Illusion Amari stands. But now I make Illusion Amari hover in the air just above the plant. It snaps viciously at her, again and again.

While the beast is distracted, Dylan and Ranger Alford dash out into the clearing. Dylan snatches the envelope off the ground and they both make it back to the jeep without the Mars mantrap even realizing what happened.

I let Illusion Amari disappear and the thing lets out a furious growl.

"I can't believe that worked," says Dylan as he rips open the envelope.

"Me neither," says a stunned Ranger Alford. "You were supposed to feed it the slumber berries in these bushes. But you managed it well enough."

Dylan rips open the envelope and pulls out the next clue. "Congratulations on not being food, but I do hope you're in a deciphering mood. Your next destination, put clear and plain, is the baffling Department of the Unexplained. Obtaining the last clue will require some wit, for it lies near the bottom of a bottomless pit."

"At least we know where to go," I say.

Dylan groans. "For all the good that does us."

As we ride back to the lobby of the Department of

Creature Control, I catch Ranger Alford looking at me in the rearview mirror.

"You can control your magic?" she asks me.

"So far," I shrug. "I really only know a few things."

"But I was always told . . . I thought that too much magic . . ." She shakes her head. "You're just an ordinary twelve-year-old girl from what I can tell. Smiling, good-natured. I guess what I'm trying to say is you're not what I was expecting."

I smile. "That's a good thing, I hope."

"It certainly is," she says. "I'll think you'll change a lot of minds while you're here, Amari Peters."

Once we're back at the lobby, me and Dylan sprint back to the elevators. I spend the whole ride down to the Department of the Unexplained praying Mischief won't snitch on me for sneaking out to go meet magiciangirl18 aka Dylan to the two agents sharing the elevator with us. Thankfully all it does is taunt them with an "I know something you don't know . . ."

The lobby of the Department of the Unexplained is pitch-black. When we step off the elevator a spotlight in the ceiling shines down on us. It follows us to the back of the lobby where a second spotlight shines down on a boy, fast asleep.

Dylan gives him a nudge and the boy jumps to his feet.

"Ah, there you are," the boy says. "Many apologies. Our department is closed during the day, so I'd usually be in bed right now. Anyway, I'll be your guide tonight—I mean today. I trust you know where you're headed?"

"The bottomless pit," I say.

"Right," answers the boy. "Unexplained oddities are on the right side of the U. Please follow me."

"Aren't you going to tell us your name?" Dylan asks.

The boy turns around. "No. And for that matter, I don't plan on answering any of your questions either. You do get that you're in the Department of the *Un*explained?"

Our Junior Curator leads us into the main hallway, which is at least a little brighter. It's still dim enough that these spotlights continue to follow us around, but a bit of light reaches us from all the great big rooms blocked off by dark red curtains.

We pass one curtain with a sign out front that reads: *What happens when an unstoppable force strikes an immovable object?* Dylan drifts closer, but the boy says, without even turning around, "Lay a finger on that curtain and you're disqualified."

"Not even a peek?" asks Dylan.

"No questions," says the boy.

The next curtain says *Cause of the Bermuda Triangle*. It's followed by *Wormhole to Parallel Universe* and *Origin of Both the Chicken and the Egg*. Finally, we arrive at a curtain labeled *The Bottomless Pit*.

We pass through the curtain. It doesn't look like anything special. It's just a boring stone well in the middle of the floor. I'm disappointed.

I lean over to have a look inside. Pitch darkness.

"Careful," says the Junior Curator. "If you fall in, they'll never be able to get you out. You'll just keep falling forever."

I don't even know how many times Dylan and I circle the pit. It just doesn't make sense. How do you get near the bottom of something that doesn't have a bottom? Dylan even tries dropping a quarter into the pit to see what happens. No surprise, it never hits the bottom.

"What now?" I say.

"Beats me," Dylan replies.

I'm starting to sweat. Even Dylan keeps wiping his face with his sleeve. I keep thinking of other pairs completing their treasure hunts and getting their invitations to the finale while we bake in this hot room.

"Don't you guys have air-conditioning in here?" I ask the Junior Curator.

He flinches.

"Wait, you flinched."

He shakes his head. "Did not."

"I saw it too," says Dylan. He wipes the sweat from his forehead. "It must have something to do with the air-conditioning."

"But what does air-conditioning have to do with a bottomless pit?" I search the ceiling, then the walls. Finally, I look on the floor. And there they are. "They've got floor vents!"

Dylan raises an eyebrow. "Which means?"

"Think about it," I say. "They cut off the AC in here for a reason."

"Oh!" says Dylan. "Because we're supposed to go down there!"

"How much do you want to bet that one of the ducts goes right under the bottom of the bottomless pit?" Once we scramble over to the vent, I know I'm right. All the screws are missing. Dylan lifts the vent up and a wide metal duct curves out of view.

"You're smaller, so you can probably get to the clue quicker," says Dylan.

I nod and drop down inside. "It's so dark down here. How will I know which way to go?"

"Wait here," says Dylan. "I'll go to the bottomless pit and shout. Tell me if you hear an echo."

A few seconds later, "Hellooo" echoes softly in the distance.

Dylan comes back. "Could you hear me?"

"Yeah," I say. "Just keep shouting."

Dylan disappears and I start crawling. It's a little scary in here but I concentrate on Dylan's voice. *Just get to that voice.*

I move down the duct, turn, and then turn again into dim light. A tiny little flashlight points upward. I crawl closer until I get to a photograph taped to the top of the duct. It looks like a large pirate ship falling over a waterfall. When I flip it over I expect to find words, but it's blank. I've got no clue what it's supposed to mean. I grab the little flashlight and find my way back.

I hand the photo to Dylan. He stares at it and then flips

it over. "The photo is all there was," I say.

"This is the edge of the world," says Dylan.

"Um, last time I checked the world is round. It doesn't have edges."

"It does have one. But it's hidden."

We lock eyes and say at the same time, "The Department of Hidden Places."

We race to the elevators and dart between the legs of a tall green ogre about to step into Lucy. "Sorry!" I call back as the doors shut. "We're in a hurry!"

Lucy chuckles. "Bet you're glad you got me. Where we headed, guys?"

She zips us down to the underground tunnels and we sprint past the neon sign that says *Department of Hidden Places this way—or is it?* The best part about this being the final destination is that the secret to finding this department was written in *Ins and Outs*. I can even remember the page, 290. We keep our hands above our heads, even as the tunnels get dark, until I feel a large button graze my fingertips. I jump and give it a good press.

Suddenly the floor beneath us shivers and then lifts us up through the ceiling and into the lobby of the Department of Hidden Places. Enormous portraits of lost cities line the walls, with plaques revealing their names as Shangri-La, Avalon, and Shambhala.

We dash over to an agent standing next to a small table. The lady looks us over. "Very good. You two have officially completed all the clues and earned invitations to the finale.

However, I must say that I find it extremely odd that the times this year were so much faster than in previous years. I'm more than a little suspicious. Did either of you hear anything about this tryout that might have given you an advantage? Cheating will not be tolerated."

Dylan and I look at one another. We did hear something. It's how we knew to study *Ins and Outs*. Now that we've been caught, it makes me wonder how we ever thought we'd get away with it. These guys conduct investigations for a living.

I can't believe I ruined Quinton's legacy like this. It's bad enough that Quinton's little sister is a cheater. I won't make it worse by lying.

The agent smiles. "It's good to know that you didn't cheat—"

"Wait," I say. "We did hear something."

Dylan starts at my words, but then he drops his head. "It's my fault. I heard the tryout was based on Bureau knowledge and I told Amari about it."

"But I didn't tell him to report it. And I definitely studied my brains out to be ready."

The agent crosses her arms, frowning. "I'm disappointed in both of you. To have elite badges and choose to cheat is a disgrace. I'm sorry to say this but . . . congratulations, you've officially passed the second tryout. You've shown the integrity and honest character befitting a future agent of the Department of Supernatural Investigations."

It takes a few seconds to sink in. "You're saying we passed? Even though we cheated?"

The lady chuckles. "We leaked that information on purpose. This was not only a test of how well you decipher clues but, more importantly, a test of whether you are honest when it is most difficult to be honest. Supernaturals must be able to trust you. As must your fellow agents."

She hands us each an invitation from beneath the table and Dylan and I laugh all the way back to the elevators.

"We did it," says Dylan. "We really made it to the finale."

I lean my head back against the wall and close my eyes. "We've still got a chance to bring them home."

"They'd be proud of us," says Dylan.

I can't get my words out so I simply nod, tears running down my cheeks.

Dylan takes my hand and for a long time we just stand like that.

T HAT NIGHT, ALL THE REMAINING JUNIOR AGENT TRAIN-
ees are called to the lobby of the Department of
Supernatural Investigations. Only six of us show up. Other
than me and Dylan, there's Josh Adams and Brian Li, and
then two of Lara's followers, Zoe Wisniewski and Madison
Klein.

Lara and Kirsten aren't here.

I overhear Madison telling Brian Li that Lara and
Kirsten were actually the first to complete all the clues but
didn't fess up to getting inside information. When they told
Lara she failed, she threw an epic temper tantrum so bad
she may not be allowed to try out again next year if Agent

Fiona has anything to say about it. Seeing as there are supposed to be eight trainees left, I guess Lara and Kirsten weren't the only ones who were disqualified.

It might be the reason Agent Magnus pulled Dylan aside for a quick talk. If his sister really did fail the tryout, then he's probably feeling bad about teaming up with me.

Agent Fiona lifts up her hands as she enters the lobby. "Congratulations! The six of ye have proven to be the best. But now's no time to be resting on your laurels. There's only seven days between now and the finale. What's your reward for getting this far? Well, I'm giving ye all your freedom. Ye can spend the next week however you'd like. Remember, the finale will test your supernatural world knowledge, your dueling skills with Sky Sprints and Stun Sticks, and your control over your supernatural ability. Spend this next week tightening up your skills in whatever areas you're weakest. The four of ye who score the best in these three areas will earn your Junior Agent badges and be assigned a Senior Agent or Special Agent to mentor ye for the last month of the summer session. You'll get to go out into the world and see what agenting is all about!"

Madison's hand goes up.

"Yes?"

She turns and points to me. "I don't think it's fair that the rest of us have to demonstrate our supernatural ability and *she* gets to skip it."

Agent Fiona glances in my direction. "We haven't

decided yet how we're handling Amari's situation."

"I heard she used a spell during her tryout," says Brian Li. "Isn't that illegal?"

"Amari got permission from her chaperone," answers Agent Fiona. "And while we aren't thrilled about it, our rules were to consult the chaperones for guidance on what's allowed."

"Seems like special treatment to me," Brian Li shoots back. "I say she should be disqualified and Lara should be let back in." The others nod in agreement.

"It's a good thing it's not up to ye, isn't it? You're all dismissed."

The others turn and head for the elevators, and both Zoe and Madison shoot me angry looks. I want to ask Dylan more about his sister, but before I get the chance, he follows Agent Fiona into the department.

As much as I don't like Lara's stuck-up friends, they aren't wrong. It really isn't fair that I get to skip one section of the finale.

I do have things I could demonstrate for them. I've been practicing my illusions for weeks. But would they ever let me show off my magic?

"I don't think I've ever seen this many people in the food court at one time," I say as Elsie sits down at a table with me.

Even though there are a lot fewer trainees than we started with at the beginning of summer, the place is packed with tutors and coaches of all kinds. For every kid, there are like five adults helping them to prepare for the finale—all retired Bureau employees. It's easy to see why Junior Agent spots go to legacy kids. Even if you manage to get through the first two tryouts, how are you supposed to compete with kids who have a whole team around them?

Elsie frowns. "It's like their parents are buying them a spot in the Bureau. But that's how it's always been."

"At least you don't have much to worry about," I say.

And it's true. Elsie did great on her second tryout. The Junior Researcher trainees had to sit in a locked room and solve seven puzzles. The last puzzle held the key that opened the door. The first sixteen kids who opened the door got an invite to their finale. Elsie finished them all in fifteen minutes flat and was the first to claim her invite.

"Neither do you," Elsie says. "I know you'll make Junior Agent."

Dylan plops down at our table.

"Sorry about Lara." I haven't been able to talk to Dylan since we found out his sister failed the tryout. Elsie and I still haven't told him about the whole Key Holder thing. Even now, it's kind of hard to bring up.

"Yeah," Dylan says. "She's pretty mad. And Dad agrees with her that it's my fault for not choosing her as my partner."

As much as Lara and I don't get along, I still feel a spike of guilt. She's Dylan's sister after all.

Dylan starts to say something more but laughter drowns out his words as Lara and a group of her friends surround our table. Lara's holding a laptop.

"Let's see here," says Lara. "Amari Peters, recipient of the Jefferson Academy Scholarship for the Disadvantaged. Oh, how sad."

"Leave her alone," says Dylan.

"Leave her alone?" repeats Lara, glaring at her brother. "But I'm just getting started." She leans in closer to the screen. "It seems you can take the girl out of the ghetto, but you can't take the ghetto out of the girl. Look at all these discipline referrals!"

"Where did you get that?" I'm so mad I'm trembling.

Lara looks to me, then her brother. "Daddy left his computer laying around. Seems like he wanted to know all about his future juvenile delinquent superstar."

Dylan stands up and snatches the computer away from Lara. "Back off."

"How dare you!" shrieks Lara. She grabs Dylan's plate of spaghetti and tries to dump it over his head.

"Stop!" I shout.

And it does stop. A shimmering illusion of me appears, and she catches the plate of spaghetti in midair. She turns to look at me over her shoulder and winks.

Gasps sound from the crowd of kids gathered around us. I stare at my outstretched hand. Did I really just do that? I decide to test it out. With a flick of my fingers, the illusion pushes the plate of spaghetti right into Lara's face.

Whoa.

Kids all around the food court point and laugh. My

illusion vanishes and Elsie scrambles around the table to where I'm standing.

Lara snarls. "You are *so* dead."

I swallow. But I'm not running away anymore. "Mess with me or my friends again and next time it'll be worse."

Lara freezes, her expression suddenly unsure. She has no way of knowing what my magic is capable of—not after what I just did. I'll bet taking me on isn't a risk she's willing to take with so many kids watching.

I take Elsie's hand and head to the elevators. Dylan stays behind to calm his sister.

Once we're inside, I breathe a sigh of relief.

"Um, Amari?" Elsie stares at me, visibly confused. "That thing with the spaghetti—I didn't know your illusions could do that."

I look down at my hands in wonder. "Me neither."

There are three reasons I never get tired of our library. First, it's just so cool-looking. Everything is made up of books—the floors, the ceilings, even the pillars between the bookcases. You can type in your book title at the computer catalog and get directions like *Three paces to the left and look down* or *Pillar closest to fern, climb up halfway*. The second reason is that there's just so many interesting things to read about, even aside from what I need to learn to become a Junior Agent.

The third reason is Mrs. Belle, the librarian. She has this knack for knowing what you'd like to read, just by looking at you. It's really helpful whenever I get burned out from studying the not-so-fun books from our booklist. I don't care what anyone says, there's a reason *Supernatural Laws and Regulations* comes with a pillow on the cover.

When I arrive at the counter, I'm glad to see that Mrs. Belle is here. Most of the other librarians aren't as nice. They either back away from the counter and talk to me from like ten feet away or they suddenly get busy doing something else and ignore me completely.

Mrs. Belle adjusts her thick glasses and grins. "Another old news magazine from the archives, hun?"

"Not this time," I say. "Any chance there's something new about Quinton that might've come in?"

"Just got a shipment of gossip magazines this morning. Sure, they might use less than reputable sources, but some of your best information comes from less than reputable sources. You remember that when you become a big-shot agent, you hear?"

I laugh but Elsie rolls her eyes. "A true researcher is a champion of facts, not make-believe. There's a reason they're shelved on the fiction side of the library."

Mrs. Belle chuckles. "Well, if you change your mind and get a hankerin' for a little make-believe, the computer catalog for the fiction section is right over there."

I ignore Elsie's protests and head straight over. What could it hurt? We've already read nearly everything else about Quinton. I type in *Quinton Peters* and a list pops up onscreen.

One headline catches my eye.

"Rumors and Whisperings: Famed Agent Kept Secrets."

"Elsie, come look at this. What do you think?"

"I think we can do better," she says, walking over. Then she reads the headline and her eyes widen. "I've heard of *Rumors and Whisperings*! The housekeepers swear by it. Maybe we *should* be thorough . . ."

We both grin.

The computer says it's located right above us, and sure enough, when I look up, the magazine drops from the ceiling and glides right into my arms. A thrill of excitement shoots through me.

Elsie and I dash to the study hall at the opposite end of the library. Once we find an empty room, I take a seat at the desk and Elsie pulls up an extra chair.

I flip the magazine open. There are only two pages—a table of contents followed by a blank page. The table of contents reads:

Things aren't so rosy as Madame Duboise
accused of stealing from rival

Great Wall of China mysteriously grows an extra
ten meters overnight. Again!

Dwarves insulted by Merlin's insinuation that
golden city is merely gold-plated

Newly elected US President faints at first
Supernatural Affairs briefing

"There has to be some kind of trick to it," says Elsie. We turn the magazine sideways, then upside down. We even shut off the lights to see if the words might glow in the dark.

"How in the world does this thing work?" I say, annoyed.

"Gotta ask me a question," comes a low, deep voice.

Elsie and I just stare. The magazine just spoke. You'd think we'd be used to this sort of thing by now.

"Let's do a test run," says Elsie. "What can you tell me about Madame Duboise stealing from a rival?"

Madame Duboise's pale green face and flowing rose petal locks suddenly appear on the blank page. Beside it is a much younger face, white petals jutting out of her bright yellow scalp like a daisy. *"Psst, listen up,"* comes a heavy whisper. *"Things got heated at an EverTree fashion show after both Madame Duboise and former understudy Vivi LaBoom both unveiled nearly identical lines of translucent apparel for ghostly spirits. LaBoom, who has long held that she was the real force behind Duboise's recent resurgence in popularity before being unceremoniously fired, has accused Duboise of having a spy within her design circle. Duboise calls the accusations 'ridiculous,' saying LaBoom was fired for being a 'LaBum.' Curious, then, that both were spotted laughing it up at Duboise's sprawling woodland estate. Publicity stunt, anyone? Course, you didn't hear it from us. . . ."*

Elsie bounces in her chair. "Scandalous!"

Grinning, I flip to the contents and then back to the blank page. "Tell me about the Special Agent keeping secrets."

"That's not a question," the magazine clucks. *"Mind your manners."*

"Fine," I say. "Can you please tell me about the Special Agent keeping secrets?"

"Why certainly," the magazine replies. An image of Agent Magnus appears on the page.

"Psst, listen up. Special Agent Quinton Peters is known for his heroics as one half of the famed agent team VanQuish. The pair went missing under highly suspicious circumstances about which the Bureau has remained extremely tight-lipped. But maybe they're seeking to protect his legacy more than anything. It's customary for an agent to create a Farewell Briefcase to be delivered to a loved one in the event of a tragedy, and it was touching indeed that Quinton Peters chose to use his briefcase to offer Amari Peters a place at the Bureau. But one has to won-der, why then would an agent of reputable stature need a second Farewell Briefcase? What secrets did the golden boy need to hide so badly that he'd send it to old Magnus for safekeeping? If the conditions for opening the briefcase are never met, perhaps we'll never know. Course, you didn't hear it from us . . ."

I slam the magazine shut and hop out of my chair, head-ing for the door.

"Where are you going?" Elsie asks.

"To find out more."

I give Agent Magnus's door a good hard knock.

"Are you sure we should bother him this late?" asks Elsie for the fifth time.

"I have to know," I say.

On my second knock, I hear movement inside.

Magnus opens the door just a crack. "Whaddya want?"

"I know you've got my brother's second Farewell Briefcase," I say.

Agent Magnus opens the door a little more. "And where'd you hear that?"

"*Rumors and Whisperings*."

"Blasted gossip rag," Magnus groans. "Bane of my existence."

"Well?" I say. "Do you?"

"Come in and shut the door behind you."

"Can my friend come in too?" I ask. "You've already met her and I'll probably tell her everything anyway."

"I'm really good at keeping secrets," Elsie says, crossing her heart. "Promise."

"Might as well," says Magnus. "Apparently top-secret work is far from secret these days."

The office looks like a tree exploded in here. Everything is made of wood. Wood paneling on the walls, a big wooden desk, and hardwood floors. He's got a pair of longhorn steer horns above his desk and lots of pictures of him and other agents along the walls. There's a really big photo with Van-Quish on a shelf next to his medals.

Elsie and I take the two chairs in front of his desk.

"All right, so maybe I do have it," he says. "What's it to ya?"

"What's in it?" I ask, leaning forward. "Why did my brother need another briefcase?"

"Here's the thing about that," he answers. "I don't actually know what's inside. I've got a guess, but I don't know for sure."

"You mean you haven't opened it?" I ask.

"Wasn't meant to be opened," he says. "Quinton didn't put anyone's name on it. Just asked me to keep it hidden. Said whatever was inside was never meant to see the light of day."

Elsie and I turn to look at one another.

Then I ask, "Do you think whatever's inside could get him in trouble?"

"That's a strange question." Agent Magnus strokes his beard. "What do you know?"

I meet Elsie's eyes again. If I tell the wrong person what we found . . .

"I bet he already knows," she says. "His aura is a reddish orange—protective. I think he's been protecting Quinton all this time."

That's why he claimed not to know about what Quinton was doing. "We know about the Black Book." I lean back in my chair and add, "We also know that Quinton discovered the Key Holder's identity. I think that's what he's keeping in that second Farewell Briefcase."

Agent Magnus jumps in his seat. "How on earth did you figure all that out?"

"Long story," I say. "What I don't understand is why he would search for the Key Holder if he knows the horrible consequences?"

"I won't say I agree with what he did," says Agent Magnus. "But I do understand why he did it. It was clear when we raided Moreau's island that he was actively trying to resurrect his fallen comrade. Seems this Black Book has the power to do just that."

"And that's why Moreau's apprentice took my brother?" I ask, wanting to be sure. "To get him to reveal the location of the Black Key?"

"That would be the best-case scenario." Agent Magnus comes from around his desk and places a hand on my shoulder. "They'd need your brother alive to learn what he knows. And if Quinton has refused to say anything, then there's a good chance he and Maria are still out there somewhere."

Please oh please let that be true.

"The Black Book is still safe inside the Great Vault, right?" asks Elsie. "Like there's no way anyone could get to it?"

"Absolutely. It's the safest place in the whole supernatural world."

I shake my head. "You guys didn't see Moreau's face. He was so sure of his plan."

"All the more reason to get our hands on this apprentice as soon as possible and put an end to this," says Magnus.

For a second I think to mention that my brother suspected Maria, but that wouldn't be treating her like she's innocent. And I promised Dylan that I would.

Instead, I say, "I want to help. I want to find my brother and bring Moreau's apprentice to justice."

Magnus sighs and crosses his arms. "Quinton didn't want this life for you. But if you succeed in making Junior Agent and officially become part of the Bureau, then you'd stand to inherit all of his belongings. This briefcase technically becomes yours. Though it's likely the information inside made your brother a target. Not to mention what it could mean for the Bureau if word got out what Quinton was up to."

"I'll keep Quinton's secret," I say. "And I don't care about being safe. Or if there's a target on my back too."

"Gathered that much when you ignored my warning and became a Junior Agent trainee in the first place," says Agent Magnus. "Good or bad, you've got Quinton's same fire in your blood. That same stubborn determination, minus a setback or two."

I remember just how close I came to quitting Junior Agent training. Twice.

"Let me help," I say again. "I'm sure my magic could help."

Something buzzes on Magnus's belt. He unclips his phone and holds it up to his face. "Would this magic of yours have anything to do with the message I just got about you dumping a plate of spaghetti on Lara Van Helsing's head?"

My face flushes. "She was planning to dump it on Dylan, and I sort of lost my temper."

Magnus snorts. "Well, if there's anybody due for a bit of spaghetti humbling, it's that Van Helsing gal. Kid was born with her nose turned up."

"Then you're not going to kick me out of Junior Agent training?"

"Oh, I'm sure those phone calls will be coming any minute," says Magnus. "It'll be a good time to trade in some of the goodwill you built up with the chief by meeting with Moreau. Besides, you've already got enough going against you. The chief is under a lot of pressure not to promote you to Junior Agent. A good many folks assumed you'd fail the second tryout. But now that you've made it to the finale, they're getting nervous. The idea of a magician inside the Bureau of Supernatural Affairs scares a lot of people."

But there have been magicians named Van Helsing inside the Bureau for centuries, I think. "What am I supposed to do?"

"Only thing you can control is how hard you try," he replies. "Make it as hard as possible to overlook you. Do that, and I'll do what I can to see that you get a fair shake. Understand?"

"I do," I say. "I'm going to outwork them all."

≋ 27 ≋

"Seriously, Amari?"

My eyes jump open to find Elsie standing in the doorway of our usual study room with her hands on her hips.

"That's got to be the most uncomfortable sleeping position ever," she says.

"I . . . I wasn't asleep," I say defensively, lifting my head. But now that I've pulled my face away from my book, I can see where I've drooled on the pages.

Elsie sits down next to me. "You've been studying nonstop for days. You need to take breaks, you know. Otherwise your head'll explode."

"I've *got* to get through this booklist," I say. "And then I have to go back over all the stuff I read when I first got here because it feels like I can't remember any of it."

"You haven't forgotten," says Elsie. "You just haven't given your brain any rest. It's practically got steam coming off it."

Maybe she's right, because I can't even remember what the title of this book is. I slam it shut and yawn. "What time is it?"

"Breakfast."

My jaw drops. "You're joking. Please say you're joking."

"Nope," she says. "You spent the entire night face-first in a book."

I rub my neck and groan. "No wonder my neck feels so stiff. . . . Wait! If it's already tomorrow then I have to meet Dylan in the training gym. It's our last chance to practice the Helsing technique. It's their family Stun Stick style and Maria taught it to Quinton. It's—"

"Amari!" says Elsie. "I know what the Helsing technique is. But maybe you should focus on going back to the room and taking a nap first. I'll tell Dylan you're going to be a little late. And brush your teeth too." Elsie pinches her nose to make her point.

I cover my mouth. "Sorry. I think I will take that nap. Hey, who needs a whole bunch of friends when I've got one Elsie."

When Dylan and I arrive at the training gym, there's a giant petition posted on the doors with the names of all the legacy parents who don't want me participating in the finale.

Most of them aren't even from Supernatural Investigations, but they are current members of the Bureau of Supernatural Affairs. They've got their names and titles listed.

"Maybe we could practice somewhere else today?" I say to Dylan.

"I say we train right in their faces." Dylan pushes open the door.

"Are you sure?" I ask. "You don't worry about people going after you because of me?"

"Never," he says. "VanQuish 2.0, right?"

I take a deep breath. "Okay, then. Let's do it."

The Helsing technique is just as hard as it looks, but Dylan is pretty confident we'll win our duels with just the basics. Quinton and Maria make it look so easy in all the footage we watch. One time they even pulled it off hanging upside down from the ceiling. Those man-eating stalactites didn't stand a chance.

We practice until we're both so exhausted we just lie on the padded floor.

I still haven't told Dylan about Quinton tracking down the Key Holder. Things were so weird between us with the whole Maria/traitor thing. And now that there's a chance we could find out who this Key Holder actually is, it feels like we're close to a major discovery.

We *did* promise to share whatever we found.

"I've got something important to tell you," I say.

"What is it?" Dylan asks, sitting up.

I sit up too and tell him everything we've learned.

"This is huge!" he says. "If the Bureau can get to the Key Holder first, then maybe we can spring a trap for Moreau's apprentice. This could be how we get Quinton and Maria back."

"Only one problem," I say. "I have to become a Junior Agent in order to inherit Quinton's second Farewell Briefcase. And there's a whole petition against me being in the finale."

"You have to do it anyway," says Dylan. "And prove that you deserve a place here."

"But how? They'll never let me go onstage and show off my magic."

"Use my turn," he says.

"What do you mean?"

"When they announce me," he says, "you go onstage instead."

"You're serious?" I ask. "We would be in so much trouble."

Dylan just laughs. "You think my dad is going to let both his kids flunk the tryouts? Besides, if you don't do this, then you're giving him the excuse he needs to cut you. All he has to say is you didn't fulfill all the requirements."

"I don't know," I say. "Agent Magnus already said he'd try to help."

"What's better," asks Dylan, "hoping Magnus convinces

enough people to feel sorry for you or going up there and taking a spot you should already have?"

A mix of nerves and excitement washes over me. "I do deserve my spot."

A sneaky grin lights up Dylan's face. "Then tell me, how *would* you show off your magic?"

Elsie dashes into our room looking way too pleased with herself.

She skips over to my side of the room, where I'm hunched over *Sovereign Cities of the Supernatural World*, and plops down on the end of my bed. "I hope you're not planning on studying all day."

"We're not all geniuses," I say, turning a page.

Elsie lifts her chin and I know immediately she's about to go on about something she's read. "You know, studies show that cramming the day before a big test is actually worse for you than just taking the day off."

"I'm not cramming," I say, without looking up. "This is the last book on my booklist."

"Fine," Elsie sighs. "Study if you want, but promise me you'll keep tonight free."

I raise an eyebrow. "Why? What's happening tonight?"

"Just promise, okay?"

Hold on. "You're *really* not going to tell me what it is?"

"Nope," says Elsie. "It's a surprise. Please just say you'll come with me. *Please?* It'll be so much fun."

As much as I'm tempted, there's a part of me that feels guilty for even thinking about it. "It doesn't feel right to have fun when Quinton is still out there somewhere."

"You've been working super hard. And once you make Junior Agent, I'll barely ever see you while you're off with Agent Magnus working to get VanQuish back. Just come with me and have some fun tonight. You've earned it."

"I . . . I guess you're right," I say.

Elsie claps her hands and squeals. "Hope you're not scared of the dark!"

It takes me all morning and most of the afternoon to finish *Sovereign Cities of the Supernatural World*. Despite the boring title, it's pretty cool to learn about the non-human cities out there. Places like the underwater city of Atlantis. Or the dwarven stronghold of Cibola, an underground city made completely of gold. It figures that it's located directly beneath Las Vegas.

When I get back to my room, Elsie is waiting inside for me with a suitcase and a grin so wide I know I'm in trouble. "What are you up to?"

"So . . . tonight's festivities may involve sneaking out," says Elsie.

Sneaking out? "To where?"

"Good question," says Elsie. "Where is much better than why. Not that I'm answering either question. Just know that it involves these most splendid cloaks."

"Are those . . . Junior Undertaker cloaks?"

"Fresh from the Department of the Dead!"

"Something tells me I'm going to regret agreeing to this," I say. "Are you sure we won't get caught?" I mean, it would really suck to get thrown out the day before I make Junior Agent.

"Don't worry, we won't be the only ones."

At exactly 8:15 p.m., we get changed and join a large group of Junior Undertakers making their way to the elevators. Bertha stops and gives us a good looking over, but with the hoods of our cloaks pulled so low over our heads, we all look alike. Still, shouldn't she know by now how many Junior Undertakers there are? It's like she's just letting us go.

Once we're on an elevator, Lucy gives us a "Tsk, tsk, someone's being naughty." Still, she zips us up to the Vanderbilt Hotel lobby without another word. Elsie and I follow the others down a side hall that leads outside where a bus is waiting. We sign the roll with made-up names.

My roommate and I head to the very back of the bus. As soon as we find seats, Elsie pulls back her hood and grins. "Done and done."

I pull my hood off too. "Maybe now you can tell me where we're going?"

Elsie rolls her eyes playfully. "You'll know soon enough."

"Amari?" says a voice I recognize. Dylan's head rises into view above the seat in front of us. "I thought I heard you." He's got on a Junior Undertaker cloak too.

"Are there any *actual* Junior Undertakers on this bus?" I ask.

"A few," he says. "Sneaking out the night before the finale is kind of a tradition."

No wonder Bertha let us go so easily.

"I'm coming back there." Dylan climbs over the seat and plops down between me and Elsie. "Is this your first All-Souls Festival?"

"All-Soul Festival?" I repeat. Are we going to a soul music concert? Mama would be so jealous.

Elsie shoots Dylan a look and says, "It's *supposed* to be a surprise."

"Oh, my bad," says Dylan, looking back and forth between us. "Well, if it's your first time going, let's just say the name doesn't really give much away."

The bus leaves the city and we end up on an empty two-lane road. We pass through thickly wooded areas and farmland until eventually the bus pulls off onto a wide grassy field. A large crowd is gathered next to the road. I try to look past them all, to get a hint at what the All-Souls Festival might be, but the only thing that catches my eye is the full moon above.

The three of us pull our hoods back on and follow the others off the bus. But when the Junior Undertakers move to the front of the crowd, Elsie grabs my hand and pulls me to the back.

"Climb on my shoulders," says Dylan.

"I'm not—"

"Hurry," he insists. "You'll miss it."

Elsie nods enthusiastically.

I take him up on his offer. On top of Dylan, I get a clear view of the Junior Undertakers spaced evenly in a straight line, their backs to the crowd. At the center is a Senior Undertaker whose cloak has a high silver collar. It looks like he's checking his watch.

"Can they get on with it?" says something that looks a lot like the boy version of Tinkerbell, his small wings buzzing in my ear. "It's been midnight for three minutes already."

Finally, the undertaker reaches into his cloak and brings a whistle up to his lips. He gives it a blow and the Junior Undertakers raise their right arms in unison. Each one holds up a baton. "By order of the Department of the Dead, working in conjunction with the foremost representatives of Afterlife, I declare before the full moon that this month's All-Souls Festival is now in session!"

The Junior Undertakers point their batons forward. Green light comes pouring out of them, and together they draw a complex symbol of glowing green. The undertaker takes a step forward and says, "Open, Says Me."

The symbol flashes and then fades into nothing. Bright colorful tents begin to emerge, spreading out over the entire field. Only they never fully take form. They stay hazy, almost translucent, like a strong gust of wind could blow them all away.

The grass below my feet becomes black pavement and little stands line the winding road ahead. Shimmering white figures swish back and forth along the road, calling us forward.

Dylan drops me onto my feet and I almost don't remember to catch myself. "Are those ghosts?" I ask.

"Yep," says Dylan. "It's why they call it the All-Souls Festival. Everyone's invited, living or dead."

I don't get very long to decide how I feel about being surrounded by ghosts because Elsie whoops and tugs me by the hand, behind the mass of people moving along the street. Dylan keeps pace, and we move through the crowd until we reach the first of the stands.

I can't stop staring. Up close, the spirits look like people, only they're as shimmery and translucent as everything else here. A slender spirit with a thick mustache waves us over to his table. "Grab a bite of Ghostly Cotton Candy! Eat as much as you want! You'll never get full!"

I pat down my pockets for show. "I'm sorry, but I don't have any money. Wait, do you even take money?"

"Joss paper," says the spirit. "Just have to burn it in my presence."

I turn to Elsie, who digs into her pocket.

Dylan stops her. "I think my dad should pay for Amari's fun, don't you?" He pulls out a thick roll of pink dollar bills and a lighter, and then sets a couple ablaze. Instead of burning up, though, the bills only turn as shimmery as everything else in the festival. The spirit happily accepts the money and stuffs it into a jar.

"A pleasure doing business," says the spirit. He hands

me a small bag of glowing cotton candy, and I can't get the stuff into my mouth fast enough. The fruity flavor melts on my tongue. I've never tasted anything so delicious.

Elsie, Dylan, and I move from stand to stand trying all kinds of different goodies. I can't stop grinning after tasting a Strawberry Smiles–flavored milkshake. Poor Elsie can't stop giggling after asking for a sample of the Chocolate Chip Chuckles flavor. Dylan and Elsie dare me to try Banshee I-Scream, which seems like plain old ice cream to me until the urge to shout my lungs out takes over after the third bite. Dylan and Elsie both go red in the face from laughing at me.

Once we've tasted everything there is to taste, we head into a large tent called *Sweet Dreams*. The dreams in here all glisten like liquid gold in little glass bottles. The sign says you only need one sip before bed to ensure you have the dream you want. *Richest Person in the World* seems really popular and so does *Most Beautiful Person in the World*. I see a few people attempt to slip *Sweet, Sweet Revenge* into their shopping baskets without anyone noticing. A group of teen-agers swarms the *My Crush Wants to Go Out with Me* counter and don't leave a single bottle on the shelf.

Eventually Dylan gets pulled away by some of his other friends, leaving me and Elsie to explore the rest of the festi-val on our own. We wander down a side street until I notice a jet-black tent with a faded sign out front.

Madame Violet's Magician Gift Shop

An actual store for magicians? Owned by the lady who wrote my spell book?

"We have to stop by that black tent," I tell Elsie.

"What black tent?" she replies.

"Right there. It's like directly in front of us."

Elsie squints. "I'm looking but I don't see any black tents."

"Just follow me." I lead Elsie closer, until we're standing right in front of the entrance. "Still don't see it?"

Elsie looks at me sideways. "All I see is an empty alleyway."

Weird. "C'mon. Maybe you'll be able to see it once we're inside."

I step through the entrance and the sharp smell of spices stings my nose. A skinny spirit wearing long dreadlocks sits cross-legged behind a black kettle. That must be Madame Violet. She grins at me from the center of the dimly lit space. "You couldn't have seen my tent unless you've magician's magic in your blood. You must be the famous Amari Peters. I read about you in this week's *Dearly Departed*."

"I am Amari Peters." I glance around at the bottles lining her shelves. A bottle marked *Broken Promises* shimmers with a soft blue light. Another silver vial says *Shattered Dreams*. *Unrequited Love* has a bright red glow. *Greatest Hopes* sparkles in gold.

Elsie comes in behind me. "This really is a tent. I thought for sure you were seeing things."

I step closer to the lady behind the kettle. "Are you the same Madame Violet who wrote my spell book?"

The spirit shuts her eyes and grins. "Do you imagine that there are many magicians named Madame Violet?"

"Probably not," I reply.

Madame Violet has a purring laugh. "Put the book to good use, child. Magic is a living thing—it does a dead woman no good. Shall we get down to business?" The spirit leans closer and strokes her chin. "The knowledgeable girl lacks courage, while the courageous girl lacks knowledge. How interesting . . .

"I'll make a deal with you," she adds. "If the dragon girl pays a small price, the magician girl can get knowledge vital to her quest."

"My quest?" I ask.

"This is not the first time I have seen your face," says Madame Violet. "When I was living, I would cast my magic far into the future and marvel at the scenes my illusions would show me. I saw who you were speaking to, Amari, and the spell you cast. I can assure you, this is a future you desperately want to preserve. And that can only happen with my help."

Elsie pulls out some joss paper from her pouch.

Madame Violet clucks her tongue. "I do not deal in common currency. For this I shall require one secret withheld from a friend."

"A secret?" My roommate shivers.

The spirit's expression darkens. "There isn't anything you've kept from your friend here? Certainly she couldn't hold it against you if revealing it is for her own benefit?"

Elsie glances to me, then drops her head. "Well—"

"Hush," says the spirit. "Don't waste it. Give me your hand."

At first, I think there's no way Elsie will agree to this but then she extends her hand.

"Wait!" I say.

"I can do this for Quinton," Elsie says.

"But . . ." I watch helplessly as the spirit takes Elsie's hand into her shimmering palm.

"Repeat these words," says the woman. "I pledge a secret withheld for a single bit of advice for my friend."

Elsie nods and repeats the words. A burst of cold air fills the tent, making me shiver.

My roommate lowers her head and turns to face me. "The first night we met I told you that I didn't know why I haven't shifted yet. The truth is that I do know. I found it in a book ages ago. Weredragons were once fierce warriors and because of that, in order to shift we have to perform a great act of courage. But I've been a worrier and a scaredy-cat my whole life. I didn't tell you because I'm ashamed."

The woman takes out a small net and swings it through the air between us. She hurriedly drops the net into an open jar labeled *Secrets Among Friends*. The black liquid swirls, going from nearly empty to half full.

"I'm sorry," says Elsie.

I take her hand. "It's totally fine. We had just met, remember? I thought you were going to say you snore like a lawn mower on purpose."

Elsie laughs and gives my hand a gentle squeeze.

"Very good," says Madame Violet. "And here is the knowledge that was promised—an illusionist should never trust that which giggles and grins."

I just stare. Is that all? "Am I supposed to know what that means?"

Madame Violet cackles as she and the entire shop begin to fade away. Soon Elsie and I are standing alone in an alley between two larger tents. It's like the shop was never here.

"Well, that was strange," says Elsie.

"Very strange."

"There she is!" comes Kirsten's voice from the main road. "I told you I saw her come down this way."

Elsie and I turn to find Lara and Kirsten coming in our direction.

Lara balls her fists. "You think you can throw spaghetti in my face and get away with it?" Whatever made her hesitate back at the Bureau is gone. She looks furious.

I glance around me for an escape but the only way out of this alley is forward. Right into Lara.

"Just let Elsie go," I say. "Please."

"So she can run off and tell someone?" says Lara. "Nope, you're finally going to get what's coming to you." She sets her jaw and steps closer.

I shove Elsie behind me.

Lara dashes forward and kicks out her leg. It's so fast I don't even have time to react. I just feel my legs get knocked from under me and land hard on my side. Next thing I know, she's on top of me, pinning both my wrists above my head with one arm. That means she's still got one hand free. She balls it into a fist.

I wriggle and buck my legs but it's no use. Her ability makes her too strong. Lara winds up her punch and I panic. I stare into her eyes and scream, "Magna Fobia!"

Lara's eyes go wide as the world around us shifts. Suddenly we aren't in an alley anymore but a big fancy office. Lara lowers her fist, glancing around, her face scrunched in confusion. "How did . . . ? Why am I . . . ?"

I push her off me and she falls backward, whipping her head back and forth like . . .

Like she can't see me. I move a little closer and realize it's true. Lara is looking right through me.

"What on earth are you doing on the floor?" Director Van Helsing stands in the doorway. His gray suit is wrinkled and he's got bags under his eyes like he hasn't slept in days. "It's bad enough you embarrassed this family at the tryout, and now I find you on the floor like a toddler?"

Lara gets to her feet quickly but I can see his words hit home. Her cheeks redden, and her normally cocky voice comes out shaky and uncertain. "I'm sorry, I . . . just got confused."

Director Van Helsing shakes his head and shuts the door behind him. Then he goes to his desk. "The phone call should be coming any minute now."

What phone call? I wonder.

But Lara just nods and takes a seat in front of the desk. She rocks back and forth in her chair.

What's going on?

The phone chimes and Director Van Helsing answers

on the first ring. Lara sits up straight in her chair, her eyes searching her father's face.

Director Van Helsing just keeps nodding and saying, "I understand," over and over. When he finally does hang up, there's a stunned look on his face.

"Well?" asks Lara, jumping to her feet. "What did they say?"

Director Van Helsing covers his face with both hands. "She's gone, sweetheart. Your sister has passed on."

Lara lets out a terrible wail. Then she falls to her knees, sobbing.

Oh no. I've got to make this stop. "Dispel!" I say, trembling.

The illusion vanishes and Kirsten flees. I run over and throw my arms around Lara's back. "I'm so, so sorry."

Lara just keeps crying. Elsie looks on from where she's standing, one hand covering her mouth. What did I just do? Lara's worst fear is the same as mine. That my brother is more than just missing. That he really is gone.

Lara pulls herself free of my grip. "Stay away from me." She sprints out of the alley.

Elsie and I meet each other's eyes, but neither of us knows what to say.

≋ 28 ≋

ON THE MORNING OF THE FINALE MY EMOTIONS ARE all over the place. I'm excited to be so close to becoming a Junior Agent and everything that would mean, and probably just as nervous about whether it will actually happen. I try not to dwell on it too much as Elsie and I get ready, but that only leaves me to think about last night and that awful spell I used. Just the memory turns my stomach.

When we got back here, Elsie asked me not to use my magic like that on anyone else, but it wasn't necessary. I had already made up my mind to never use foul magick again. Ever.

No matter what.

There's no big ceremony or encouraging speeches to kick off the finale for the Junior Agent trainees. The six of us report to the lobby at 9:00 a.m. and we're given a schedule that tells us where we need to be and at what time in order to complete each section of the finale. We're all fidgety and anxious and look over our schedules quietly.

First up for me is supernatural world knowledge. I walk into this little room with just a number 2 pencil, the test, and an answer sheet. I thought for sure we'd take the exam on a computer like we do when we practice, but they insist that this is tradition. My hard work completing that booklist definitely pays off. I know a lot of the answers. When I get to the last question, I smile. It's the same final question I had on my first exam. *Which two great beasts reside in the Atlantic Ocean?* Easy peasy. The kraken and the leviathan.

After the test, me and Dylan practice our steps for the Helsing technique for about thirty minutes and then report to the dueling gym. First up are Zoe and Madison. It feels so good to zap them into giggles on the floor mat. The next duel is harder, and I get zapped, but Dylan wins it for us.

I should be excited that things are going so well, but still no one's told me how they're going to grade me for the supernatural ability demonstration. They only made it clear that I'm not allowed to do one, with a big red *X* on that section of my schedule. It makes me think that maybe Dylan is right, and Director Van Helsing plans to disqualify me.

Guess it's a good thing I plan on performing a demonstration anyway.

"Would Dylan Van Helsing please come to the stage?" Director Van Helsing speaks into a microphone. Even though it's the final demonstration, the briefing auditorium buzzes at the sound of Dylan's name. It's filled with Agents and Junior Agents, with Director Van Helsing and the rest of the grading committee getting the last row to themselves.

A few seconds later Dylan appears from behind the curtain. He's brought a microphone and a chair with him that he places at the center of the stage.

Director Van Helsing says, "You may either display your supernatural ability first and announce what it is to the spectators later or vice versa. It's your choice."

Dylan moves to the microphone. "I'll be allowing my partner, Amari Peters, to have the stage. She has a demonstration she'd like to perform."

Shouts go up in the crowd as I walk out onstage to join him. People leap to their feet.

"I'm very sorry but that won't be allowed," announces Director Van Helsing. "Come down off that stage at once, young lady."

My partner and I exchange a grin and then he darts behind the curtain, leaving me the stage.

Director Van Helsing is practically growling into his microphone. "I'll give you one more chance before I send someone up there. You will not perform that vile sorcery here among these good people."

But I don't move. And when I raise my hands it goes silent. People cower in their seats like they think I'm about to attack or something.

"Get her off that stage!" barks Director Van Helsing.

Two agents run onstage and try to scoop me up into their arms. But I'm not onstage—it was just an illusion. With a wave of my hand I fill the room with darkness.

Whispers break out across the room and I take a slow deep breath as I tiptoe up to the stage. My whole body tingles with nerves and it feels like my tummy has balled itself into a knot. But if this is what I have to do to prove myself, then I will.

"Hello," I say into my own microphone. "My name is Amari Peters, the magician girl. You guys have heard all about magicians, but most of you don't actually know any. So I'd like to welcome you all to a very special Supernatural Immersion class—magician edition."

There are rumblings in the crowd, but thankfully no one leaves.

"Habitat," I continue. And I paint an illusion, letting the image pour out of my fingertips. Suddenly, the auditorium looks like a street in my neighborhood. A few people gasp, some keep turning their heads back and forth while others reach out with their hands to see if they can touch anything. "I've lived in the Rosewood Projects for as long as I can remember. It's basically a low-income apartment complex for people who need a little help getting by. People joke and call it the 'hood' or the bad side of town, but it's full of good people if you give them a chance."

I change the illusion to my apartment and have the audience glide through like one of those virtual house tours on the internet. "This is home for me. It's probably not much compared to where a lot of you guys live, but it's all I've ever known. This is my room, junky as always. And this is where the famous Agent Quinton Peters used to sleep when he was just my big brother. We would lie in here and dream about the things we were going to do. He made me believe I could actually do anything I set my mind to. He made me believe in me.

"Hobbies. Well, usually I compete in the summer swim meets at the rec center but I got a little busy this year trying to make Junior Agent." My joke gets a few laughs, and it's enough to encourage me to keep going.

"Go to the Department of Undersea Relations," someone shouts.

"Oh, good point," I say. "Guess it's hard to complain about missing the pool when there's a whole floor that's underwater."

That gets even more laughs.

"I also like to read books. The fun ones, not *Supernatural Laws and Regulations*. That author should definitely be investigated for crimes against good moods and staying awake. I'd much rather read books about magic and adventure—though I never imagined my own life would ever come close! Recently I've taken up another hobby, and that's practicing magic, which is mostly just me playing around with illusions." I flash an image of Elsie freaking out that time I turned her hair pink.

"I think I've gotten pretty good. Tell me what you guys think . . ."

And then I put on a show. I turn the ceiling into a cloudless, starry night sky and let the aurora borealis glimmer just beyond their fingertips as shooting stars zip across the auditorium. I turn the room dark again, and suddenly fireworks explode and sparkle overhead one after the other. Then the auditorium becomes a circus, with performers doing flips down the aisles and trapeze acrobats twisting and flipping above them. Clowns spill out of a car onstage while tigers jump through hoops of fire. I put us aboard a pirate ship in the middle of a terrible storm. People clutch their seats as the ship rocks back and forth amid crashing waves that tower above us. Finally, I put us on a calm sandy beach with the sun setting into the horizon. "The End."

I sweep away my illusion and step out onto the stage in front of the microphone Dylan left for me. Awed faces stare up at me. "Supernatural Immersion class usually ends with us asking questions. So here I am. I'll answer anything you guys ask."

"Is it really you this time?" someone asks.

"Yep, it's really me," I say. "Hopefully Director Van Helsing will let me finish?"

Agent Fiona's voice answers. "Go on."

There are so many questions, from "Does using magic make you grow horns?" to "Did Quinton know you're a magician?" to "What makes you different from all the magicians that committed so many awful crimes?"

That last question is the hardest and I have to think before I answer. "I don't know that anything makes me different from those other magicians. Honestly, there's a lot to being a magician that I still don't get. But what I *have* learned is that it's my choice what kind of magician I'm going to be. I'm trying to learn from my mistakes and not be like those bad magicians you guys know about. I guess I'm just asking for a chance to prove myself."

And when Agent Fiona finally calls time on my presentation people actually clap. Not everyone, but some. And it means everything.

I head backstage to find two agents waiting. I figured I'd get in trouble for this no matter how good or bad it turned out. "Just a few more seconds." And I close my eyes, still listening to that applause.

Screams from the auditorium pop my eyes back open. Suddenly alarms go off and agents rush past me. I step back onstage to find the whole place going nuts. People dash up the aisles toward the exit, others climb over their seats. But most everyone is looking up.

I lift my head to find three huge bat hybrids, flashing long fangs. I'm too stunned to even react, my feet rooted to the stage. But then I blink—and suddenly there are twenty.

≈ 29 ≈

Piercing screeches hurt my ears as the giant bats descend from the rafters, fangs bared. Dozens of agents scale the walls to meet them head on.

"Amari!" Agent Magnus's voice snaps me out of my daze. He stands at the edge of the stage, waving me toward him.

I run over, and he throws an arm around my shoulder. He leads me off the stage and up the aisle toward the exit, where Director Van Helsing and a few agents are helping people out of the auditorium. We're almost there when there's an enormous crash and something massive bursts through the wall.

A hulking gray hybrid standing upright on two legs turns to face us. Its long snout has a pointed horn at the end. A rhino hybrid.

Magnus puts himself between it and me. "When I say go, you hightail it outta here and don't look back, got it?"

"Got it," I say.

The rhino hybrid growls, its massive muscles bulging. Then it lowers its snout and charges.

"Go," shouts Magnus. He gives me a shove, sending me stumbling into the seats. I whip my head around in time to see Magnus and the beast tumble down the aisle.

Magnus is one of the best there is. He'll be fine. I make myself believe it. I have to get to Director Van Helsing so I can make it out of here in one piece. But a glance through the giant hole that the rhino made in the wall stops me cold. It's total chaos. Dozens of hybrids—bears, panthers, gorillas—run roughshod over the place. I mean, the agents are amazing, taking down monsters more than twice their size, but every time one falls, another appears out of thin air to take its place. They can barely keep up.

It also doesn't help that so many agents have to stay back to protect the spectators Director Van Helsing is sending out of the auditorium.

I grip the Stun Stick at my waist. Shouldn't I try to help? What would Quinton do?

I step out into the chaos, eyes darting in every direction. Agents and monsters move in blurs around me. Deafening roars and bone-rattling growls come at me from all directions. My fingers tremble around my Stun Stick.

I'm in way over my head.

I scream as something snatches me back into the auditorium. But it's only Agent Magnus, sporting a nasty bruise on his forehead. He's furious.

"What's the matter with you?" he shouts.

"I—I just w-wanted to h-help," I stutter.

"This ain't a fight for a kid," Agent Magnus snaps. "Get over to Van Helsing and make for the lobby. Go!"

This time I listen. Agent Magnus follows behind me just long enough to make sure I don't get any more dumb ideas. Then he balls his fists and I watch his skin harden into metal. He flicks his wrist and his Stun Stick becomes a giant ax. Flames erupt along the blades and he leaps through the hole in the wall, back into the battle.

I reach Director Van Helsing just as he sends off the last group.

The director's eyes dart back and forth between the battle with the bat hybrids overhead and the fight going on in the hallway. He frowns when he notices me, but it doesn't last long. "Hurry and catch up with the others."

I duck through the doorway. The agents have stopped this last group from making a run for the elevators because a group of scary-looking gorilla hybrids are close to breaking through the line of agents protecting the escape route.

I recognize Elsie's brown curls and white researcher coat in the group and take the spot next to her. Her eyes are wide and panicked.

She nearly jumps out of her skin when I throw my arms around her.

"Oh, thank goodness," she says. "I tried to wait for you, but Director Van Helsing made me leave."

"Thanks," I say.

Elsie shrieks as a gorilla hybrid gets frighteningly near, but it's beaten back by a female agent with a laser whip. That was too close.

Elsie clutches my jacket. "Are we going to be okay?"

"Definitely," I say.

As soon as the word leaves my mouth, a sea of beige appears over Elsie's shoulder, and a wave of Wilderness Rangers from Creature Control charge out of the lobby, each with a flaming bird perched on their arm.

"Phoenixes!" Elsie exclaims. In one synchronized motion, Wilderness Rangers point out targets and the birds take off, colliding against hybrids and exploding on impact. As soon as the fiery ashes hit the floor, the birds re-form and strike again. The agents use the attacks to get the advantage in the battle, pushing the hybrids farther up the hall.

"Kids, get to the lobby!" yells an agent.

None of us need to be told a second time. A wave of relief surges through me as we start down the hall to the bottom of the U, away from the danger. I turn to get one last look at the fighting and freeze. A masked figure in black sprints across the ceiling, straight toward the hybrids. Only none of the beasts attack—if anything, they're clearing a path. I gasp.

Moreau's apprentice. It has to be.

The figure is down the hall in seconds, headed into the hallway leading to the Great Vault. No one else seems to notice.

Except Dylan, who turns and gives chase.

No! What's he thinking? But I already know the answer. This is his chance to not only stop this, but to prove Maria isn't a traitor.

"Amari!" shouts Elsie. "What are you waiting for?"

A terrible knot settles in my gut. "We aren't just being attacked. I think we're being robbed."

Elsie's eyes go wide and she glances down the hall in the direction of the Great Vault.

"You two by the door!" shouts a Junior Agent near the entrance to the lobby. "Either come on or we're leaving you behind!"

It's now or never. I turn to Elsie, "Go on without me."

"Whatever you're thinking, don't do it," she replies. "You'll get yourself hurt."

That's what I'm afraid will happen to Dylan. I won't let him do this alone.

One of the agents shouts, "Hold the position! The hybrids are retreating!"

But they aren't retreating. Not really. They've backed up to form a wall in front of the Great Vault. That can't be a coincidence. I still have on my Sky Sprints . . .

"I know what I'm doing," I say, and dash up the nearest wall. I keep close to the ceiling, away from the fighting below. Someone calls my name, but I can't turn around. I have to get to the vault before it's too late.

The old wooden door protecting the Great Vault is wide open. A shiver creeps down my back. That door is supposed to be impenetrable.

I drop to the floor and run inside. The vault is a wide, dark space with little spotlights shining down on long rows of pedestals. It reminds me of the pedestals in our first tryout. I look around for Dylan or the intruder, but I don't see anyone.

"Amari!" Dylan steps into the spotlight of a pedestal. "There's someone else in here."

"I saw. How did they get past the door?"

Dylan shakes his head. "It was open when I got here."

We step farther into the vault, looking for some sign of the intruder.

"Looking for me?" a voice whispers into my ear.

I spin around to find a girl dressed in all black, backing away from me. She fades into the shadows. "Dylan, over here!"

He's at my side in an instant. "What happened?"

"I saw the thief," I say with a shiver. "She was right behind me."

Dylan points his Stun Stick out in front of him. "We

know you're in here. You might as well come out."

The thief snaps her fingers and all the spotlights shut off at once.

"She's a technologist," says Dylan. "That must be how she got in."

"Are you two trainees going to arrest me?" she teases.

Dylan gasps.

"What?" I ask. "What is it?"

"A-Amari," he stutters. "I know that voice."

Shouts pull my eyes to the door. Blinding overhead lights click on.

"There!" Agent Fiona calls, and a crowd of agents rushes in our direction.

"Dylan? Peters?" says Director Van Helsing. "What on earth are you doing in here?"

"There was a girl in black," I say quickly.

Dylan looks sick. "Dad, it's—"

"Above us!" someone shouts.

The girl in black races along the ceiling and the agents fire blast after blast, but none of them even comes close. Once she reaches the hallway, she drops to the floor and pulls off her mask.

Gasps ring out from the agents around me.

Maria Van Helsing smirks and gives us a bow. Then she taps at her transporter armband and vanishes.

Quinton *was* betrayed by his own partner. Knowing it's true makes my chest ache. Worse, that terrible thought is followed quickly by another. "Director, where's the Black Book kept?"

But Director Van Helsing doesn't seem to hear me. He's frozen in place, staring at the spot his daughter just teleported from. A few of the other agents dash farther into the vault. Still dazed, I follow.

Agent Fiona stops suddenly, throwing a hand over her mouth.

A pedestal sits empty.

"GOOD AFTERNOON, CHIEF CROWE SPEAKING. EARLIER today, the Department of Supernatural Investigations suffered an unprecedented attack by hybrids somehow capable of teleporting directly into our facility. It is still unclear exactly how our various security systems were breached, but I can assure you that we are in the process of a most thorough investigation. For now, all training activities are suspended until further notice. All trainees and junior personnel are to remain in their dormitories unless given express permission to do otherwise. Dinner will be delivered directly to your rooms."

"Will you please tell me what's wrong?" Elsie asks again

once the announcement is over. "You've been pacing non-stop since you got here."

I don't answer her. I can't. I wish so badly that I could've knocked that stupid smirk from Maria's stupid face.

"Hey!" says Elsie, jumping into my path. "You're scaring me, okay? I've never seen your aura go this red before. Tell me what's wrong!"

So I do. I tell her what I've hoped wasn't true for weeks—my brother was stabbed in the back by the person he trusted most.

"Are you sure?" Elsie's voice goes soft. "But that would mean she's a magician too. That can't be right, can it?"

"She *is* a magician," I say. "And Moreau must've given her the same choice he gave me—Bureau or magician. And she dragged my brother down with her."

A loud knock makes us jump.

Elsie hops up and opens the door. It's Bertha.

"Your presence has been requested by Special Agent Magnus ASAP."

I'm up and out the door in seconds.

Lucy the elevator asks me a million questions I don't have answers for, but she goes quiet once we arrive at the lobby of the Department of Supernatural Investigations. An agent steps into the elevator. "State your business," he says in a stern voice.

"I'm supposed to see Agent Magnus."

The agent taps his earpiece. "I've got Peters here to see Agent Magnus, confirm." I start to worry that maybe no one will answer, but then the agent nods and asks, "Do you know the way?"

"I do," I say.

"Go straight to his office and then come right back to this lobby, understand?"

"Yes, sir," I say.

He steps aside and I head through the lobby and into the main hallway. The whole area is a mess. Papers are everywhere, and big chunks of the walls are either dented or missing entirely. It looks like a bomb went off. There isn't a person in sight.

I've never heard it so quiet in here. A heavy, sad feeling settles over me as I walk around the U and turn into the hallway where all the offices are. This place belonged to my brother, and I've worked this summer to make it belong to me too.

Director Van Helsing is in the hallway surrounded by other agents. He's changed into a different suit, but his face still looks haunted. He does a double take when he sees me. "Peters? What on earth are you doing up here?"

"I was called by Agent Magnus," I reply.

The Director frowns. "Whatever business you have with him, make it quick. We'll be locking down the entire Bureau within the hour."

I move a little faster as I squeeze past them all.

When I knock on Agent Magnus's door, he rushes me inside and shuts the door.

The office looks like a hybrid got loose in here too. File

folders are scattered across his desk, the floor covered in loose papers.

"Maria," I say. "It was her all along."

Magnus's face flushes. "I won't lie and tell you it don't break my heart. But there'll be plenty of time later for the cursing and the shouting. Right now we need to focus on our next move." He places a briefcase on his desk. It looks just like the one Quinton sent me weeks ago.

"Is that—"

"It is." Agent Magnus waves me over to his desk. With a few taps on his keyboard, my Bureau of Supernatural Affairs webpage pops up onscreen. "Good," he says. "All four of us judges submitted our marks before the hybrid attack."

AMARI RENEE PETERS—Junior Agent Trainee

First Tryout: **Pass**

Second Tryout: **Pass**

Finale—Supernatural Knowledge Score: **91% Pass**

Finale—Stun Stick Duels: **2 Wins 0 Losses Pass**

Finale—Supernatural Demonstration:

    (3/4 passing marks obtained) Pass

Magnus—**Excellent**

Fiona—**Excellent**

Kozy—**Satisfactory**

Van Helsing—**Fail**

Trainee Peters has met all requirements for

    promotion.

"Don't worry about that Fail," says Agent Magnus. "You only need three out of four to pass this year. Fiona put in that rule change early—she thought the Director might not give you a fair shake."

"I really did it, then?" I'm so relieved.

"You done good, kid." Magnus types his name beside Promoting Agent and taps Enter. Then he puts a finger to my moonstone badge and says, "By the power vested in me as a training agent, I promote you, Amari Peters, to Junior Agent."

My moonstone badge warps from a circle into an oval, *Department of Supernatural Investigations* engraved above the image of an evenly weighted balance. Bureau of Supernatural Affairs is etched across the bottom.

Despite everything, I can't help but smile at the sight. After all the hard work, and the bullies, and the doubters— especially myself—I actually made Junior Agent.

Agent Magnus points to the briefcase. "Quinton's things are yours now. Go on and grab the handle."

The moment my fingers make contact the locks click open.

I lift the lid to find several folders inside. Magnus and I take them out and set them down on his desk. It's not till we reach the bottom of the briefcase that we find a manila folder so thin it looks empty. It's marked *Key Holder*.

I pull it out and open it up. There's a single sheet of paper inside.

"Dag gummit," says Magnus in an awed voice. "Quinton actually did it. He tracked down the Key Holder."

KEY HOLDER
Name: Dr. Henry Underhill, MD
Shapeshifter
Location: Boonies Medical Clinic

"I'm putting in a formal request to be allowed to retrieve the Black Key and bring it under our protection," says Magnus.

"A request? Maria already has the Black Book! She could be on her way to the Black Key right now!"

"The honest truth is she could have the Black Key already," says Magnus. "And if that's true, the supernatural world is in a lot of trouble. We can only hope that's not the case."

"I'm tired of hoping. I've been doing that since I got here. Quinton went missing trying to stop this!"

"Our hands are tied," says Magnus. "As caretakers of the Black Book, the Bureau was founded on the oath that it would never pursue the Black Key. The Black Book and the Black Key are never to be brought together for any reason."

"But they won't be," I say. "The Bureau doesn't have the Black Book anymore."

"And we'll be sure to make that point clear when we ask for permission. Rules are rules, Amari. If an emergency session is called, we could probably have an answer in about twenty-four hours."

"That's a whole day!" I say.

"It's time we can spend gatherin' as much info as we can," says Agent Magnus. "Maybe we'll try Moreau again, see if we can't get a sense of what Maria is planning to do next. It's a long shot but he'll probably be in the mood to gloat."

I start to protest but Agent Magnus has already pulled out his phone. "I need to be connected with the chief immediately."

"Now entering Blackstone Prison."

I'm back on Lord Kensington, the elevator, only this time it's with Agent Magnus. While the Bureau waits to hear back from the Supernatural World Congress for special permission to go after the Key Holder, Chief Crowe agreed with Magnus about questioning Moreau again.

Maybe he won't tell us anything helpful but I guess it's worth a try. Better than sitting around doing nothing.

"Heavens," says Lord Kensington, "how did those nasty hybrids even get in?"

"Somebody shut off our shields." Magnus crosses his arms. "But only a few people have access to those codes, and I'd trust any of 'em with my life."

"Did Maria have the shield codes?" I ask.

"Yeah, every Special Agent does in case of emergency," says Magnus. "But her codes would've been deactivated the moment she and Quinton were declared missing in action. The main computer would've done that automatically."

That's when I realize something. Back in the vault, Dylan said the thief was a technologist. "Maria is a magician, like me. So she wouldn't need codes to shut down our defenses."

For a moment, Agent Magnus just stares, incredulous. He shakes it off. "You're telling me magicians have the power to control computers with their magic?"

I bite my lip. "It's called tech magic."

"And how do you know this?" When I don't answer, Magnus's expression darkens. "This ain't a time for secrets, kid! How do you know this?"

"It's just . . . something I've learned," I say.

Magnus groans and turns away from me. "Then we're still vulnerable, even now. We've gotta get you kids home and away from danger."

"You can't send me home," I say. "Not until I've found Quinton. You said you'd let me help with the search."

"That was before the Bureau got turned into a war zone! I owe it to your brother to keep you safe, Amari."

"But—"

"No buts," he says. "After we speak to Moreau, I'm gonna personally see to it you and your mother are placed in a safe location until this is all sorted out."

I'm so annoyed I could shout. It's so unfair. I don't need protecting.

Lord Kensington races us down the spiraling rail to the level Moreau has all to himself.

Just as he was the last time, he's sitting in a chair facing away from us.

Agent Magnus steps out of the elevator first and I follow.

The moment my foot hits the smooth black floor of the prison, the inside of Moreau's glass cell transforms into a scene of a fancy party full of people celebrating. Moreau appears next to the glass.

"Is that Agent Magnus?" asks Moreau. "My, it has been a while, hasn't it?"

Agent Magnus's face turns serious. "I take it you know why I'm here."

Moreau's thin lips curve into a small grin. "I've heard talk from the guards about your precious Bureau being attacked. And by hybrids no less. Such pests. I do hope you called the exterminator."

"Enough with the games. We know Maria is trying to resurrect Vladimir for you!" Agent Magnus pounds the glass. "Tell us how to find her!"

"You know nothing!" snaps Moreau. "I do, however, confess myself disappointed. I warned you when you captured me that another would take on the mantle and return us to our former glory. You laughed then at the idea that other magicians existed outside the Bureau's knowledge. And today you show up with your brand-new magician in tow. It seems it's my turn to laugh now!"

Agent Magnus turns and starts toward Lord Kensington. "This is a waste of time."

Moreau is eyeing me now. "You had your chance to choose the winning side. Perhaps we can teach you to be less trusting. But then, maybe all Peters are gullible."

"Just shut up, okay? I told you, I'm on my brother's side." I turn to follow Agent Magnus, frowning at Moreau over my shoulder.

But Moreau just shrugs. "Ah, well. I do appreciate your stopping by. Even if it amounted to little more than giggles and grins."

My whole body goes stiff. *Giggles and grins.*

I hear Madame Violet's voice in my head. "An illusionist should never trust that which giggles and grins . . ."

I swallow. The words suddenly make sense. What's the most obvious reason for an illusionist not to trust? Because we know that eyes can be tricked. It's the very first lesson in her spell book: *Never trust. Take absolutely nothing at face value. In viewing anything, assume its appearance is false until otherwise proven.*

The rest of what she said comes back to me. "When I was living, I would cast my magic far into the future and marvel at the scenes my illusions would show me. I saw who you were speaking to, Amari, and the spell you cast."

But she couldn't have meant right now, could she? That's when I remember what Moreau told me, the very first time we met. *"There will only be one lie between us."*

Right after he introduced himself.

Slowly, I raise my hand toward Moreau, lifting two fingers. "Dispel."

The party scene vanishes. All that's left is Moreau and his rocking chair. He tries to stand, his body shaking violently. Still he moves closer, limping on his left side . . .

Agent Magnus steps up next to me. "What did you do to him?"

But I don't answer. Because I can already see the wrinkles and gray hairs begin to fade away. A shorter, paler, much younger man sneers at us . . .

This can't be happening.

"Good!" the man grins darkly. "Very good. For now you truly understand the danger you are in. My master—a magician whose magic dwarfs your 100 percent—now possesses the Black Book!"

"Who are you?" Agent Magnus demands.

"I am but a lowly servant who has played his part in the grand scheme," the man says. "Join us, girl. You won't want to find out what we do to those who betray their fellow magicians!"

It takes a second for me to process what it all means. Moreau was never captured. He's the one behind all this.

The most dangerous being in the supernatural world has the Black Book.

Agent Magnus grabs me by both shoulders and crouches. "How did you know?"

Voice shaky, I tell him about my trip to Madame Violet.

"This changes everything," says Agent Magnus, his eyes wide and panicked. "If we don't get our hands on that key, the world might not last another twenty-four hours."

We dash to Lord Kensington. Agent Magnus shouts, "Take us directly to the chief!"

31

T*HIS ISN'T THE CHIEF'S OFFICE.* THAT'S MY FIRST THOUGHT
when Lord Kensington opens its doors.

Instead, we've been brought to the Department of
Supernatural Investigations.

"I'm sorry," says Lord Kensington. "I've been ordered to
bring you here."

Director Van Helsing stands in the lobby, arms crossed.
Behind him is a whole squadron of agents.

"We ain't got time for whatever this is," says Agent Magnus. "Didn't you get the alert? Moreau is free! The person
who has the Black Book isn't simply some apprentice magician. It's one of the *Night Brothers.*"

"I received the alert," says Director Van Helsing. "Peters, come stand next to me."

"But—"

"Do as he says," Agent Magnus interrupts.

I don't feel good about it, but I do as I'm told. Director Van Helsing's face hardens at the sight of my Junior Agent badge. "If I haven't made this clear enough, there will be no magicians in my department as long as *I* am director." He puts a finger to my badge and says, "*Demoted!*"

And just like that my moonstone badge shrinks back into a trainee badge. I ball my fists at my sides. Dylan was right—his father never meant to give me a real chance.

Director Van Helsing's eyes return to Agent Magnus back in the elevator. "How curious that your first move would be to head to the prison to make this remarkable discovery. Convenient, wouldn't you say? Look at Magnus the hero, instead of Magnus the accomplice. Despite our differences, not in a million years would I have pegged *you* for a traitor."

Magnus shakes his head. "Not even you're dim enough to believe that, Van Helsing. Just what are you gettin' at?"

Director Van Helsing makes a motion with his arm and the agents move forward, surrounding the elevator. Van Helsing waits until they're in position before he answers Agent Magnus. "We've discovered how the hybrids were able to teleport into the Bureau. *You* deactivated our shields."

"He didn't!" I say. "It was—"

"Quiet!" says Magnus.

"Yes, Peters. Save your breath," says Director Van Helsing. "This man doesn't deserve your loyalty. No one has access to your codes but you, Magnus." Director Van Helsing steps forward, his jaw clenched tight. "How far back does your treachery reach, I wonder? Maria looked up to you! Did you convince her to betray both her family and the Bureau?"

"I'm being set up," Magnus pleads. "Why would I be dumb enough to use a code that can easily be traced back to me? Why wouldn't I run off instead of sticking around here?"

"Both are questions I'm asking myself," Director Van Helsing replies. "I've simply followed the evidence, just as we're taught. It leads to you, Magnus."

Agent Magnus huffs. "And I suppose you want me to make this easy on you and just turn myself in."

"Young Miss Peters is present," Director Van Helsing replies. "I hope, for her sake, you'll keep this a civil affair."

Agent Magnus's intense eyes find mine and I can see he's trying to tell me something. He raises his hands. "I'm surrendering."

My mind is spinning as I'm led by two agents back to the youth dormitories. Neither says a word till we get to my room. That's when the taller one says, "The Bureau is on lockdown tonight. The director wants you available for questioning first thing tomorrow."

They don't wait for me to answer. Both turn and head back down the hall.

As soon as I step through the door, Elsie rushes over and pokes her head into the hallway, looking back and forth before closing the door behind me. "You've got a visitor."

That's when Dylan crawls out from under my bed. It's the first time we've seen each other since we followed Maria into the Great Vault.

"What are you doing in here?" I ask.

Dylan pulls himself up to a knee. "I heard about them tracing the codes back to Agent Magnus. There's no way he would betray the Bureau like that. It had to be Maria." His voice falters and he shakes his head. "She must've framed him or something. I should've listened to you about her."

Elsie throws a somber glance at the magazine covers framed above her bed. This goes against everything she's ever believed about Maria. But she didn't see Maria's smirking face—Dylan's sister enjoyed every second of betraying her father and the rest of the Bureau.

"I know you may not trust me since I'm her brother," says Dylan, "but I feel like it's my responsibility to do something about it."

"It's worse than Maria stealing the Black Book," I say. "If you've been here then you probably haven't heard that Moreau is free. I think one of his other apprentices was using an illusion to take his place."

Elsie's hand goes to her mouth. "He's free?"

Dylan's eyes go wide and he stumbles over his words

before he's finally able to say, "For how long? Was he ever even captured?"

"I don't know," I say. "But I don't think Magnus would want me focused on clearing his name. I think he'd rather I do what he can't anymore—what my brother started before him."

"You can't mean what I think you mean," says Elsie.

"I'm going to go after the Black Key," I say. That has to be what Agent Magnus was trying to tell me with that look. And why he stopped me from telling Director Van Helsing about how Maria's tech magic is capable of shutting down the Bureau's shields. He doesn't want me stuck here answering questions. He wants me out there getting that key.

"Wait," says Dylan. "You know where it is?"

"Magnus was right about my brother hiding the location in a Farewell Briefcase," I say. "We just have to get there before Moreau does and convince the Key Holder to give us the Black Key."

"I don't know about this." Elsie falls heavily onto her bed. "You'd be breaking the Bureau's biggest oath. They could disband the entire Bureau for this. Amari, they'd throw you into Blackstone."

I swallow. "My brother went missing trying to prevent this. I have to try."

"If you're really going to do this," says Dylan, "then I've got your back. I won't let Maria hurt anyone else."

Elsie sighs. "Then . . . I guess I'm coming too."

"No offense," says Dylan. "But I don't think that's a

good idea. Amari and I at least have Junior Agent training to defend ourselves."

"I've got all the gadgets I've been working on." Elsie reaches under her bed and grabs a book bag full of contraptions and then looks to me. "Every time you get into trouble I just sit back or I hide. I'm sick of being that person. *Please* let me help."

"It's my idea, so it's my call," I say. "Elsie comes."

"Fine," says Dylan. "But if something happens to her that's on you."

"Deal," I say. "Now we just need a plan."

"Leave it to me," says Dylan. "Just be ready to go."

At eight o'clock an announcement comes over the intercom.

"Attention junior personnel and trainees, this is Chief Director Crowe speaking. In light of this morning's attack, and after meeting with the directors of each department, I have decided to suspend this year's summer camp. Until we can verify that none of our other security protections have been compromised, we cannot in good conscience allow children to remain inside the facility. We are in the process of notifying your parents. For those from non-legacy families, the cover story will be that our organization ran into a funding mishap that caused us to end summer camp prematurely."

My phone buzzes at the same time that Bertha stomps into the room. A quick glance shows it's Mama. She must've gotten the news about camp being canceled. I slip my phone into my pocket.

Bertha holds up a slip of paper that she reads from. "This is a Level Five notification. Amari Peters and Elsie Rodriguez are to report to the Transporter Room in the Department of Supernatural Licenses and Records right away." Her face scrunches, but she continues reading. "They are to bring the necessary equipment, and they will already know what equipment that is. Signed Director Van Helsing, Department of Supernatural Investigations."

Bertha looks up at me. "Get to it, then! Director Van Helsing made his wishes pretty clear, I'd think!"

"Oh yes, very clear," I say. How in the world did Dylan pull this off?

I grab my Stun Stick and Sky Sprints and Elsie straps on her backpack.

Bertha hands me the note as we step out of my room. "You'll need this to get by the security checkpoints."

I walk to the elevators in total disbelief.

Mischief is waiting for us. "ID card or hall pass, please."

Elsie puts a hand on her hip. "Since when did you start acting like a proper elevator?"

Mischief sighs. "My dirty-rascal chip gets deactivated during lockdowns. ID card or hall pass, please."

I hold up the slip Bertha gave us, and Mischief scans it.

"Permission to travel to the Department of Supernatural Licenses and Records granted."

The large lobby of the Department of Supernatural

Licenses and Records is completely empty and only one lady is seated at a booth. We walk over, and she clears her throat loudly. "Please grab a ticket."

"But we're the only ones here," I say.

"Rules are rules," she says.

The lady makes us walk all the way across the lobby to grab a ticket, then waits for us to sit down before tapping the button that causes the speaker to chime, "Now serving A1 at the first window."

We show her the pass and she lets us into the main hall. An agent is stationed here, and I show him the pass too. He reads it, scratches his head in confusion, and then calls another agent farther down the hall to have a look.

Finally, the agents let us through, but they watch us closely until we turn the corner into the Transporter Room.

Dylan pops out from behind one of the glass tubes. "You made it. Wasn't entirely sure that was going to work."

"Me neither," I say. "But you do know we can't teleport out of here during a lockdown. The security computer will shut us down."

"True," says Dylan. "But only if you're trying to teleport someplace outside the Bureau."

"You want to teleport us someplace *inside* the Bureau?" asks Elsie.

"Yep," says Dylan. "Just trust me on this one. I've already plugged in the destination."

Dylan leads us over to the teleporter he's got powered on.

I step into the glass tube and Dylan follows. Shouts come from behind us. It's the agents we handed the note to. They must've triple-checked.

"Stop!" one of them shouts, sliding to a stop in front of us. Poor Elsie is between the agents and the teleporter. "Step aside, girl, and you two exit the transporter. Now!"

Elsie takes a deep, trembling breath and looks back at us over her shoulder. "Go!"

Dylan mashes a giant red button and the transporter begins to hum.

At the sound, the agents rush toward us and I expect Elsie to run. But she stands her ground.

And then my best friend breathes fire.

Dylan and I reappear inside a wide concrete room. Along the walls are large stalls with all sorts of crazy vehicles parked inside them, everything from floating bicycles to flying saucers. Dylan starts forward but turns to look at me over his shoulder. "Did Elsie just . . . ?"

I grin. "I think she really did."

It isn't until we're halfway across the large space that I see where Dylan is taking us—the *Jolly Roger*. The ship that belonged to my brother and his sister.

"And just where do you think you're headed?" Agent Fiona steps out from a stall labeled *Winged Chariot*.

We stop cold. And three thoughts jump into my head. One, we're so caught. Two, Agent Fiona is definitely cool enough to pull off a winged chariot. And three, we are so, *so* caught.

Dylan and I each give completely different explanations at the same time. Agent Fiona just crosses her arms and looks me right in the eye. My whole body goes stiff.

Agent Fiona blinks in surprise. "Magnus put ye up to this? Or do ye just think he wants you tracking down that key?"

"He said that we've got to get our hands on that key," I say, remembering Agent Magnus's words.

Agent Fiona claps her hand against her forehead. "I don't understand what the man could be thinking! You're just trainees, for heaven's sake!"

"He wanted to do it himself, but he got framed," I say. "It's a long story."

Agent Fiona grumbles. "Told that bumblin' idiot director there's no one more loyal than Beauregarde in the whole bloody Bureau." She holds up her left wrist, where a device has been cuffed. "Van Helsing's even tracking *my* movements in case I'm guilty of helping. Can't step one foot outside the Bureau without setting off an alarm that'd have fifty agents come after me. Like I don't have a kiddie of my own at home to check in on. The *audacity* of that man."

I step forward, realizing Director Van Helsing may have done me a favor when he decided to demote me. "I'm just a trainee and not officially part of the Bureau yet, so I can't get the Bureau in trouble for going after the key." I decide to be a little bolder. "I think you should trust Agent Magnus's judgment."

Agent Fiona shakes her head. "Heaven help me, this is

what we've come to. Take down my cell phone number. The very first sign of trouble, ye text me your coordinates and I'll be right there, tracking device or not."

I type the number into my phone. Agent Fiona gives us another look like she can't believe this is happening and then heads to go open the hangar doors.

It's not till we get into the ship that Dylan admits he's only ever flown the *Jolly Roger* on *Called to Action: Agents Against the World*. That boy then has the nerve to say, "How much different could real life be from the video game?"

Turns out a lot. But after backing into the wall twice, he gets things under control. Thankfully Agent Fiona can't see our rough start from inside the hangar control room. Dylan guides us slowly out of the stall and into the landing area.

The real *Jolly Roger* is even fancier than the Wakeful Dream version. I type "Henry Underhill, Boonies Medical Clinic" into the navigation system.

Route found. Autopilot?

I look to Dylan and he nods. Then I press my finger to the GO button and the two of us dash into the night sky.

32

J ust like in the Wakeful Dream, the Jolly Roger moves
impossibly fast. The world blurs and I close my eyes against
the streaking stars. *This will work. We're going to find the Key
Holder and get him to safety. Maria and Moreau won't win.*

We're here, I think as the ship glides to a slow stop in
midair. The trip took all of ten seconds. I glance back at
Dylan at the captain's wheels and notice his troubled expression.

I feel so bad for him. All this time he's been so convinced
Maria was innocent. And now they're on opposite sides.

I lean over the railing. A vast forest stretches out beneath
us. The only sign of civilization is a small log cabin and
a long dirt road that curves out of sight. Here, the sun is

only just beginning to set, hurling up streaks of purple and orange as the night pushes it away.

Dylan comes over to take a look.

"We should hurry and park this thing," I say. "We don't want the Key Holder to look out his window and see a ship hovering over his house."

Landing the *Jolly Roger* ends up being trickier than I'd imagined. Dylan brings the boat down a little too fast, causing a boom that echoes through the trees. "Sorry."

"I'm just glad we got here in one piece," I say.

We hop down off the ship and head over to the doctor's cabin. The grass around here reaches up past my knees. It hasn't been cut in a while. Weird. It makes me wonder if anyone is really using this cabin.

We pass a sign that says:

THE BOONIES MEDICAL CLINIC
COUNTRY DOCTORIN' AT ITS FINEST!
Henry Underhill, MD

This is definitely the place. The front door is only a few steps away but Dylan grabs my arm and says, "Just hear him out, okay? Give him a chance."

Huh? "Give who a chance?"

Dylan sighs. "Why don't you come inside and find out."

Without even knocking first, he walks inside.

Confused, I move to follow him but freeze in the doorway. The doctor's office has been completely trashed. Papers and medical supplies scattered all over the floor. Chairs and cabinets overturned.

And seated at a fancy golden table in the middle of it all is a smiling gray-haired man in blood-red robes. He looks identical to the illusion except there's a presence to him that I never felt back at Blackstone Prison. Something old and very dark.

It raises the hairs on the back of my neck.

The real Raoul Moreau leans forward in his chair. "Nice to finally meet you, Amari Peters."

Please don't let us be too late. "Where's the Key Holder?"

"I'm afraid Dr. Underhill was dealt with some time ago," says Moreau. "Do you really think I would risk attacking the Bureau for the Black Book without already possessing the Black Key?" He pulls a piece of twisted black metal from inside his robe.

"But how?" I ask.

Moreau's grin widens, flashing his pointed canines. "Being so young in your magic, you wouldn't know this, but there are ways to make truths spill from lips like water from a fountain."

I grimace. My brother didn't stand a chance. "Where is Quinton?"

"Right here." Moreau sweeps his hands forward and a medical gurney rolls out from behind the counter.

My breath hitches at the sight of my brother, lying still. Too still. Shimmering green mist hovers in the air around him. "What are you doing to him?"

"Extracting his life essence—your brother has been dying a very slow death." Moreau grins. "The spell I shall perform tonight requires it. A fitting end, wouldn't you say?"

I draw my Stun Stick but Dylan knocks it out of my hand.

Moreau laughs and, with a twirl of his fingers, yanks my body forward through the air and drops me into a golden chair at the table.

I'm totally defenseless.

Dylan takes a seat across from me—right at Moreau's side. I feel like I could throw up.

"You've been lying to me all along," I snap at him.

Dylan doesn't respond. He doesn't even look at me.

Moreau laughs. "I'm afraid *my* partner has played you for quite the fool, child. And for a very long time too. It might shock you to know that it was he who stole the Black Book from right under your nose. He walked out with it in his jacket pocket while you, Chief Crowe, and a dozen other agents stood only feet away!"

"But Maria," I say. "I saw her. We all did."

"You saw what Dylan wanted you to see." Moreau throws his head back and laughs some more. "She was an illusion, and all the tech magic she supposedly performed was actually Dylan here."

I can't believe it. "You disabled the shields to let the hybrids in. *You're* the one who set up Magnus." Maria was a victim just like Quinton.

Dylan still won't look at me.

I shake my head. "But why? All those times you said you wanted Maria back and you knew where she was all along."

Dylan stares me straight in the eye. "Maria is a coward! Just like all those other weakling Van Helsing magicians before her. For centuries they've stayed silent while the Bureau locked away magician after magician. It's like I told you, we're special, Amari. And we deserve to be treated like it. We shouldn't have to hide what we are. Moreau helped me to understand that a true magician cannot serve two masters."

With a wave of Moreau's hands, Maria is rolled out on a gurney, too, her eyes closed. That same green mist surrounds her.

I just keep shaking my head while Moreau chuckles in delight. "Tell her everything, child. Let her see how thoroughly she has failed. Just like her fool brother."

And he does. Dylan tells me that he and Moreau first bumped into each other over the othernet while using tech magic. And two years ago, it was Dylan who warned Moreau that VanQuish was coming to arrest him, giving Moreau time to wrap his former apprentice in an illusion so he could escape. Dylan was the one who set up Quinton and Maria's kidnapping. He tells me how every triumph in those tryouts kept me close, while also allowing him to remain inside the Department of Supernatural Investigations long enough to use his tech magic to figure out its wards and security systems from the inside.

It was all Dylan. Attacking his sister wasn't enough; he wanted to destroy people's memory of her too. It's just so cruel.

My heart breaks into pieces. "So those hybrids destroying your house—that bruise you supposedly got—that was just to convince me to come back?"

"Whatever it took." He shrugs.

"You can't be like this," I say. "You just can't."

"We're at war with the entire supernatural world," Dylan says bitterly. "We're fighting for magicians' right to exist, Amari. We have to do what's necessary. You should want to be a part of this—"

"A toast," Moreau interrupts, lifting a glass. "To Amari Peters, the most powerful illusionist I've sensed since Vladimir himself. A shame that you must be sacrificed for the return of the Night Brothers."

"Wait," says Dylan. "You said that she didn't have to die. That she could join us."

Moreau frowns. "Don't be stupid, boy. The girl clearly has no interest in our cause. I gave you the chance to win her over and you failed. But not to worry . . ." Moreau pauses to drink from his goblet, letting the blood drip down his chin. "She will go to her death knowing that it was her sacrifice that righted the world. All those who have cursed and vilified what we are, they shall get their just due. They will all be punished!"

I flinch. I've had those same thoughts. Wanting revenge

on all those people who've hated me for something I can't change about myself. Those people who gave me dirty looks or the parents who signed that finale petition on the training room door. Isn't it exactly how I felt when I'd finally had enough and shoved Emily Grant on the last day of school? It was payback for all those times she made me feel bad about being the poor Black kid from the other side of town. For daring to say that Quinton was dead. And it did feel so good standing over her while all those other kids laughed.

I felt totally justified.

But that's not how I feel anymore. "We can change people's minds about magicians without hurting anyone. I've seen it happen. We just have to give them a chance to see who we really are." Didn't Elsie become my friend because we gave each other a chance? And what about Ranger Alford at the second tryout or those people who clapped for me at the finale. I was changing minds by simply not shutting myself off. No matter how many times my efforts got thrown back in my face.

"A touching sentiment, but I have no interest in changing minds," says Moreau. "A lion does not concern itself with the opinions of sheep. The supernatural world shall fall in line or it shall die. Sadly, a great many will have to perish before this message is fully understood."

Without looking down, I slowly reach into my pocket for my phone. If I can send Agent Fiona a message . . . But when I glance at the screen, Moreau's image appears, wagging a finger at me. The phone shorts out.

Moreau stands and pulls the Black Book from his robe. With another flutter of his fingers, it opens. He sets the book down in front of him. Then he balls both hands into tight fists and slams them together. He hisses the words, "Death's door."

The green mist around Quinton and Maria swirls in the air before colliding into the far wall. It re-forms into a shimmering green door, as ghostly as the tents at the All-Souls Festival.

With a swish of his cloak, Moreau glides over to the door. He gives it a single knock and shouts, "Come forth, my old friend. Come forth, Vladimir!"

The shimmering door begins to creak open . . .

Moreau's gleeful eyes return to me. "You shall supply the magical blood he'll require to nourish himself back to a proper magician."

With a wave of his hand, Moreau lifts me out of my chair and drops me in front of the glowing door. A ghostly, skeletal arm reaches out from behind it, scratching and clawing to reach me. Moreau's magic is so strong that I can't move an inch.

I can't even move to perform an illusion. I'm helpless.

No, no, no!

A blast of energy streaks through the air, hitting Moreau square in the back. The old man's arms snap to his sides and he collapses. Dylan stands over him, pointing his Stun Stick.

Moreau hisses up at him. "You would challenge me now, when we are on the brink of victory?"

Dylan closes his eyes. "You know what we are to each other. I can't just watch her die."

"*Weakness.*" Moreau snarls. "To put sentiment before power. You are unworthy of being called a magician."

Dylan growls back. "You've had *centuries* to restore magicians to their rightful place. And yet *I'm* the one who got you the Black Key and *I'm* the one who took the Black Book. No, I think you're the one who's unworthy. Time's up, old man."

"You do not have the power to steal my magic, boy!" Moreau shouts.

Dylan says a series of strange words and his hands erupt into silver flames. He balls them into fists and streaks of silver light pour out of Moreau and into Dylan.

"Impossible!" Moreau wails.

I scramble to my feet as Moreau does his best to crawl away from Dylan. The guy fades into dust right in front of me. The Black Book slams shut, and the skeletal figure is yanked back through the ghostly green door before it dissolves into mist.

Dylan glows with silver light. "I wouldn't have believed I could do it until you told me about Director Horus's vision. A non-magician wouldn't know this, but two-headed snakes represent magicians who have stolen magic from another magician. Twice as dangerous."

"*Please*," I beg. "Let me have my brother and Maria. Let us go."

Dylan just shakes his head slowly. "Forget about them.

They'll only get in the way." He meets my eyes. "This is about us, Amari. We're the born magicians of this age. I realize now that this is *our* time, not the Night Brothers'."

"Y-you're a born magician too?" I ask.

"I know I've told you so many lies, and you have no reason to trust me. But we share a bond that's more powerful than anything else in the world. Why do you think I was strong enough to steal Moreau's magic? Our magic calls to each other."

I think back to when I created that Amari Blossom without even really trying. Or when I made my illusion throw that spaghetti at Lara. And the fire illusion at the table during the Welcome Social. . . . Even my very first illusion at the Crystal Ball—Dylan was in the front row. Every time my magic has overflowed into illusions, he's been right there.

"Help me do what the Night Brothers couldn't. The Bureau won't stand a chance. We have the Black Book and the Black Key. We've got the power to do whatever we want. This world could be *ours*." Emotion flickers across his face. "I don't want to be alone."

"Then you shouldn't hurt the people that care about you," I say. "I don't want power. I just want my brother back."

"You're no better than Maria!" Dylan snaps. Tears drop down his cheeks. "I should've known it by your reaction to foul magick, but I guess I hoped . . ." His expression goes ice-cold. "Then I'm going to have to take your magic."

"Even if it kills me?"

"This is *your* choice!" he shouts. "Defend yourself."

I shake my head, tears welling in my own eyes. "I don't know how."

"Then this is goodbye, Amari Peters."

I have to do something. *My Stun Stick.* I make a run for the front door but Dylan knocks me off my feet with a wave of his hand. My shoulder crashes into the wall and I get up to my knees. He really does have Moreau's magic.

I throw open my arms. "Solis!"

I begin to glow, but Dylan puts out my light.

"You'll have to do better than fair magick." His hands erupt in silver flames. "Your life depends on it."

The Magna Fobia spell is on the tip of my tongue, but I can't bring myself to say it. I promised myself I'd never use foul magick again—that I would be a good magician, no matter what. Someone Quinton would be proud of. I close my eyes, my whole body shaking.

I'm sorry, Quinton. They were right all along. I'm not good enough.

No! I shake those doubts from my mind. That's not me anymore. I'm not the girl who gives up.

I'm the girl who tries. The girl who fights. The girl who believes.

My eyes open with a burning realization. *I'm unstoppable.*

Something inside me bursts and my whole body goes

white hot. The Black Book flips open and dozens of Amaris appear around the office, each with their hands lifted to the sky. Finally, an Amari in glittering armor appears at the center of the room. She winks at me.

Dylan staggers backward. "How . . ."

This isn't like the other times my magic has overflowed. Because I'm not just reacting, this is me *deciding*—Dylan won't win. At that, the armored Amari lifts her hand to the sky and says, "Finis."

Thunder booms overhead and lightning explodes through the roof and into her hand. The last thing I see is an eruption of blinding light.

≋ 33 ≋

Nomination for Consideration

Nominating Party: Quinton Javon Petre
On behalf of: Amari Renee Petre

To be used no sooner than the
latter's twelfth birthday and no
later than the latter's eighteenth
birthday.

Please bring this nomination, in
person, to:

1440 X. Main St. Atlanta, GA 30305
for the requisite interview.

Upon arrival at this address, note
the leftmost elevator door. Use
the device class, press the lowest
button (B) twenty-six time and await
further intruction.

Normally I'm not a fan of music that doesn't
have a beat. I mean, if I can't bounce along to it, I'm
just not interested. But there's something about this soft little voice I hear. It's just so nice. And the melody is so catchy.

My eyes open to the bluest eyes hovering above me. I
blink a couple times and Agent Fiona leans back a little, a
big grin spreading across her face. "There ye are."

Agent Fiona turns around. "She's awake."

Next thing I know, Elsie is on top of me. Hugging
me and kissing my cheek like I just rose from the grave or
something. Wait, did I?

"I'm so glad you're okay," says Elsie. "If you weren't, I
don't know what I would've done."

"Let the kid breathe, will ya?" laughs Agent Magnus.

"Yeah," I say, with a small laugh. "Let the kid breathe."

Now that I've got a little space, I can see that I'm in a hospital room. It looks and *feels* like a hospital room anyway. My mom works at the hospital, so I've been in enough of them to know what it feels like when you're inside of one. But where's all the equipment? The only thing I see is a lady in white in front of a microphone. That's when it hits me. She's the lady from the departmental presentations who sang that guy out of a coma.

I've just been sung back to health.

I blink and everything comes back to me all at once. Then right out of my mouth. "Moreau! The Black Book! Dylan! Did you stop them? Wait—Elsie, did you really breathe fire?"

Elsie laughs. "Sure did. It's not a full shift yet, but I think I'm finally starting the process."

"As for the rest of us," says Agent Fiona. "We didn't do anything. By the time we tracked down the *Jolly Roger*, ye were slumped over the Black Book and the Black Key, and Dylan was unconscious inside a cage of lightning. Had a devil of a time getting him out."

"Then we won?" I ask.

"We did," says Agent Magnus. "Thanks to you."

"Can I see my brother?" I ask quickly. "And Maria?" I've got so much I want to say to both of them.

"They're still being operated on by the cursebreakers," says Agent Fiona. "But we're hopeful."

I lay back on my pillow and close my eyes. *Thank goodness.* But as good as this moment feels, I always pictured sharing it with my partner.

"It was Dylan the whole time." I get a rush of emotions thinking about him, though I couldn't even say what they all are. I should hate him for lying to me, but there's still a part of me that wishes I could go back to when he was still my friend. The Dylan in Dr. Underhill's office feels like a different person. I wonder if I ever even knew the real him.

"We know," says Agent Fiona. "Dr. Underhill was a paranoid fellow, as any Key Holder has a right be. He kept surveillance cameras all over his office. We've got the whole incident recorded."

"Where is he now?"

Agent Fiona and Agent Magnus both frown a little. "I'm sorry, but that's classified information."

"But don't go fretting over it," says Agent Magnus. "The day is saved. Not bad for your first day as a Junior Agent."

Did I hear that right? "I'm a Junior Agent? I get the scholarship?"

"That's right!" says Chief Crowe, walking over to my bed. "Congratulations!"

"You aren't mad that I went after the Black Key?"

"Well," says Chief Crowe. "As you so eloquently explained to Agent Fiona, you were only a trainee, so you weren't technically a member of the Bureau yet. Oh, they grumbled and groaned for six hours straight at the emergency session of the Supernatural World Congress, but no one could fault your logic. However, I do hope you'll take something like this to an adult in the future."

"What in the world were you thinking?" asks Agent Magnus.

"I was following that look you gave me," I say, sitting up a little. "When Director Van Helsing accused you of letting the hybrids in."

"That was a 'help Agent Fiona get the Black Key' look." Agent Magnus goes red in the face. "Not a 'Go save the world on your own' look!"

I bite my lip. "Well, you might want to work on your looks then."

"I'm with Peters," says Agent Fiona, laughing. She gives Agent Magnus's scruffy beard a tug. "It's like I'm always tellin' ye, things would go a lot better if ye only put a little more effort into your looks!"

Later in the evening, once everyone has cleared out of my room, I get a visit from the last person in the world I expect. "Mama?"

Mama runs over to my bed and throws her arms around me. "Oh, Babygirl, I'm so glad you're all right. When they called me to say that you were recovering from something called severe post-magic overexertion, I didn't know what to think."

"I can't believe they let you visit me," I say.

Mama leans back a little. She looks so lost. "I can't even

pretend to understand half the things I saw on the way down here. There was a man with no face in the elevator with me!" Mama shakes her head. "But face or no face, nothing was gonna keep me away from my daughter."

I smile.

Mama swallows and says, "They also said you found Quinton?"

I nod, and Mama covers her face. "Oh man, you're going to make me cry."

She reaches out and we hold each other, crying and laughing.

Quinton's room is located in the ICU of the Department of Supernatural Health, aka the Intense Curses Unit. Me and Mama hold hands as we walk the halls to his room. The cursebreakers were able to revive Maria, but Quinton hasn't woken up. The Senior Cursebreaker who came to meet with us explained that he'd done all he could and now it's just a matter of waiting. My brother could wake up tomorrow, or he might never wake up.

I won't lie, it wasn't the easiest news to get. But I've got to keep hoping that my brother will be okay, that he'll wake up sooner rather than later. Hope has brought me this far; surely it'll get me my brother back healthy.

I don't know what to do with my hands when Lara Van Helsing runs over and throws her arms around me. Even though it's just a hug, it still feels dangerous coming from her.

"Thank you for bringing my sister back," Lara says, taking a step back. "I know I'm probably the last person you want to talk to, but thanks anyway."

I give her a small smile. "I told you I'd do it."

She nods and says, "About Dylan, I had no idea . . ."

"He fooled all of us," I say.

Lara's eyes turn sad and she runs back up the hall toward her mom.

When we enter Quinton's room, we find him resting peacefully on the fluffiest pillows you can imagine. Maria sits in a chair beside the bed holding his hand. When she notices us, she flushes and stands.

"Maria Van Helsing," she says, extending a trembling hand. I can't get over how much prettier she looks in person.

Mama shakes it first, and then I do.

"Thank you," Maria says to me. "I'm so sorry that it was me who woke up and not Quinton. The cursebreakers think it's because he was giving off more of his life essence, so I'd have to give less. It's just like him to try and one-up me like that."

"That's Quinton," I say softly. "Never lets anyone beat him in anything."

Maria smiles and relaxes a little.

Mama says, "There's nothing to be sorry for, sweetheart. I'm sure your family is happy to have you home again."

"Are you the reason Mama gets to come down here?" I ask Maria.

She flushes again and nods. "My family pulled some

strings to get special permission. After Dylan, it's really the least we could do."

"Thanks," I say.

"Do you want to talk to Quinton?" Maria asks.

"Huh?" I say. "What do you mean?"

"That's what I was doing when you came in," says Maria. "My supernatural ability—no, I'm sorry. There's no point in pretending anymore. It's really just a simple bit of blood magic that allows me to communicate telepathically with anyone I'm touching. If I'm touching two people at once, those two people can also speak telepathically."

"You go first," I tell Mama.

Maria takes Quinton's hand again and then she takes Mama's. Mama gasps and then come the waterworks. I try to focus on something else, so that they can have their moment. But Maria meets my eyes while Quinton and Mama talk.

"I'm so sorry about my brother," Maria whispers. "I feel like this has all been my fault. I should've seen him for what he was and not who I wanted him to be."

"Did you know about him being a born magician?" I ask.

She nods. "I taught him how to keep his magic a secret from the rest of the family. At some point he started keeping secrets from me too."

"What makes being a born magician so special? It's like . . . Dylan and I are connected somehow."

Maria's expression saddens. "There are rules against me explaining." With a flick of her fingers, she produces a card out of thin air. "Keep this on you and don't let anyone see it. As long as you have it, they can come to you."

"Who?"

But Maria just hands me the card.

International League of Magicians

"You can't be serious?" I say.

"Even the supernatural world has its secret societies," says Maria. "They'll find you when the moment is right."

My mind spins at the idea that there is a whole organization of magicians out there that not even the Bureau knows about. It also makes me wonder if Dylan knew about them, and what he thought about it.

I think of Elsie, my *real* friend, and decide to ask the question I know she'd want to get an answer to. "Was Van-Quish really breaking up? Dylan said that you didn't get along and that you were fighting and you really wanted to be a training agent like Fiona. . . ."

Maria raises an eyebrow.

"And I answered my own question," I say. "Dylan said whatever it took to make you out to be the bad guy."

Maria gives me a sad nod. "Although I *did* put in my training agent transfer papers. But Quinton was going to transfer as well. When we graduated from Junior Agent training, we agreed, five years as field agents and then five years as training agents and, at the end, we'd stick with the one we liked best."

I smile. Well, that sounds totally normal. "And did you know about Quinton talking to Director Horus about you?"

"Dylan was stealing classified files using my security codes and Quinton found out. It's actually what Quinton and I were meeting to discuss when we were taken."

I just shake my head. "Is it weird that I still miss Dylan a little, even though he lied over and over?"

"If it is, then I'm just as weird." After a moment Maria says a little more cheerfully, "Maybe some good can still come from this. Dylan can't hurt anyone where he's going. And now that I've been outed as a magician, I promise you won't have to be alone anymore. We'll do it together."

It's my turn to talk to Quinton. It feels like there's static inside my brain when I touch Maria's hand.

"Chicken Little?" comes Quinton's voice in my head.

How's it going? is all I can think to say.

"Oh, you know, just having the best nap ever."

I laugh at that. *Are you okay in there? Are you hurting?*

"I'm dreaming. Remember how I always said I wanted to go bass fishing, and you would tease me that nobody under fifty goes fishing?"

Yeah, because it's true. I grin.

"True or not, I'm in the middle of a big, wide lake, with my feet kicked up on the edge of the boat. I could get used to relaxation like this."

I shake my head. *Only you would dream about fishing.*

"You don't know what you're missing." Quinton's tone turns sad. "Magnus came by earlier. He told me about you being a magician like Maria. About all the things you've had to deal with since you touched the Crystal Ball. I never meant to throw you into a situation like that."

It's cool. If I didn't come to the Bureau then I never would've found you.

"I should've known if anyone could, it'd be you. You've always been amazing, sis. You did this all on your own."

I don't like doing things on my own. It's scary and I never know if it'll work out.

"That's part of growing up, Amari," says Quinton. "You don't need me anymore. As long as you bet on yourself and believe you can do anything, you can. That's why I need you to make me a promise, okay?"

Okay.

"Mama told me how obsessed you were with finding me. *Promise* me you won't spend your life beside this bed waiting for me to wake up. Go out and do and see everything. That's what I want for you. Be as great as I know you can be. When I do wake up, and I will, I expect to hear lots of stories!"

Mama has to stop by her job on the way home. She was worried she might get in trouble for missing a couple days to be with me and Quinton, but one call from Chief Crowe to the president of the hospital and not only is it okay, she's even getting paid for the time she missed.

It gets hot sitting in Mama's car with no AC, so I cross

the street to a supernatural newsstand tucked inside an alleyway. You'd think I'd get some slack on the price since my face is on the cover of so many magazines, but that only makes the hobgoblin charge me double. "Yous can obviously affords it," it smirks. "Big shot like yous."

I take a copy of *Harper's Bizarre* and find a seat on a shaded bench under a tree. The magazine caught my eye because me and Maria's faces were both on the cover beneath the headline, "The Good Magicians?" It's proof that at least some people are rethinking how they feel about us.

"May I sit here?" asks an older man in a dark blue suit. He's got messy salt-and-pepper hair and a handlebar mustache.

"Sure," I say, scooting over a little to give him some room.

He takes a seat and places his cane in his lap. "Lovely weather, isn't it?"

"I guess so," I say. "Maybe if it wasn't this hot. Wouldn't be so bad if I was on the beach, though."

The guy snaps his fingers, and suddenly our bench isn't next to the hospital anymore. It's sitting in white sand leading to a clear blue ocean that stretches out to the horizon. The sun sets behind us and a cool wind whips across my face. "Better?"

I turn and look at the man, hoping this is the meeting I've been waiting for. "Are you from the League of Magicians?"

He dips his head. "Cosimo Galileo Leonardo de' Pazzi

at your service. But my colleagues call me Cozmo. My ancestor helped Vladimir create the spell you conjured to save yourself the other day. Knights of the Round."

"Is that what happened? I didn't really know what I was doing."

"It's why your magic took over," says Cozmo. "Through sheer willpower and self-belief, you summoned up all your magic and demanded it take action. And, my dear girl, it heeded your call."

I think about that. It makes me wonder if the smaller snake in my constellation with Director Horus was actually my own magic. It was separate because it was acting on its own, responding to what I wanted and how I felt—*unstoppable*.

"Who are you guys?" I ask. "Have you always been around?"

Cozmo wrinkles his brow. "The terrible magicians the supernatural world has come to know these last seven centuries have all been newly made apprentices of Moreau. The League of Magicians, on the other hand, are the recipients of magic handed down through the years from a spare few of Vladimir's original apprentices. We exist entirely separate from the Bureau, although we have allowed the Van Helsing magicians into our ranks—the latest being Maria Van Helsing."

"Is she in trouble now that everyone knows she's a magician?" I ask.

"You and Maria represent a situation the league has never dealt with. While many of us, including myself, have long advocated revealing ourselves to the Bureau and the rest of the supernatural world, the majority of our order still believes it's safer to continue to pose as ordinary people. But then, perhaps *you* will tell us how to proceed?"

"*Me?*" I ask.

The corner of his mouth lifts. "Or will it be Dylan Van Helsing?"

I lean closer. "What are you saying?"

"I'm saying the next two born magicians have both been identified! That makes it a brand-new age! Like all those born magicians that came before, your connection—be it as friends or rivals—has the potential to shape the world, child. Consider these words both a courtesy and a very dire warning."

I lean back, eyes wide. Suddenly we're back on the side street next to the hospital.

"You are hereby invited to join the League of Magicians, Amari Peters." He grins as he gets to his feet. "With all that's to come, I do hope you accept the invitation." And with a bow of his head, Cozmo shrinks into a bird and flaps away.

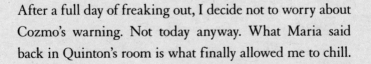

After a full day of freaking out, I decide not to worry about Cozmo's warning. Not today anyway. What Maria said back in Quinton's room is what finally allowed me to chill.

With Dylan locked away for his crimes, hopefully for many years to come, whatever connection we share won't matter for a long time.

For right now, since summer camp at the Bureau is still canceled until next year, I've decided to put my thoughts and energy into something else.

And since I kinda-sorta saved the supernatural world from a second war with the Night Brothers, revealed Dylan as the Bureau's traitor, *and* retrieved the Black Book and the Black Key, the Supernatural World Congress and the Bureau of Supernatural Affairs granted me a Congressional Request as a reward. After talking it over with Quinton, I knew exactly what request I wanted to make.

Mama would kill me if she knew I was headed to a boy's house in the middle of the night. Hero or not, there's just some things I can't get away with. Especially when I've already kissed her goodnight and told her I was headed to bed. But what she doesn't know won't hurt her.

I head down the stairs of the apartment building until I get to the door I'm looking for. I give it a good knock. Most times, knocking on somebody's door in this neighborhood, this late, is asking for trouble. No telling what's liable to happen. But I already know Jayden's mom isn't home.

Jayden answers the door, rubbing the sleep out of his eyes.

"Would you put a shirt on?" I say.

"'Mari? What you doing here in the middle of the night?"

"Um, I'll explain after you get dressed."

"Dressed? For what?"

I cross my arms. "You trust me or not?"

"Uh, give me a sec."

I wait in the doorway while he throws on his Food Mart T-shirt. He's been working there since last week. He's not old enough to do anything but sweep the floors, and I'm sure he's not making the kind of money he used to, but it's a change for the better.

"Sorry," he says. "It's the only thing I got that's clean."

"That's totally fine," I say.

"You know I don't run with those boys up the street no more. Trying to leave that stuff alone, man."

"That's actually why I'm here," I say. "Follow me."

I wait for him to ask me where we're going but he just shuts the door behind him and says, "I thought maybe you forgot about me. Haven't seen you around much."

"Oh, I've just been busy saving the world and stuff."

He laughs. "If you say so—wait, we're going to the roof?"

"Yep," I say. "Promise me you won't freak out, though."

"Girl, please, don't nothing freak me out."

"Okay, Mr. Tough."

I step out onto the roof first and turn around to watch Jayden come up after me. His eyes go so big they nearly pop out his head. He ducks back down the stairs and I can't help but laugh.

"I know I'm not *that* sleepy," says Jayden. "Is that a boat?"

"Sure is," I say. "You coming or not?"

"Oh, I'm cool. Just give me a sec to get myself right." He takes a few deep breaths and then steps onto the roof. I lead him inside the *Jolly Roger 2.0*. "I don't know what's going on, but this is some next-level stuff. How'd you get a boat up here?"

"Let's just say I borrowed it from a family member," I say. "Besides, you haven't seen anything yet." I lead him up onto the deck and hand him an envelope.

Jayden takes it and reads it aloud. "Nomination for Consideration for the Bureau of Supernatural Affairs . . . Wait, am I being pranked?"

"No, just listen, okay? You used to be a part of Quinton's tutoring program. But I also know that you gave up on school after he went missing. Well, I'm going to restart the program."

"For real?" he asks. "You really gonna start it up yourself?"

I nod. "I know I'm not Quinton, but I think it could be just as helpful. Because you *are* smart, Jayden. You just need someone to have your back the same way Quinton always had mine. That nomination won't make much sense yet, but if you promise to really give the tutoring a shot, it will. Tonight, I'm going to give you just a taste of what I mean."

I touch the wheel just enough that it lifts off the roof. Jayden's jaw drops.

I give him a wide grin. "Tonight, we're going to go look at some trains."

ACKNOWLEDGMENTS

This is the book of my heart. A book many years in the making, and a story that both scared and thrilled me to write. There are countless people who have helped this novel find its way into your hands. Far too many to ever thank properly. But I'll do my best.

Thank you, first and foremost, to God, who has blessed me far more than I could ever hope to deserve.

Thanks to Gemma Cooper, SUPER-agent and captain of #TeamCooper, for just being such a great human being. That first phone call when you offered rep was one of the happiest moments of my life. Your endless enthusiasm and guidance through what has been a whirlwind of a publishing journey has been invaluable.

*A special thanks to everyone at the Bent Agency: Jenny Bent, Molly Ker Hawn, Amelia Hodgson, and Victoria Cappello and all the assistants and co-agents around the world.

Thanks to my utterly brilliant editors, Kristin Daly Rens and Lindsey Heaven, my companions in turning this book into the best story it could possibly be. Kristin, you've been wonderful since our first conversation and I don't think there is a smarter, more patient person in the whole universe! Lindsey, your enthusiasm and expertise are unmatched! I've learned so much from you both and look forward to learning so much more.

*A special thanks to everyone at Balzer + Bray, Egmont UK, and the entire HarperCollins family. To the editing team, the sales and marketing teams, the art department, and everyone else who works tirelessly on my and so many other book's behalf behind the scenes. You all rock!

Thanks to Mary Pender, my amazing film agent who I can never thank enough.

*A special thanks to Orly Greenberg, Akhil Hedge, and everyone at UTA!

Thanks to Estelle Laure, freelance editor extraordinaire. The first person to read Amari who didn't share my last name. And the first person to say that I might have something special.

Thanks to those authors who've most inspired me and paved the way. It's my hope to tell you how much you've meant to me whenever I'm lucky enough to meet you all. And thanks to the authors who've been so generous in freely sharing what they know about the craft and the industry.

Thanks to all of my family and loved ones. Especially my brother Steven (who got the height and the hair), and his wonderful wife, Stephanie. Thanks to John Lakin for the constant laughs these past twenty-five years (man, we're old!). Thanks to Marquise and CC Ramey for the much-needed game nights. Thanks to Cousin DJ, Uncle Dib, and Aunt Judy. A special thanks to Uncle Mel and Aunt Carol for stepping up when they didn't have to.

Thanks to my parents who have always been shining examples of what it means to be "good people." So often it's not until you grow up that you can appreciate what a commitment being a great parent truly is.

Thanks to my loving wife, Quinteria, for always believing in my writing even when I didn't. You are absolutely the best thing that's ever happened to me.

Turn the page for a sneak peek at the sequel,
AMARI AND THE **GREAT GAME**

≫ 1 ≪

I SPRINT DOWN THE SIDEWALK, PAST DESIGNER BOUTIQUES, luxury shops, and a fancy art gallery. A few blocks ahead lies the sprawling downtown campus of Whitman Preparatory Academy. The main building's all-glass exterior sparkles in the morning light, and a short line of cars circle the large fountain out front, dropping off kids who might actually get to homeroom before the 8:15 tardy bell.

Late or not, school is where I should be headed too.

Instead, I stop in front of a rundown little shack that looks like it's been crammed between two larger, much nicer buildings. The faded sign out front reads Marco's Mini-Mart.

I take a few seconds to catch my breath and pull out my phone to double-check my messages.

Voicemail from Elsie
Come to Marco's before school. Emergency!

If there's one thing I've learned about my best friend during our first year as classmates, it's that the girl can exaggerate. If I say something's an emergency, then best believe something major has happened. If Elsie uses the word "emergency," it could just mean the delivery guy is late with some robot parts for her latest science project.

I head into the store. If the outside is sketchy, inside's even worse. The place is dimly lit, just bright enough to reveal sections of paint missing from the walls. This is supposed to be a convenience store, selling soft drinks and snacks, but every time I've picked anything up, it's already expired. That soda cooler hasn't ever worked.

And did I mention the store always has the faint smell of rotten eggs? Like, *always*.

I scrunch up my nose and cut through the candy aisle. Up ahead, some poor guy looks completely unimpressed by the chip selection. *Can't say I blame you.* I scoot past him and head for the register.

A big, bald bodybuilder guy in a *Muscles Win Tussles* T-shirt stands behind the counter. His eyes narrow at my approach.

I squint right back at him. And suddenly, tufts of bright

red fur appear on his head and neck, and two curved bones jut out from his jaw-like elephant tusks.

But then I blink and he looks human again. That must be a pretty expensive disguise if my Truesight only last a few seconds. Definitely something from the Vivi LaBoom: City Camouflage Chic collection.

I clear my throat and politely ask, "May I use your restroom?"

He crosses his thick arms and looks me over before grumbling, "And why should I do this?"

I grin and roll my eyes. "C'mon, Tiny. I'm already running late for school."

A smile splits Tiny's face and he lets out a bellowing laugh. "No 'hello' . . . no 'how is your day?' . . . just 'give me key.'"

"Pretty please?" I say.

"Fine, fine. Anything for a fellow human."

I wince and lean in, lowering my voice to a whisper, remembering we aren't alone in here. "Just so you know, we don't usually call each other humans."

Tiny scratches his bald head, his confused eyes flashing bright yellow before changing back. "But why? You are human, yes?"

I nod. "It's just . . . well, we tend to assume everyone we meet is human, so there isn't any reason to mention it."

His shoulders droop dramatically. "So many things to remember to fit into human world."

I give him a reassuring pat on the arm. "You'll get the hang of it."

Tiny nods and reaches under the counter. I hold out my hand and he drops the restroom key into my palm.

"Um, excuse me?" That guy from before pops out from behind the chips rack. "I asked about the bathroom a few minutes ago and you said it was out of order."

Tiny frowns. "Out of order for *you*. Perfectly fine for her. Any questions?"

The guy looks ready to protest, but an inhuman growl from Tiny seems to change his mind.

"Be careful," Tiny says to me in a low voice. "That one has look of a Watcher."

I bite my lip. Watchers are folks who're convinced there's more to the world than meets the eye. According to them, there's this huge worldwide conspiracy to hide the fact that supernatural creatures from myths and legends are real and secretly live among us.

These guys have websites and chat rooms and members all over the world. Sometimes they'll even have public demonstrations demanding the truth. Most of all, they try to find evidence that will prove to the world that they're right. Which is probably why Mr. Watcher guy is hanging around a convenience store that's clearly not *really* a convenience store.

Most people think Watchers are just conspiracy theorists and don't pay them any attention. But me, I have to take them serious. Because not only are they right, but I'm part of an organization, the Bureau of Supernatural Affairs, that's committed to making sure the proof they're so desperate to find never ever gets out.

Sure enough, when I glance back over my shoulder, I find the Watcher guy's eyes on me. He fumbles through his pockets for a phone—and then has the nerve to start recording us!

"Can you give me a distraction?" I whisper to Tiny.

He grins and steps from behind the counter. "This I *can* do well." He throws his arms open and shouts, "Congratulations, sir! You are big winner!"

The man furrows his brow as Tiny puts a thick arm around his shoulders to guide him toward the counter. "B-But I didn't enter any contest . . ." The poor guy whips his head around frantically, trying to find me, but I've already ducked back down the candy aisle toward the restroom at the rear of the store.

I ignore the giant out-of-order sign plastered across the door and stick the key into the lock. Before I turn the knob, I take one more glance behind me to make sure the coast is clear.

The Watcher guy frowns up at Tiny. "You're saying I won . . . a mop bucket?"

"*Quality* mop bucket," Tiny answers. "Used many times and never have leak."

I cover up my laugh and slip through the door.

The *real* Marco's, the one behind this door, isn't just a different kind of store, it's practically a different world. *Marco's Fine Desserts* is only open to the city's supernatural community—meaning no disguises or glamours necessary—and it's got the best magical treats in all of Atlanta. Midas Milkshakes that stain your teeth bright gold, Stardusted Scones to give your skin a faint glow, and even the World's Worst Best Coffee, which tastes so good it actually puts you sleep. The moment I step inside, the sweet smells fill up my nose and I'm instantly in a great mood.

I squeeze through a couple of harpies, careful to duck beneath their wings. A tall yeti in a chef's hat literally barks a hello at me from behind the counter and I wave back. "Hi, Marco!" But the distraction nearly causes me to trip over a boggart, who thumbs its hooked nose at me. It mumbles something about "rude humans" before waddling off.

I spot Elsie at a table beside another Bureau kid, Julia Farsight, whose heavy eyelids always make her look sleepy. Elsie waves to me and I rush over.

"Okay," I say, slipping into the seat across from them. "What's so important that we needed to meet here before school?"

Elsie frowns. "I don't think I used the word *important*."

"You literally said it was an emergency," I reply.

"No," she says. "I said 'emerge and see.'" She grins mischievously. "As in 'emerge and see' what I've got for you!"

Julia giggles.

"*Els* . . . this could've waited till after school. It's going to cost me a perfect attendance certificate. And you know how much Mama cares about stuff like that. The lady has already got a spot picked out for it on her wall."

"Don't worry," she says. "Bear's bringing his dad's spare

transporter so we can literally be at school in an instant. As long as we're on the bus when it leaves for Georgia Aquarium, Mr. Ames will count us as present."

"And teleporting to school is allowed?" I ask. "Because I've been catching the city bus to school all year . . ."

"*Allowed* might be a strong word," says Elsie.

"As far as I know, it's not *not* allowed . . ." Julia adds in her singsong voice.

I wince. "I'm really looking forward to going back to summer camp this weekend, so maybe let's not get kicked out of the Bureau before then?"

Elsie just grins and starts tapping on her phone. "Would they really kick out somebody who's getting headlines like this?" She flips the phone around and scrolls through all the search results she's found on the othernet—the protected portion of the internet reserved for the supernatural world—from just typing in my name. "They're all *nice* articles."

"Even *Better Gnomes & Gardens* wrote about you," says Julia, leaning in. "We've got a colony of gnomes on our property and it's a real pain to get them to talk about anything other than flowers, so that's a real accomplishment."

"Let me see," I pick up the phone and tap on the first link I see.

Amari Peters: The Good Magician?

Magicians are known for two things: Off the charts magic levels and a long history as our world's greatest villains. Despite this, a thirteen-year-old girl seems poised to prove that magicians don't have to be bad. She's already saved the world once—what else could the girl wonder accomplish as a force for good? The entire supernatural world is watching!

Honestly, I'd be lying if I said I hadn't been keeping up with articles like this all year. The fact that something I did is making people rethink how they feel about magicians is what I'm most proud of about last summer. It's one of the reasons I can't wait to go back to summer camp—unlike last year, I might actually be accepted by the rest of the Bureau.

I grin, handing Elsie back her phone. "I'm not the only magician the supernatural world discovered last summer. And Maria Van Helsing is a way more famous agent than I'll ever be."

"You should both be thrown out of the Bureau," comes a grumpy voice.

Ugh. Bear.

This kid got his nickname because he's the tallest at our middle school, and an even bigger bully. He's also the fourth member, and only eighth grader, in our school's Soup Club—short for SUPErnatural club. It's for Bureau kids who know about the supernatural world. Lots of middle schools and high schools have them—they're even listed in the student handbook sometimes. Lucky for us, non-Bureau kids have zero interest in giving up their free period for a club where you don't actually eat any soup.

"Bear . . ." Julia wags a finger. "Be nice."

Bear falls heavily into the seat beside me, making sure to lean as far away from me as possible. As much as the supernatural world has come to accept magicians over the past year, there are still many who will always hate us. No matter what I do.

"We're all here," Bear grumbles. "What's this dumb meeting even about?"

Elsie sits up straighter. "Well . . . I just wanted to say that I've really enjoyed being president of this Soup Club. And I thought I'd gather the four of us together one last time before we're off to camp. I got you all a gift!"

Julia claps. "I love gifts!"

Even Bear perks up a bit.

But I recognize the look in Elsie's eyes—my best friend is up to something. "What did you do?"

Elsie waves to Marco behind the counter, and four plates come floating toward our table. "I ordered fortune cookies. As in, real ones."

I gasp as the plates land softly before each of us. "But these things don't just reveal your fortune—they cost a fortune too."

Elsie nods. "But only because they're so incredibly difficult to make. You have to infuse the dough with used tea leaves from a successful prediction, a magic 8-ball has to be present in the room, the stars have to be in the proper alignment, the fire pit you bake it in has to have yielded at least one vision in past year . . . and that's just the requirements

I can remember. Not going to lie, this totally drained my science fair winnings, but I happen to think you guys are worth it."

Julia grins and cracks hers open, pulling out the tiny slip of paper and setting it down. It's blank. But then she closes her eyes, whispering to herself before placing a piece of cookie in her mouth.

Suddenly red letters appear on the paper.

"What's it say?" asks Elsie.

Julia holds it up for us to see.

The grass isn't always greener on the other side.

"I asked it whether or not I should switch to a different department this summer. Guess that means I should probably stay put in the Department of the Dead. The fact that my supernatural ability is being a medium *does* make things pretty easy for me there."

Bear goes next. He frowns when his fortune comes back as:

Sometimes the real enemy is in the mirror.

He crosses his arms and turns away from us. No chance he's gonna tell us what he asked his cookie.

Elsie goes next, and when our eyes meet, I already know what she's going to ask. Elsie is a weredragon. Only she's never been able to shift into a full dragon. The closest she's come is blowing fire a few times. As the last of her kind, it's something that really bothers her.

My best friend closes her eyes and places the cookie into her mouth. She holds her breath as the letters begin to appear.

Your hard work will pay off.

That girl hollers so loud . . .

"Does that mean—" I begin.

"I think so!" She beams. "I might actually shift into a full dragon this summer! *Finally.* Of course, the cookies are only right about 70 percent of the time, but I feel so much better."

"That's amazing!" I say. "I'm really happy for you."

My turn—I break my own cookie. I already know what I'm going to ask.

The whole reason I joined the Bureau last summer was to find out what happened to my missing brother, who'd been working there for years. And even though I eventually found him, it wasn't before he'd fallen victim to an awful curse that's kept him permanently asleep ever since.

At first it was easy to believe that he'd eventually get better. That any day now he'd come home to me and Mama, and everything would go back to the way it used to be. But that never happened, and every day it's a little harder to keep my hopes up. He's spent the last two months getting experimental treatments from cursebreakers in Sydney, Australia, but even they couldn't help him.

"Will my brother ever get better?" I ask.

Elsie grabs my wrist before I can eat the cookie. "Sorry. I should've known you'd want to ask about Quinton. But you have to ask a question about yourself for it to work."

"Oh," I say, deflated. I'm not sure what else to ask. So I place the cookie in my mouth and think. After a few seconds I shrug and ask, "Is there anything important I should know?"

Gasps sound around the table and I look down.

Beware of Unseen Dangers.